DRAGONBAND
SAGA

THE HUNTERS AND THE HUNTED
TALES – VOLUME TWO

Edited by
Kim Huther & Joel Norden

Knights of the Northwest, LLC
NAPOLEON, OHIO

Copyright © 2017 by Knights of the Northwest, LLC.

All rights reserved. No part of this publication may be reproduced, distributed or transmitted in any form or by any means, including photocopying, recording, or other electronic or mechanical methods, without the prior written permission of the publisher, except in the case of brief quotations embodied in critical reviews and certain other noncommercial uses permitted by copyright law. For permission requests, write to the publisher, addressed "Attention: Permissions Coordinator," at the address below.

Knights of the Northwest, LLC
Napoleon, OHIO/43545

Publisher's Note: This is a work of fiction. Names, characters, places, and incidents are a product of the author's imagination. Locales and public names are sometimes used for atmospheric purposes. Any resemblance to actual people, living or dead, or to businesses, companies, events, institutions, or locales is completely coincidental.

Cover art by Jamie Noble.
Project Manager: Aaron Wulf
Edited by Kim Huther, and Joel Norden.

The Hunters and the Hunted -- 1st ed.
ISBN 978-0-9997727-0-6
Library of Congress Control Number: 2018902152

TABLE OF CONTENTS

THE MONSTER HUNTER'S DOG – *Jack Gabriel* 1

THE BRONZE DRAGON – *Jacqueline Abela* 49

CURSE IN HIS BLOOD – *Nikolas Monastere* 75

DUOS NECROSIS – *David Burman* 114

WITCH'S CURSE – *Joel Norden* 127

THE DARK VILLAGE – *Katie Lawrence* 178

GARRETT'S TALE – *Anna Warkentin* 189

FAIRY TRAIL – *Richard A. Knaak* 233

REQUIEM FOR A FISHERMAN – *Chanté Van Biljon* 278

BLOODIED – *Stuart Thaman* 301

SHE CALLED FROM BELOW – *Aaron Wulf* 325

Acknowledgements

A special thanks to Aaron Wulf for all his hard work managing this wonderful project.

The Monster Hunter's Dog

By Jack Gabriel

1307BM
Age of Destiny

When the horn sounded, Fell dropped his spoon into his breakfast broth. Across the room, his mother put her whittling knife and half-carved wooden horse on her lap, tilting her head to listen. Fell's father, who had been cursing over the new bowstring he was braiding, let the frayed ends loose to writhe and unravel.

The deep lowing of the horn startled the few birds living in the roof. Through the frost-misted windows, Fell watched clumps of snow hiss off their neighbors' roofs and crunch to the ground. The village of Halven was shaken awake. The silence after the horn was broken by the enthusiastic opening of window and door latches.

"She's back," Fell whispered.

"So it seems." Fell's mother clucked her tongue and sighed—either at the continuing rattle of the birds above, or the mess Fell had made on the table.

Fell's chest tightened at the thought of the grey-skinned woman with the white braids. The sword at her hip. The symbol emblazoned on the leather armor she wore under her traveling cloak. "Do you think she…?"

"She'd better have brought proof," his mother said, returning to her whittling. "The village Fathers are paying her enough."

"Now, Hild," Fell's father said. "Best let that rest. The Fathers made their decision to pay the hunter. Nobody thought she'd do it. But it seems likely she's followed through, and the Fathers will pay her the agreed price. On their honor, and the honor of Halven."

Fell began to wipe the spilt broth off the table with the side of his hands. "Do you think we could—"

"And that's that, is it, Garth?" Hild twisted her wrist, drilling the knife into the chunk of wood. "Leave it to the Fathers. The wise Fathers. Self-appointed and self-important."

Garth Holm snorted. "They know what's best." He tucked the end of the bowstring back between his toes and took up weaving again.

Fell knew his father's position on the subject well. For Garth Holm, it was bad enough when the outside world came to Halven. When the wandering misfits and vagrants stole through the town, threatening and thieving their way through to wherever they were going. Garth Holm could handle that well enough if it meant that his village was left alone. But when some foreign monster began lurking about, taking livestock and scaring off all the good hunting, then it was trouble. And if a vagrant wanted to gamble her life against a sack of gold to try to kill the thing, then good luck to her.

But she was no vagrant. Fell knew what she was. "I want to go and see," he said.

"Too dangerous," Garth Holm said immediately.

"The creature is dead!" Fell said.

"Still scary."

"I'm fifteen. I think I can handle seeing a dead thing. No matter how scary."

Fell's father frowned. He grunted. As good an assent as Fell would ever get.

"We'll all go. But you'll finish your food and tidy that mess you've made first, young man," his mother said. "And you," she pointed at his father, "get rid of that bloody bird nest in the roof. I've had enough."

Outside, the crunch of footfall on snow, the hubbub from the village square, and the morning how-do-you-dos were all growing. The monster-hunter must be close to the gates now. Fell picked up his bowl and swallowed down the meaty water. He mopped up the spilt broth with a chunk of bread and stood.

"That's you cleaning up, is it?" his mother asked. But the twitch in the corner of her mouth told Fell it was fine. He could go. "Stay warm," she said.

Fell veered around his father, grabbed his coat, and burst outside into the biting air. The sky was pink-grey, filled with cold smoke. The mountains to the north were shrouded, and the forests at their feet looked like shadows hovering in the sky. He dashed through the narrow alleys towards the village square, kicking snow drifts apart and apologizing as he dodged villagers and horses.

A real-life monster-hunter killing a real-life monster! In Halven! Where nothing ever happened. Finally, something exciting in this frozen little nothing of a village. People had nothing to do here except drink and make babies, and Fell wanted to escape before either of those things trapped him here forever.

He wasn't surprised to see a great deal of the village's population already gathering around the outside of the square. They stood outside shops and hung from windows. Pipes smoked, and gossip flew as they all stared up at the watchtower guard—the one who had blown the horn when he first spotted the far-off movement as he peered into the forest below.

Soon enough the guard called down, "She approaches! She brings the beast!"

The village gates stood open, and beyond them snaked the path that led from the forest. A shape moved there, among the skeletal trunks and heaped snow. Something small, human-shaped, leading a horse, and behind the horse followed something much larger.

At last the trunks parted and all could see what came, and all gasped.

The vagrant stomped towards the village, a blank stare on her blood-smeared face. The horse she led was also blood-smeared, but showed no signs of injury. Dragged by the horse was a kind of makeshift sled made of branches bound with twine, and strapped to this was the monster. It was a boulder of white fur, dirty and matted with blood and grime. One of its great clawed hands hung over the side of the sled and dragged in the snow.

The woman's dog stood, panting, on top of the beast. The blotchy mutt rode the slain monster proudly, how Fell imagined a ship captain might look from one of the tales he'd read, staring over the ocean in search of a new land.

As the woman led the horse and her prize through the gate, the villagers both gasped surprise and huffed disappointment. Muttered about the beast being so small. Witnesses claimed that it couldn't be the thing they saw.

Fell, too, was surprised at the size of the monster. This beast was little more than half again as tall as the tallest villager. Its hands, however, were big enough to grasp a fully-grown man around the torso. Its feet were thick and wide, its legs like stumps covered in white moss, and the patch of fur that covered the beast's chest was thin enough to reveal a mass of knotted muscles.

Fell felt embarrassed for the bravado of his fellow villagers. Their mocking frowns were frowns of ignorance. Of course, the monster looked impotent now, dead on the crib of criss-cross branches. But this creature had been a powerful thing. Look at those hands. And what about its size? Plenty big enough to do damage. Even something human-sized was something to be feared. After all, look at what horrors humans had caused.

The vagrant woman scowled at the whispered comments as she scanned the crowd for the village Fathers. Berg, Velem, Jorgmund and Freg—the four men Fell's mother had always hated—waited ceremoniously for the woman in their fur cloaks and chains of office. Their grey hairs blew around in the morning wind.

The woman stopped. She dropped the reins, and the horse dug its hooves into the dirt under the snow. It was well-trained. A farming horse. Given to her by the Fathers as a deposit.

"Killed your monster," the vagrant said.

The dog atop the monster barked. It pawed and whined at the body, as if punctuating the woman's statement.

And Fell thought he saw, for a moment, a twitch in the chest of the beast. But the dog did not move. Surely the dog would sense danger. Dogs were like that.

"So, it seems," Father Bern said.

"Although," Father Jorgmund added, "It doesn't look quite so impressive now. Not quite a monster as a…"

"A regular animal," Father Freg said.

"All monsters are animals," the hunter said.

"Indeed!" Father Velem boomed. Any mutterings in the crowd now ceased thanks to Velem's magnificent voice. His curly black eyebrows danced. "And all animals are monsters, to those who hunt them. Which would mean," he opened his palm and indicated the monster, "that to this poor beast, you were the monster. So, are you a monster, my good lady, or a monster-slayer?" Velem asked.

The woman showed her fangs when she smiled.

In the weeks since she'd arrived nobody in the village had failed to notice the blue-grey tinge her skin took on in the half-light, or those luminous spots that passed as freckles during the day. That her height and build matched any of the strongest and proudest men of the village. Her differences marked her as a common target for mocking challenges between drunken young fools in the taverns. Some called her half-breed, though they couldn't be more specific about what breeds. Others called her names. Outsider. Goblin Woman. Troll-hag.

If the woman had been aware of the names, she didn't show it. She showed nothing now, when Father Velem was calling her a monster to her face.

"Depends who's paying," she said. "Or who doesn't pay."

"Straight to the point," Jorgmund said.

"And a veiled threat," Berg said, clapping.

A hand dropped on Fell's shoulder. He spun to see his mother standing above him. She smiled.

"Where's Father?" Fell asked.

"On the roof." His mother winked down at him, then frowned at the Fathers. "Look at these four fools."

"I'm curious," Freg was saying. "Now that our problem is apparently solved, now that our livestock and children and hunting grounds are safe, what would happen if we were to," he waved his hands about as if thinking, "not pay you?"

The woman ran her tongue over her fangs and drummed her fingers on the hilt of her sword.

"You would kill for gold?" Freg asked.

"I just have," the woman pointed back at the beast.

"Oh, do stop teasing her, Freg." Velem clapped his fellow Father on the back.

Father Freg smirked. He toddled forward and produced a clinking bag, which he held out for the woman. When she went to grab it, he tugged it back a little, giggled to himself, then let her take it from him.

"We thank you for services to the Village of Halven," Father Velem announced. "You have made our village safe once more."

Light applause broke out in the crowd.

"Pompous idiot," Fell's mother muttered.

Sniggers rose around them. People glanced at his mother, and Fell wanted to sink into his shoulders. She just had to embarrass him every chance she got.

"Take off its head!" someone yelled.

"Nail it to the gatepost!" another added.

"I want its fur for my hearth!"

The vagrant woman spun on the crowd, her sword already out before her cloak had settled back around her. "Nobody touches the body!" she yelled.

Her dog barked furiously.

"Nobody!" she repeated.

Once again, Fell swore he saw the creature twitch.

The woman rounded on the four Fathers. She pointed her sword tip at Velem. "We had a deal."

Father Velem held his hands up. The crowd froze.

"Yes. Of course. The body is yours, good lady," he said. Then again, louder, his eyes not leaving the blade levelled at him, "The body is not to be touched!"

"Look at her go," Fell's mother whispered as the woman sheathed her sword.

"May I ask," Jorgmund said, "what you will do with the body?"

"Take it apart," the woman said. "Sell what I can to alchemists and sorcerers."

"Huh," Berg said. "And you get a... good price?"

The woman said nothing. She picked up the reins and led horse and sled in a large circle around the square before leaving the village again and disappearing into the trees. Nobody moved until she was out of sight. When the trees swallowed up the last sight of the creature's feet hanging off the end of the sled, everyone moved as if a spell was broken. Now that three weeks of terror had overshadowed the town, it seemed odd to go back to a normal routine. Nevertheless, a normal routine was what waited. And what they had all wanted back when they agreed to pay the monster-hunter.

Is that what they all wanted?

A great cloud of pressure swallowed Fell. He felt as if the curtain hiding the world had been pulled aside for a moment, then dropped back into place. Now the threat was gone, he realised what his life would be like. Unless something like this happened again, from this moment until he died every day would be the same.

He would live every day exactly as the one before. Like his father.

Fell looked at the deep ruts left by the sled, cutting through the snow, slicing through to brown grass and into deep, rich soil below. Leading out of the town. Out there where no day was the same. Where other people lived who had grey skin, or were short and lived in mountain kingdoms. Where there was grass and warmth and oceans and ships and monsters.

*****

Fell checked the fastenings on his pack one more time as he shoved the portion of lard-soaked bread into his mouth. He stood up and studied the ground again. With the early afternoon's falling of fresh snow, he'd lost the trail of the sled tracks some time ago. Nevertheless, his father had always taught him that there were other ways to track your quarry. The disturbance of the low branches, where only fresh snow had piled, told that something big had brushed past. And there were only so many gaps big enough to accommodate the woman, the horse, and the thick sled. Every now and then he could see the remains of a snow-smoothed indentation that had to have been made by a clomping horse.

He was closing in on the monster-hunter, he was sure of it.

Anyway, the sky was turning a darker grey already, and it was too late to turn back to Halven. He did have a torch to light his way back to the road, but he'd still have to avoid the wolves and survive the cold.

He laughed. If he did turn now and make it back, his parents wouldn't even notice he'd left. It wasn't uncommon for him to be back after dark. And if his own parents hadn't noticed he'd run away to become a monster-hunter, then he was hardly brave enough to become a monster-hunter in the first place.

He'd told his mother it was a hunt. She'd even helped him pack his bag. Didn't ask questions when he packed a little more than usual for a day out hunting rabbits.

"Stay warm," his mother had said, rubbing his shoulders. "Stay safe."

He'd walked out through one of the hunter's tunnels under the wall, acting for the whole village as if he was leaving for a rabbit hunt. But as soon as he was under the cover of the trees he'd doubled back to the main gate and the road. There, waiting for him, were the footprints of the woman and the horse, and the twin slices of the sled, only just then filling in with a light snowfall.

It was then that it stopped being a hunt and became the moment he chose a new life. He could have still turned back, but he didn't. He followed the road away from the village, sticking to the treeline. The tracks moved west, along the road for some time, before veering sharply into the surrounding forest. Fell followed.

Shortly after that, the snow fell harder for a while, but had thankfully stopped again. Fell was still on the trail.

A wolf howled, and something broke a branch to his right and fluttered off into the sky. Fell swore and punched his leg. Punishing it for freezing up. Something they always did when he was scared. It was only fear, he told himself. Trying to stop him. Trying to turn him around. Only fear.

But fear followed Fell as he followed the trail in the twilight. He knew where he was going. He was sure of it. But the light faded, and the shadows between the trees shifted and moved. Trunks that were there a moment ago stepped out of view. Branches reached down and swept fingers across his hair. Owls and wolves called his name from a distance. Every time he stopped at some half-heard voice, it seemed another pair of boots close by stopped walking, a fraction of a moment after his.

"*Wolves and ogres and trolls and bears,*" Fell sang to himself. "*Jump out to catch you unawares.*" It was only when the night had fully fallen, and the tightness in Fell's chest came from cold and panic rather than excitement, that he smelled smoke. Meat smoke.

He squinted between trunks for any sign of light, but ultimately followed the sweet scent of the cooking fire. He abandoned the trail his eyes had followed for the one his nose had found. He hoped they led to the same place.

At last, an orange glimmer sparked into view. Through a tunnel of trunks Fell had a clear view of the fire. Someone was silhouetted against it, eating from a bone. A braid fell against the person's face and she tucked it away. That was her. The grey woman.

Fell almost called out, but didn't want to waste his breath until he'd warmed up a little more. He trudged through the snow towards the fire. By the size of the joint of meat she ate, he was sure she'd have enough to share. He'd brought ale from his father's cellar to try to sweeten her.

Fell huffed forward, ignoring the fear. Forcing his legs to move. Voices still whispered from somewhere, and he was sure he still heard another pair of boots in the snow, but there was safety right ahead. Fire and safety. Fear wouldn't get him tonight.

The woman's face was clearer now, and across the fire from her lay the massive shaggy bulk of the monster's corpse. Atop it was the dog, curled up, nuzzling a bone.

Fell realized with a sick lurch that they were probably eating a part of the monster. That's what she was doing, wasn't it? Selling off parts of the monster. Why not eat the parts that weren't worth much?

In the dancing light of the fire, it almost looked like the huge creature was breathing.

Then, the dog pricked its ears. Looked right at Fell through the trees. Growled.

The woman paused for a moment, then slowly put down her joint of meat. She spoke swift words and the dog leapt to the ground.

A shout, and three armed men leapt into the firelit clearing. The woman's sword was out and blocking the first swipe before she was standing. The dog barked, in a frenzy.

Then the mound of matted white fur rumbled and spun. Heavy hands hung from heaving shoulders, a great jaw jutted open in a scowl and tiny, too-human eyes sparkled in the firelight.

The monster was very alive.

The woman threaded her sword through the chest of the closest stunned attacker. The monster lazily flung its arm out and crushed another man against a tree. It pulled back its fist, the shaken-loose snow cascading over the gore that now slumped against the trunk.

The third man dodged a thrust from the woman's sword. He dropped his ax and ran. Right towards Fell.

The dog bolted after the man; the monster roared, thumped its chest, and came after the man, too. It ran on its short legs, but pounded its fists on the ground as it ran, flinging itself forward.

Fell screamed and stumbled away as fast as he could. The whining pleas of the man were gaining. The dog barking. The monster grunting and roaring.

"What?" the man was screaming. "Why is it alive?" he yelled. Then, when he was so close Fell could almost feel his panicked breath on his back, the man made a throttled yell. "Who are—"

But the question was interrupted by a wet crunch. Not even a scream.
Fell ran on, feeling now the presence of the monster looming behind him. The dog barking on his heels. The branches whipping and scratching his face.
Something grabbed his ankle.
He tumbled forward, his face slamming into the snow.
This was it, Fell thought. Any moment now, that monster's great fist would pound his little skull into nothing. Some great adventurer, getting half a day away from his village before ending up a stain of bones and blood on the ground.
But the pounding never came. Instead, he could feel something digging and snuffling around him, nipping at the fingers of his gloves. He pushed himself up and dared to look. A wet tongue darted over his face, stinging on his cold skin. The dog barked and nuzzled into his shoulder, wagging its tail.
"Hey, pup," Fell squeaked, and patted the dog. Slowly, he turned himself around and lay on his back.
The monster stood at his feet. Watching. Heaving twin clouds from its flaring nostrils.
"Please. Don't," Fell pleaded.
But the monster didn't move. It only looked down at Fell and the dog, its eyes darting from one to the other. Its arms hung limp, face passive.
"Get out of it!" the woman yelled, storming up behind the monster.
The dog backed away from Fell and trotted over to the monster's feet. The dog sat down, tongue hanging. The monster slowly raised its massive hand and gently stroked the dog. The woman crunched up behind the monster and patted its thick arm.
"And who are you?"

"What?"

"Your name is 'what'?"

"No. You…"

"You? Did the village send 'You' to get the gold back, too?"

"What?"

The woman sighed. She reached down and pulled Fell to his feet. As easy for her as lifting a rabbit. "Gods, you're only a kid," she said. "Who are you?" she asked again. Kinder this time. "What are you doing here?"

"My… my name is Fell. I followed you."

The freckles on her skin glimmered. "Well, Fell. Despite what your villagers may have told you, my name is Brenna." She snapped her animal teeth. "Did you come to kill me, Fell? To get the gold back for your Fathers?"

"What? No."

"Then what, in the name of my gods and yours, are you doing out here?"

"It's alive again," Fell said, pointing.

The monster was focused entirely on the dog now, patting it gingerly, grinning like a child.

"It was never dead. Focus, Fell of Halven. Why did you follow me?"

"I want to become a monster-hunter."

The woman chuckled, her fangs reflecting the soft glow of her skin. "No, you don't."

The pressure of panic welled inside Fell again. His throat closed. He couldn't speak. "I…"

"Come on," Brenna said. "You can't go back to the village now." She turned around and stalked away. "Come and get warm. Have some meat," she called over her shoulder.

Fell stared up at the monster, legs locked. Afraid that if he moved he'd end up merely a stain on those huge white knuckles.

"Alva! Come!" Brenna called.

The dog yipped and shot off after the woman. The monster slowly turned and ambled off after it, lazily kicking at the mashed remains of a man. The ruined body flew off into the darkness, crashing through branches.

Fell stepped forward, and the monster didn't kill him. He followed the monster and the dog and the woman to the fire. The monster didn't kill him. He didn't look at the body next to the fire, or the mound of red-stained snow under the tree. He sat on a log. He ate the chunk of meat that was passed to him. All the while he remained astonishingly not murdered by the monster.

"What is going on?" he asked eventually.

"Do you mean the men who tried to kill us, or the fact that the yeti is still alive?"

"Yeti?" Fell pointed to the monster.

"Yeti," Brenna nodded. "It's called other things. Depends where you go. But in most books, it's called a yeti."

"Yeti," Fell tried the word on again. It was only a short word, but still sounded so foreign.

The yeti's stumpy legs were crossed to form a nest in which the dog was resting. The great white arms formed a further wall of protection around the dog. Both animals watched Fell with fire-glazed eyes.

"It's a game," Brenna said, picking meat from her teeth.

"A game?"

"A dishonest way to get money."

"So, you're not a Valon?"

Brenna coughed. She raised her eyebrows and flung a picked-clean bone into the fire. "Now, how does a little boy from a nowhere little village know what a Valon is?"

"Monster-hunters," Fell said, remembering the book of history he'd found in Halven's ill-kept library. "They're what's left of the Dragonband. A remnant of the great Feltarian Empire."

"Valons. Dragonband. The great Feltarian Empire." Brenna poked the fire. "Something like that."

"And the men who came after you?" Fell again tried not to look at the body of the man that had bled out, or the mess under the tree.

"I was expecting them," Brenna said. She laughed then. "They weren't expecting Kang."

The monster grunted at what Fell realized must be its name.

"Kang," Fell said.

The monster snorted at Fell, frowning, as if he wasn't worthy of saying that name yet.

"Sorry," Fell said to him. "Why were you expecting them?" he asked Brenna.

"Happens a lot. Village Fathers, chiefs, councils, whatever. They're all the same. Pomp and grace in front of their subjects, but deep down they're all nasty little backstabbers. Your Fathers saw how small our Kang here actually was, and decided my services weren't worth the price we agreed. Those three men were sent to get the gold back." She belched and leaned back, loosening the buckles on her leather armor and taking off her sword belt. "Quite dishonest, really."

"Dishonest!" Fell stammered. "You're the one bloody pretending to kill a monster and collecting a bounty for it. You're the one who tricked my entire village. You're the..." He stopped talking when he saw the satisfied smirk on her face.

Brenna shook her head. She drew her blade, then shoved it down through the snow and into the dirt underneath. She unpacked a small stone and a skin of oil, pulled out her blade again, and set to sharpening it.

Fell sank into silence. He chewed on his meat and watched the fire as he listened to the slow hiss of the stone sliding across Brenna's blade. Fire sparks crackled and danced, spiralling up into the branches high above. Kang's fur glowed orange. It was free of blood now, but was speckled with tiny singe marks. Fell saw a ragged scar across his thinly-haired chest. The monster's eyelids drooped as he gently dragged a thumb the size of a man's forearm across the back of the sleeping dog, Alva.

Brenna, satisfied with her sharpening and oiling, put away her sword. She yawned—what impossibly big teeth she had—and smacked her lips. Burped again.

Fell knew he should have been disappointed. He'd gambled his life away to follow a monster-hunter and beg to become her apprentice. He should be furious that she'd robbed his village. But all he felt was admiration. Valon or not, honorable or not, here was a woman who made her own money, who slept outside, and who walked with monsters.

He was still determined to follow her. More so, in fact. Remembering his bribe, Fell reached over and tugged the two bottles of ale from his pack.

Brenna's eyes lit up. "Brilliant."

"I brought these," Fell said, "to help convince you."

Brenna's eyes narrowed. "Convince me of what?"

"To take me with you."

"And you think two bottles of malty piss will help sway me?" Brenna held out a hand.

Fell passed her a bottle. She waited until he'd popped his bottle and drank some, then ripped out the cork of her own bottle with her teeth, took a deep swig, and whistled.

"Fantastic. That's a terrible ale. Exactly what I expected. Well, I'm glad you want to come with me, young Fell," she said.

"Really?"

Brenna nodded. "It was either that or kill you."

Fell sputtered out his mouthful. "What? Why?"

"I told you. You can't go back to the village."

"I thought you meant just tonight because it's too dark and... you know... wolves and ogres and trolls and bears."

"Oh no. I meant you can't go back ever again. You'd promise not to tell, but I can't risk it. You're coming with me. If I were the dramatic type I would say, Fell of Halven, that our fates are now intertwined." She waved her hands vaguely in the air. "Now get some sleep. We're quite safe with Alva and Kang on watch. We're up with the sun, and it's a hard walk to the next village of idiots. Several days."

Fell searched around the campsite. Something had seemed missing the entire time and he only just placed it. "Don't you have a horse?" he asked.

"You've just eaten it."

*****

"It's a simple game, really," Brenna said as they clambered along the leeward edge of a rocky ridge.

They'd been walking for three days since Halven. Fell had seen more than he'd ever thought existed in all the world. They'd passed between mountains, forded freezing rivers, and even wormed through an ancient tunnel. Brenna never followed a path—a yeti tended to attract attention on a path, she said—but she never appeared lost. Always they walked in same order: Brenna leading, Fell and Alva following Brenna, and Kang stomping along behind Alva.

"Simple," Fell said, to show he was paying attention. He stumbled on a loose stone and landed heavily. He groaned as he watched the stone tumble down the slope.

Kang grunted several short coughs, a sound Fell had come to realize was a kind of laughter. Fell ignored him.

Brenna had been promising to share the way she played the game since they set off that first morning, but had held off, claiming that she'd had to work him into the plan. Fell suspected that she was stalling to ensure he didn't escape until he was properly lost.

"First, we locate a village," Brenna said. "The one I have in mind is a couple of days away still."

Not that he wanted to escape. Fell had never felt so alive as when he was forging a path through the wilderness with this woman, her dog, and her yeti.

Brenna paused, and pointed to the horizon. A white and black patchwork of rocky hills and woods. "Somewhere over there," she said.

Alva nudged Fell's knee, and Fell ruffled the fur around her neck. He had learned that it was important to shower Alva with affection whenever possible. A delicate stroke across her head or scratch behind her ear was always noticed by Kang. The yeti seemed to understand that objects of Alva's returned affection were not things to be squashed or eaten.

As long as Alva was in sight, Kang lumbered without rest or complaint. Sometimes he'd lurch off suddenly with incredible speed. The first time he did this Fell screeched with terror. But the yeti reappeared moments later, holding the body of some animal he'd already started eating—a deer, a wolf, a fox, or some other wild thing. He'd always come back to Alva. Share some of his meat with her. Sometimes, if the dog seemed tired, Kang would pick her up and cradle her like a toddler with a puppy.

"We skirt the village," Brenna said, stomping on. "We find a cave or somewhere for Kang to sleep and hide. We stay there for a day or so. Kang wanders about. Hopefully gets himself spotted. Then, when he's comfortable and has been promised a fresh horse if he's a good boy, you and I and Alva make our way into town. Just a couple of vagrants and their dog looking for a bed. At whatever tavern we end up in, we make sure two things are communicated. First: The fact that I am a Valon."

"You just tell people?" Fell asked.

Brenna turned around and flashed open her coat to show her leather armor. The sigil of the Valon was burned into it. She held her fist out to Fell and he saw the sigil on the seal of her ring. The pommel of her sword, too, showed the woven blades of the Valon.

"Small town folk are nosey. Small things are noticed. Word gets around."

"All right. So, then what?"

"Next, we make casual mention of seeing something white and large out in the woods. Ask a few questions about large wolves or bears. Never use the word 'monster'. Someone else will start that rumor. You'll always have a drunk or two who claims they've seen something, if you suggest the right things. Then we sit for a couple of weeks. Stay quiet. Play cards at the tavern. Don't talk much to anyone. Spend some money. Meanwhile, Kang is out there getting anxious. He's sneaking about. He can smell Alva, you see, but he won't come into the village."

"Why not?"

"Yetis are timid by nature. They're generally afraid of large groups of people. He won't like being by himself, but he weighs that against being around lots of people, and he always stays away. Anyway, people start to spot Kang. Rumors grow. A few sheep go missing. Sightings go up. A bounty is offered. And then suddenly," Brenna slaps herself in the head, "someone remembers! Where did they see that sigil? The strange woman! The large, quiet one with the grey skin. The one they've all been making fun of. The one they call the Troll's Whore or Orc's Bastard…" She trailed off into mutterings that Fell couldn't hear over the whistle of the wind.

Fell stepped into each of Brenna's massive footprints as he followed in her silence. He remembered the names he'd called her, too. Remembered laughing at her when she was the subject of his boastful friends' claims of conquest.

"Sorry," Fell said after a while.

Brenna sniffed. "And they come to you for help," she said, talking louder now. "And you refuse. And they beg that they need you. They need you. And so, you set your price. A high price." She scoffed. "They laugh at first. But then more of their livestock disappears. Sightings go up. Soon enough they fear for their children. At last, desperate, they agree to your terms."

Her voice croaked, and she fell silent again. Fell trudged on behind her, oddly comforted by the heaving breath of Kang and the little pants from Alva.

"Idiots," Fell said.

Brenna laughed. She turned and clapped him on the shoulder. "That's right, my young apprentice. Idiots. All of them."

"But how do you make Kang seem dead?"

"Simple. Smear him with blood and convince him to lie still."

"How do you do that?"

"Magic," Brenna said. She clicked her fingers and pointed along the ridge. "There's a sheltered little glade in the valley over that rise."

"Good place to camp?" Fell asked.

"You're learning," Brenna said. "Come, Fell! Onwards to treachery and fortune."

*****

This town was larger than Halven. Twice the size, Fell reckoned. He'd had plenty of time to look at it. They'd spend a full day circling it from the cover of the forest before finding a cave. They'd let Kang wander about for a couple of days. Hopefully have him seen by a few people.

The town was a dirty smear over a few bare foothills at the foot of a handful of forested mountains. Apart from its size, Fell was surprised at how similar it was to Halven. The clang and murmur of the place was the same as Halven. The same thin lines of smoke rose from chimneys and threaded into the grey clouds above, just like Halven. Even the smell was the same, a smell he didn't realize was there until he found it again—horses and sweat. He couldn't wait to sit next to a fire.

That morning, walking without Kang was oddly unnerving. Fell felt naked without the powerful promise of protection the yeti provided. After they'd left him, pouting and sniffing in the cave, Alva had whimpered and sulked. More than once Brenna had to stop and rub the dog behind the ears before she'd take another step. They weren't usually this upset, she'd claimed.

Once they'd emerged from the cover of the forest and onto the muddy, busy road leading to the village, Fell began to notice little differences. Travelers on the road wore clothes like folks in Halven, only with different patterns, or darker fur, or cut short in some places and left longer in others. The buildings were that tiny bit different, too. They were squatter, and their eaves hung out more. As they entered the village Fell noticed that, like Halven, its name was carved into the crossbeam above the gate.

"Gelriven," Fell said.

"Cheerful bunch, aren't they?" Brenna said.

Fell saw now that the folk of the town were blank-faced and sullen. They dragged their feet and sighed with each movement. It was as if an avalanche of despair had buried them all. Even the horses hung their heads.

"What's wrong with them?" Fell whispered.

Brenna leaned down slowly. "I think the problem might be," she nodded sagely, "that they live in Gelriven." She thrust her finger out suddenly, pointing at a low, thick building with a slosh of well-trodden mud beneath its doors. "A tavern! We'll find smiles in there, my young apprentice."

Fell hurried after Brenna, who had found new vigor with the promise of a drink. She strode with purpose, letting her coat billow out behind her. Some heads turned to watch her walk, and Fell saw their eyes dart to the sword pommel.

Fell expected good cheer and the sweet smell of roasting meat when he followed Brenna through the tavern doors. What he found instead was a smoky den of hang-faced drinkers. There was neither the musicians on stage nor the good-natured landlady of Halven's tavern. There was nothing but a scabby-cheeked publican staring at them.

"You clean up after your dog," the publican said. "Or you'll be eating it."

"Right you are, sir," Brenna said. She tapped her ring on the counter, holding a few coins in her fingers. "Two ales."

The publican nodded. As he busied himself with their order, Fell saw his gaze flicker over them. Trying to read their clothes. Trying to figure out, no doubt, exactly what Brenna was. That green-grey tinge to her skin. Those pointed ears and white hair.

"You two travelers?" he asked, thumping down two tankards.

"We travel," Brenna said. "Here and there." She slid the coins along the counter.

The publican flicked the coins into his hand and took a moment to examine them before dropping them with a clank into his drawer.

Fell was certain that Brenna must have noticed the frowns, nods, and hand gestures that the publican was sharing with some of the other patrons. But she merely drank, and sighed at the roofbeams.

A man approached the bar, and communicated that he wanted another drink without saying a word. Fell was certain the man tried to smell Brenna before going back to sit down.

"Dangerous 'round here lately," the publican said finally.

"That a fact?" Brenna looked uninterested.

"How dangerous?" Fell said, as casually as he could. He couldn't believe it. Could it be that they had already instilled such fear? Only a couple of days of Kang wandering about in the forest and already people look terrified.

Brenna glanced down at him and frowned. She flicked her head out towards the rest of the tavern. Fell turned to see all eyes on them.

"You. Grey woman." A bearded, fur-covered man in the back corner of the tavern shuffled out from under a pile of tankards. He glowered across the room and raised his finger at them. "Have you seen the white beast?" he demanded.

Brenna's eyes shone. She slowly put down her tankard. "The white beast?"

Fell nudged her as secretly as he could. They were saying exactly what she'd said they would! Almost as if she'd written their words and they were players on her stage.

"Now, Geir," the publican said, holding out his hands.

"You shut up," the man called Geir snapped. He staggered towards Brenna and Fell. "I know what I saw. Out there in the woods."

"Aye. We know what you saw," someone said.

"I seen it, too," another voice piped in. Then, quieter, "I think I have."

Fell almost felt guilty. They were terrified! Of Kang! The biggest, dumbest thing he'd ever met. If they'd ever seen Kang pick up and cradle Alva, they'd all be ashamed of themselves.

"What kind of beast is it?" Fell asked.

Geir had staggered his way across the tavern now, and spoke in a rasp. "Bone-white. Muscles like twisted tree branches. Thrice the height of a man."

Fell could barely contain a smile behind his tankard. That was quite some exaggeration.

But then Brenna reached down and clutched Fell's arm. She squeezed hard. Fear laced her eyes.

Blank terror fell over across Geir's face. "I saw it eat my son," he whispered.

Fell's stomach sank through the bottom of the stool.

What did the old drunk mean? Surely Kang hadn't eaten someone?

"Three weeks ago," Geir said.

Fell sputtered out his ale.

"Three weeks…?" Brenna breathed.

Fell swallowed. They'd been here for two days. What was happening? Were they all confused about time?

"Since then, more have gone missing. Children have disappeared."

"My cousin's boy," someone yelled.

"My neighbour's daughter," said someone else.

"I'm sorry," Brenna said. She swallowed deeply, and held her head in her hand. "Oh no."

It hit Fell finally.

Nobody was talking about Kang.

This was something else. This was a different monster altogether.

"We sent men into the forest to kill the beast. None returned. We sent word for help," the publican said. "No help came. Maybe the beast killed the messengers. Maybe they got the message through and nobody believed us."

"But we know what we saw." Geir pointed at Brenna's leather armor. "And I know what I see now."

Brenna twitched her coat around herself.

"You're a Valon!" Geir announced. He grinned, yellow and cracked teeth showing. He turned and held his hands up. "A bloody monster-hunter!" he yelled at the rest of the tavern.

A roar of triumph erupted in the smoky room. Geir clapped some nearby punters on the back. Tankards smashed together with oaths of justice and revenge. The publican poured Brenna another drink and winked at her. Fell laughed weakly, not knowing what else to do. Brenna only stared at her newly-filled tankard.

Suddenly, Alva's ears pricked up. She whimpered, and pawed Brenna's leg. Then Brenna stared at the door of the tavern as Alva yipped and pawed at it. It was still a few moments before the noise died down enough for Fell to hear it, too. A low wail. Mournful and frightened. Coming from outside.

Brenna exploded from her stool and crashed through the door. Fell stumbled after her, ignoring the shouts of alarm from the tavern. The first screams from the village had begun.

Fell already knew what was happening, but as he sprinted and slid his way into the main square of the village there he was. Kang, back hunched and trembling, scurrying into the village. His face down, and his huge knuckles sweeping the snow, he crooned like a mourning widow.

Villagers lined the streets, hiding behind each other as they stared at the thing. But screams and calls of surprise soon gave way to awed confusion. Some even began laughing nervously to see this shaggy beast cowering as it walked into their village.

He was scared. Fell could think of nothing so terrifying that Kang would be frightened. The thought made his legs heavy.

"Alva!" Brenna yelled. "Get back!"

"Alva!" Fell echoed. He stepped after the dog, but Brenna's arm smacked across his chest.

"Don't."

Alva had reached Kang now. She began circling him, licking his arms and face, wagging her tail furiously. At her attentions Kang stopped walking. His wails turned to sobbing, then silence. He sat down in the snow. Alva climbed into his lap and curled up between his legs. Kang gently patted her head and grunted, ignoring the stares all around him.

And stares there were.

Fell thought the entire village must have come out by now. All staring and still. They glanced at each other, holding hammers, half-sewn clothes, tankards, or the detritus of whatever they had been doing before Kang arrived. Geir, the publican, and everyone else who had been in the tavern, leaked out onto the street.

"Don't move," Brenna warned. "Don't approach him."

"But Alva!" Fell hissed.

"Shut up. I'm thinking."

A rustle and murmur grew now from the crowd. The conversation was curiously similar to what onlookers had said in Halven.

"This is the beast?" someone said.

"This is not the beast," another answered.

"It isn't?"

"Oh good," Brenna muttered. "Here come the village Fathers."

Three bearded men wreathed in long furs and chains pushed to the front of the crowd. Surrounding them were a dozen armed men, half of whom had crossbows already nocked and aimed at Kang. Others held shaking swords and spears.

The foremost Father rubbed his beard. "What is it?"

"A yeti," the oldest-looking of the three said.

"And this is not the beast of the forest?"

"That is not the curse!" Geir yelled. "That is not the creature that ate my son!"

As if he were some authority, Geir's words rippled through the crowd. This was not the beast that had terrorized the village. This was something else. This was nothing to be frightened of. Look at it. Patting a dog like a child.

"What is it doing?" another Father demanded.

"It is frightened," the oldest Father said.

The number of people laughing at the absurd sight grew. Fell couldn't believe it. If any of them had encountered Kang in the forest, they'd have been terrified. They'd have exaggerated what they saw. But now, with Kang so obviously afraid, lost in his own world where only he and Alva existed, he seemed no threat at all.

"This is not our curse!" the lead Father yelled. "This creature was drawn away from the forest. This yeti, too, can smell, and is afraid of the monster that hunts us. Look at it petting the dog. It is more like us than the thing out there." He pointed at the mountains.

The Fathers turned to each other and spoke in low voices.

"I knew something was wrong," Brenna whispered. "He seemed more jumpy than usual. Didn't want us to leave. Must have sensed something. This other monster. He must have been frightened enough to come and find us. Damn your simple mind, Kang."

"What did he sense?" Fell asked. "What's the other monster?"

But Brenna only shook her head slowly and exhaled.

The mutters and laughs of the crowd began to turn to jeers. From among the armed men came the sound of clanking.

"We will chain this beast while it is docile," the head Father said. "And tonight, we will leave it outside the gates as an offering to our curse. Let beast feast on beast tonight."

Four men dragging a heavy chain stepped forward. They took long, deliberate steps, keeping their heads low and their eyes trained on the yeti.

Kang's side was turned to the men, but he didn't seem to register their approach at first. Only when Alva's head turned to look at them and she let out a small yip did Kang suddenly turn his head and bark, too.

The men paused. Kang bared his teeth.

Alva slipped out from the safety of Kang's lap and put herself between the men and the yeti. She barked. Kang's body tensed; his shoulders unhunched as he turned to face the four men.

"Alva," Fell breathed.

Alva leapt at the front man, and he kicked out at her.

Kang's roar thundered. Immediately on his feet he thumped the ground with a mighty fist, sending a shock of snow into the air. The four men dropped the chain and leapt backwards. Kang knuckle-walked his way over and loomed above them. He raised a fist.

"Kang!" Brenna darted forward, holding her hands up. "No! Kang. No!"

Kang paused. He puffed his cheeks, watching Brenna.

Fell ran after her, unable to match her long strides in the snow.

"No, Kang!" Brenna yelled.

Kang dropped his fist to his side. He panted, pushed out his cheeks. Roared half-heartedly at Brenna.

"No!" Brenna scolded. She pointed at Kang. "Kang. No."

Fell sprinted to Alva, who received his hug with licks and a wagging tail.

"Look, Kang!" Fell yelled. He ruffled Alva's neck fur. "Look, she's all right. Alva is all right."

"Alva isn't hurt," Brenna cooed, stroking the fur on Kang's huge forearm. "She's not hurt."

Fell walked with Alva over to Kang and Brenna. The four of them stood there in the middle of an entire village of confused and frightened people.

"What now?" Fell said.

"I'm thinking," Brenna said.

"Somebody," the head Father said, crossing his arms, "had better start talking."

*****

Fell had never been locked in irons before. He'd always imagined they'd be easy enough to slip out of by tucking his thumbs into his palms. But these were tight. They dug into his wrists. The chains they were attached to were heavy, and it was hard to scratch his nose.

Brenna wasn't bothered by hers. She had looped the chains up over her shoulders to lessen their weight.

Fell copied her. "Not your first time in chains?" he asked.

"Just shut up and let me think and it won't have to be my last."

Kang was bundled up in the chains, too. His ankles and wrists were locked together, and the chain looped around his body several times. Alva sat on his lap still. Brenna, under threat of death, had wrapped him in chains herself. As mocking as they were, nobody else in the village dared to get close to Kang.

The day had been long. At first, Fell had expected they would try to fight their way out of the town. That's what heroes did when they were outnumbered. But the people of Gelriven were not hordes of evil. They were innocent, scared villagers. They were angry, certainly, but they had a right to be.

It hadn't taken long before Brenna's game was figured out. Some of the villagers knew of it. They told second-hand stories about the game, heard from distant relatives in other places. And Brenna admitted it all. She tried to tell them that Fell was innocent, but nobody listened to that and Fell was roughly chained up, too. Brenna calmed Kang down. When she put the chains around him, she'd made sure there was enough slack for him to pet Alva so he'd keep quiet and calm. Fell knew Kang could easily break the chains apart if he was angry, or if Alva was threatened again, but it seemed enough to keep the villagers confident.

"What will they do to us?" Fell asked.

Brenna snorted.

The Fathers had been gone for some time. They had disappeared to consult with each other, leaving an armed guard circling the prisoners. Weapons were pointed both without and within. Many villagers had gone on with their day, but there were enough still loitering to call out names and threats. Brenna took the brunt of the insults, but a few were thrown at Fell, too. Other things were hurled. Rotten things smashed near their feet. Half-frozen horse dung rained over them from upper-storey windows.

"I've never been hated before," Fell said.

Brenna laughed. "What a life of privilege you've enjoyed."

"Couldn't Kang help us escape?"

"Kang would be cut down by these archers. He'd kill a few before he died maybe, but he probably wouldn't escape. Besides, these are innocent people, and I don't murder innocent people."

"But—"

"Shut up, they're coming."

The Fathers walked back to the makeshift open-air court in the middle of their village. They were making a clanking sound, but the noise seemed too loud to be just from the metal.

"What are they going to do?"

"Hang us."

"Hang us?" Fell's throat tightened. "Hang us?"

Brenna's chains rattled as she shrugged. "Probably."

The head Father silenced the muttering. He pointed a finger at Brenna. "You are a woman who preys on fear and grief. Forming a dark fellowship with this... creature, you employ superstition and trickery for your own gain. There are people here who have lost loved ones to the curse that has come into these woods."

Brenna didn't reply. She let the silence settle until somebody else spoke.

This time it was the oldest Father. "You wear the mark of a monster-hunter, yet it is you who are the monster."

Agreeing murmurs and hums rose up all around them.

Fell winced, remembering similar words spoken to her in Halven.

Brenna growled. "You're all the same," she said.

"If we were to catch you in this lie under ordinary circumstances," the head Father said, "perhaps we would have you hanged."

More murmurs of agreement.

"But these are not ordinary circumstances," he said. "It has been suggested that we tie you all up outside the gates and let the beast devour you all. It was this fate for you I was particularly keen on. But it was Father Felren's idea that eventually won out."

The oldest Father, who Fell assumed was Felren, now stepped forward. He pulled his hand out from his robes, and in it was a bulging purse of coins. He shook it. "This is the purse of money you had on you. If we were to double it, I assume it would be sufficient to cover your usual fee?"

"What?" Brenna said.

"It is hard to kill a monster-hunter. And so, we concluded that you must be a real Valon. Perhaps strayed from their noble path, but you are a Valon nonetheless. Yes?"

Brenna coughed a laugh. "Noble."

"Are you a Valon?" Felren demanded.

Brenna clucked her tongue. "Yes. Yes, I am a Valon."

"So, if you call yourself a monster-hunter, go hunt our monster. Our real monster. I imagine having a yeti with you will be an advantage in a fight."

"If I fail?"

"If you die, you die. Nothing changes for us. If you win you have saved us, and the fee is yours." The bag of money disappeared back into the robes. "When you bring back the head of the beast. The real beast."

"And if I refuse?" Brenna asked.

"A gallows can be erected by morning."

A dark tint closed in over Fell's eyes. He felt a rising sickness. He had left Halven to begin an adventure that would end by his being hanged in the very next town he walked into.

Brenna sighed. To Fell's shock, she laughed. A bitter laugh, but a laugh nonetheless.

"Do we take your mirth as agreement?" the head Father asked, cocking his head.

Brenna nodded. "Got any spare horses?"

*****

"As near as we can guess," Geir slurred, "the beast comes down this valley. We found out once when we followed the... marks in the snow. The blood." He pointed down, and almost fell from his horse.

"Careful, old-timer," Brenna said.

"Snowed over now," Geir mumbled. "Like it never happened."

The Fathers hadn't appointed Geir to accompany them, but the old drunk wouldn't leave them alone, insisting that he could point them in the right direction.

The shallow valley they rode along had a thin stream cutting a line down a lazy slope between two peaks. Trees lined the tops of defined banks on either side, and Fell guessed that this must be a stronger river in the summertime, when the mountain waters thawed. A light snow was falling now, and the milky afternoon light made the surrounding forest dance with shadows. Not even the footfalls of the yeti could calm Fell's heart.

"Most people disappear from hereabouts," Geir went on, waving his hands around.

They had come to a bend in the valley, where the little stream meandered and pooled around a snow-capped boulder.

"And this is as far as I'll go," Geir said, bringing his horse to a halt. He watched with suspicion as Alva lapped from the stream, and next to her Kang collected water into his palm to drink. The horses, unused to a yeti, were jittery, and shied away from Kang as he passed by.

"They do everything together?" Geir asked. "The dog and the yeti?"

"Loyal," Brenna said.

Geir patted his horse's mane. "If you avenge my son..." He stared into the mane for a while, picking clumps of snow from it. "Well, you'll always have a seat at my table. Thief or not."

Brenna nodded quickly in reply. She didn't watch as Geir drove his swerving horse back down the well-trodden path. Didn't see the old man stop and look back once, as if to say something, then jab his mount's ribs into a trot and away.

"What are we going to do?" Fell said, turning back to Brenna. She had dismounted, and was filling up a small glass vial with water. She corked it and shook it violently.

"What we said we'd do," Brenna said. "Kill a monster."

"But..." Fell didn't want to suggest what he was thinking. "Geir's gone now. They wouldn't know," he said lamely.

"Won't get far without money," Brenna said, frowning at the swirling particles in the vial.

Fell wasn't sure if he was about to apologize, or suggest that they could make more money. When saw the tears prickling in Brenna's eyes, he said nothing.

She nodded softly and sighed. "Yes. We could run, Fell of Halven. We could disappear into the trees. Let Gelriven deal with its own curse. More will die. Those who aren't killed by the beast will abandon the village. Some will die traveling. Sickness. Cold. Beasts. Bandits. Those who survive will tell of their cursed village and the disgraced monster-hunters who ran instead of helping."

"You're doing this for honor?" Fell would never figure out how Brenna's mind worked.

"I am still a Valon. Whatever else that means, and whatever baggage I bring with me, I'm still trained and sworn to kill monsters that threaten the peace."

"I'm frightened," Fell said. He clapped his hand over his mouth when he realized he'd spoken aloud.

Brenna nudged her horse close to his. "Me, too. But you followed me for adventure, didn't you? You're not going to run away now, are you? Come on, my fresh apprentice. Your first real lesson. Let's kill a monster."

Fell's chest swelled. "Yes." He laughed despite his fear. "Let's kill... wait. What is it?"

Brenna dragged a fang across the flesh of her palm until blood welled from the cut. "What we're dealing with sounds like—and I hope I'm wrong—something that's twice the height of Kang." She uncorked the vial and squeezed in several drops of blood before re-corking and shaking it again. "It's strong and thin. It looks like a gnarled white tree. Bark-like skin. Hair like strands of moss. Long arms and legs that can be cut off, then crawl right back and reattach." Brenna breathed heavily. She closed her eyes. "I never thought I'd see one."

"What is it?"

"A slender troll."

"Slender troll," Fell echoed. A half-remembered picture from a book brought him visions of long fingers and gaping teeth. "All right. All right. How... do we kill it?"

"Destroy its body completely."

"How do we do that?"

"Fire." Brenna held the vial up to the failing light. It glowed a swirling purple. "And magic."

Kang grunted suddenly. He reached out and picked up Alva. Dog and yeti looked up the valley, then Alva struggled until Kang let her down again. She growled at the mountains.

"Looks like our guide led us to the right place," Brenna said. She remounted and kicked her heels in. The horse was reluctant, but eventually yielded and plodded up the valley. Alva yipped, and scurried along behind them. Kang, of course, followed Alva.

"What's in the vial?" Fell said.

"Magic."

Fell huffed.

"Herbs, mostly," Brenna said. "It's what I use to get Kang to appear dead."

"Ah. You're going to use it on the troll."

Brenna winked. "That's the idea. How good are you at throwing snowballs, kid?"

Fell was the best at throwing snowballs. "I'm all right," he said.

"Good at catching?"

"What?"

Brenna had already thrown the vial of magic. Fell snatched it out of the air.

"Nice," Brenna said. "Listen. When we get close enough you mix that with some snow, make a snowball, and aim for the troll's mouth. The blood will make it want to swallow. Once it's knocked out, we take it apart and burn its body."

"Is that really the plan?" Fell asked. "Throw a snowball?"

"That's *your* part of the plan," Brenna said.

Fell waited for more elaboration, but it never came. He figured he knew what to do and that was enough. Simply throw a snowball into a troll's mouth. Get close enough to a terrifying monster to throw a snowball into its mouth. Fell laughed. It was absurd.

"What's so funny?" Brenna muttered.

"Adventuring," Fell said. "It isn't really what I thought it would be."

"What, you always wanted to be a hero?"

"Yeah."

"Small town kids are like that."

They rode on in silence for a while. The afternoon faded towards twilight, and the snow began to glow the deep orange-blue of the sunset. Alva paused every now and then, and Kang was barking and grunting more than Fell had ever heard before. He sniffed the air, growling, but always followed Alva.

Brenna's eyes glowered at the valley ahead of them, flicking her face to the treeline, following things that Fell couldn't see or couldn't hear. Her skin was luminous in this light.

"Where are you from?" Fell wondered aloud.

Brenna grinned her fangs at him. "Why is everyone so obsessed with where I'm from and what I am?"

Fell shrugged. "Just wondering."

"They always wonder. Then they guess. Half-orc, half-human. Half-dark elf. Frostreaver. Half-something, half-something else. They never guess I might be a whole."

"All right. So, what is that whole?"

Brenna shook her head and laughed. "You're missing my point, Fell."

"Am I?"

"Truth is, I don't know what I am. Didn't know I was different until other people started pointing it out. I was raised in a human city by human parents, but it was made clear to me that I didn't belong there. At first, I hated that I was different. Ugly. I tried to find my own people, but nobody came close. I got good at fighting. You do when you're different from everybody else. Then I found the Valons. A group of people who belonged together because of a skill, a talent, not the color of their skin or the length of their teeth. I'd found a home. Or at least I thought I had."

"What happened?"

"The truth is, Fell, people like to look for those differences. They—"

A raspy squeal seared Fell's ears. Birds exploded from surrounding trees, their black silhouettes dancing against the darkening sky. Kang barked, and Alva tucked herself between his legs, yipping defiantly.

Brenna jumped from her horse and hissed out her sword. "Get on your feet."

Fell hurried from the saddle and slumped to the ground. He picked up the dropped vial of magic herbs and clutched it tightly.

Brenna stomped over to Fell's horse, raised her sword, and brought the flat of the blade down hard on its rump. The horse shrieked and shot off up the valley, sending up clumps of mud and snow behind it.

"What are you doing?"

Brenna turned and slapped her thighs. "Alva! Come here, girl."

Another squeal echoed through the forest from all directions. Fell spun, convinced it was behind him, but saw nothing among the trees.

Alva whimpered.

"Alva!" Brenna demanded. "Here!"

Alva slinked out from the cover of Kang's legs. Kang growled, but didn't follow. He was watching the horse, which had slowed now, but still trotted, confused, up the valley.

Brenna ruffled Alva's hair. "Good girl," she soothed. She unraveled a piece of rope from her pack and tied it around Alva's neck. "You're my good girl," she whispered. The other end of the rope went around a tree trunk. A knot pulled tight.

"Alva stays here," Brenna said to Fell. "You come with me, but hang back until it's time to throw... Where is the snowball?"

"Oh!" Fell dropped to the ground, tipped out the contents of the vial into the snow, and began shaping his snowball.

"Kang!" Brenna snapped.

Kang turned to face her.

"Horse? You want that horse?"

Kang grunted.

"You're a brave boy, aren't you?"

Kang thumped his chest.

Then the horse in the valley screamed. From the trees stepped the slender troll. A thrill like a cold hand gripped Fell's neck at the sight of it. A twisted mockery of a creature, exactly as Brenna had described it. Its huge trunk-like legs propelled it towards the retreating horse. Fingers like vines wrapped around the horse's back legs. The horse bucked and thrashed, but the movement had no effect on the troll's grip. The troll twisted its arm, and ripped the horse's back legs off.

Fell vomited, narrowly missing the ball of snow. The other horse was already running into the woods. Alva barked.

Brenna yelled and ran at the troll, and Kang, glancing at Alva, charged at it, too. Fell's legs were soupy, but he eventually got to his feet, holding the snowball, and ran after them. They were an odd pair, the strange woman and the yeti, but he certainly wouldn't want them running at him.

The troll watched with curiosity for a moment, then dropped the horse's legs. Its misshapen mouth opened in another shriek. Fell froze at the sound as if it held some magic. His chest tightened again, and his legs were filled with iron. Maybe it was the size of those teeth. And a mouth that could swallow him whole.

He tested the weight of the snowball. At least that mouth was a big target. He stepped forward again, the spell broken. An adventurer had to be brave. Even in the face of a slender troll.

The troll sidestepped, assessing the three threats approaching. It swiped its long arms out. Shrieked again.

Kang roared. A mighty, thick sound in answer to the troll's high-pitched call.

Behind Fell somewhere, Alva barked.

"Keep close enough to throw that, Fell!" Brenna yelled.

Fell saw that she was keeping her distance from Kang, mirroring his movements but keeping separate so that the troll had to deal with a threat from two directions. This was clearly infuriating it. One thing Fell knew about trolls was that they weren't smart. The slender troll shook its head and bared its teeth, swiping its arms out in turns at its two attackers.

"We've got it confused, Fell! Come closer!" Brenna yelled.

The troll wailed at her in reply and Kang answered with another deep bellow.

Fell hurried forward, wielding the snowball, but then froze in fear when the troll's attention was briefly on him again.

"Use the fear, Fell!" Brenna shouted.

Fell shoved himself forward again, willing his heavy legs to move faster.

Kang suddenly launched. He clasped one fist in the other and slammed it down on the troll's foot.

The troll flailed at the attack, wrapping its fingers around its foot. It yelled at Kang and swiped at him, but the yeti was now safely out of range. While the troll was still occupied, Brenna pulled a dagger from her thigh and threw it, hitting the troll in its side with a wet *thunk*. It screamed and bucked. Wiggling its fingers, it found the dagger and wrenched it out with a spurt of blood before flicking it away onto the snow.

"Get ready, Fell!" Brenna yelled.

The troll groaned, then inhaled. Fell saw that it was about to shriek again. He readied his arm, set his aim. The troll's fingers curled in rage. The knotted muscles around its mouth tensed. The keening shriek sent a shock through Fell's head just as he released the snowball.

And with horrific certainty, Fell watched his throw go wide. The snowball sailed past the troll's open mouth and splattered onto its shoulder.

Brenna's yell of frustration mingled with his own.

The troll paused for a moment and looked at the pink-tinged snow running down its arm. It then turned its head curiously towards Fell. It took a lurching step between Brenna and Kang. Towards Fell.

Fell's legs wouldn't move. He shook in the grip of cold fear.

"No!" Brenna yelled. She bolted at the troll's legs and slashed. Dark blood hissed out onto the snow. The troll pulled his leg back in a rage, then bent down and spun to attack her. But Kang was already in the air and clamped his teeth into the troll's arm, wildly flailing his fists.

"Yeah!" Fell yelled.

The troll leapt away from Brenna, spun, and dropped. He fell right on top of Kang, whose muffled bellows of pain were answered with frantic barking from Alva. The troll swiveled its limbs and found its feet again. It scooped Kang up from the ground in long fingers and threw him. Kang flew a short distance before crashing into the waiting trees and slumping in an unmoving pile.

"Kang!" Fell yelled.

"No!" Brenna ran at the troll, who now rounded on her and shrieked in response. She raised her sword and screamed an oath that curdled Fell's blood where he stood. She brought the sword down on the troll's descending hand, slicing off a finger.

But Fell watched on in horror as the troll ignored its severed digit and wrapped its hand around her. It brought her up to its face, opening its tombstone teeth.

Fell cursed himself as he hurried forward. If only he had another magic snowball.

A horrible crack echoed through the valley. Brenna wailed in pain. She spat blood and yelled at the monster as it squeezed the life out of her, snapping her bones in its grip. Fell began sobbing. Alva was hysterical behind him, yapping and whimpering.

The sword. The sword was lying in the snow under the troll.

Fell punched his legs. "Use the fear," he commanded himself. He sprinted for the sword, barely noticed by the troll. Another series of horrible cracks, and Brenna wailed again. Blood had started to drip from the fingers of the troll. Fell ignored it all, focusing on the sword. A last desperate hope.

Suddenly, something darted past him. Something trailing a frayed end of rope.

"Alva!" Fell yelled.

The little dog threw herself at the troll, clamping down on one of its ugly toes and whipping her head, growling fiercely.

"Alva, you get!" Fell sobbed uselessly. He couldn't even make words properly.

The drips of blood on the snow grew heavy, until suddenly Brenna dropped to the ground in a mess of flesh and bones. The troll had let her go and was staring, apparently amused, at the little dog.

Brenna didn't make a sound, but shifted her weight slightly. She was still alive. Fell rushed to her.

The troll gave Alva a little shove with its toe. She tumbled back, then jumped up and attacked its feet again. The troll frowned.

It then lifted its great foot and stomped Alva into the ground.

"No!" Fell retched. He started crawling towards the sword again, but made the mistake of looking up to see the troll now watching him.

The troll bent down.

"No. No," Fell pleaded.

From somewhere came a low grunt. The troll paused. Looked up.

Fell spun to see Kang, bloodied but whole, standing at the treeline. His face was blank, staring at the troll's foot, where a moment ago had stood his beloved Alva.

Kang's massive hands slowly curled into fists, and the muscles of his shoulders bulged. He bared his teeth. Thumped his chest. Roared with such fury that the trees around him shook off their snow and the boom echoed into the mountains.

Then he attacked. Leaping the full length that the troll had thrown him, Kang slammed into his opponent. A fist the size of a sheep cracked the troll across the head. Another punched into its chest and cracked the bone underneath. The troll wailed and stumbled backwards. But Kang was there when he landed. Pummeling, stomping, and beating the troll, not letting it gather itself, not pausing for anything. The troll's fingers reached out and wrapped around

Kang, but he snapped those fingers off, bit down on them. With roars of grief and unhindered rage, Kang's fists kept punching until they were wet with the troll's dark blood. Until the troll stopped fighting back. Stopped moving entirely. And then Kang punched some more. The cracking of bone soon gave way to the slush of flesh pounded into snow. Still Kang punched. He punched until the heat of his rage melted through the snow and he had punched the troll apart entirely. Until all that was left was a red hollow of gore-strewn mud.

At last, Kang stopped. He stepped from his carnage, fur pink with troll blood. Ignoring Fell, he walked over to where the broken remains of Alva lay in the snow. Sinking to his knees, Kang threw mournful sobs to the sky.

"Kang," groaned Brenna.

"Brenna!" Fell gasped. He went to her, lay down in the snow with her. "Brenna. Are you...?"

Brenna's ruined face smiled. She winced as she tried to unfold herself from way the troll had crumpled her. Something in her body crackled, and she yelled out. Her breathing was short and ragged. "No... Not all right... Kang?"

Kang pushed his great shaking hands under Alva. He slowly pulled her up into his arms, cooing softly. Tears rolled down his glowing cheeks as he cradled the dead dog.

Fell stood up. "Kang," he said.

Kang pulled Alva tighter to his chest, narrowing his eyes at Fell. He barked and stepped forward. Fell stumbled back down to the ground. Kang stood over Fell and Brenna, frowning down at them. He grunted, cuddled Alva's corpse to his cheek, then turned away and walked into the trees.

"Kang!" Fell called.

"Let him go," Brenna wheezed. "Let go."

*****

"I can still smell that troll's burning flesh," Fell said, readjusting his grip on the stretcher. He had built a fire in the trench made by Kang's rage. Had stayed to ensure it was properly alight before leaving. It didn't seem like anything could regenerate from being completely punched apart like that, but Fell had to be sure. They'd stayed the night next to that huge fire to be sure it wouldn't come back. Maybe, also, to see if Kang would come back. But he never did.

"You're heavy, you know," Fell said. "I'd take a rest, but if it's all the same to you I'd rather get back. I am hungry, though. You?"

He looked back at Brenna's quiet face, her eyes staring up at the web of branches meeting over the road above. Her blood had frozen around her in clumps. A deep slash trailed behind them through the snow from the pointed end of the triangular stretcher, cutting through into the mud below. It was hard work when the stretcher caught on a root or stone, or when Brenna's foot flopped over the side. Kang would have been a big help.

"I wish we'd brought something to eat." Fell smiled. "Maybe they'll give us a hero's welcome when we get back to Gelriven. What I wouldn't give for a hot bowl of my mother's breakfast broth and a chunk of soft bread."

He adjusted the stretcher handles again so it didn't pinch his finger where the ring was. It was too big for him. And he didn't think he'd ever get used to wearing a sword.

"Hopefully we can find you a nice place in Gelriven," Fell said. "I know it's not your kind of town, but I can't really take you with me."

He sniffed, annoyed that he couldn't wipe the cold wetness from his face.

"When I return your sword and ring to Valonholm, maybe they'll come and get you," Fell said. "Maybe they've got a place there for you."

Fell rounded a corner in the road and saw the gate of Gelriven ahead of him. From somewhere came the low moan of a horn.

"You hear that, Brenna?" Fell said. He slumped to his knees, dropping the stretcher into the snow. He scrambled around to look her in the eyes. "You hear the horn? They're announcing our victorious return."

Brenna's bright eyes stared back, unblinking.

The Bronze Dragon

By Jacqueline Abela

53BM
Age of Destiny

Trading was well underway at the market in Isatarist when Mallory emerged from The Bronze Dagger Inn. She rubbed her eyes with the heels of her hands as they adjusted to the harsh sunlight that bounced off the many steel and gold items. Just as she stepped forward, a woman who had been running tripped over her extended foot and fell into the dirt beside her.

"I'm so sorry," Mallory said as she gripped the woman's thin arm to help her back to her feet.

The woman, whose face was marked with scars and dirt, flicked her eyes between Mallory and someone over her shoulder. Mallory, noticing that the arm she was holding was in a tense, bent position, looked down to see that it was gripping two fox furs. She looked back at the woman and saw a familiar glint in her eye, the one that came before the decision of fight or flight, but Mallory tightened her grip before she had a chance to try to get away.

"Mal!" the familiar voice of Anders called between puffed breaths. "How can I repay you?"

He ripped the furs out of the woman's grip, which fell open as she quickly realized her defeat. Mallory let go and noticed how easily her fingers left a mark on her malnourished frame. It was definitely going to bruise. The woman glared at her, then turned and walked away. Mallory had already returned her attention to Anders and forgotten all about the woman's presence, as did all the others who had stopped to watch the commotion.

"I need work, Anders," Mallory said.

"Yes, I know." Anders looked down at the foxes, stroking the fur where the woman's tight grip had matted the coat.

Mallory had been in Isatarist for eight days and was yet to hear of her next job. She didn't like to stay in one place for too long, unless it was her home in Darvalon. Isatarist was far too crowded for her. Even an early morning stroll resulted in bumping into a stranger.

"There is actually word of a job," Anders started, still looking down at the furs.

"Where?" Mallory asked, suddenly wide awake.

"You've been asked for directly," Anders added.

"Who?" Mallory frowned.

Anders lifted his eyes but not his head, so that he looked her in the eye from beneath his thick, red eyebrows.

"Anders," Mallory prompted.

"Havelock," Anders finally answered.

"*Havelock?*" Mallory repeated.

"Yes." Anders nodded once.

"Huh…"

Mallory raised her eyebrows as she focused on the busy scene of the Trades over Anders' shoulder. She could see him frown and tilt his head to try to catch her attention, but her mind was too far gone in thought to return to him. Havelock was a sorcerer and one everyone was warned to stay clear of, though Mallory was sure it was Havelock himself who had spread that warning. He wanted to be known as powerful and dangerous, no doubt striving for the most powerful in all of Draston. And he wanted Mallory to hunt a monster for him.

"Okay," Mallory said, and stepped around Anders to go to Havelock.

"Okay?!" Anders gripped her arm and she pivoted back around to him. "What do you mean, okay?"

"Anders, I've got a job," Mallory stated what she thought was obvious, and gestured over her shoulder with her thumb to indicate where she planned to continue going.

"Mallory, didn't you hear me? The job is from *Havelock. The* Havelock." Anders emphasized the words as though she were stupid or hard of hearing, or both.

"Yes, Anders, I heard you. Havelock has a job for me, so I'd better..." She gestured over her shoulder again and took a step back as though to continue on her way.

"Mal, he's dangerous," Anders said.

Mallory laughed, and folded her arms. "So am I."

"Yeah, but—"

"Anders!" Mallory threw her hands up as though to defend herself. "It's fine. I'm a monster hunter, and Havelock apparently has a monster for me to hunt. I'm not going to turn down a job."

Anders' shoulders dropped as he became the second person that day to lose a battle to her, and it wasn't even lunchtime. He set his mouth into a tense, straight line, then nodded once and took a step back to give her space to go.

"Okay. Just... Consider the job before you agree to it. There will be other jobs; you don't have to say yes to this one just because it came first," he said.

"Yeah, sure."

Mallory smiled and patted his arm in what she thought was a comforting gesture, but was no doubt just as awkward as it came to her. She turned and left him standing there, watching her retreating back until he could no longer spot her amongst the crowd.

She knew where Havelock's home was, everyone did, but she had never actually been there or seen it. It was memorized after being warned so many times to not go there. Everyone stayed away from the area for fear of getting on his radar. Mallory shook her head as she realized that she had subconsciously avoided the area with the same fear.

As she walked uphill, past boarded shopfronts that were impossible to rent, the number of people she came across drastically lessened. She felt relief from being out of the hordes of people, but her heartbeat also quickened as she neared the house she feared.

While all the buildings around were sandy in color, Havelock's was a dark brown-black. There was only one other person in the cross street, and he quickened his pace as soon as he was walking by Havelock's home. The man realized he was being watched, and his head snapped around to look at Mallory. His eyes were wide, wondering why she would willingly be there, and he didn't drop his gaze until he was walking down the next street, out of sight.

Mallory felt goosebumps travel down her neck as she, too, felt that eyes were on her. She looked up to where she was sure the watcher was, behind the tall, arched window on the top floor of Havelock's home. All the windows were tinted so no one could see in, which Mallory was sure was just an illusion, but she didn't have the skills to be able to look past it. She stared at the window until she felt the feeling go away, and she knew he was on his way downstairs. She walked to the front door and went to knock, but it swung open right away.

"There's no need to be creepy," Mallory called out as she stepped inside. The lighting was low in the small entryway, with low-burning lanterns hung around. There was a wide staircase that went straight up to the second floor, and at the top of the stairs was Havelock, silhouetted by the daylight coming in through the window. "I'm here for the job— you don't need to show off or anything."

"You don't even know what the job is," Havelock called out.

Mallory stepped one foot on the first stair, then paused, unsure if she should go upstairs or wait for his direction. She stayed there in the awkward position, one foot on the stair, one foot on the floor of the entryway.

"That's why I'm here, to find out more." Mallory shrugged.

"Come upstairs," Havelock said, then turned and walked to the left.

Mallory slowly ascended, and turned the corner to find him in a small library. He was seated in a brown leather armchair with his back to her. She walked past a desk piled with papers and books and stood at the side of his chair.

"I have a job for you," he said, looking out the window to the street below.

"Yes..." Mallory prompted.

"A hunting job," he said.

"That's what I do." Mallory crossed her arms impatiently.

"For a dragon," he said, then looked up at her to gauge her reaction.

Mallory frowned. She waited for him to say something more, but he sat in silence and waited for her.

"But... I hunt monsters. I think you want someone from the Dragonband to hunt a dragon," Mallory offered, starting to feel deflated as she realized that she wouldn't be getting a job after all.

"I don't want the Dragonband; I want to hire you, Mallory," he said.

Mallory sighed and looked around for somewhere to sit, but there was only the occupied armchair and the desk chair behind him, which was holding a teetering stack of books.

"Look, I've never hunted a dragon. I thought those jobs were a myth these days," she said.

"I will pay you three times the going rate," Havelock offered, and Mallory's eyes just about popped out of her head.

"Three times?!" she said, and Havelock nodded once.

She breathed out all the air in her chest and looked around the room again. These days, only royalty could afford to hire a dragon hunter, but not even they would offer more than the going rate. She could hear Anders' voice in her head: 'Consider the job before you agree to it.' She frowned skeptically and stared into Havelock's dark eyes.

"Why?" she asked.

"What do you mean?" Havelock didn't budge.

"Why do you want a dragon hunted at such a high price? What's the catch?" she pressed.

Havelock sighed as though she had got him, but the smirk that appeared said otherwise. She was playing right into his game, and she knew it.

"It's a bronze dragon," Havelock said.

Mallory threw that around in her mind, recalling everything she knew about dragons and why that would make any difference. Then the penny dropped, and her mouth gaped open.

"Bronze dragons aren't a threat. I can't hunt a protected dragon!" she said.

"I'll pay you four times the going rate," Havelock offered, watching her carefully.

Mallory blinked hard, opened her mouth to speak, closed it again, frowned at him, then opened her mouth again. As she tried to think of the right thing to say, he continued to watch her with that amused smirk.

"Why do you want a bronze dragon?" she finally asked.

"That is not your concern. You can either do the job and get paid, or you can walk away. The choice is yours." Havelock clasped his hands under his chin. It could've been misinterpreted as a pleading gesture if you didn't already know of Havelock and his wicked ways. Mallory saw it for what it was: calculated and conniving. He knew she wouldn't walk.

Mallory groaned. "Okay. I accept."

Havelock grinned.

"But—"

Havelock's smile dropped then turned into a frown.

"I want to be paid a 25% deposit, and I want something for protection," she said.

"You…" Havelock's frowned deepened, and Mallory was pleased that she had done something he hadn't expected. "You actually want to use sorcery?"

"I want a charm that will hide me from anyone who will want to do me harm as a result of this hunt, because…" Mallory leaned down and placed her hands on the armrest, putting her face directly in front of his, "it's in your best interests that I'm protected. If I get caught, I won't hesitate to give away my client's name."

He stared Mallory down with critical eyes, waiting for her to flinch. Though her heart was beating faster than it ever had, she didn't move an inch or lower her brave façade. Havelock sighed.

"All right. We have a deal."

Mallory left Havelock's with her bag full of coins and the protection charm secure in her pocket. She had to walk back to the inn to pick up the few possessions she owned, always traveling with minimal items so that it was easy to leave at a moment's notice. But going through the Trades meant going past Anders. She kept her head down and tried to melt into the crowd. Unfortunately, Anders had been keeping an eye out for her since the moment she left.

"Mal!" he called, once he had spotted her.

She pretended she hadn't heard him over the noise of the crowd, and picked up her pace just a little to try to get inside the inn before he caught up to her.

"Mal!" he called again.

She could hear him jogging just behind her and knew it was too late, so turned around as though she was unsure if she had heard her name called or not, and then smiled when she recognized Anders.

"Oh, Anders, hi!" she said.

When he stopped in front of her, his cheeks were already red from the short sprint in the heat.

"What happened?" he asked.

"Huh?" Mallory frowned.

"With Havelock. What's going on?" He searched her face as though he were looking for the answer to his question there.

"Oh, right. I took the job, so I was just going to get my things." She gestured to the inn behind her and took a step backward as though to leave. Almost all of her conversations with Anders ended with her trying to slip away.

"You took it?" He raised his eyebrows.

"Yeah, I took it."

"But... what is it?"

"Ah," Mallory said, and winked before adding, "client and contractor confidentiality, I'm afraid."

She smiled and turned around to walk away to the inn, but Anders followed her, staying right on her heel.

"But you did consider the job first, right? You didn't just take it without knowing all of the details?" Anders pushed.

"Yes, Anders, I considered it before I accepted. Don't worry," she responded, rolling her eyes, though he didn't see that.

"So, where are you going?"

She stopped at the front door to the inn and turned around to face him. There was a brief moment of thought, her eyes scanning the space in front of her as though she were looking over something he couldn't see, then she focused on him again with a smile.

"East."

*****

The first place Mallory traveled to was Wellsford in Northern Glandstone, where a retired Dragonband member who owed her a favor lived. She knocked on his front door and waited. Compared to Isatarist, it was like she had stepped into an entirely different season. The day was rainy and cold, which Mallory much preferred to the dry heat she had been stuck in along the Storm Coast.

The door opened, and Thoren frowned when he realized who had knocked.

"Mallory," he said, with a sigh of remorse.

"Hi, Thoren, how are things?" she asked, and pushed inside without waiting for an answer.

"Good," Thoren said quietly, knowing that she hadn't heard and had already let herself into the sitting room, then added, "I hope."

Thoren closed and locked the door, then followed her inside. She had made herself comfortable in an armchair and smiled up at him. He didn't sit down, not wanting to make her stay any longer than necessary.

"What do you want, Mallory?" he asked.

"Most people call me Mal—"

"I know you're not here for a social visit. You said one day I would pay up for what I owe you, and now here you are, so what do you want?" he asked, folding his arms.

"I want to know about bronze dragons," she said.

Thoren frowned and waited for something else, but nothing came. It was too simple a request from someone who owed a Valon her life. Was it a trick? Was she looking to humiliate him, again?

"Bronze dragons?" he asked.

"That's right. Tell me everything you know about bronze dragons."

Thoren let out a puff of air and sat in the opposite armchair. He told her the basics: about their curiosity and love for talking to other races, how they can polymorph into a humanoid form to observe them, how they attack and can use bolts of lightning.

"Where will I find one?" Mallory asked.

"Why do you need to find a bronze dragon?" Thoren frowned, wondering if he was getting himself involved in something he shouldn't. But, what the hell, he was old and retired anyway. As a retired Dragonband member at thirty-five, his life was pretty much over anyway.

"I just do. Tell me where to find one and I will consider your debt paid," Mallory said.

The deal was indeed sweet. If giving her the information meant that Thoren no longer owed anything to anyone, then there was no doubt that he would do it. He thought about the day that he had made a grave error when hunting a dragon and Mallory, as a young teen, had saved him in front of many races. He had been mortified.

"In Bola," he answered.

"Bola?" Mallory frowned. "Only the Minotaurs live there."

Thoren shook his head.

"A Dragonband member lives in the rocky cliffs along the Crystal Coast with a bronze dragon," he said.

"With? As in, linked with the dragon?" Mallory asked, and her eyes dropped when Thoren nodded. She suddenly looked tired and beyond her years, but that quickly passed when she returned to her mask of the fearless hunter. "Who is it?"

"Tuva. She used to train Dragonband members, but when she linked with her dragon she moved to Bola. She counsels the ruler of the Bolan Minotaurs with their politics," Thoren explained.

"How well do you know her?" she asked.

"Not well," he answered honestly, and Mallory's shoulders slumped in disappointment. Thoren stood up and pointed a foot towards the exit. "Is there anything else you need, Mallory?"

Mallory stood up and gripped her bag tightly.

"No, nothing." She kept an eye on Thoren as she walked past him to get to the front door, not trusting him now that he owed her nothing. Once she was outside, she turned to say goodbye, but he had already closed and locked the door behind her. She huffed and walked away.

*****

The journey to Bola took six weeks from Wellsford. She was glad to have negotiated the payment with Havelock. Otherwise, she would've needed to take on other jobs along the way to sustain herself. When she reached Katar, she had to be careful not to draw attention from the Katarian Minotaurs, who would gladly enslave her. When she made it to Bola, she crossed the desert and reached the coast just as a tropical storm hit.

Scaling the cliffs during the storm was not the smartest thing she could've done, but knowing how intense and prolonged the storms could be she knew that she would be safer on higher grounds. She was muscular and agile and knew how to use her body to her advantage, so she found rock climbing to be an almost leisurely activity. With the winds ripping at her from all sides, however, she knew that this climb would be a challenge.

Mallory slowly navigated herself up the cliff, being careful to make sure that she was secure on every foot and handhold. The rain grew heavier, though, and the rock surface slipperier, and soon she found herself shaking from the effort of keeping herself attached to the cliff. She didn't know how far she had climbed, refusing to look down, when her hand slipped and she almost fell backward. She was able to support herself with one hand and caught a glimpse of the shore far below. She sucked in a shaky breath and quickly righted herself back against the cliff to continue climbing. After a few more hauls, however, her foot slipped and left her hanging on with both hands, flailing as she tried to find somewhere to hold her feet. Everything she attempted was too slippery, and she could feel her fingers starting to slip and lose strength. Just when she thought she was about to lose her hold and plummet, a hand grabbed her wrist and pulled her up. She had been holding onto the entrance of a cave in the cliff face and used her free hand to help the rescuer pull her in.

Mallory rolled onto her back inside the cave and stared up at the rock ceiling as she tried to catch her breath. She was drenched, cold, exhausted, and her limbs wouldn't stop shaking. A woman, at least twenty years her senior, with blond hair tied back in a long plait, leaned over and looked down at her with a scowl.

"What the hell were you thinking?" she said.

Mallory felt for her bag, remembering where she was and what she was doing, and found that it was still on her person. She held it tightly as she sat up and wiggled back along the floor to put more distance between herself and the woman.

"You would've died out there if I didn't happen to see you climbing up here," the woman said, and shook her head.

"Well, I didn't," Mallory said with a shrug, refusing to thank her when she was sure she would've been fine. She would've worked it out.

"Who are you?" the woman demanded.

"I'm a Valon," Mallory started off with, testing the waters. The woman relaxed instantly, so Mallory offered her name. "Mal."

"Tuva, Dragonband," she returned, and Mallory suddenly perked up.

The challenge of the climb and being pulled into the cave made her momentarily forget who she was here for and what she was doing. She frowned and tilted her head, pretending to be confused, and not at all expectant of finding her.

"Dragonband? What are you doing *here?*" Mallory asked.

Tuva stood up and brushed the dirt from her pants. She offered Mallory a hand to help her up, then gestured toward the inner workings of the cave, suggesting she follow her inside. She took the lit torch from the cave wall and held it ahead of her as they walked in.

"I moved here on my own. I was done with the Dragonband. Needed... a change of scenery," Tuva said.

"But why?" Mallory asked.

"Well... you'll see."

As the cave opened up into a vast cavern, and Mallory's eyes adjusted to the light, she noticed the bronze dragon, curled up and asleep at the back of the area.

"Is that..." Mallory trailed off, her eyes wide.

"A bronze dragon," Tuva offered, smiling proudly at the dragon.

"I thought they were all gone," Mallory gushed.

"Not all. A lot, unfortunately, but some were able to find safe spaces and tribes to protect them. Raynor took an interest in the Bolan Minotaurs, and they liked his curiosity, so they decided to honor him by allowing him to live here with their protection. And mine," Tuva said.

She sat down on furs that were laid out beside a fire, and gestured with her hand for Mallory to join her. Mallory sat and watched as she split her meal in half to share with her unexpected guest. Mallory nodded her thanks and dug right in. She hadn't realized just how hungry she was until the food was right in front of her.

"That storm isn't going to pass anytime soon. You can stay here until it does. Thanks to the severity of the drought here, the storms are more intense than any other in Draston. I hope you don't have anywhere you need to be," Tuva said.

Mallory could tell that she was digging for information. It was lucky that she was well practiced with lying, and she shook her head.

"I just finished a job and was traveling through until I found my next one," she said.

"What did you hunt?" Tuva asked.

"A vampire," Mallory answered readily, since that was the last job she had.

"Ah," Tuva nodded, satisfied with her answers. "Nasty beasts."

Tuva made up a bed for Mallory in a corner that was sectioned off by a makeshift screen. While she was just sleeping on furs on the cave floor, it was more comfortable than The Bronze Dagger Inn. Probably because she couldn't hear the drunken sounds coming from the bar below, and didn't have to worry about someone breaking in her door. That night was the best sleep she'd had in years.

She woke to the feeling of being watched. She turned onto her back and noticed a shadow on the wall that was bigger than that of the makeshift screen. She looked above the screen and saw two yellow eyes looking down at her.

"Hello?" Mallory offered.

"Raynor!" she heard Tuva yell, and the dragon scurried away.

Mallory got up and emerged from behind the screen. Tuva was making breakfast, and smiled apologetically when she saw her. Raynor was nearby, watching Mallory's every move.

"Sorry about that. Like I said, he's curious," Tuva shrugged.

"It's okay, I don't mind," she said, watching the dragon.

"I've made you breakfast. Come, sit."

Mallory sat on the furs beside Tuva and took her serving of porridge. Raynor continued watching, even as he fed on his breakfast of raw meat.

"He's just shy," Tuva said as she dug into her meal.

"How did you come across him?" Mallory asked.

"I was looking for work in this area when he found me on the coast. I was setting up camp on the beach when he flew down and warned me that a storm was coming, and quickly. He allowed me to climb onto his back, and he flew me up into this cave and let me stay here with him until the storm passed. When I returned to the Minotaurs for work, I made them an offer to let me help them govern their land against the Katarian Minotaurs in return for my being able to stay here with Raynor," Tuva explained. "Now, this is my home. I'll never go back."

Mallory couldn't imagine calling anywhere else home, but she also didn't understand how the whole linking-with-dragons thing worked. Tuva wasn't the only one to have a link with a dragon. There were a lot of Dragonband members who had done the same.

When Raynor turned his head to rip off a chunk of meat, Mallory noticed a dull area on his neck amongst his glittering scales. As she focused on it, she realized that the scales were missing there.

"What happened to him?" Mallory asked, staring at the scales.

Tuva followed her gaze to his neck and knew what she was referring to right away. She sighed and shook her head, as the thought of what happened to him still affected her so.

"A sorcerer tried to kill him. How anyone could hurt a kind creature like Raynor is beyond my comprehension. Not to mention that he's protected," Tuva said.

"No, I can't imagine who'd do that," Mallory muttered quickly. She could see Raynor glance up at her over his meal.

"Greedy people, that's who. People would put their life and personal gain above another's," Tuva said.

Mallory just nodded, focusing on the sum of money she would be receiving once she returned to Havelock. She couldn't allow herself to think about whether she was one of those greedy people. It was something she would just have to deal with after the fact, but right now she had to remember why she was there and what she would be rewarded with.

*****

The next few days stretched on much the same. They talked, and ate the food that Tuva had stockpiled for the storm. Raynor spoke now and then, but was otherwise quiet, which Tuva said was quite unlike him. Finally, they started to see the end of the storm. The rain eased off and the sun peeked out from behind the gray clouds.

"Now that the storm has cleared, I have a meeting to attend with the Bolan Minotaurs. You are safe to leave," Tuva said as she gathered her climbing equipment to scale the cliff.

"Thanks for everything. I'll just get my things together and go." Mallory gestured to her corner where her things were, even though she didn't have to get anything together. She could just pick up her bag and leave.

"Take your time," Tuva said as she walked toward the entrance of the cave.

Mallory walked over to her bag and pretended to organize and pack her belongings. She could see Raynor in her peripheral vision; he was watching her. She put on her bag, keeping her hand concealed inside it, near the handle of her dagger. She walked over to the dragon and smiled at him.

"It was nice meeting you, Raynor," she said.

He sighed and said, "The same to you, Mallory."

She reached up to stroke his neck, but he flinched and moved away from her. She frowned, thinking that she had earned his trust these past few days. His eyes flicked to her hand inside her bag, and she saw it in his eyes—he knew. She pulled her dagger out without any hesitation, and he retaliated with a blast of lightning that knocked the blade out of her hand. She flew backward and landed on her back, dropping the blade by the dragon.

He flew up toward the ceiling of the cavernous room, hovering above her and staring her down with angry eyes. Her heart was pounding; she could feel the energy building around him. Her hair stood on end as though an electrical current was nearby, and she knew that he was getting ready to strike again. She rolled right at the moment that the lightning blast was released; it hit the spot where she had been seconds before, charring the ground.

She rolled again, but not quickly enough. The lightning brushed her right arm, searing her skin with a hot flash that caused her to scream. She cradled her arm against her chest as she got to her feet and ran for her dagger. Her fingers brushed the hilt as the next lightning blast threw her off her feet again. She rolled against the wall with a thud.

Raynor flew back and forth in an angry frenzy, screeching with every turn. Mallory knew she didn't have much time left. Since he was connected to Tuva, she would've already heard his cries and felt his anger at being under attack. She realized that there was something in her left hand, and looked down to see that she had picked up her dagger after all.

Her left arm was not her strong arm at all, but she knew it was the only chance she had. She tried to think of it as her right arm, to pretend that she threw best with that arm. She threw her dagger toward Raynor as best as she could.

It wasn't the best throw she could muster, and Raynor had just changed direction. She was sure that it would missed, but it sliced his leg in the nick of time. He cried out from the shock of the contact, but it wasn't enough to have any effect other than annoyance. It was precisely what Mallory needed.

She stood up and ran for the dagger. If anything, it gave her an extra minute to run beneath Raynor, as the scrape had distracted him for a brief moment. Once he had recuperated, however, he turned on her and focused on her back as he began to descend towards her.

Mallory took the dagger in her hands, seeing a bit of blood on the blade from where it had cut the creature. She thankfully rubbed it along its length. The hilt glowed as the blade marinated in its target. She tossed the dagger up into the air and rolled out of the way just before Raynor would've snapped her neck with his jaw. The knife flew through the air and followed Raynor, who pumped his wings furiously in a bid to get the magical weapon off his trail. It never faulted and, when it caught up to him, began slicing and stabbing at the dragon as if a living creature.

He tried to at first attack the blade and destroy it, but it was too quick for him. Eventually the slices built up, and loss of blood caused Raynor to descend to the ground, crying in sorrowful pain. The blade dropped, satisfied with the outcome, and the hilt dulled to its standard color. Raynor was flailing, spilling blood from several cuts. He tried to shoot more lightning at her, but his wounds weakened him too quickly. He screamed in pain, breaking Mallory's heart.

Immediately after the dragon was too weak to lift its head, she took the empty jar out of her bag and rushed to collect his blood in it. She patted his neck to comfort him.

"I'm sorry," she said, and she really meant it. "I'm so sorry."

Once the jar was full, she replaced the lid and wrapped it in cloth before putting it back into her bag. She wiped her hands and arms clean of his blood on the fur she had been sleeping on and looked back at Raynor, who had become still and kept his eyes on her as the life drained out of them. Mallory swallowed the tears that wanted to spill, feeling guilty for murdering such a kind, beautiful creature. She righted her bag, then left the cave.

Her body was bruised, burned, and in a lot of pain, but she didn't have time to stop. She knew she was already on borrowed time. She took a deep breath and forced her limbs to start the climb down the cliff face. When she was halfway down, she heard a scream directed at her from above. She looked up to see Tuva, whose face was blood red with murderous fury. She began her descent, abandoning her climbing gear to try to reach Mallory quickly. Mallory picked up her pace, climbing more carelessly than usual in a bid to reach the ground quicker. Though the storm had cleared, the stones were still wet and slippery. She was far enough down that she could survive the fall if she had to. It might hurt, but so long as she landed on the sand and not the rocks, she would be okay.

The adrenaline that Tuva had from her grief, however, meant that she was faster and keen to get revenge. Mallory thought she was winning the race, when she felt a sharp kick to her fingers. She lost their grip instantly, and cried out in pain. Tuva was directly above her, and she looked ready to kill. Mallory had just replaced her grip when Tuva kicked her other fingers, causing them to let go. This happened a couple more times until Tuva had been able to kick her before she had managed to get a grip with the other hand, and she fell the rest of the way down to the sand. The fall was short, and she landed on her feet with a slight stumble. Once she righted herself she ran as fast as she could, looking back to see that Tuva had made it down and was running after her. She ran more quickly than she ever had, knowing that her life depended on it. It was lucky that she'd had the few days' rest and was recovered enough to expend as much energy as necessary.

When she made it over the border and into Katar, Tuva screamed, communicating her anguish and sending a shiver down her spine. Mallory stopped and turned to her. Tuva's alliance with the Bolan Minotaurs meant she couldn't cross into Katar, unless she wanted to threaten war. Thankfully, the Katarian and Bolan Minotaurs had a shaky relationship.

"I *will* hunt you," Tuva yelled.

"I'm sorry," Mallory offered, then turned and continued running. She may have escaped Tuva's wrath, but she still had to get through Katar without being captured.

As she made her way back to Isatarist, her bag felt more cumbersome than it actually was. The blood gave her nightmares, and weighed heavily on her conscience. How many bronze dragons were left in Draston? What if she had killed the last one? She questioned her own morals constantly and wondered if the money was worth living with what she did.

Mallory arrived at Havelock's and walked in without knocking. She took the stairs two at a time and entered the library, where she just had a feeling he would be, and she was right. She walked up to the desk where he was seated and slammed the jar down beside him. She expected him to be surprised that she was inside his house unannounced, but he didn't even flinch as he continued to read.

"Your payment's on the table," he said, gesturing at the small table beside the armchair, where a bag of money sat on top of the pile of books.

"That's it?" Mallory frowned.

Havelock placed his book face down, and looked up at Mallory with a look of disdain at having been disturbed.

"Should there be something else?" Havelock drawled.

"I just killed an innocent creature," Mallory explained.

"No creature is innocent," Havelock said.

"I *murdered* a dragon that was linked to a Dragonband member," Mallory pressed.

"You have to live with your choices, not me." Havelock picked up the jar of blood and looked at it as he got up from his desk. The deep red blood was marbled with bronze glitter. "You did not have to accept the job. That was your choice."

Mallory glared at him as she watched him gather supplies and begin mixing them with the blood in his small cauldron. Her annoyance gave way to curiosity, and she stepped closer to get a better look at the ingredients he was using.

"What are you doing with it?" Mallory asked as he stirred and boiled the ingredients together.

He held up a finger and shushed her, so she watched on in silence as he murmured a memorized incantation, speaking louder and louder as he went. The mixture glowed a brilliant green during the last verse, then returned to the red-bronze color of the blood. He poured some of it into a vial and held it up to the light.

"I've wanted to do this for a very long time," he said with an excited smile.

He held the vial to his lips and drank the potion. Mallory took a step backward, worrying about what would come next. He put the vial down and stared at his hands; he could feel power instantly rippling through his entire being. He laughed manically as lightning began to play across his fingertips.

"Finally," he marveled. "Finally, I can be as powerful as I'm meant to be!"

He laughed again, his chest puffing proudly with his glee. Mallory noticed his skin was starting to turn green.

"Ummm... Havelock?" She cringed.

"What?" Havelock asked, his voice lilting with his greedy happiness.

"Your skin..." She pointed.

He paused and picked up a metal spoon to see his reflection. He pressed his fingertips against his cheek and then checked to see if any green had come off onto them. He looked in the metal spoon again and saw that the green was still there, plus his forehead had a sweaty sheen to it. He wiped the sweat away with the back of his hand, but it kept coming. He was starting to feel hot and cold at the same time, and a burning sensation began in the back of his throat, making him cough.

"No!" he cried out as he collapsed to the floor from exhaustion and intense body aches. "No—" A fit of coughing cut him off, sounding like he was going to hack up a lung. He doubled over, clutching a hand to his chest and wheezing in between coughs. Mallory didn't know what to do. She stood there and watched as, eventually, he coughed up blood and suffocated when he wasn't able to get any air into his lungs. His upper body crumpled to the floor and lay still.

Mallory was frozen to the spot. She didn't know if she should call for help or what she should do for the sorcerer. A voice told her to leave him be, that he did this to himself and there was nothing anyone could do for him. Besides, the city would be happier without him there. Now, they could finally get people to move back into the area surrounding his home and open up their stores again.

She picked up the bag of money and quietly stepped away, taking one last look at Havelock's grave face before leaving.

"Where will you go now?" Anders asked when Mallory returned to the Trades to say goodbye to him.

"I'm going home. I need a break from hunting for a little while," she answered.

"And you won't tell me what happened on this job?" he asked, raising his eyebrows.

Mallory shook her head.

"All right," he sighed, and gave her shoulder a friendly squeeze. "Come back soon."

"I will. Goodbye for now, friend," Mallory said, then turned to leave.

Mallory preferred to travel by foot, but she was too weary and too keen to be in her familiar city. She bought a horse to take her home, happy to be seated and carried the rest of the way.

*****

Mal rode north along the Storm Coast, through the cities of Lundkirk, Askimstad, then to the west and into the mountains. She was riding through the chilly forest of the Orclands, when her horse was suddenly frightened and reared up onto his back legs, throwing her off. Before she could tell what was happening, something hit her horse from behind, prompting him to run away at full tilt.

Mallory jumped up to her feet and looked in the direction it had come from. Tuva stepped out from behind a tree, holding a sword in one hand. She twirled it to show it off as she slowly stepped closer to Mallory.

"How did you find me?" Mallory felt for the protection charm in her pocket, but there was nothing there.

"A charm no longer exists after its sorcerer is dead," Tuva said.

"How did you know about the charm?" Mallory frowned.

"I had friends try to find you with magic. They said that there was no trace of you, that you were probably hidden by a protection charm. But we kept looking, trying to find you. Then, magically, you showed up in their search. The protection was gone. Apparently, your sorcerer chose to cast a spell on your charm, instead of giving you an actual enchanted item. So, when your sorcerer was found dead by his assistant, after drinking a potion with *my* dragon's blood, the spell left the item. Luckily, I was in Duskvar, so could travel south to meet you halfway."

Tuva stood a few feet away from Mallory, who poised herself, ready for the attack.

"You killed the dragon I was linked to. Which meant that you killed a part of *me*," Tuva said, banging her hand against her chest.

"I am sorry," Mallory said.

"No, you're not. You got what you wanted, so you're not sorry at all. People like you are a plague to the Valon organization," Tuva spat.

Mallory had nothing left to say. She waited on edge for the attack to come. She knew she could take Tuva. What she didn't expect was to step into a trap that Tuva had hidden beneath the foliage on the forest floor. The rope tightened around her ankle and turned her upside down as it hauled her up off the ground. Her bag slipped off her and spilled open on the ground, her magical dagger glinting up at her amongst some coins that had fallen out. Tuva walked up to her until they were face to face.

"You killed a protected creature. You are a disgrace," Tuva said, right before she slit Mallory's throat.

She walked away as Mallory's blood drained from her, letting her retreating back be the last thing Mallory saw before she died. The death of the hunter wouldn't replace the loss of her dragon, but it was reasonable punishment for what she had done. She would leave her body there for the forest creatures to feast upon. Let Mallory's death be a warning for any other hunter or sorcerer who planned to kill for personal gain.

Curse In His Blood

By Nikolas Monastere

283AM
Age of Magi

The funeral was over quickly. Villagers offered Fronsac their condolences—handshakes and a couple teary-eyed hugs, soft voices trying to impress upon the young man how much his grandfather would be missed, how he'd been such a kind man. Fronsac accepted their sympathy with stoic resolve, making eye-contact with each one but offering little by way of reply. He knew most of it was a lie; his grandfather had been a cold man. Not a bad man in any way, but he'd shown little inclination towards friendship. Still, the old man was the only family Fronsac had ever known. He was going to be missed.

Fronsac knew the villagers wouldn't stick around for long. The funeral was held during the hottest part of the day, while everyone was taking breaks from their labor. Now that the niceties had been observed, they would go back to work. There were crops to reap and food stores to stockpile; after the blazing summer a harsh winter was guaranteed. The death of one villager only meant there was one less worker gathering food.

Then again, that was also one less mouth to feed.

After everyone left, Fronsac went to Blind Allen and his son, Samuel, who stood a respectful distance away with their shovels. Fronsac passed Samuel a few copper coins.

"Do the job well," said Fronsac, already turning away.

"Hey!" Samuel called. "This pays for the burial. What about the headstone?"

Fronsac waved, never looking back. "Just make sure animals won't be able to dig him up, Sam. He doesn't need a marker."

Fronsac watched the villagers going back to the fields as he walked to his hut. The funeral, the time for the dead, was over. Now all that mattered was gathering food for the living.

Fronsac reached the clay dwelling he'd once shared with his grandfather. He paused in the doorway, gazing upon his inheritance. A few tools hung on one wall, rusted with age, dented from use. A large pot hung inside the fireplace, a single pan on the mantel. Two stools next to a table with two dining sets resting on top. His grandfather's bed with its thin mattress high off the ground; Fronsac's pile of hay in one corner.

Some inheritance.

Loneliness overcame him. He hadn't allowed himself a moment of introspection since he'd woken up and found his grandfather cold and dead. He'd alerted the cleric of the goddess Marthna, who'd told the priest, who'd told Blind Allen and his son. The entire community alerted and the old man laid to rest in a couple hours, then back to the fields. The quickness of it all, the practiced efficiency of death, made Fronsac tired. For the first time in memory, he sat down on his grandfather's bed and hung his head.

He was alone.

He was also incredibly uncomfortable. The mattress was lumpy and hard beneath his buttocks. He shifted his weight but found no relief. Squirming, he wondered how his grandfather had slept on such a thing. Fronsac's pile of straw on the floor was more comfortable. Frustrated, Fronsac stood and flung the mattress aside, revealing the chest beneath.

He felt as though he was looking at something he shouldn't, like a boy spying a neighbor woman changing through a window. Fronsac put the mattress back in place and stared uneasily at the bed.

Grandfather had secrets.

Fronsac glanced at the closed door of the hut, half-expecting to hear his grandfather's booming voice telling him to get away from there, go back to the fields.

Silence.

Fronsac pulled the mattress aside. Massive iron rings lay flat on the surface of the chest, iron straps traversing the width. Strange runes were engraved on the red wood, an elegant script the likes of which Fronsac had never seen. He looked for a keyhole or a latch, but found none. He tried to lift the chest from the bed frame but it refused to budge. He would have to dismantle the frame itself to get to the sides.

Fronsac grabbed a shovel from the wall and drove the tip of the blade between the chest and the box-frame. He pushed and pulled the handle like a pry bar, but the bed frame held fast. Grunting, Fronsac put all his weight against it. The handle groaned and snapped, piercing his hand with long slivers of wood. He yelped and jumped back.

A few drops of blood splattered the iron and wood. Fronsac looked up from his bleeding palm as the chest started humming like two pieces of metal tapped together. The runes absorbed his blood and radiated fierce light as the iron fastenings sizzled and hummed. The chest rattled violently and knocked the bed frame loose. Fronsac backed away, terrified, too stunned to react. The iron bands whined and snapped from the chest, slapping the floor in puffs of dust. The wooden sides of the chest groaned and bowed outward, threatening to burst. The light of the runes was blinding; the roar was deafening. Fronsac threw his arms across his face and squeezed his eyes shut.

Silence.

Fronsac lowered his arms and opened his eyes. The chest was still now, silent. The runes faded into faint afterglows of the fierce brilliance they'd originally produced, and the bands were cold and stiff on the floor. The lid of the chest was cracked open ever so slightly, ready to reveal its secrets.

Fronsac went to the door to make sure it was locked, afraid the villagers would come to investigate the ruckus. He could hear them in the fields, swinging their scythes and bagging their wheat. Maybe he was the only person who had the heard the noise. Maybe he was the only one who was *meant* to.

Tentatively, he went to the chest and lifted the lid, sealing his fate.

*****

Fronsac had been riding hard for two months, unsure of which direction to go. The map he'd found in the chest amongst the books, dagger, and robe was beautifully illustrated, but offered nothing by way of legend. A forest, a few paths, a cave, and what looked like a castle. The castle had three towers, an emblem of which was featured on all the objects he'd found. Without explicit instruction, he gave himself to the mercy of Fate.

The three books covered metallurgy, poisonous plant botany, and bestial anatomy. The pages were filled with painstakingly accurate illustrations, with notes and paragraphs recording the most mundane and uninteresting facts. Despite the size of the tomes, they were deceptively light. Fronsac knew there to be magic at hand.

He'd called for Blind Allen's son, Samuel, who had just finished burying Fronsac's grandfather. After taking his father home, Samuel rushed over to Fronsac's hut. Samuel was a strong boy, tall and broad-shouldered. He was a hard worker but dimwitted. The cart accident that had rendered Allen blind had also given Samuel a horrible blow to the head, largely robbing the lad of intelligence. Samuel's excess of empathy replaced his lack of wit, and anyone who treated him with kindness was a friend. The community had rallied around Allen and Samuel after the cart accident, watching out for their own. Since Allen could no longer work in the fields, he was the handyman for everything outside of farming. Tool sharpening, fence building. Grave digging. Samuel helped his father with all those tasks, following every order to the letter. Fronsac knew he could be trusted.

Samuel ran to Fronsac's hut, face red with exertion. "Did you call for me, Mister Fronsac?" He gasped between breaths, hands on his knees.

"Samuel, you didn't have to run," said Fronsac, rubbing the lad's broad back.

Samuel shook his head, sweat running from his brow. "Mister Fronsac is a friend. Friends always come when asked."

Fronsac smiled, and retrieved a bucket of water from his well. He passed it to Samuel. "Cool off, my friend."

Samuel poured the bucket over his head, drinking some but mostly letting it splash down his body. "Whew!" He passed the bucket back to Fronsac. "Thank you, Mister

Fronsac." His eyes narrowed with worry when he saw Fronsac's bandaged hand. "Mister Fronsac, you're hurt!"

"It's fine, Samuel, just a small cut. Listen, I was wondering if you could help me with something."

"Anything, Mister Fronsac." Samuel wrung some water from the hem of his shirt. "Is it about your granddad's grave? I can still order a gravestone. You or Papa can tell me what to write in the letter to the quarry-man—I'll just need help with some of the spelling."

"No, no; this doesn't have anything to do with burial, Samuel. Actually, I was wondering if you and your father still had that mule."

"Tina? Yes, she's still out in the stables. Papa says she's useless since she won't take to the cart harness."

"Do you think he'd be willing to trade her?"

"Trade her? What do you want with a crotchety mule, Mister Fronsac?"

"Does she take to saddle?"

"Yes. But she won't pull a cart. You won't be able to take your harvest into town with her."

"I'm not looking for a cart animal, Samuel. I need something to ride. Will she carry me and a small pack?"

"She sure would."

"Excellent." Fronsac clapped the lad's shoulder. "Follow me."

Fronsac led him inside the hut. Ashes smoldered in the fireplace—all that remained of the chest. The mattress was resting on the floor, the head of the shovel lay tucked away in a corner. Fronsac pulled a stool away from the table. "Please sit down, Samuel."

Samuel took a seat and leaned forward. "What do you need help with, Mister Fronsac?"

Fronsac went to the fireplace, the only brick structure in the clay hut. He grabbed a loose brick and pulled it free. Reaching into the cavity, Fronsac retrieved a coin purse and a faded envelope. He pulled a letter from the envelope, read the headline, then tucked it back in. He pocketed the coin purse and passed the letter to Samuel. "Samuel, you can read a little, right?"

"Oh, yes, Mister Fronsac." Samuel nodded happily. "I can't spell none too good, but I can read."

"I want you to take that letter to your father and read it to him. Ask him if he'd be willing to trade that for Tina."

"Yes, Mister Fronsac. I can do that."

"Thank you. If he agrees, just bring Tina and a saddle on your way back. I hope to see you soon."

And that was how Fronsac traded his hut and his field for a mule. She was temperamental at best, with a will stronger than any animal Fronsac had ever known. She never tried to buck him, though, and at times she would trot along for miles without so much as a snort of argument. On other occasions, it was all he could do just to make her walk.

When he could, he'd find sleeping arrangements in a town. He couldn't afford to spend much money on luxuries like a room or bath, but he'd been able to budget the gold coins, his life savings, so that he could always afford a meal and a spot in a barn, sleeping in the hay next to Tina. He tried to keep the map out of sight. He knew most travelers were good men and women, seeking work in the cities or riches and adventure in the uncharted territories of Draston, but there were equally as many thieves and murderers traveling the roads. Anyone who offered to lead him to his destination was just as likely to rob and murder him in the night. He decided the wisest course was to ride to the northern mountainous areas, explore for a few days, then move on.

The first frost of the season caught him unprepared and out in the open. He woke up shivering, in the woods just outside a small town called Garbagan. The innkeeper had been a rude fellow, refusing to give Fronsac so much as a stable without a payment of two silver coins. Fronsac had argued with the man over the price, pointing out that two silver coins could buy him a proper room and daily baths for three whole weeks at a finer establishment in any other town. The innkeeper noted Fronsac's coin purse, claiming wealthy travelers should pay whatever was asked, especially considering his was the only inn in town.

Fronsac argued with the man, whispering, trying to keep any of the ruffians in the tavern from overhearing. The innkeeper took note and raised his voice, remarking time and time again how fat and heavy Fronsac's coin purse was. Fronsac watched the men at the bar, caught their greedy glances. Even the brownies sweeping the floor and wiping down the bar were eavesdropping, their goblin-like ears twitching. Fronsac shoved the innkeeper into a corner and drew his dagger, holding it low and out of sight from the other patrons.

"Stop talking so loud," Fronsac whispered.

The innkeeper stared at the dagger and turned green. He held his tongue.

Fronsac sheathed the blade. "I'll find lodging elsewhere." He walked to the door, fastening his cloak with a brooch that bore the castle emblem as he went. The unscrupulous patrons watched him go, sizing him up and wondering if they could take him.

Fronsac turned in the doorway, meeting their stares. "My home is far from here. I'm a stranger with little to lose. Think long and hard before you mark me as easy prey." He left.

Not knowing if his bluff had been successful Fronsac took no chances, taking Tina through multiple paths, crossing and crisscrossing his route, riding on the roads and skirting them, backtracking, throwing off anyone who might be following. Tina didn't object, even after it was far past her usual bedtime. The moon rose fat and heavy in the cloudless sky, permitting Fronsac sight without a lantern or torch. After several hours of riding he heard a howl far off in the distance, one that gave Tina pause and scared them both. It was too high-pitched to be a Kiroth wolf, too guttural to be an orc. It was faint enough that Fronsac knew the beast was miles away, but he wasn't going to take any chances. Though he'd never seen or heard one until now, he knew there was nothing as dangerous in the woods at night as a werewolf.

He found a small cave carved into a cliff face. After making sure there were no bears or other animals within, he coaxed Tina inside. Using shrubbery and leaves, Fronsac disguised the shelter. He wrapped himself in his cloak and lay down next to the mule, throwing a thick blanket over them both.

He woke up shivering after a few hours of fitful sleep. Tina slept comfortably, exhaling great puffs of mist from her nose. Fronsac pulled the cloak and blanket tighter around his body and moved to the cave entrance, tossing aside the bushes. Thick frost covered the leaves on the forest floor and lined the bark of the trees. The innkeeper had not only tried to price-gouge him and have him robbed, but he'd also nearly sentenced him to death. Blood boiled in Fronsac's freezing chest.

Tina was as grumpy as she was cold. Fronsac's anger and frustration grew as he tugged at the mule, urging her to her feet. Once he finally got her to stand, Fronsac put the saddle and pack on her. He rode back to the village, eager to exact revenge on the unscrupulous innkeeper.

Fronsac was just outside the Garbagan town limits when five hooded riders overtook and surrounded him. Long-swords hung from one side of their saddles, a quiver full of black arrows on the other. They held bows in their hands, arrows nocked, though they kept them pointed at the ground.

Fronsac wanted to reach for his dagger, but he knew it would be useless against so many well-armed men. He held the reins tight in his hands and sat up as tall as he could in his saddle.

"Knights," he said. "I assure you, I am no scoundrel."

They looked at Fronsac impassively, quietly, their mounts breathing softly. Tina nervously stomped one hoof. Four of the men wore blue cloaks, one wore green. Fronsac assumed the man in green was the leader. He addressed him directly.

"Sir," he said. "I have no business with the crown, nor am I a wanted man. I wish only to have a word with the innkeeper of Garbagan. I nearly died thanks to him, and I seek compensation for his transgression. I have no murder in my heart, and it is hardly a concern of the crown. I will go to him and demand a room and meal for his offense to me."

"We care not about your disagreement with the innkeeper, traveler." The rider in green walked his horse closer to Fronsac, the other men tugging their arrows ever so slightly. The green rider grabbed the edge of Fronsac's cloak and cast it aside, grabbing Fronsac's dagger. He pulled the blade from the sheath and inspected it.

"The innkeeper mentioned this blade; apparently you introduced him to it." The rider in green ran his thumb over the three-towered castle emblem. "How is it you came to possess this blade, traveler? And your cloak and brooch—where did you get those?"

"They were part of my inheritance, sir. Left to me by my grandfather."

"Really?" The rider didn't sound convinced. One of the other men came forward and cut Fronsac's pack from Tina's saddle. Tina whinnied and Fronsac protested, but a stern look from the green rider stalled Fronsac's argument. The other rider dropped the ground and inspected the pack.

"Brother Acel," said the rider, holding up one of Fronsac's books. "He carries tomes from our library."

The rider in green, Acel, put his hand on his sword hilt. His eyes flashed. "Those tomes have been sorely missed; their worth cannot be overstated. They have been charmed with ancient sorcery. I ask you one more time: where did you get your belongings?"

Fronsac raised his hands. "I inherited them, I swear!" He showed Acel his scarred palms. "My own blood unsealed them from my grandfather's chest. I cut myself trying to open it, and my blood caused the chest to burst. I'm trying to find where it all comes from." Fronsac pointed with his chin at the book in the other rider's hands. "I found a map as well. The map is folded and tucked into that book. I promise you, Sir Acel, I did not come across them by nefarious means."

Acel eyed Fronsac wearily. "I am no nobleman," he said. "I'm a brother in the Order of the Night. Your cloak is an abbot's cloak, though you are certainly not an abbot." The rider on the ground pulled the map from the book and passed it to Acel. Acel scanned it for a moment, then handed it back to the man on the ground. "You really have no idea about your heritage, do you?"

Fronsac stared at the hilt of the sword in Acel's hand, noted the three-tower castle emblem engraved at the crossguard. "My heritage?"

Acel's grip loosened on his sword, but he did not let go. "Yes. A ward created from blood magic is impossible to unseal, unless a drop from the original Spellbinder's bloodline is applied. Blood magic is one of the trickier forms of magic, and those books combined with that cloak tell me your grandfather must have been someone great in our Order."

Fronsac accepted that with ease. His grandfather had been too wise and too educated to be nothing more than a farmer. He'd carried himself as a leader, a warrior, conducting himself as a nobleman.

"Acel," said Fronsac, "what can you tell me about my grandfather?"

"I can tell you nothing for certain," said Acel. "You will come with us, if you wish to know more. The other brothers and I will present you to our abbot, Brother Henri. He will be able to answer your questions."

Fronsac forgot about the innkeeper and the night before. Acel made him take off the gray cloak of an abbot and instead wear a spare blue one that one of the riders had. "You are not a brother of the Order and no more worthy to wear the blue cloak than the gray," said Acel, "but it is better you ride into Castle Kaarlo wearing a brother's cloak than an abbot's."

Fronsac nodded, draping himself with the blue garment. "How did you find me?"

"We weren't looking for you," said Acel. "We were looking for a werewolf, rumored to be in this area. There hasn't been a were-creature recorded in these parts for more than three-hundred years. Abbot Henri sent us to investigate."

"So, you're monster hunters? Valons?"

"We belong to the Order of the Night. We are scholars, trained in the battle arts. The reports we received at Castle Kaarlo said the werewolf was on this side of the mountain, but by the time we arrived it had already moved to the opposite side."

"My name is Fronsac Leodegrance," Fronsac offered.

"Leodegrance?" Acel cocked an eyebrow. The other riders exchanged looks of surprise.

"Yes."

The riders looked to Acel, who was pensively stroking his chin.

"Abbot Henri is definitely going to want to meet you."

*****

Castle Kaarlo was another month's ride, further north. Right up into the wilds of the Orclands. Fronsac wondered how many years he would have spent searching if the riders had not chanced upon him when they did. They had ridden back to the village to one of the stables, and Fronsac was urged to sell or trade Tina for a more reliable mount. He sold the mule, and that and a single gold coin bought him a red mare, long-legged and powerful. He warned the stable-master that Tina was stubborn, even for a mule. The man had said that was fine, if she took to saddle he could turn a profit from her. Fronsac patted the mule's face and wished her a long and happy life. He mounted the red mare and followed the brothers north.

Acel was the most conversational of the riders, but even so he was a quiet man, never delving too deeply into any of the explanations he gave to Fronsac's questions. The other riders, who never offered their names, barely spoke at all, except to ask Fronsac if they might read the three books he carried. Fronsac told them they could, and they all took turns passing around the books every morning and every evening, before and after the day's ride. Fronsac realized that the men held knowledge as being of the utmost importance in life, and no information was useless in their eyes.

Approaching the castle with a blizzard to their backs, Acel produced a curved horn from his pack and gave three mighty blasts: one for each of the grey towers that pierced the foreboding sky. The gates creaked open as the final notes of the horn were snatched by the cold wind. Once they rode through the entrance, several men in blue cloaks ran forward to tend the sweaty horses.

Fronsac wanted nothing more than a hot bath and a warm bed; even just a pile of hay with a thick blanket. Acel made no doubt that it would have to wait as he grabbed Fronsac by the arm and pulled him to one of the towers.

"Abbot Henri must speak to you first," explained Acel as they climbed the winding stairs inside the tower. "Then we will find you a bed."

After climbing several flights, they came to a landing and a closed door. Acel knocked three times. "Abbot Henri? It's Acel. We've returned."

The door opened and there stood an old man wearing a grey cloak, identical to the one Fronsac had found in his grandfather's chest. He glanced at Acel then stared at Fronsac. "I do not recognize this brother," said the old man.

"Abbot Henri, this is Fronsac Leodegrance. We stumbled across him near Garbagan as he was seeking out our Order from the back of a mule."

Abbot Henri's eyes went wide with shock. "I send you to investigate a werewolf and you return with a *legacy*?"

"Yes, Abbot; his dagger and brooch all bear our seal, and he claims to have inherited his items from a chest guarded with blood magic. Here," he passed the abbot Fronsac's map. "He also carried this."

The abbot's jaw dropped as he inspected the map. "Leodegrance," he whispered, looking from the map to Fronsac in awe. "By all the gods of all the planes—*Leodegrance*."

Fronsac's cheeks reddened, and he fought the urge to fidget and look away, embarrassed. "How are you, sir?" he murmured dumbly.

Abbot Henri smiled broadly. "*How am I*, dear lad? I'm absolutely thrilled!" He grabbed Fronsac's arm and vigorously shook his hand. "I'm so glad to see you! Everyone will be! We thought for sure the Leodegrance bloodline was wiped out during the Kromen raid two decades ago, yet here you stand!" He clapped his hands and laughed. "Brought to us on a mule, no less!" He handed Fronsac the map and pulled Fronsac and Acel into the room. "Such an event like this is unheard of; a prodigal son returns!" The abbot closed the door behind them.

Fronsac looked around the room in awe. Scrolls of paper as broad as a man hung from the ceiling and covered every inch of the walls; small, delicate script flowing across every inch of parchment. Ink blotters and quills were scattered haphazardly about the floor; no matter where someone stood they were always within arm's reach of writing material. A single desk dominated the center of the room, piled high with books. A large window dominated the wall behind the desk, allowing just enough of the sun's fading rays to illuminate the chamber.

"Did you write *all* of this?" Fronsac asked Abbot Henri, treading carefully across the floor. The script on the scrolls was elegant but incredibly small. Fronsac had to squint to read it. "How long did it take?"

The old man laughed. "Lad, this is but a month's worth of work." The abbot paced behind Fronsac as he circumnavigated the room. "From dawn's first rays to evening's final light, I translate tomes and codices of all the nations and of all the planes. When the Rangers of the Order such as Acel return with new knowledge, that too goes into the scrolls. Every full moon, the pages and the clerics take these scrolls down to the library where they are copied and bound into books that will be studied for generations to come. The Order of Night's goal is as simple and as noble as it was when Castle Kaarlo was first built: to gain and to preserve knowledge, no matter how unimportant or seemingly inconsequential." The abbot grabbed Fronsac by the elbow and turned him around. "It is a noble purpose you have chosen to dedicate your life to."

Fronsac pulled away from the man. "What?" He looked to Acel for help, but the ranger looked on in silence. "I beg your forgiveness, Abbot, but I did not come here to take any oaths or to join any orders."

Abbot Henri looked at Fronsac with jocular confusion. "But of course you have, you are a Leodegrance! I was elected to be abbot after your grandfather. I trained and educated your father. You are a legacy."

"Abbot, I'm not a scholar," apologized Fronsac. "I'm a farmer. I know everything I need to about planting and harvesting crops; academically I know how to read, but not much else besides. I know when rain is coming, and I can read the signs well enough to predict a harsh or mild winter. It might not seem like much to you—" Fronsac gestured to the walls of paper and ink. "—but it's all the education I have."

The abbot grinned. "If you know everything you need to know about *all* you need to know, why did you seek us out?"

Fronsac's reply died on his tongue. Why was he here? He'd traded his meager land and holdings to a blind man for a mule and a saddle, and for what? He hadn't allowed himself any introspection regarding his decision to leave; it'd only seemed like the natural thing to do at the time. His brow furrowed and he looked at the floor. "I honestly don't know."

Abbot Henri smiled and grabbed Fronsac by the shoulders, gently shaking him. "You came because you were curious! Curiosity is the first step to enlightenment. Knowledge is not given to those who do not seek it. I have no doubt that you are well-versed in the specifics of farming. You probably even know a thing or two about cattle. But that clearly wasn't enough for you, was it? Tell me, how far have you come since you first began your journey?"

Fronsac tried to find a good round number for the leagues he had traveled, but he wasn't sure himself. He'd never stopped to consider it. "I began in Jayco, less than ten leagues from the Ritco Sea. I rode north until I reached the Sea of Barancha, then north again until I found myself in sight of The Great Wall of Cobracorpen. I traveled further north, following the expanse of The Wall. After that, I went east, exploring the mountain passes and many winding trails of the hobgoblins, orcs, and kralle. I've passed through forests of pine, forded rivers of ice-melt, traversed seas of grass. I've seen men and women from all the territories and all the fiefdoms. I've met dream-walkers and farmers, peasants and nobleman. I have come far, Abbot; so very far."

"You've come all this way with only your wit and dagger to protect you? Only a mule to carry you and curiosity to guide you?"

"Yes."

"You might not realize it, Leodegrance, but you thirst for knowledge more than you consciously realize. Why else travel as far as you have; who else would have braved the dangers you've braved?"

Fronsac was silent, unsure how to reply.

"If it makes you feel any better," Acel's deep voice made Fronsac jump, "we *are* permitted to marry; we are allotted alcohol, in small doses. You won't be like a monk who has devoted himself to one of the gods. There are no vows of celibacy, and you abstain from nothing wholly. The terms 'abbot' and 'brother' are more categorical than clerical."

"Your grandfather had a wife," added Abbot Henri. "As did your father. We all have the occasional evening of drunkenness, to celebrate certain events. Events such as the resurrection of an extinct bloodline." He smiled and placed a hand on Fronsac's shoulder. "All we ask is that you do your part to help the progression of mankind, to assist in the gathering and cataloging of information and wisdom."

"And to take up arms to defend our sacred knowledge," Acel added quietly. "Should that time ever come."

Abbot Henri nodded. "All knowledge, even martial knowledge, is studied at Castle Kaarlo."

Fronsac held his tongue. He didn't know what he'd hoped to find when he first left his home months ago but he'd found it, and he didn't know if it was what he wanted. A warrior-scholar. Was that a better life than farming? These brothers lived not nearly as pious or boring lives as he suspected other monks of other orders lived, but he was not yet convinced this was the best life for him. His grandfather had always seemed to house some deep discontent for the simple life of farming, but Fronsac hadn't found it terribly unappealing.

It wasn't terribly enticing, either.

"You don't need to make up your mind now," said the abbot. "Whether you choose to stay or leave is entirely up to you. I will not turn you away, especially not with a blizzard nipping at your heels as you rode through these gates." As if the storm was eavesdropping on their conversation, the light from the window faded entirely as dense clouds overpowered the setting sun's weak light. "I will find you a bed; you will eat in the dining hall. Anything you ask that is within reason will be yours, Leodegrance."

Fronsac's gaze shifted from the floor and met Abbot Henri's. "Why is my name so important to you?" Fronsac asked. "And what happened to my family?"

Snow and freezing rain pelted the window, and Abbot Henri's grin faded away entirely. He gently grabbed Fronsac by the arm.

"Come, Fronsac," said Abbot Henri. "A dark tale requires a bright room, lest we let the darkness touch our souls. We will go to the library and sit before the fire. That is where your education will begin, with the knowledge of your bloodline."

*****

Years passed quickly at Castle Kaarlo. Fronsac read, and he learned. In the village he'd never read or written anything more than shopping lists or supply catalogs. Now he read broadly and voraciously. He read about the Lining that separated the planes of existence, the Elementals that sometimes broke through. He read about the beasts and the gods and legends, and the men and women who had helped shape Harthx, from the legend of the Cursed Witch King to the orders and deeds of the Cobracorpen Knighthood, to the adventures and misadventures of the famed monster-hunters, the Valons.

"Are we not like the Order of the Scroll?" Fronsac once asked Abbot Henri. "We, too, seek knowledge of the planes to better the people."

"The Order of the Scroll seeks knowledge to better the Cobracorpen Knighthood," corrected the abbot. "The knowledge and wisdom they acquire is strictly for their brothers in arms whereas we seek information for all people, provided they seek us out.

"Those who value knowledge will seek it."

Fronsac read books on geography and cryptozoology; learned the histories of each region and their religions. Never satisfied with one field of study, he read books every evening until his eyes throbbed, and every morning he gained martial knowledge under Acel with the same fervor.

Acel tossed him a weapon. "Explain."

"Cimmatarian bow," recited Fronsac. "Single piece, flexible wood. First rose to popularity in 803BM with the invasion of the Cimmatars. Accurate up to fifty feet, armor-piercing up to thirty-five. Lightweight wood, brownie-gut string. Popular among assassins for its size and stopping power, frowned upon by the Knighthood due to its limited range."

Acel nodded. "Good." He walked behind the line of trainees and young monks. "Brothers, nock your arrows."

As one, Fronsac and the other seven pulled bolts from their quivers and nocked them to their bowstrings.

"Draw. Back!" Acel ordered, enunciating each word as its own sentence.

The sound of stretching string and flexing wood filled the air.

"Take. Aim!"

Cloth rustled as the trainees brought their weapons to bear.

"Fire!"

Wood whined and strings twanged as Fronsac and the others let go simultaneously. Each arrow slammed into their creature-sized targets, all of them hitting center mass.

All except for one.

Fronsac's target was a bit smaller than a man; a hay-filled plaster stand-in for an orc. Fronsac's arrow had cleaved the top of the target's brow from the body, hay spilling from the head like blood.

The group lowered their bows in silent unison.

Acel came up behind Fronsac and put his hand on the younger man's shoulder.

"Hear me now," Acel addressed the group. "Go to the armory. Draw morning-stars and whip-chains. Practice controlling the rebound of your blows against the training posts. Remember, flow with the direction of recoil, not against it!" The trainees silently jogged to the armory to exchange their Cimmatarian bows for other weapons. Acel's grip turned hard and he spun Fronsac around.

"Why won't you aim for the chest? No matter how good a shot you are, *always* aim center mass. A chest shot will drop everything from an orc to a minotaur. You could drop a dragon with a chest shot, provided you had the proper arrow-heads! Why must you always risk head shots?"

"To the best of the Order's knowledge," Fronsac recited, "Kromen have only one weak spot: the crown of the head."

Acel's face flushed with anger. "We are not Valons!" He shoved Fronsac, causing him to stumble. "We are not monster-hunters! We are scholars. We seek knowledge of beasts, not to kill them."

"Kromen killed my family," retorted Fronsac.

"A family you never even knew," spat Acel. "You've said yourself that you don't remember anything about your parents. You were scarcely more than a baby when the castle was attacked. Why do you hold such a grudge?"

"Why do you not?" Fronsac countered. He had never raised his voice to Acel before. "You told me you trained alongside my father, on this very ground, with these very weapons!" Fronsac shook the bow in his hand. "You and the abbot say that the bonds of this brotherhood run deep, yet you do nothing to avenge those you've lost!"

Acel rubbed his temples, gathering his patience. "You cannot blame monsters for the death of your parents. The Head Ranger before me trained your father and me to know the dangers of any reconnaissance mission. Abbot Leodegrance, your grandfather—"

"I know who he was!" Fronsac spat.

"—taught us there is no such thing as an evil beast. Orcs and dragons and other creatures are different; they are self-aware enough to choose whether they will be good or evil. Kromen aren't. They hunt for sustenance; they kill for food and protection. They did not harm the Order out of spite."

"You don't know that," said Fronsac. "You can't *possibly* know that. Before the recon party stumbled across the cave, Kromen were nothing more than legends. Then it was you and the rest of the scouting party who awakened them, and it was you who led them back here in the first place!"

Acel slapped Fronsac across the cheek, hard. Fronsac fell to the ground, shocked.

"You listen close and you hear me now," Acel whispered, standing over Fronsac and pointing his finger. "I loved your father as a brother, cared deeply for your mother as a friend. And they weren't the only two we lost that night. There were dozens more; the next day the other survivors and I cut down scores of trees to gather enough wood for the pyres. Bodies burned for almost a week; the smell of cooked flesh filled my nose at all hours of day and night. The screams of those carried away to the mountains rang for two days straight before the Kromen had had their fill, and we knew we could do nothing to help our brothers and sisters inside those black caves. That's not to mention the centuries of precious knowledge we lost when the library caught fire, nor the heartache felt when we thought you and your grandfather were dead or carried away." Acel angrily wiped his eyes before the tears could fall.

"Don't you dare so much as imply that the others and I were cowards, Fronsac. Don't you even consider it. We fought hard, we saved ourselves, and we saved who we could. We were unprepared for the nightmare we awoke in those mountains, but now we know what hides in those caves. We have the knowledge, and we paid for it dearly. I lost more than you did on that day; I have memories of those who were killed. Your parents are more than just stories to me. They were real. But the biggest difference between you and me is this: I won't give in to my animal instincts." Acel stepped back. "The Kromen will stay in their caves unless we disturb them. They lack the awareness to hold grudges or seek revenge. That's what makes them animals. If you honestly believe that taking revenge on a creature that has no concept of right or wrong is the noble thing to do, you are sorely mistaken and you are more beast than the Kromen themselves...and you are unworthy of your name."

Fronsac glared at Acel, indignant tears burning his eyes.

"Enough weapons-work for today," said Acel. "Turn in the bow and go to your book studies. I recommend you read up on ethics." He turned and walked away.

Fronsac considered yelling a retort, angering the head ranger even further, then thought better of it. He dusted himself off, deep in thought. He knew his anger was a flaw and would be his undoing. What he *didn't* know was where it had come from. He'd never been an angry man before; even as a child he hadn't been prone to tantrums. Why now?

He passed Abbot Henri as he walked to the library. "Good morning, Abbot," said Fronsac. "How goes your translation of the Mythilis chronicles?"

Abbot Henri nodded enthusiastically. "They go well, Leodegrance. I'm sure you and other trainees will be just as excited to read them as I am to translate them." His eyes narrowed. "Speaking of which, why aren't you with them now? You usually spend at least another hour with weapons." Before Fronsac could reply, the abbot frowned and touched his cheek. "Disregard the question, young brother; the answer is literally staring me in the face."

Fronsac's cheeks turned red, but he held his tongue. He would not dishonor himself again. "Abbot Henri, I need to speak with you."

"Of course, lad, follow me." The abbot held Fronsac's arm for support and led the younger man to the Tower of the Abbot. "We'll talk when we reach my chamber," explained the old man. "I can scarcely climb the stairs without being winded, let alone hold a conversation." They climbed the stairs in silence, Fronsac helping the abbot navigate the steep stairs and the twisty path.

"At my age, I'd rather my chamber be on the ground floor," the abbot wheezed. They reached the chamber door and went inside.

The abbot let go of Fronsac's arm and hobbled over to his desk, collapsing into the chair behind it, breathing deeply. "Forgive me, Leodegrance; I'm not as young as I once was."

"Take your time, Abbot," replied Fronsac politely. He looked at the walls, still covered with rolls of parchment, only they hung lower than they had a few years before. The ladders were gone now, and the writing wasn't nearly as eloquent as it'd once been.

"I'm guessing," said the abbot, "you want to discuss your anger."

Fronsac nodded. "Yes. How did you know?"

Abbot Henri nodded his head and sighed. "It's obvious to everyone. You've been training with the Order for three years now. You started happy and eager, exciting us all with the thought that the famous Leodegrance bloodline had returned. But you've been changing. We watched you go from inquisitive and eager to competitive and ambitious to, most recently, combative and condescending."

Fronsac nodded. "I know, Abbot Henri. I don't know why I'm like this."

"I think I know. It all goes back to your grandfather."

Fronsac cocked an eyebrow. "My grandfather?"

"Yes. When the Kromen attacked, he watched his son and daughter-in-law torn apart. He saw the library and the stables catch fire. He saw his brothers torn in half and eaten before his very eyes. As abbot, he was sworn to protect Castle Kaarlo, and he undoubtedly felt like a failure. I remember that night well, lad; I relive it in my nightmares. After the library caught fire, it seemed as though all was lost; I doubted any of us would survive. Your grandfather likely thought the same, so he gathered the three books he had in this very chamber, grabbed you from your crib, and stole away in the chaos."

Fronsac nodded. He'd heard this all before. "What does this have to do with my anger, Abbot?"

"Blood magic is a tricky thing at best," said the abbot. "You used blood magic, albeit unknowingly, to open your grandfather's chest, did you not?"

Fronsac nodded.

"When the chest was sealed," wheezed the abbot, "your grandfather had to have been angry and upset. Distraught, even. His blood would have been boiling with rage and shame as he enchanted the chest, despite his belief there are no such things as 'evil' beasts." The abbot coughed dryly into his hand. "The rage your grandfather felt as he recited the incantations had an unexpected effect. Tell me, young brother; do you know the difference between a spell and a curse?"

"The spell-caster is the deciding factor," Fronsac quoted from his studies. "The intent of the person saying the incantation is what separates a spell from a curse. If the enchanter has good intentions, the magic is pure and serves its intended purpose. If they are angry or spiteful, the magic could be corrupted and possibly have unintended side effects."

Abbot Henri nodded. "Your studies have been going well, I see."

"How do I break the curse?"

The abbot frowned and looked away, massaging his left shoulder. "You'd have to avenge the slight against your grandfather."

"Kill the Kromen?" Fronsac asked excitedly.

"I would not be so happy were I you," chastised Abbot Henri. "That goes against the teachings of our order. Were you to kill them out of spite, you would be excommunicated and forbidden from ever studying here again."

"What you call spite I call necessity."

The abbot shook his head. "Leodegrance, be not a fool. You're not thinking this through."

"Thought without action is meaningless!" Fronsac's face turned red as he stood, fists clenched.

"You're trying to justify genocide! Calm down and sit, Leodegrance. Let us think this—"

"I'm sick of thinking!" Fronsac knocked the quills and ink blotters from the desk. "I've thought too much and acted too little since I've come here. This curse must be broken, and there's only one way to do so." Fronsac turned and moved for the door.

"Leodegrance!" The abbot followed him out the door. "Leodegrance, pause for just one moment!" He grabbed Fronsac's arm. "Please, if only you'd—"

Fronsac wheeled on the old man, eyes wide and burning with demonic hate. "I'm through thinking things through!" He grabbed the old man by the shoulders and flung him to the stairs. The back of the abbot's head landed with a hollow crack. His eyes went wide then drooped sleepily. He put his hand on the back of his head and touched the blood pouring from his skull. He looked from his bleeding hand to Fronsac, concerned and confused.

Fronsac knew he should call for help, but his rational thoughts were giving way to the curse. A humorless smile stretched his lips.

"Will thinking things through help you now?" Fronsac stood over the abbot, one foot on either side of the old man's head. Abbot Henri tried to roll away, but Fronsac delivered a swift stomp to the old man's face.

"Leodegrance..." Blood sprayed from the abbot's mangled lips. "It is not you, it is the curse..." Fronsac's smile turned to a frown. "It is necessary."

Fronsac lifted his foot and stomped down on the abbot's head three times in quick procession. The abbot's hand twitched and rose in the air, pleadingly, but a fourth and final stomp completely crushed the old man's skull, and the limb dropped.

Fronsac's mind wrestled control from the curse for a moment. His satisfaction faded to horror as the realization of his actions became clear.

"Abbot..."

He looked at the gory mess that had once been a head.

He glanced down the stairs, wondering if he should seek help.

Curse or not, they won't forgive you for this.

Fronsac ran his fingers through his hair, trying to calm the panic rising up his spine.

You must leave.

But where? Back to the village? *Could* he even go back to his old life now?

End the curse. Find the cave. Kill them all.

The panic faded and was replaced with cold fury.

This is the Kromen's fault. This never would've happened were it not for them.

Fronsac nodded—the voice was right. The Kromen set this entire thing in motion, and now it was hurtling forward with increased inertia. He was past the point of no return; all that remained now was to exact vengeance. He looked at the bloody body at his feet.

He shouldn't have tried to interfere.

Fronsac nodded.

Go.

Fronsac scraped the blood from the bottom of his boot, then calmly walked down the stairs of the Abbot's Tower. He passed the training ground, saw Acel training the would-be rangers. Fronsac smiled and waved at his former friend as he walked towards the gates. Acel cocked an eyebrow, wondering where the young man was going. Fronsac waited for the gates to open, rocking back on his heels impatiently.

It was then that Acel noticed the blood on his boots.

"Fronsac!" Acel called, instinct telling him something was wrong. "Where are you going?"

Fronsac waved but didn't turn to face the ranger. He walked into the woods.

Acel took a few steps to follow, then turned abruptly and ran to the Abbot's Tower.

Fronsac made it to the wood-line then sprinted ahead, eager to put Castle Kaarlo far, far behind him.

*****

Weeks had passed since Fronsac had seen another human soul, and he had no idea where he was. The first few days of his flight had been spent always moving, stopping only for a few hours of sleep before waking and moving haphazardly to throw off pursuit. If he didn't know where he was going, the brothers wouldn't be able to predict his next move. They came close several times, the sound of the braying hounds alerting him whenever they caught his scent. The forest was dense and full of streams and rivers. Every time he heard the dogs he would run until he found a water source, then he would flee upstream if the creek was shallow enough or let the current carry him downstream if it was swift enough.

The wild stripped away every ounce of fat and he became taut with corded muscle. He became a predator, a shadow in the forest. Stalking prey with a feline grace, attacking with wolfish savagery. His senses heightened to the point he could smell berries and nuts hidden beneath the undergrowth; he could hear the padded paws of the apex predators as they slunk through the forest. Fronsac was becoming more like them with every passing day.

The blood magic in his veins grew in correlation to his animal instincts. Rage drove him forward, anger kept him strong in spite of sleep deprivation. His cheeks hollowed and his eyes sunk further into his skull. A skeleton, animated solely by baser instinct, he sought the Kromens' cave.

Whether it was the curse in his blood or his unconscious mind drawing from his studies at Castle Kaarlo, he found the cave on the mountain. Blood pounded heavily at his temples, the curse urging him onward. The conscious part of his mind heeded warning; to rush in blindly would be suicide. Plans had to be made. The enemy had yet to be observed.

The curse acknowledged the wisdom of the mind. Fronsac slowly backed away from the cave, his feet making not a single sound on the fallen leaves underfoot. He crept away slowly, eyes darting and finding all possible places of cover and concealment, noting choke-points and avenues of approach, plotting his attack.

He found a toxic stream not far from the cave, the water black and thick and undoubtedly the waste of the creatures. Fronsac put his hand in the foul liquid and began smearing it all over his body. He took a deep breath and stuck his head into the noxious elixir. He made sure none got in his eyes, and he spat every drop from his lips. He shuddered to think what would happen if any of the liquid were to enter his body.

Fronsac snuck back to the cave. He sought the perfect hiding spot; close enough to observe while offering concealment. The accounts of the raid of Castle Kaarlo said the creatures possessed night vision beyond that of a panther, having picked off the initial recon party one-by-one in the dead of night, following them all the way back to the castle, where the real bloodshed began...

A large tree stood near the cave. At the crook of two large branches sat a hole, undoubtedly the nest of some great bird of prey. Fronsac climbed the tree as easily as an ape. The nest was empty, save for a few animal skeletons and some feathers. Fronsac theorized that the avian inhabitants had either been killed or driven away by the Kromen. Judging by the size of the skeletons the birds must have been massive, yet even those raptors were unable to stand before the fury of the Kromen. He crawled in and stared at the cave.

Fronsac fed on insects and small lizards as the day turned to dusk, snatching them from the tree branches. He no longer thought in sentences or thought of himself as a person, he was a creature now, more jungle-cat than man. He sniffed the air, tasting the difference in quality as day gave way to night. Every noise in the forest amplified, from the hum of insects to the wings of predators snatching prey from the forest floor. Night fell, and he heard motion coming from the cave. His body coiled and he tightened his grip on the dagger, his eyes adjusting to the darkness with supernatural ease.

Kromen emerged from the cave. They walked upright, slightly hunched. Their wide-set eyes glowed green, seeing more than even Fronsac's predator eyes. Two small ears hung low on their brutish heads, twitching as they sought to hear whatever the night would offer. Fronsac steadied his breathing, willed his heart to slow. One of the beasts crept forward, staring at the tree. It stepped in front of the first

Kromen and was slapped to the ground, the leader glaring down and roaring, massive canine teeth glinting in the moonlight.

The one that had been struck screeched in reply, and the leader roared once more. The other three beasts jumped up and down, slamming their massive fists against their broad chests. The fallen slowly rose to its feet and slowly backed to the rear of the pack. The leader snarled and sniffed the air for a moment, finding a scent. Its eyes went wide as it caught Fronsac's scent from earlier. The leader hooted and screamed and pounded its chest, motioning the others to follow. They lumbered away, toward the foul-smelling creek Fronsac had used to cover himself. Fronsac wondered what they would do once they realized the human scent vanished at the creek.

The curse in his blood urged him to chase down the beasts, to end them all. What was left of his civilized brain urged patience; wait and observe. He knew too little of these ape-like creatures. Even the account of the attack on Castle Kaarlo was vague by the Order's definition of detail. Fronsac would wait, and he would watch, and he would observe. When the time came, he would kill.

Each night the Kromen left the cave, and each night they chased down a new scent. Fronsac changed his hiding spots each night, worried they might backtrack his scent when he left to bathe in the foul stream. Each subsequent night saw more Kromen leaving the cave, due to the lingering scent of man. The first night he'd seen five creatures total, but now the party was holding strong at twelve.

Fronsac fashioned himself a bow, not unlike the Cimmatarian bow he'd trained with the day he'd fled the Order. He killed a river rodent the size of a cat and used the animal's intestines for the bowstring, fashioning himself a sling from its hide. He avoided the Kromens' cave for several days, using the time to fashion arrows and find stones for his sling, using the remnants of his shirt to make a quiver and several bags to carry stones.

The curse in his blood drove Fronsac to madness. He obsessed over the notes on the Kromen back at Castle Kaarlo, the images dancing through his mind in a haze. The Kromen were thought to have lived side by side with the other ape-like creatures who would evolve to create modern man, a distant cousin to the barbarian clans of the North. The Kromen were cannibals, attacking the weakest of their neighbors, generally the injured, the sick, the old, and the young. Kromen raiding parties attacked the neighboring tribes by night, targeting the nurseries or infirmaries to hunt the most defenseless members of the communities. The early tribes of man banded together to drive the Kromen away, hunting them almost to extinction and forcing them deep into the earth.

The Kromen evolved, shrinking to better move about the low-ceilinged underground labyrinths. Their eyes became more attuned to darkness than light; their noses grew, and their hearing improved so they could better hunt at night. Thinking them vampires or werewolves, the Order investigated.

Fire terrified the creatures, but it didn't cause any physical harm the way it would a vampire, and neither silver nor enchanted wood could pierce their hide. Only the crown of the Kromens' heads were susceptible to damage. Be it due to some genetic flaw in their shallow gene pool, or possibly a curse from the gods, the top of their head was soft as a newborn's. The one chink in their armor.

As the sun set, Fronsac took his grandfather's dagger from its sheath. He cut a thin, shallow line across his palm and ventured into a small corridor made by the rocks, near the cave; smearing his bloody palm as he went. Reaching a natural cul-de-sac, he prepared for his first altercation in the coming battle.

Blood hummed in his veins, the coming slaughter exciting the curse in a way Fronsac had never felt before. The full moon slowly rose into the dark blue sky, the heavy orb and the twinkling stars bearing witness to the coming confrontation like the eyes of so many wrathful gods. Fronsac lit a small fire using two stones, then wrapped one of his arrows in a swath of cloth. He stood next to the fire, holding his bow in one hand and the arrow in the other, waiting.

He heard the excited hoots and roars of the Kromen as they caught his scent. Fronsac's heart galloped and he let out a primal scream.

Let them smell me, let them hear.
Let them come.

The sound of hide scraping along rockwall. They were in the corridor. Fronsac dipped the cloth-wrapped tip of the arrow into the flame and crouched in a corner, waiting.

A dozen raiders ran shrieking into the cul-de-sac, eyes glowing murderously in the moonlight.

Their eyes first focused on the burning low in the corner, dumbfounded. Fronsac drew back the flaming arrow, and all eyes moved to him.

The creatures roared.

Fronsac fired his arrow, the gut-string popping into place with a satisfying snap. It struck the line of kindling Fronsac had laid out during his preparation, behind the Kromen. The creatures jerked with fear and looked from Fronsac to the inferno building behind them. They shied away with terrified hoots and shrieks, backing themselves against one wall. Fronsac dropped the bow and placed a stone in his sling, twirling it underhand.

The leader of the creatures was the first to shift its attention to Fronsac. The whir of the sling confused the creature, the fire terrified it. The smell of blood drove it insane with hunger. It beat its chest and sprang forward with a roar.

Fronsac let the stone fly. With a sickening crunch and a splat, the stone burrowed into the beast's skull. The creature fell from the air and landed at Fronsac's feet, twitching.

The other raiders stared with animal confusion, shocked at seeing their prey drop their leader so easily. Fronsac grinned, the curse filling him with sadistic pleasure as the blood-letting began.

Fronsac smirked as the Kromen hooted in confusion.

He screamed, a loud and inhuman raging, unlike anything a man has ever felt finding its way into his voice. The creatures flinched, and Fronsac fired another stone into their midst, dropping one of them with ease. Fronsac sprang past them and over the fire, trusting the light of the flame to disorient the Kromens' night vision. He raked his knuckles across the rockwall, drawing blood. With the same hand he twirled the reloaded sling, sending droplets of blood into the air and riling up the creatures further.

He laughed

The Kromen, dimwitted and dangerous, attacked. Their fear of the flame was over-shadowed by their blood-lust, but the narrow corridor meant they had to attack one at a time. One by one they came through the flame, and one by one they fell beneath Fronsac's sling. Red and gray gore splashed from the wounds, drenching Fronsac and the cave walls in a grotesque collage of blood and brains. The stench of burnt blood and cooked brain filled the air, worsening the blood-lust that flowed in the veins of the adversaries. The bodies piled up and eventually smothered the flame.

Fronsac leapt to the top of the heap of corpses, twirling the stone in his sling as he glared down the final two beasts.

One stepped forward and threw back its head with a roar just as Fronsac let loose the stone in the sling. The stone caught the Kromen in the mouth, knocking out the majority of its teeth. It put one long-clawed hand to its mouth and shrieked in pain and surprise. Fronsac loaded another stone to finish off the beast, when the other creature attacked. Fronsac caught it with a killing blow as it jumped towards him, but inertia kept the body sailing forward. It slammed into him before he could step aside and he tumbled off the pile of corpses, dropping his sling as he fell.

Fronsac rolled to his feet as the broken-toothed Kromen leapt over the pile of bodies. The creature roared, spraying Fronsac with blood. Fronsac backpedaled, desperately ducking and side-stepping the furious overhand swipes of the creature as it drove him backward through the rock corridor. Finally, they reached the opening and Fronsac spun on his heel, sprinting towards a tree. He knew the creature would catch him in no time out in the open.

The Kromen crouched and leapt after Fronsac, using all its considerable strength to attack the former acolyte of the Order. Fronsac placed one foot on the tree and kicked upward, arm outstretched and reaching for the bag of rocks he had stored in the crook of two branches. His hand closed around the cloth as he kicked away from the tree, twisting in the air. He swung the bag downwards mid-flight, the Kromen's claws just missing his stomach as Fronsac brought the bag of rocks down onto the beast's head. The creature dropped, twitching.

Fronsac landed with a roll, coming to his feet with the bag of stones held high. The Kromen twitched and gurgled angrily, not yet dead. Fronsac strode forward.

The creature glared up at Fronsac, a mixture of hate and fear in the dying thing's eyes. Fronsac smiled.

"You weren't the first to die on this night," Fronsac said, hoisting the bag over his head. "And you won't be the last."

Fronsac laughed and brought the bag of rocks down on the creature's head, again and again. After the beast was dead, Fronsac calmly retrieved his weapons and made his way back to the cave entrance.

His eyesight had sharpened and his hearing improved, the curse giving him the abilities necessary to complete his task. He looked into the cave and saw them, crouched in a corner deep within the earth, more Kromen, eyes wide with fear as Fronsac looked on with a sinister smile. He reeked of death and pulsed with raw power.

Fronsac cackled and drew back his bow, taking aim at the nearest creature. The bolt thudded into the Kromen's crown, dropping it in place. The others shrieked and ran deeper into the cave.

Nocking another arrow and laughing with sadistic joy, Fronsac stalked the fleeing beasts into the bowels of the earth, the moon and stars staring down with impassive judgement.

*****

Fronsac emerged sometime later, the rising sun illuminating his gore-caked figure. He'd killed them all; from the smallest newborn to the weakest elder. At first, they'd shrieked and gone deeper into the caves, seeking refuge, but it did them no good. One by one they all fell beneath his arrows and his stones, dying with shrieks of pain and confusion, their warriors all dead in the cul-de-sac or rock corridor. Too late the creatures had tried to mount a defense, but by then their numbers were so few it hardly mattered. The final three Fronsac killed in close combat, his dagger in one hand and a fist-sized rock in the other. He could have killed them from a distance, but he chose not to. He wanted to look these final three in the eyes as they fell, he wanted to see the life leave their bodies. And so he did.

Fronsac exited the cave feeling mighty; strong and proud and god-like. He relished the scent of the gore splashed across his bare chest, salivated at the taste of blood on his lips. Drunk on battle, he laughed in the still morning air. He saw the body of the Kromen he'd killed with the bag of stones, lying lifeless and twisted before the tree. Fronsac laughed even harder and walked forward to inspect the corpse.

Fronsac grinned at the mess of the creature's head, relishing the memory of the kill. His grin faded as he looked at the creature's wide eyes, the fear frozen in them forever. Fronsac's joy abated the longer he stared at the creature. He suddenly thought of Samuel, Blind Allen's dimwitted son. Fronsac hadn't thought of Samuel in years. Now, memories of Samuel's slow speech and dim wit filled Fronsac's mind. The curse left Fronsac quickly, its purpose fulfilled now that all the Kromen were dead. As the blinding rage and the animal instinct dissipated, Fronsac came to his senses and realized what he had done.

Shaking, he dropped next to the corpse, running his hands through his hair.

"No," he whispered. "By all the gods, what have I done?"

The dead Kromen didn't reply.

"No," said Fronsac once more. "No!" He furiously wiped at the gore on his chest. Worse than murder. Genocide. An entire race wiped from the planet by his own hand. He shook and he screamed and he scratched his chest raw, a new madness replacing the old.

He ran for the freshwater stream and dove in, using sand to scrub the blood and gore from his body. He sobbed and he apologized over and over to whatever deity was frowning upon him. He screamed apologies to the creatures he'd killed; he turned to Castle Kaarlo and shrieked for forgiveness. Samuel—even the blind man's son had more mental capacity than the Kromen, more understanding of good and evil. Acel's words rang loud in his mind. *If you honestly believe that taking revenge on a creature that has no concept of right or wrong is the noble thing to do, you are sorely mistaken and are unworthy of your name.*

Fronsac shrieked.

The Order found him that night, naked and babbling in the stream. They grabbed him and pulled him to shore, reassuring him as he continued to apologize. Green-cloaked rangers scouted the area and found the corpses at the cave. They went back to where Fronsac was shivering near a fire, wrapped in a blanket, reason returning to his eyes.

Fronsac glanced at Acel, but couldn't bring himself to meet the ranger's gaze.

"I killed him," Fronsac confessed in a quiet, shaking voice. "The abbot. I killed him."

Acel nodded, his stomach turning. "It wasn't you. It was the curse."

"How do you know about the curse?"

"I figured it out." Acel sat next to Fronsac, neither man looking away from the fire. "After I saw you leave the castle and I found the abbot, I knew you weren't in control of yourself. I thought back on all your time here, and the story of your grandfather's chest. I can't believe that none of us thought you'd be cursed—it makes so much sense in hindsight."

Fronsac started crying.

"Does it matter?" Fronsac sniffed. "The abbot's dead, and by my hand. I know as well as you that murder is no more forgiveable than genocide."

Acel looked away, his own heart breaking at the thought of putting his friend on trial. Exile would be the least of Fronsac's worries.

"You'll escape in the night," whispered Acel. "I'll take the final watch. I'll loosen your bindings, and you'll knock me unconscious. You'll have a few hours to run, possibly more if I'm still 'unconscious' and unable to wake the others." He turned to Fronsac, and the younger man met his gaze for the first time. "You must run far and you must run fast. Go as long and as far as you can; eat as you move and don't chance sleep until you're beyond the mountain ranges. Change your name, your appearance. Change everything and start new."

Fronsac knew he'd be hunted for the rest of his days. He wondered if that was appropriate penance for his crimes, or if he deserved death instead. "What am I supposed to do, once I'm away from here and I'm a new man?"

Acel's gaze turned to steel and he gripped Fronsac's arm. "Find redemption, Leodegrance."

It would be quite some time before Fronsac would hear that name again.

Duos Necrosis

By Drunken Clarity (David Burman)

570AM
Age of Gloom

The two men faced off, to the delight of all patrons drinking that night at The Broken Sword Tavern.

"I'm go'na crack ya jaw so hard ya dog'll bleed," said Jacob, six-feet-two-inches of solid, muscular, twenty-four-year-old farmstock. His opponent, Hargrad, was a mere five-foot-five, stout, dumpy, and had twenty-something years on the farmboy. But still, Hargrad seemed very little if not at all perturbed by the situation. He just raised his fists, planted his stance, and smiled.

Both men were surrounded by a ring of patrons in what had become a regular event in the tavern over the past few years, much to the delight of its owner, Grismol.

Jacob let out an almighty battle cry, launched forward, and took a wild right-handed swing at his smaller opponent's head. This left him open, and Hargard ducked and planted a short but powerful right hook square to the solar plexus of the younger man, stopping him where he stood.

There was the distinct sound of multiple ribs cracking, a cry of pain as Jacob collapsed to his knees, and the awful stench of warm ale as he spewed his night's fill all over the stone floor. The tavern erupted into laughter, and two of Jacob's friends rushed to his aid. Hargrad turned, bowing to the crowd. He stood a little taller as walked to the tavern bar to retrieve his fresh winner's tankard and collected his take of the evening's festivities from Grismol, minus the tavern's cut.

Grismol was very happy and went to place his easy earnings into the coffer box, when he spotted the two hooded figures standing at the dark end of his bar.

"And what might I do for you fine gentlemen this night?" asked Grismol with a slight tremor in his voice, placing the winnings in the box and closing it.

"We are here for the job," said the shorter of the two, no tremor in *his* voice.

"And what job would that be?" asked Grismol, soon to regret his cheeky question.

The tallest of the hooded pair went to step forward, but Velidah put one hand on his partner's chest as he pulled back his hood with the other. "Easy, Gardarsh; I will handle this." Gardarsh grunted and stepped back into the slightest of shadows, and was all but removed from the room visually.

Grismol was mesmerized and intimidated by Velidah; it's not often you see a Dalanik Elf in the flesh, and he was the first to grace Grismol's tavern that was for sure. He stood around five-foot-five with skin darker than the night abyss, and frost-white hair that looked magical. They could have been classed as a race of beauty if it not for their dark past and fanatical ways.

"I'm sorry, my lord, I meant no disrespect." Grismol was backtracking at great speed. "Yes, the job, of course."

"It is my understanding that you are losing patrons at an alarming rate," said the Elf, cutting Grismol off mid-sentence.

"Yes, my lord, it was just a few at first, but now there is one every other night from all over the city. People are becoming aware, and are less likely to venture out at night," said Grismol, looking over the Elf's shoulder towards the near-invisible Gardarsh. "Can I get you gentlemen a drink?"

"No. Payment now and we will fix this problem." Velidah was straight to the point.

"There is a collection of coins from all the businesses affected. I'm sure they would want to see proof before payment, my lord," said Grismol, still with a tremor in his voice.

Two words came from the dark corner, where Gardarsh had been overseeing the conversation. "Dous Necrosis."

Grismol went pale as the words uttered sank in, and he reached into his coffer box and removed a cloth pouch. "If Darvalon has sent the Duo of Death to fix our problem, then who am I to argue?" Grismol handed the pouch to Velidah.

"Your problem will be no more this night," said Velidah. He took the bag and slipped it into a hidden pocket. Velidah kept full eye contact with Grismol as he reached back and replaced his hood, doing it with such style that Grismol would remember this meeting for all eternity. With that, the pair left the tavern as quietly as they'd entered.

*****

"Duos Necrosis, really?" asked Velidah, feeling the weight of the pouch as the pair walked through the night streets on their way to the docks.

"It got us paid up front didn't it? And who the hell says no to a free drink?" replied Gardarsh.

"I thought it was better for us to just get out of there before he tried to start haggling on the price," replied the Elf.

"Oh, and you did that thing with your hands again," said Gardarsh, a little excitement in his voice.

"What thing?"

"You know that thing where you stare at the customer, reach back and slowly put your hood on, and then flick your hands and fingers forward like you're silently saying, 'ta-da!'" Gardarsh could hardly contain his laughter and excitement. "It's really weird to watch."

"Well… you're weird—you don't even have a nose!" said Velidah.

"Now that's just mean. Genetically I have no nose, and I was born that way; instinctively you learned to act like a dick," replied Gardarsh.

Both men laughed, and Velidah slapped his friend on the back as they continued to the docks.

*****

"It's there, I can smell the death!" said Gardarsh, pointing to an opening in the stones large enough for a man to enter crouched.

It was an opening or, better put, a vent for part of the town's sewers to release into the open bay. Tonight, though, it was to be used as the entrance to another fight for the pair.

Both men entered the sewers through the gap until they found themselves in a sizeable man-made cavern at the end of the sewers' central cisterns. There were several large and small passageways leading off in all directions, but Gardarsh knew precisely which would lead them to their prize.

Both men removed their robes, placing them in a canvas sack. Gardarsh hung it from a stone protruding from the wall of the dark, dank, musty cavern. They both did this as a ritual, but also so as to not dirty their fine robes or to be confined by them when the fighting began.

Velidah was clad in such exquisite leather armor with intricate designs adorning it, that you would have thought that only a master craftsman with a lifetime of skill and experience could have produced such a marvelous set. But it was one of his own designs and his favorite build. He only wore it on the most harrowing of jobs, and it had the scars to show them all. Strapped to his back was his pride and joy, the magical Mysturian sword of fire and ice. This blade was like no other; it was balanced with precision to its wielder, and kept an edge without the need of sharpening. It also had the designs of an ice dragon on one side and a fire dragon on the other; a clear stone was set in the pommel that appeared to be glass as clear as water but perfect in its crafting. Of all the treasures he had found on his adventures this was his favorite, hands down.

Gardarsh, also now free of his garb, was standing tall in all his Darkholder glory. Though he was entirely lean at six-foot-three, he looked similar to an ordinary human, except for the fact that Darkholders have leathery brown skin and no nose, which leaves them with two holes in the center of their faces. Darkholders also have an extra eye in the middle of their foreheads more significant than the other two, and have three fingers on each hand. He chose to wear a lighter tunic with leather straps crossed to hold his daggers, light greaves, and crafted boots with a metal rim and toe to allow his agile frame the ability to move with speed. His only visible protection were the thick leather bracers that covered his forearms from wrist to elbow, with hooked blades on the elbows of both. These were formidable combat weapons to the trained, and deadly for an expert, of which Gardarsh was both.

Gardarsh was in meditation, chanting to collect his thoughts and praying to his gods for a good fight. Velidah was picking his teeth with his little finger.

Gardarsh finished his preparation and turned towards his friend.

"Ready?" said Gardarsh.

"Let's do this, my brother!" replied Velidah

Velidah took a tight grip of his sword and concentrated until the stone in the pommel began to glow with a blue aura. The blade turned from steel to that of ice; it was a truly magical thing to witness, and one that neither of them ever got tired of.

"Levadelvora," said Gardarsh as he cast delving, a simple yet effective spell to produce the light required for their journey through the passageways.

Gardarsh pointed the way, but it was Velidah who led the duo; it was always the Elf who would lead the way so that the Darkholder could use his skills to the best of his ability. They were the Valons who got sent in to do the jobs that no others would, or possibly, couldn't do.

The unlikely pair had become bonded brothers from a young age. Both had joined the Valon academy at the same time, and both were shunned, ridiculed, bullied, and victimised, forming an everlasting bond that proved to be unbreakable. They were slowly becoming legends among not only the other Valons, but their notoriety had now spread from towns to cities. If a monster or worse needed to be dealt with, it was becoming the norm to ask for the duo.

"There is something strange in the air; be ready," cautioned Gardarsh.

"I was born ready!" replied Velidah with a cocky head shake.

"No, you were born small, wet, and crying, pretty much as you are now!" Even in the midst of danger, Gardarsh couldn't help but have some fun at the expense of his friend.

"Just point the way and keep an eye out, since you've got three of them," said Velidah. It was a weak retort, but it did make him feel a little better.

They entered a large catching chamber filled with various larger pieces of debris from crates, waste material, and even dead animals, but it was the live ones under the debris that caught the Darkholder's attention.

"BLOODROACHES!" cried Gardarsh as the hoard exploded from the piles and mounds on the chamber floor.

Gardarsh started casting spells in all directions; Velidah began to disperse a wave of swordplay that was not only deadly in its accuracy but poetic to watch in its beauty. Had he not become the masterful Valon that he was, he would surely have made a renowned dancer like the ones who performed for the elite and even the crown at festivals and the like.

Bloodroaches are not the most dangerous of enemies in that they are small, about the size of a medium dog, and relatively predictable in their movement, but they inject the blood taint into their victims from the fangs on their jaw mandibles, which means they need to be close to be effective. If you are lucky, you will be attacked by a male whose blood taint will only kill you in twenty-four hours or so. It's the female that injects her eggs into the bloodstream, and they hatch on the inside and work their way out.

Gardarsh was using primarily fear to turn the bloodroaches away from his position, and both the slowing and paralyzing ray spells to allow Velidah to do his thing. The duo made quick work of the room, not leaving a single bloodroach alive.

"How many do you reckon?" asked Velidah.

"I would say you destroyed around twenty-five in little over two minutes, which has to be a new record!" replied the Darkholder, who paused now that he had the scent of their prize. "Got you!"

"What is it?" questioned the Elf.

"Death, lots of death…" said Gardarsh, removing two crystal daggers from his belt and looking a little sterner than usual. "This one, we need to go down this one…"

Velidah led the way as they walked for what seemed an eternity, switching from passageway to passageway until they came to a massive chamber. It appeared to be about thirty sewer inlets, or tunnels, on various levels of the thirty-foot-high chamber wall. Dark little recesses were everywhere, and perfect for the use of hiding when being hunted. The chamber floor was scattered with bones and half-eaten body parts that the bloodroaches had probably been feasting on. There was also a single passageway on the other side some forty feet away.

"Something is not right," said Gardarsh, looking a little perplexed at the situation. "I am not sure which tunnel holds our prize."

Velidah was about to question his friend when an Icorii appeared from one of the higher tunnels. It let out a screech as hideous as any living creature could bellow, threatening to deafen the duo. The creature was only visible from the head and shoulders, but it still made for a creepy vision.

"Not Icorii—I hate Icorii!" shouted Velidah.

"Then you are not going to like what comes next," said Gardarsh, getting into his battle stance, daggers up.

Several Icorii appeared from their individual tunnels and released similar screeches. The Icorii were not usually known to congregate in groups, but they had, and this was going to be a hell of a fight, if not a severe problem.

Icorii were not the easiest monsters to fight, in that they were hard to kill with their regeneration ability. Their sheer numbers were going to be a problem, not to mention they were just plain ugly with their little bat-like faces, hunched-back posture, and saliva-dripping fangs.

"Nasty, just plain nasty!" Velidah wasn't happy. He took a firm grip on his sword, the pommel stone turning from blue to blood red, and the blade erupting into fire to the dismay of the visible Icorii.

The first of the Icorii took the leap from a high tunnel some twenty feet above Velidah. This would be the only easy kill of the night as Velidah swung the blade with perfect precision straight through the beast, cleaving it from neck to chest, then out the abdomen. The body lay lifeless in two pieces on the cavern floor.

"And that's how it's done," said the Elf, maybe just a little prematurely, but uttered nonetheless.

The remaining bloodborn—or Icorii—were not happy with what had just happened, and in unison expressed their disdain with a song of death, their shrills and shrieks seeming almost sad.

One by one the bloodborn crawled and slithered their way out of the tunnels and the darkness to join the duo in the chamber and on solid ground. The pair was surrounded by Icorii, and things looked like they were about to get worse. Icorii were not known for their co-operation and teamwork and, apparently, the books of knowledge at the academy severely needed to be updated. These particular bloodborn seemed to be working together with purpose and for a unified outcome.

"Why have you come to my domain?" called a voice from the darkness, holding all Icorii at bay and demanding the total and utter attention of Velidah and Gardarsh. "I am not to be trifled with; you are but worms in my garden of death." From the opposite passageway emerged a figure, not Icorii but similar, almost human but not quite.

"Who and, more importantly, what are you?" demanded the Darkholder.

"I was Grayson Brice, a night guard of the docks for twelve years." His grin was pure evil, showing his yellow teeth and the fangs that were now part of his smile. "Now I am the life in the darkness, the gatherer of death, master of the night and the..."

"You are a turd in the sewers, and you are nothing!" said Velidah, interrupting the stranger mid-speech.

"My coven gave me the gift of everlasting life, and for your insolence I shall take yours! Destroy them!" commanded Grayson. The bloodborn began to move on the duo as if collective in nature and purpose. Gardarsh stepped closer to his partner and simply said, "Keep me alive, or we die."

Gardarsh went into a trance and began to mouth some unheard chant while Velidah braced for the onslaught of Icorii. The first attacked and the Elf cut him down with a single blow, not as poetic as the first, but it did the job and made the rest think about their attack plan. The Darkholder was in full chant mode and of no use, not something that Velidah was used to; they were a team and worked well as a team, but this was something entirely new for him and not wholly within his comfort zone.

Velidah was holding his own, keeping the Icorii at bay—a hand here, a decapitation there. At last count he had maimed three and killed four, but as they grew bolder his job became harder and harder. The group seemed to realize that, should they attack as one, they would have the upper hand, and so they started to advance.

Velidah was preparing for what could possibly be their last battle; it was not what he had expected but, then again, he was surprised that they had lasted this long. He raised his sword and prepared to say something witty in his last moments, when Gardarsh opened his eyes; they were all white, with the center one glowing.

"VASTELLA NOCTURA!" The words burst from Gardarsh like a shockwave.

The majority of the bloodborn dropped dead where they stood, the rest withering with a pain and an agony unseen by either Valon in their long career, but it was Grayson that Velidah had his eye on. Gardarsh was now back in the real world, and this allowed Velidah to have a word with the so-called master of darkness. the Elf dispatched three Icorii on the way by removing their heads from their shoulders, not a lot of sport in his actions but satisfying anyway. Velidah reached Grayson and knelt beside his body.

"Any last words, Mr. Gatherer of Death?" asked the Elf as he knelt beside Grayson.

"Change is coming. The world that you know is in the crossover; death and life will become one!" Grayson seemed to be speaking from a place beyond this world.

Velidah took his flaming blade and slowly drove it into the heart of the being that used to be known as Grayson Brice.

"Sleep now; you do not deserve to walk the halls of wonder!" said the Dalanik Elf as he removed the blade and closed Grayson's eyes. Velidah was utterly unaware that his friend was dispatching the last of the Icorii with a sleep spell and a short, sharp stab to the heart with his crystal daggers. The sleep spell would not usually work on the bloodborn, but they welcomed the rest to relieve the pain, and allowed the spell to work.

"So what the hell was that you cast?" asked Velidah.

"We are brothers, and as brothers you must swear not to repeat what I am about to tell you," replied the Darkholder.

"I swear. I swear on my life and all that is sacred to me." Velidah was shocked that Gardarsh would need to ask this of him.

"I found a hidden page in the Scrolls of Darkness when I was tasked with cleaning the backrooms of the academy library; it mentioned the incantation of an unnamed spell," said the Darkholder.

"And?" asked the Elf.

"I studied it, incanted it, and tried it on bugs and rodents."

"So what was the spell?" he asked.

"I cast a Ray of Darkness." Gardarsh lowered his head so as to not look at his friend.

"How? I thought that spell was a myth," said the Elf.

"It is the forbidden Spell of Death that my kind once used, and I believe I am the only living practitioner," said Gardarsh.

The pair looked around the cavern at the destruction and death that had befallen it. Tonight was a night for the books but also a night to be learned from. Something was not right with the world, and Grayson's warnings may actually have some merit to them.

The pair worked their way back through the endless caves and chambers until they reached the first that they had entered. They were silent during the endless walk, so Velidah put his hand on his friend's shoulder.

"You know that you saved our lives tonight, right?" said the Elf.

"Yes, but I used a forbidden spell from the darkest of arts!" the Darkholder replied.

"Only you will know when it is forbidden and when it is not; you are the holder of a spell not known by another, and the keeper of its truth," said the Elf.

Gardarsh just smiled. His friend was right in that he and only he was the keeper of his oldest and most powerful spell—a spell that killed on the spot.

Gardarsh retrieved the canvas bag from the stone on the wall, retrieved their robes, and handed one to Velidah. Once they were both dressed, Velidah turned to Gardarsh.

"Tell me why we do this again?" asked Velidah with a grin, already knowing the answer

"Because it's what we do!" said Gardarsh.

"And we do it well!" they said together.

"Bet you wish you had that free drink now," said Gardarsh, slapping his friend on the back. "Yes, I bet you do!"

Witch's Curse

By Joel Norden

596AM
Age of Gloom

Sweat trickled from the man's furrowed brow. Bugs swarmed around him, attempting to bite every chance they got, and he cursed them for it. There was no getting away from the damned things in this damp forest that lay on the edge of the swamps. Aeric had heard that a Red Robed Magi had discovered a potion that would hide a person's scent from the bugs. Making you invisible to their humming wings and stinging blood-suckers.

Aeric took a deep breath, ever so slowly raising his yew bow. His fingers rested on the bowstring, yet he did not draw it. The red stag before him raised its majestic head, a tuft of grass hanging from its mouth as it eyed him. Their eyes met for a moment; Aeric met that gaze, wondering if it realized it was staring a man right in the eyes. Aeric lowered his eyes as if that might save him from being spotted. He didn't dare take a breath, and it felt like an eternity.

The stag, deciding Aeric was not as exciting as it had previously believed, twitched its ears, lowered its head, and continued to eat.

Aeric drew the bowstring to the corner of his mouth in one practiced motion. He concentrated all his willpower to one spot on the stag. Right behind its muscular shoulder was a small patch of fur that was a brighter red than the rest. Aeric had been taught by his father some thirty-five years ago; his father had called it instinctive shooting. Concentrate on something small, and the brain would naturally calculate the aim of the bow.

The bearded man took a deep breath and exhaled, only letting half the air out of his lungs. At that moment, he released the arrow.

It darted from the yew bow with a *twang*. Aeric's shot was perfect and he had only a moment's glance of the arrow's impact before the stag flinched and jumped. Then it darted into the underbrush at a mad trot. The arrow had entered the red stag's flesh right behind the shoulder, and stuck there in the mounds of healthy muscle.

Aeric observed as the animal disappeared from sight. He mentally marked the direction so he could track it later.

Aeric let out a thankful breath and sank to his knees. His callused hands shook, the adrenaline from the hunt running rampant through his veins. It was something that always happened to him while hunting big game.

Leaning up against a nearby tree, he tried to relax a bit. But with his concentration on the hunt gone, the heat of the midday sun was getting to him. And those Nether-cursed bugs!

He waited a good fifteen minutes, giving the stag time to calm down and find a spot to bleed out and die. Aeric then quickly retrieved his arrow and found the blood-trail. It wasn't long before he saw the stag dead in the brush, some sixty yards from where it had been shot. It always amazed Aeric how far they could run after taking an arrow to the heart.

Aeric field-dressed the deer, gutting it and cutting off the large antlers, which he shoved into the large chest cavity of the stag. He then tied a rope tight to each back leg of the animal, also tying it around his shoulders, and began to pull.

Three hours later, Aeric dragged the four-hundred-pound stag onto the trail where his horse and small flatbed wagon waited. He breathed a sigh of relief—it had been slow and painful going. Aeric's body ached and burned, despite the many breaks he had taken. He had been lucky that the stag had died not too far from the wagon.

Sighing, he slid the stag up onto the flatbed wagon, and it groaned in protest. Aeric patted his dun-colored horse and mounted up.

The ancient trail was thick with weeds, for few used it now. In other ages, the road had led to the large city of Khrolim. It had been a massive city, bringing merchants from all over Harthx. But during the mass conquest of Tenthrolen in the Age of Destiny the city had been destroyed, and the roads had since fallen into ruin, much like Khrolim itself.

Aeric glanced at the falling sun; there were maybe three hours until dusk. The wagon rattled behind him on the uneven road as he crested a large hill. Aeric took a deep breath of the humid air around him. At least on the hilltop there was a breeze. And that sight. The rolling hills covered the landscape, and turned into the forested swamps of Kitherlund. Within the wetlands of Kitherlund, Khrolim could be seen. Its walls crumbling, dark clouds of birds flew there. From this distance, no one would have known the clouds were swarms of crows, but Aeric had seen them up close many times.

He avoided going near Khrolim at all costs now, since the last time he had traveled close to that dreaded place he had almost died at the hands of a group of flesh-eating ghouls. He had been unfortunate enough to have gotten turned around within the wetlands, and had stumbled across the necropolis of Khrolim during a full moon.

Those undead creatures still haunted his dreams. Pale, blotchy skin, hungry eyes, the glint of hunger for human flesh bright in their gaze. Thick globs of drool pouring from gaping jaws.

Aeric shivered as the thought danced across his consciousness. Just as quickly, he pushed the thought away. He didn't need to worry about the ghouls anymore, for he wouldn't be returning to the area near Khrolim.

He descended a slope of another much smaller hill and pulled up to his little cabin. Furs hung in front of the house, dotting the porch overhang. Spears leaned against the outer wall, and a large barrel of black-fletched arrows sat on the porch next to the spears. A large firepit and spit were not far from the porch, for here he had cooked many a meal.

He had made everything around the small clearing by hand; spears, arrows, spit, cabin. Aeric was particularly proud of the cabin. Something he had built around twenty years ago for his wife and himself.

Lately, every time he returned home with a kill, his heart yearned for the old days. His wife, Nina, would come out to meet him, a smile on her lips. His daughter, Alicja, would be swaddled gently against her chest. Both of them happy to see him safely return with food for the dinner table.

Those days were gone now.

Aeric's daughter currently lived in Kraos to the south with his wife's uncle; she prefered the city and disliked her father's hermit-like way of life. Nina had been killed some fifteen years ago. After her death, Aeric had found it increasingly hard to socialize with people. With impressive speed he had folded into himself, avoiding people at all costs. When he did have to speak to someone, he did so with anxiety and dread.

Aeric jolted, realizing the presence of two horses at the side of his cabin. Their reins were tied to the rail of his porch. His eyes fell upon two figures sitting on the edge of the porch. Cursing himself, Aeric's hand inched for his bow.

"Hail, stranger! We mean you no harm, and we apologize for intruding on your abode. The woods are dangerous to those who were raised in the city." The stranger on the right spoke—definitely a woman. Her voice was smooth as silk, and had a melodious quality to it that immediately calmed Aeric. "We wish to spend the night if you will have us."

Aeric eyed the woman and her companion. The woman was perhaps one of the most beautiful creatures Aeric had ever laid eyes on. Her long blonde-brown locks flowed over her shoulders, reminding Aeric of a lioness. Her brown eyes had a calming, peaceful effect as she looked at him. A white robe covered her body; around the hem of the sleeves were embroidered moons and stars. A silver medallion hung from her neck, depicting a quarter moon.

A cleric of the goddess, Vala, Aeric noted. He was not a religious man by any standards, but his teacher had forced religion down his throat. Aeric relaxed, for Vala was a supposed deity of good. A goddess of the moon, beauty, and women.

Aeric's gaze brushed over the figure next to her, soaking in every detail possible with those hunter-eyes in one quick glance.

This stranger was rather shady, though not a threat. Dark brown robes covered the body; where its arms would have been exposed, they were wrapped in cloth. Its face, too, was covered with a cloth mask, and those eyes… Those green eyes had seen and endured much pain.

Neither carried weapons, so Aeric let his hand fall from his bow.

"Who are you? What is your business in these parts?" Aeric questioned. It had been a while since he had conversed with another person, so he may have come across as rude, but he was tired and didn't care.

The strange figure eyed Aeric, then gave the beautiful woman a knowing look.

"I am Lydia, and this is Ellyn, a Cleric of Vala," the wrapped figure said. Lydia's voice sounded like a strange mixture of a snake's hiss and gravel being ground underfoot.

From her name Aeric realized the figure was a woman, though her voice had fooled him.

"We plan on entering the Kitherlund swamps, and we are looking for a guide who knows the area," Lydia continued.

"A village south of here sent us to you, saying you might be interested in helping," Ellyn added, her voice gentle and sweet.

"I don't enter the swamps anymore. They're too dangerous," Aeric said, dismounting his horse. He unstrapped the stag and unceremoniously slid the dead animal to the ground. "You both can stay the night here if you'd like. It's safe; animals wander through occasionally, but nothing to be worried about."

"Maybe this will help you understand why we are asking for your help," Lydia hissed as she let her robe drop to the ground.

Aeric turned from the dead animal to look at Lydia. Her entire body was covered in a cloth wrap, almost like the legends Aeric had heard of mummies haunting the desert tombs. Lydia's haunting green eyes watched him as she unpinned the fabric at her wrist and started to unravel it from her arm.

Aeric's eyes widened before he could restrain himself. The woman's arm was covered in thick blueish scales. Lydia lowered her cloth mask as well; scales covered her face like some kind of crossbreed between human and lizard. She looked very much human, despite the lizard-like appearance.

"The Witch of the Kitherlund swamps did this to me. She laid a curse on me for not worshipping her," Lydia spat.

Aeric sank to the ground as if he had just been punched in the stomach. He couldn't stop staring at the cursed woman's scaly face.

Ellyn nodded her head, sorrow in her eyes. "She will not be accepted in society anywhere with this condition. I've tried to break the curse, but it is strong and unyielding. I believe if we kill this witch, the curse will be lifted."

"I've been chased out of more villages than I can count. Mobs with pitchforks and torches chasing me," Lydia said. She slowly approached Aeric; her green eyes pierced the depths of the bearded man's eyes. "We have heard that you've had dealings with the Kitherlund Witch in the past, and even a possibility that you tried to hunt her down at one point but failed. Rumors are thick across the countryside. So, what say you, Hunter; will you help us kill this witch?"

Tears burned Aeric's eyes, but none fell. The pain within him was resurfacing, a dullness in the pit of his stomach that churned upward, dragging up to his chest. It was like a chunk of his heart or soul had been violently ripped out. The loss of his Nina had exacted a tremendous toll.

His life and entire villages of people had been affected by this witch. They had followed the "laws" that the witch had created over their society like sheep, instead of standing together as one and breaking her evil grip.

I will finish what I started. I will avenge my wife.

Aeric Krull looked up at the two women with a hard look. "I will help you kill the witch."

He meant that with his whole heart and soul, or at least what was left of it.

*****

Aeric crept down the earthen tunnel's sloped path. The tunnel reminded him of a groundhog's hole: shoddily dug, and roots hanging from the low ceiling. The damp and muggy air caused sweat to roll down and gather in his brows. He swiped a hand over his forehead before it started stinging his eyes again.

He worried about the choice his wife and he were making. Was it wise to overthrow the witch's governing? For life, yes, he knew it was. Aeric could feel the anger building in his chest. No child is worth that price.

Aeric turned to Nina. His wife's long black hair stuck to her face; her jade-colored eyes met his. She was so strong.

Aeric glanced at the short sword that he held with a white-knuckled grip. He was scared. Never would he admit it to Nina, as she had no need to know. It would only plant the seed of doubt in her mind. Aeric needed her strength.

As they continued their descent, a dim light illuminated the bottom of the sloping tunnel. Aeric could see that it opened up into a vast chamber. An acrid smell filled the air, making Aeric wrinkle his nose.

They crept up to the doorway and peered in. The room was quite large. The walls of the cave were covered in shelves which held many books, most falling apart and ancient. Potions and other occult objects were on a rickety wooden table. In the very center of the room was a large kettle, red bubbles forming and popping slowly within it. But Aeric's eyes were drawn to the painted symbols on the wall in the back. It was a giant, glaring, red "S". He hoped it wasn't blood that had been used to paint that horrid letter. But he had the sick feeling that was indeed blood. Anger and fear mixed in his chest. Those mixed emotions were for Alicja; what if that was his daughter's blood...

He shoved those thoughts away with a savagery that surprised him. At that moment Aeric halted, and his eyes were drawn back to the kettle.

Slender, crooked fingers stirred the pot slowly. The witch stood there, eyeing them with her one good eye. The crone smiled, showing off her crooked, blackened teeth. They were razor-sharp, Aeric noted with a shiver. Wispy, greasy hair fell over her thin shoulders and hunched back. Red, gory stains covered her hands.

In his rage, Aeric had chosen his short sword instead of his bow for this journey. He had wished to feel the steel as it entered the witch's body. But now, doubt and regret surfaced through his fear and anger. This could have been done and over with already if he had brought his bow... But something told him that it wouldn't have played out as easily as he thought it would have.

"So... You have come for your child?" the witch cooed, turning to glance behind her at a cradle that Aeric had failed to notice before.

"Release our daughter, witch," Aeric growled, now fearing that perhaps his Alicja was in the cookpot.

The witch cackled and, as if reading his mind, gestured to a corner. Aeric's fear turned to hope upon seeing his newborn baby swaddled inside the cradle. The witch gave Aeric an amused look. "Call me Corina, Hunter."

"Our daughter," Nina said, a motherly fierceness in her voice. That tone said, give me my child or I will end you, without saying a thing.

"I think not... But I am willing to trade... Blood for blood. You for her."

"No, you will give us our daughter, or you will die," Aeric spat, giving the witch—Corina—a hard look. His tone was blunt, saying explicitly in the most threating voice possible what he planned.

"You would sacrifice your entire village to kill me, oh brave hunter? I, who use my magics to make the winters less harsh? I, who keep frost and drought from killing your crops? I, who help your farms and animals grow ripe and plump? I, who make childbirth smoother for your women? I, who protect you from disease? You would be a fool, oh hunter. My magic makes this region go 'round."

"The price of blood is too high. I've seen too many mothers mourning children they will never see again. Please, give us our daughter," Nina said, tears trailing down her rosy cheeks.

"All I ask is the first child born of every year. You have already let the village take your precious child from you. The babe is yours no longer. Now leave before I boil your blood, as I will boil your daughter's!"

"No!" Aeric shouted, charging forward, sword raised high.

The witch cocked her head, and smiled as if she knew this would happen. That black-toothed smile was a gleeful one.

"You have made the fool's choice," Corina said, and darted to a bookshelf with a speed that turned her figure into a blur. Snatching up a vial containing a greenish liquid in it, she hurled it at Aeric.

Instinctively, Aeric threw up a hand. As the potion hit his flesh, the glass shattered. The green sludge slopped over his fingers. He instantly fell to his knees in agony, the green ooze sizzled his skin. Aeric twisted in pain, everything around him a blur.

His wife ran past him at the witch, dagger raised. The witch shouted something and Nina fell, screamed and writhed in pain, brown hair sticking to her sweat-covered face.

Soon, no sound left her lips.

Aeric swore, pushing against the pain and trying not to gag at the smell of his own burnt flesh. He had to get to his *wife's side—he was supposed to protect her. It was his job as a husband. And their baby...*

The witch was standing over Nina now, cackling.

"No!" *Aeric shouted, lurching to his feet.*

He swung his sword. It was a blow that was weak; the pain had somehow sapped some of his strength. Corina's one good eye widened in surprise and she lifted an arm in a humanly reflex of defense. Corina's arm was scrawny, and Aeric had time to notice an S-shaped scar on her arm that seemed to be scabbing over before his short sword sliced through her hand.

With a screech the old crone fell back, holding her stump. It spurted blackish-red blood. She looked from it to Aeric. He would never forget that look. It made the hair on the back of his neck rise. In the witch's eye was neither fear nor pain, only hatred.

Aeric quickly raised his sword to strike a killing blow, but paused. A swishing noise sounded behind him. He glanced to the opening where they had entered not long before.

Nothing.

He turned back to the witch and tensed for the blow he was about to inflict. There came the sound again, closer this time.

Too late.

Hundreds of crows burst into the underground chamber, swirling about, shrieking wildly. The witch's cackle could be heard through the cries of the creatures. Aeric swung his sword in panic. The crows were shredding him with their talons and beaks. There were so many. Did he come all this way just to die? He almost laughed.

Already, he was bleeding from numerous cuts. Deciding he had to try to ignore the birds, Aeric charged towards Corina. Hoping that maybe, just maybe, killing her would turn these birds into ordinary crows, not the bloodthirsty kind.

Corina seemed to slump or shrink in an odd hunched posture. Aeric could barely see her with all the crows swirling about the room. He blinked, and where she had been sat a crow. The crow stared at him with its one healthy eye.

*****

Aeric awoke, sucking in a large breath. A sheen of cold sweat covered his body, causing his clothing to stick to him uncomfortably. A dream. It had been a damned dream... Or had it been? Aeric cursed in confusion. Giving his head a shake, he attempted to remove the sleepy fog from his mind.

After a few moments, it came to him.

It had, in fact, been a dream. A dream replaying a slightly twisted version of the reality of what had happened to Aeric and his wife. With a yearning passion, Aeric wished he could go back fifteen years and end the witch while the moment had been within his grasp. If only he had cleaved her skull open before those birds had burst in. Then there was the oddity that the witch had escaped in the form of a crow, something he could never entirely wrap his mind around. What sort of magic could do that?

"Are you okay, Aeric?" Ellyn's sweet voice called from the other side of the campfire.

Aeric rolled over to face the woman. Ellyn sat there across from him, staring at him with a worried look on her face. Behind her, Lydia appeared to be asleep on her bedroll.

"Eh... a nightmare."

"You've had nightmares every day since we set off two days ago. If you don't mind me asking, what are they about? I may be able to help you. I am a cleric, after all." Ellyn smiled.

It was such a gentle smile. Too bad there were no gods and that this poor woman, with her soft smile, had been very much misled in life. It wasn't his place to point this out, though; Aeric strictly believed everyone was free to believe in what they wished.

Aeric cleared his throat. "I'll be fine, no need to worry."

He got to his feet, stretching off his stiffness, and started walking towards the forest.

"The witch killed your wife, is that what you dream about?" Ellyn murmured.

Aeric stopped, turned, and looked at her for a while. She met his eyes without fear. He winced but nodded once, then turned and walked into the trees.

Dawn came fast, pink light from the horizon streaming through the canopy. The woods echoed with noises: squirrels searched for acorns, and a mother raccoon eyed him from a tree stump as her little ones wrestled in front of her.

Aeric strolled back into the camp, just as he had done the last two nights. The two women had stopped asking if he was okay by the second night. His answer was always the same: He needed to scout the area.

In reality, he didn't want to talk about his dead wife. It was something he already struggled to shut from his mind.

Lydia asked if there were any signs of the witch, in that rasping voice of hers. Aeric shook his head in response.

"We are getting awfully close to the edge of the swamps. I suppose the witch will be hiding somewhere in the heart of the marsh. We need to avoid Khrolim, though. It's too dangerous for just the three of us."

Ellyn and Lydia nodded in agreement as they turned to set off into the swamps of Kitherlund.

Lydia wore just her black robe now, no wrappings, as they made their way to the edge of the wetlands. The sun glinted off her scaly, blue skin. Aeric found her skin odd, but who was he to judge? Could he judge? After all, it wasn't Lydia's fault she was cursed with the scales. In truth, he and the cursed woman had hit it off rather well—finding common ground in the fact that both of their lives had been affected by this witch.

It had taken Lydia three days to finally pry the story out of him. After he started talking, Aeric felt an odd sense of comfort in telling her his nightmare, explaining the situation. That, in its own sense, made him feel uncomfortable at the same time.

"Something you haven't told me, Aeric," Lydia said quietly. "How do you know your wife is dead? Did you find her body?"

Aeric was shocked at her direct question.

"Well?"

"Nina's body was there," Aeric replied after a while. "After the crows escaped with the witch, her body lay there on the cave floor. She had no pulse, and her skin was cold and hard to the touch."

Aeric paused for a second before continuing his story. A pained look passed over Lydia's face, and Aeric wondered if he should stop; he didn't want to upset her. Well, he had told this much, so he might as well finish.

"Alicja, my child, was freezing. I had to make the choice of staying and burying my dead wife or saving my baby. I returned three days later, but her body and all the witch's belongings were gone."

"You made the right decision." Lydia smiled, her scaly face wrinkling up.

Aeric nodded. "I hunted the witch for a while after that. I could never find her. She was always one step ahead of me. What I don't understand is, why she fled after my wife and I were defeated. She had won... She could have killed us easily."

"Perhaps losing her hand caused her to flee. Or maybe she wanted you to live with the knowledge of your failure," Lydia replied.

Aeric turned away, and Ellyn gave Lydia a stern glance.

"Did you ever return to your village?" Ellyn asked, behind them.

Aeric said nothing for a while. Finally, though, he spoke, "Yes, once. I was deemed an outcast for making the witch turn on us. I was chased out of the village with pitchforks and torches. I was treated as a villain."

"You mean to tell me, the people couldn't see that the witch was evil?" Ellyn asked, troubled.

"This had been going on for several generations within our village. The first child born every year was given to the witch in return for her protection. Over the centuries of doing this, it was viewed as 'the right thing to do' within our society. A sacrifice to better our community.

"When we first decided to fight back against the witch, I had just gotten back from some business in the North, and being part of the outside world I could see this was wrong. When Nina and I fought back, the community turned to coercion and took Alicja to the witch as they'd promised. So when we attacked the witch, it was viewed almost as a form of blasphemy," Aeric explained, anger rekindling in his voice.

Ellyn replied, sorrow marring her beautiful face, "The world saddens me sometimes. It can be such a dark place, so filled with hate. Society puts all its faith in something that is so clearly wrong. Yet when you stand up against it and show them how wrong it is, the people want nothing to do with it. The only thing you can do is pray for them and hope they find their way."

"Or you can let them look down the shaft of your arrow or the tip of your sword. Let society know you aren't afraid to die for what you believe in. Most people will stand down at the thought of losing their life," Aeric said, a bit more sharply than intended.

"How did that work for you?" Ellyn queried, not meeting Aeric's eyes.

Aeric seethed inside. He found himself wanting to backhand the Cleric of Vala. He took a deep breath and forced himself to release his clenched fists.

Don't let her get to you, Aeric. So what if she believes in a fairy tale of a god?

He suspected it was his lack of being around people these past few years.

They continued forward in silence. The forest floor was quickly turning into muck as the group entered the swamp of Kitherlund. The hickory and oak trees disappeared, being replaced with stunted red maple and draping willow trees. Shrubs surround the area as well, such as spicebush and dogwood.

An hour of travel into the swamp and dry spots of land were becoming harder to find. Most of the time they were hip-deep in swampy water that was covered in green flecks. Occasionally, a large patch of dry land could be found, but it wasn't long until they had to slosh into the murky waters again.

Aeric led the trio; several times he saved them from falling into quicksand, and avoided several huge alligators.

At one point Aeric had held up his hand, calling for a halt. They had just come to the edge of another pocket of water. He eyed the water for any possible dangers.

Aeric moved with caution as he pointed to a dark silhouette in the water. Two toad-like eyes stared at the group. Its eyes were as big as Aeric's balled fist, if not bigger. As if it knew they saw it the creature's eyes disappeared beneath the water, not even leaving a wake.

"By Vala, what was that?" Ellyn asked, eyeing the still water.

"I'm not sure, couldn't see enough of it to tell," Aeric replied.

The calm marsh water abruptly churned some twenty feet out, a large wake heading for the shore where the three stood.

"Look out!" Aeric called as he nocked an arrow.

The wake was aimed at the shore nearest to Ellyn, and the three scrambled away from the waterside in haste.

To the trio's astonishment, the creature launched from the water in full force at Ellyn. The thing's skin was covered in warts, giving it a resemblance of a giant toad, except it had no legs. It did, however, have two huge bat-like wings and the tail of a tadpole. The wings, though large, apparently couldn't support the thing's body weight. It used them to create more force on its jump to hit its prey.

The only thing that saved Ellyn from being grabbed in its massive maw and smashed into the ground was Lydia's bravery.

Lydia dived, and tackled Ellyn out of the way as the creature was in mid-air, mere inches from its quarry.

An arrow penetrated the creature's wart-covered hide, right near its large gills, with a wet thunk before it even hit the ground. The beast flopped for a few moments before dying.

"By the gods, what in the Nether was that?!" Lydia swore.

"A gratkar," Aeric said, still eyeing the dead creature.

"Have you seen one before?" Ellyn asked, looking at the dead creature with disgust.

"No, but I read about them in *The Book of Monsters* while I was in Darvalon." He nudged the gratkar with a boot to ensure it was dead.

Ellyn stopped staring at the creature and looked at him with curiosity. "*The Book of Monsters*? If I'm correct, you have to be a Valon to read from those volumes."

"That's right."

"You're a Valon, then. Interesting. Makes you the perfect man for our mission."

Aeric looked at Lydia; she hadn't said anything, and really didn't seem too surprised at the news.

After the encounter with the gratkar, they were even more careful of entering the water.

*****

"What is she going to do, pray up a fire?" Aeric gritted his teeth with annoyance.

Lydia touched his shoulder gently. "Have faith, Aeric."

Aeric was taken back for a moment. That was something his wife used to tell him.

Have faith.

That is what Nina would say when he thought the winter would doom them, or the game was nowhere to be found in the forests.

"Have faith; the gods test those they love," his wife would say then. They had always pulled through, and she would laugh at him.

Lydia's words gave him comfort. The fear was still there, but it was the fear of entering a fist fight. The fear of the possibility of being knocked out, that hid just below the adrenaline rush. It was no longer the fear of going into a sword fight, your life on the line.

Branches cracked from a different area this time and Aeric realized there was more than one danger, which made a bad situation even worse. He tried to judge which creature was closest to him or what it was. It was impossible; the woods made the sounds feel as if they were coming from all angles.

Blue light flared behind him. Ellyn had done it! Aeric was stunned—he wasn't sure how she had done it. He guessed she used sorcery and claimed it was channeling Vala's power.

Aeric and Lydia whirled to see Ellyn, a small blue flame flickering in her hand. The blueish flame burned in Ellyn's palm, extending a dim flickering light. Aeric had another shock when the fire didn't burn the woman.

Ellyn lit the moss. The fire changed from blue to orange in a flash as the flames caught on to the moss and branches. It quickly roared up, splashing light into the darkness.

A deep, soul-searing screech pierced the night. It caused the hair on the back of Aeric's neck to rise.

The trio turned their backs to the fire as they peered into the dimness.

There were three sets of eyes watching them from the edge of the light. Each of those eyes burned with hatred and malice. Aeric's heart beat faster, seeing the three humanoid figures. He knew right away that these were undead; they were covered in rotting flesh that was peeling off in what seemed like strips, showing the oozing dead muscle below.

The undead were closing in. Gaunt skin covered their faces like that of some kind of plague victim. At first sight in the darkness Aeric would have sworn they were zombies, but at the sight of their giant oversized lips and sharp fangs, he knew better.

"Grolirs. They are undead minions," Ellyn said, with a calmness that neither Lydia nor Aeric felt.

The grolirs smelled heavily of the putrid rot of something that's slowly decomposing. Aeric had to fight not to gag; Lydia, however, failed that battle as she dry-heaved.

Aeric was also thankful to see the undead didn't enter the ring of light, something he had also learned in his time with the Valons. These creatures of darkness would be weakened considerably, if not harmed by it, Aeric remembered. He had to dive deep within the caverns of his psyche to recall those lessons he had learned as a Valon. Sometimes, it almost felt like he had gone through training to become a Valon in a different life.

Aeric took aim at one of the grolir's fish-like eyes and loosed an arrow from his bow, though he knew it wouldn't matter. Magic was the only thing that could kill these undead beasts. The arrow thunked into the grolir's eye socket, and the creature reeled backward. The grolir regained its balance quick enough, then gave a nasty, dry laugh that showed off its fangs. It yanked the arrow from its face with a nasty sucking sound, and the leftover rotting eye oozed down its dead cheek.

Ellyn stepped forward, her gentle face calm. There wasn't any sign of fear on her face.

"Get back, Ellyn—these creatures will tear you limb from limb!" Aeric shouted. He wasn't sure whether to applaud the woman's bravery or shake her to clear her insanity.

The grolirs gnashed their teeth, hungry for blood. Ellyn looked at them, pity and a deep sorrow in her eyes.

"Vala, it is I, your ever humble follower, asking again for a favor. Provide me with light to shatter the darkness before me. Help me send these poor creatures of dark to the next world, where they belong. Free their souls."

Aeric heard himself continue to shout. This damn woman would get herself killed! His cries died on his lips, however. The grolirs screamed angrily as a bluish light exploded from Ellyn's palm. Screeching, the trio of creatures fled into the swamp.

They didn't make it far, however.

The powerful light that the cleric of Vala wielded pierced their undead bodies. Flesh began to crumble under the heat of the holy, radiant light. Their skin peeled off their bodies like burning paper drifts into the wind. It wasn't long until they were just a pile of bones, sinking into the swamp from which it seemed they had come.

"Thank you, my Goddess," Ellyn whispered as she slumped to her knees. Fagitude now slipped over the place where the awe of her goddess' power had dwelt.

Lydia rushed to her friend's side to steady her before Ellyn completely fell over.

Aeric stood in shock, feeling slightly like a fool for doubting this cleric and her magic. "Thank you," Aeric said. He didn't know what to think, to be honest. Maybe she was a sorcerer; whatever she was, Ellyn had saved their lives. For that, he was grateful.

Ellyn met his eyes and smiled. That smile carried a feeling of gentleness and love. Aeric could feel something building in his chest, and his eyes burned. Just another thing the once-Valon couldn't explain.

Ellyn looked tired to the bone. Dark spots had formed under her eyes, and she looked much older than she was. Channeling that power of Vala, even such a minute fraction of it, had drained her.

The flames roared, keeping the darkness at bay. Aeric knew that fire kept more than just the void of emptiness at bay. Other things lurked in the darkness; his keen senses from years of hunting told him so.

If he could have seen into the dark, he would have noticed a crow roosting in a dead oak not thirty paces from the group's fire. It didn't sleep like most of its kind were at this time, instead watching the trio with its one good eye.

*****

Aeric awoke from sleep, jumping up in alarm. He cursed himself for falling asleep on watch. Looking around, he realized all was okay. The fire still blazed, and plenty of firewood lay nearby. He had only dozed off for maybe an hour.

Ellyn slept fitfully next to the warmth of the flames. She was still tired from working her magic. Lydia, however, was not sleeping.

She stood at the edge of the light of the fire. Her back was to Aeric. No robe or wrappings covered her body, as when they had first met. Lydia still wore the robe while traveling, but around the campfire she preferred just her tunic and trousers. They were snug on her, letting Aeric see every curve. He found himself swallowing hard, trying to shake the sudden rush of arousal.

Aeric sighed, and forced those thoughts from his head. "What are you doing up? You should get some sleep."

"I couldn't sleep. Then I saw those... They are beautiful, are they not?"

The way Lydia spoke still confused Aeric. Her words were gentle for the most part, but the tone of her voice was harsh and grating. He was curious to see this woman without this curse that had turned her skin into scales. He couldn't help but wonder, would she be beautiful, and what would her voice sound like? Something inside his mind knew Lydia's voice and outer shell would be gorgeous.

Aeric went to her side, and Lydia lifted her head to meet his eyes. Something in the depths of her eyes made memories stir.

"That they are; dangerous, too," Aeric said, breaking eye contact by looking to the creatures she spoke of.

Before them, many glowing lantern-shaped globes floated gently throughout the marsh. They drifted aimlessly through the air like a jellyfish pumping away within the depths of the sea. They were curious in their nature, almost as if asking the trio to follow them.

"My wife and I used to sit on a hill near my home that overlooked the swamp. We would spend many late nights there in the summer, watching the will-o-wisps float about.

They have such a unique beauty. We would talk for hours, trying to figure out what they consisted of. What kind of magic or energy," Aeric reminisced.

"Do you yearn for your wife still, Aeric, or have you moved on?" Lydia asked, looking back to the will-o-wisps.

Aeric was taken aback for a moment. What kind of question was that? Then he realized she was asking for herself, and decided to ignore her question. He wasn't ready for something like that, and perhaps he never would be. Aeric kept many old views close to his heart, including marrying only once. For he had already given his only heart away.

"Everyone knows, though, that to follow a wisp into the darkness means death. The old tales tell of them leading men into quicksand pits, then devouring their souls somehow, causing them to grow larger."

Lydia gave him a look and opened her mouth to speak, but instead bit her scaled lip and said nothing more.

The two stood for a long while, watching the orb-shaped wisps glide about, spreading their pale ivory light in the darkness of the Kitherlund swamp.

Inside him, a sort of war raged. He didn't even know what Lydia looked like without the curse of the scales. But somehow it felt right, Aeric thought. Like now, they stood here enjoying something he and his wife had enjoyed. His head screamed that it was wrong, but his heart told him it was right. The feeling left him utterly confused.

Perhaps this was a sign from his wife, an indication that he could move on and find someone new to spend his time with. For this reason, when Lydia slipped her cold, scale-covered hand into his, he didn't pull away.

They sat and watched the will-o-wisps for a long time. Only two thoughts swirled inside Aeric's head: *How can I be falling in love with someone when I don't even know what she truly looks like?* And, *What would Nina think of this?* He couldn't shake either question, they just continually took turns in his thoughts.

*****

A day had passed since the night Aeric and Lydia had spent watching the will-o-wisps. They didn't exactly avoid each other, but they did avoid the topic. They moved on and pretended they had never held hands. Aeric wasn't sure why, but it just didn't feel like it was something that needed to be talked about.

After spending all that time slogging through the swamps, they had finally stumbled upon what they thought was an animal trail.

They were wrong.

The trail had brought them a lot closer to the ruins of Khrolim, much to Aeric's displeasure. The trail had seemed normal enough until Aeric had noticed something tied to a string on a low-hanging branch.

The outer rim was wooden, in the center dead grass had been woven into strange and intricate designs around a dead, stretched-out crow. Maggots wriggled from the dark-feathered bird's now-hollow eye sockets.

Seeing that bird, Aeric knew immediately where the trail led. Anxiousness lay heavily in his gut. He was aware that Lydia felt the same.

Fear crept up inside him, like an earthworm wiggling its way through the ground in a desperate attempt to find the surface, all while the rains howl down from a night sky.

Who will I lose this time? Aeric caught himself thinking as he looked at his two companions. Ellyn gagged as they passed, causing flies to scatter from the dead crow. Aeric wrinkled his nose and continued on.

They moved on in silence. Each hoped that there would not be another of the grizzly trophies that had been hung artistically.

They were unfortunate, however, because in another two hundred yards or so another wooden object hung from a tree branch. This held no crow, but a bloody finger.

"Is that a…" Lydia didn't finish her question, as she already knew the answer.

"A finger," Aeric stated as he studied the strange pagan symbol. Dread grew within him.

"Why would she do this?" Ellyn asked, disgust chiseled across her face.

"Maybe it is a payment of the people from nearby villages," Lydia murmured.

"It's possible. The witch does things to amuse herself. For example, after I attempted to hunt the witch down after my wife died, I traveled through many villages under the witch's sway. Some gave fingers, toes, ears, or even worse in payment. Or, like my village, children."

"That's terrible… Wh-what kind of person would do such a thing?" Ellyn asked.

"She is no longer a person. Long ago she traded her soul to evil. She is the embodiment of darkness in these swamps," Lydia said

"Lydia is right; those three grolirs you killed were created by the witch's occult magic. She has held a dark hold over these lands for too long. The bitch must be stopped."

Ellyn nodded in agreement. Her face was pale, and Aeric worried she might become sick. As they continued, Aeric noticed Ellyn holding her moon medallion and muttering prayers to her goddess, Vala.

He couldn't say why, but it angered him. There was so much wrong in this world, so much hate and anguish. If these gods were real and they held a so-called balance, the scales were clearly off. Evil covered the lands of Draston, and it seemed to get darker by the year.

The group continued down the small trail that zig-zagged through the swamps. The path was strangely dry, while wetlands spread out on both sides of the trail.

To the group's dismay, every seventy yards or so there hung a gory talisman. Fingers, then toes. Ears followed, then a kidney. After the kidney, each was a more significant organ, and fresher than the last. They walked in dark silence, not even stopping to examine the hanging objects.

They walked another quarter mile, ignoring the hanging talismans. The trail before them widened and created a clearing. Only one tree grew in the center of the clearing. A massive oak, its bark covered in red moss. Surrounding the circular clearing was murky, algae-covered water. Aeric spotted several alligators in that water, each around fifteen feet long, if not bigger. Short, stunted trees grew from the shallows, somewhat hiding the alligators.

Aeric stretched his shoulder, a nervous habit he had picked up a long time ago. The trees growing from the water made Aeric feel as if he were fenced into this clearing. His eyes returned to the large oak in the center of the clearing. His breath caught in his throat. A mutilated human body was nailed to it.

Crows sat on the branches next to the corpse, and they were greedily feeding upon it. Aeric watched in disgust and horror as one ripped a strip of flesh from the body and, cocking its head up, swallowed its grisly treat.

Lydia turned away and vomited. Ellyn looked green, but she held down her food.

The crows stopped their gruesome feasting and turned to eye the trio. Those black eyes caused gooseflesh to break out on Aeric's neck and back.

The last meeting with the Witch of Kitherlund skittered through his head. Corina had defeated him with crows.

Nocking an arrow, Aeric took aim at one of those beady black eyes and loosed his shaft. There was a cloud of feathers from the impact and then all the crows took flight, squawking with anger at their meal being interrupted.

"Let's keep moving... I'd hate to find the witch near dusk," Ellyn suggested, shivering.

Lydia and Aeric nodded in agreement.

*****

As the group walked, more and more dry land could be spotted and the setting water lessened. It wasn't long until no more water or muck surrounded them. Thankfully, there were no more fresh hanging items. The few they found now were just broken sticks hanging from a string, as if something had greedily torn away the gory piece in the center, not caring if it broke.

Aeric was not paying attention to his surroundings. He was caught up in his own thoughts. Because he was quite sure that the ripped-open talismans were a sign of ghouls, he prayed to every god that he didn't believe in that it wasn't ghouls. But his Valon training told him a different story.

The Hunter stopped dead in his tracks. Farther up ahead he could see high, crumbling stone walls through the trees.

"Damn it!" Aeric hissed.

"What is it?" Lydia asked, eyeing the stone structure.

"Khrolim. Damn it, I thought we had passed it. That trail must have led us in a circle," Aeric muttered angrily.

"Wouldn't surprise me. I've felt lost for the last two days," Ellyn murmured.

"What is your reason for avoiding this place, Aeric?" Lydia asked, her eyebrow raised.

Aeric shook his head. "When I attempted to hunt the witch down before, I got too close to the graveyard on the south side. Ghouls leapt at me from everywhere, clawing, teeth gnashing. I barely escaped with my life."

"Fear not, Aeric. Vala smiles upon our mission. She will guide us and repel those undead creatures if they try to attack us." The cleric smiled. It was the first smile Aeric had seen from her today.

"I doubt you could stop so many."

"You still doubt my faith to Vala?" Ellyn asked, a hint of edge in her voice.

"It isn't you I doubt, or your faith. I doubt your goddess. Why are you so sure she will come through for you? All it takes is one time for her to fail you and you could die. *We* could die." Aeric stalked farther ahead, anger causing him to pick up his pace.

Ellyn stormed in front of him, cutting him off. "How can you question Vala when she has come to our aid several times already!"

"This isn't three grolir, this is like a horde of ghouls. And if Vala watches over us so closely, where was she while I battled the witch the first time? Where was she when my wife was taken from me? Where was she when my own people threw me out? Where was she when Lydia was cursed?" Aeric shouted, his voice echoing through the wooded area.

"Enough! Listen, Aeric, I need to tell you someth—" Lydia was cut off by a fiendish howl on the other side of the wall.

Whatever Lydia had been about to say, Aeric knew deep down in his soul that it was something he needed to know. Something he had to know. But there was no time now.

The two women stopped, staring wide-eyed. Birds squawked and flew into the sky, leaving the swamp in eerie silence. Aeric could hear his own breathing. He waved the two women to follow him and ran up to the base of the wall and crouched there. The two women followed.

The trail they had been following led to the wall and abruptly stopped in a dead end. The wall here had at one time been a gate, but it had collapsed and was filled with tons of collapsed jagged stone.

The three crouched against the wall in silence. Aeric held his breath, as he felt his breathing was too loud to his own ears; he wanted to hear what was coming. He already knew, though. He would have known that screech anywhere.

It belonged to a ghoul.

Something scrambled along the wall from the left, and then it was right above them.

Aeric held his breath as it stopped right above them. His heart hammered inside his chest. He was sure it would give them away. Stones fell from above, pelting them, yet none of them dare cry out.

There was a little growling hiss, followed by another piercing screech.

That shriek made his blood run cold. Panicking, he stood to run. Ellyn was there before him, hand on her medallion. Aeric saw her mouth words and a rush of calm overcame him. Without a sound, he hunkered back down and realized the creature wasn't attacking. With an odd yell the beast was off again, scrambling along the wall.

The group waited for what felt like forever, but the creature wasn't heard again.

What had come over him? He was no coward, and it angered him that he had reacted in such a way.

"The creature's screech is a call of evil, striking fear in even those with the bravest of hearts," Ellyn reassured, her voice soft.

Aeric was thankful she didn't mention her goddess saving them again. "It was not just any kind of ghoul. It's an alpha ghoul. They are much quicker, and as we just saw, they have a peircing screech. But, it sure didn't seem to both either of you ladies."

Ellyn smiled, and Aeric knew what her reason was. Vala.

"My curse must have made me immune. Feelings have seemed dim for me since this curse was bestowed upon me." Lydia looked right into Aeric's eyes and added, "Now let's hurry along before that creature comes back."

They muttered among themselves for a few minutes, each wanting to go a separate way. Aeric wanted to follow a small lane which hinted at once being a trail along the wall of Khrolim. Ellyn wanted to backtrack and see if perhaps the path the witch had littered with grisly trophies led off another way. Lydia wanted to enter Khrolim itself and search for the witch. In the end, the ladies decided to take their guide's advice and follow the trail on the outside wall.

They traveled at a slow pace at first, nursing sore thighs, calves, and feet. But the sound of a ghoul's screech behind them set them to a fast walk. The cry would sound every few minutes, and soon there were more than one.

"*Kurva!*" Aeric cursed.

Both women looked at him, shocked at his language. Ellyn very much disapproved; Aeric could tell by the twisting her lips made. He didn't care—this was no time for her to scold him on his language like she was tempted to do at this moment.

"They have found our trail; ghouls thirst for living beings," Aeric said as his leisurely pace turned into a trot.

"What else did you learn about ghouls in the Valons?" Ellyn asked, slightly out of breath.

"Avoid them." Both women gave him a sidelong glare, so he continued, "And a bite from them can transfer a rotting disease that will turn you into a ghoul in the end. The alphas are fast, have sharp teeth, and love a nice bloody meal."

They ran full speed now, the screeches getting closer and the screams overlapping. Maybe fifteen, he guessed. They raced down the narrow path, low-hanging branches scratching them as they passed, uncaring of the wounds they inflicted.

The trail gradually swung away from the wall, and they continued to follow it. Aeric was more than happy to put some distance between them and Khrolim.

The path abruptly widened into a clearing and the three stopped dead in their tracks, causing them all to skid and almost fall down into a shallow ditch.

The clearing was dark and menacing. Wrongness emitted from it. Tall, crooked trees seemed more than willing to stretch out their overhead branches, like taloned fingers reaching down from the heavens. Those rows and rows of taloned branches created the shade over the clearing. The trees were not the only darkness in the clearing; twisted trunks only added to the atmosphere.

To the group's right sat a giant gate. The portcullis was open, and the path led right back into the ruined city. It had probably remained that way since Khrolim fell. Creepers, ivy, and what looked like morning glories, but were covered with black flowers instead, covered the ancient, crumbling stone gate.

None of this was what caught Aeric's eyes, for he had seen the gate long before. What he stared at worried him much more than Khrolim, the damned ghouls, or any possible danger in this swamp could.

Not fifty yards on the left side of the clearing was a large hulking shape that stood eleven-feet tall. It had grayish mottled skin, almost looking like stone. Thinning white hair stuck to its greasy, bump-covered skull. Its back was severely hunched over, and rock-like bumps protruded all along its spine.

Any Valon would recognize this creature, and apparently Ellyn's goddess hated them. First ghouls, now a cave troll. Perhaps Vala wanted them to die.

Aeric was about to turn and slink back from where they had come, as it hadn't seen them yet. However, the ghouls who were closing in were screeching louder than ever and had caught the troll's attention.

It turned and eyed the trio, a dumb look on its ugly face. It looked as if it had been bashed in the face with a mace several times, and its nose was jammed in. The troll's eyes kind of bulged, as if it had stolen that feature of its bloodline from a frog.

"Run," Aeric said.

Not waiting to see if the two women followed he ran with all his might to the right, towards the gate of Khrolim. They did not have the tools to take down a cave troll, and if he had seen what he had thought they were dead. Very, very dead. Aeric could have sworn that the troll had smiled a bit, showing two large fangs.

As the three ran as fast as their legs could carry them, ghouls burst from the underbrush where they had just been standing. With a roar that seemed to send quakes through the ground, the troll charged after Aeric, Ellyn, and Lydia. This caused the ghouls that were also on the heels of the group to chatter, and they turned to attack the troll.

This gave Aeric time to turn and eye the troll over his shoulder, and he didn't like what he saw. The troll was unnaturally pale, blue veins showing under his skin. Aeric moaned. It was a cave troll that had contracted Icorii Vampiris, also know as vampirism.

A vampiric troll. The worst kind of troll.

As it blurred into movement, it confirmed what Aeric had suspected. The speed that the troll used was unnatural and it smashed into the oncoming ghouls, sending them flying in all directions. A few climbed its back and gnawed on its neck. The thing tried to shake them off as it battled those around it, but they had sunk their talons deep into the troll's stone-like flesh. Finally, the troll snatched both of the creatures which had climbed onto his shoulders at the same time and smashed them together. The result was a substance much like jelly, that had long ago gone bad and was now a brownish-black color.

That was all Aeric could see as they ran under the gate, trying their best not to trip over the broken cobblestones. Khrolim, that had once been splendorous, was now a ruin. Stone houses that lined the streets varied; some were nothing but a pile of collapsed rubble, others were in good condition for two hundred years' abandonment. Others were standing, but the roofs had long ago collapsed. Trees grew everywhere, looking as if they had fallen from the heavens and smashed into the cobblestones. This caused even more problems. The evening had set in, and though the sun was still out it was well hidden behind the buildings and trees.

Aeric shouted with hope, pointing to a large spot of sun that had found its way through the evening clouds, in between two large crumbling buildings, to spill its radiance upon the shattered cobblestones. It was like a signal from the gods of light. Lydia and Ellyn followed Aeric without question as he ran as fast as he could. They all were breathing hard, and he felt as if his heart would pound right out of his chest.

They wouldn't be quick enough, he knew.

"Get in the sunlight, and don't leave it!" Aeric shouted, slowing to nock an arrow.

The troll slammed through the gate, causing it to tremble and stone to fall onto the beast. The large chunks of rock only bounced off its skin, not slowing it down at all. Using its hands to boost its speed, the troll looked like a charging gorilla.

Ghouls still ran about the ugly beast, and Aeric witnessed one unlucky creature get caught in front of the charging troll. It was smashed into the soft mud, its body broken and useless.

Raising his bow, Aeric loosed. The arrow sank deep into the troll's shoulder, causing the creature to roll in a cloud of dust. To Aeric's horror the troll looked at him and plucked the arrow from its skin, and the wound sealed up at a steady pace, its fleshing knitting itself back together.

Aeric hadn't thought it would heal instantly like that.

The troll gave him that smile, fangs bared as it didn't even harm the thing.

Turning, Aeric ran for all he was worth. The sunlight that splashed between the two large buildings called to him. Behind him, he could feel the ground tremble as the troll closed in. Aeric imagined the fetid breath of the vampiric troll rolling over his shoulders. He could hear the heavy breathing of the creature as it struggled for oxygen in its watering mouth. Gooseflesh prickled his skin, and every hair on his neck stood on end as if the body sensed its own death approaching.

Twenty steps.

Lydia and Ellyn stood on the other side of the sunlight, screaming and shouting. They waved to him and bid him run faster.

Fifteen.

A bestial roar behind him, caused him to stumble slightly, but he regained his balance in a flash and continued to run.

Ten steps.

Five.

The pain that exploded in his back was quick and excruciating. He could feel his backbone and hip snap, the bones grinding together. Just as fast as the explosion of pain had come, sweet darkness closed in.

Then, there was nothing.

*****

Ellyn shouted as the cave troll's stone-like fist smashed into Aeric's lower back. She could hear his bones shatter on that terrible impact. He crumpled from the force of the blow, and his body flew into the air.

Everything moved in slow motion in Ellyn's mind. Lydia let out a shriek. Aeric flew through the air, eyes staring at them blankly. His brain hadn't realized it was unconscious yet, Ellyn thought. Aeric's face sank into that blessed sunlight that shone down through this horrible ruin of a city. Then his neck and shoulders felt that light. The vampiric cave troll reached with the hand that hadn't hit Aeric and snatched Aeric's leg with desperate fervor.

The troll couldn't stop himself quick enough, however, and Aeric's body caused it to tip further off balance. Its clenched fist crossed that threshold; flesh turned with astounding speed into stone. The weight of the statue-like arm and the speed at which the troll had been moving made it unable to stop itself. The rest of the troll's body followed, turning to stone as it touched that last light of day.

The giant body smashed into the ground, shattering the arms of the now troll-like statue. Aeric didn't escape more harm in that fall; his shin had been crushed as the rock-hard grip had met the ground. It was blood-covered pulp, a few tendons still connecting it to his ankle.

Lydia and Ellyn stood in shock. They had no idea that the troll was going to turn into stone. They hadn't been quite sure why Aeric wanted them in the sunlight to begin with, but now it connected.

Lydia was there in a heartbeat, leaning over the fallen Valon. Tears fell down her scale-covered face, and Ellyn was positive he was dead. Calling aid from her deity from the link created through the strength of her belief, she channeled an anti-undead blast in front of her.

The ten or so ghouls were loping towards the two women. They had fallen back from attacking the troll and waited to see the outcome. When they entered the anti-undead blast, they immediately turned and fled. They ran like defeated dogs; she knew they would attempt to return later, though.

"Ellyn, can—can you do something? You have to. You promised you would bring us together," Lydia said. Her voice was thick with panic, and it rolled off her cursed tongue with an odd tone.

"I did, Nina. And still plan to. Now hush, I need to concentrate. Do you know how to use a bow?" Ellyn asked as she leaned down and inspected Aeric.

Lydia did. Ellyn told her to watch for danger while she tried to heal Aeric. His breathing was shallow, heartbeat faint and fading fast. Ellyn sought to avoid looking at his leg, as it was smashed into a blob of red with shattered bone chunks mixed in it.

Again, she prayed to Vala. A subtle warmth grew in her, and that warmth also pulsed from her palms in a blueish, healing light. She placed her hands on his waist, and could feel the bones in Aeric's hip and spine started to mend. Ellyn then moved down to his leg, and the slush knitted itself back together with increasing slowness as she weakened. There were plenty other injuries on Aeric, but his breathing was steadier and heartbeat stronger.

"He is better—not completely healed, but his injuries are no longer life-threatening, thank Vala."

Lydia threw her scaly arms around the other woman. "Thank you and Vala."

"Now we must find somewhere to hide," Ellyn said, looking at the horizon where the sun was beginning to disappear behind the hills.

Lydia nodded, and Ellyn would swear the other woman muttered something like, 'You will be mine soon' as she looked at Aeric's unconscious body.

*****

The water rippled in the bowl as the witch's gnarled fingers clutched it in a rage. How, how had those three survived the stupid vampiric cave troll? She'd been sure that the thing would tear them limb from limb and feast upon their blood. She had found pleasure in that scene, even though it wouldn't have been her causing their deaths.

Corina. She wasn't sure if that was her actual name, as it had been so long since someone had used it, but it worked well in the past few decades when she had needed it. She wanted the three to live so her little surprise could be sprung.

She disliked to admit it, but she was beginning to fear them. Corina worried that, perhaps, she had underestimated the trio. Hate still outdistanced fear, but there was that nagging doubt within her.

Corina scratched at the scabbing wound on her bicep as she looked back into the scrying bowl. The wound from the brand was old and shaped like an "S", with a bit more of a snake quality. It was her only marked connection to the Demon Lord who called itself Saiv, and through this brand-like wound was the link that allowed her to tap into the black magic.

Corina smiled an almost toothless grin as, in the scrying bowl, the two women struggled to drag the unconscious man down the street before the ghouls could return.

It was time to move.

Throwing the bowl to the side it shattered on the floor, spraying water and clay shards everywhere. She grabbed a few potions from the shelf, each a trick up her sleeve. Then, walking to the window, Corina muttered a few words and pulled a black feather from her pouch and shoved the crumpled thing into her mouth and chewed. With incredible speed, Corina morphed from a witch into a raven.

With a few bounds and hops she landed on the window sill, then she was off from her little hut, heading for Khrolim.

*****

The pain was the first thing that greeted Aeric, and he knew what that meant. He was alive. Moaning, he tried to sit up but yelped and fell back to the ground. The floor was stone, he realized. He opened his eyes. Aeric was in a stone room by himself. The walls were covered in a greenish moss that had grown from years of moisture and not being used.

Slower this time, he sat up and was successful, if having to deal with some aches and pains in doing so. Fifteen or twenty minutes passed before he decided to stand and stumble to the lone window in the room.

The sun was rising, a beautiful pinkish color that lit the ruins below. Aeric immediately felt trapped. Not only was he surrounded by a haunted city, but hundreds of ghouls as well. None were in sight at the moment, but he knew that would change soon.

Aeric judged the building he was in from the window, and guessed it was some kind of a small tower.

Hearing a boot scuff the stone floor, Aeric turned toward the noise. Ellyn and Lydia stepped into the room from a staircase that Aeric hadn't even noticed.

Lydia approached him without saying anything and gave him a small hug, and Aeric patted her back awkwardly.

"I can heal you, but it will weaken me enough that we will have to stay here another night. Honestly, we may have to anyway, Aeric. You look terrible." Ellyn smiled as she said this. The smile was a beautiful one that spread warmth throughout Aeric's insides.

He opened his mouth to say he'd manage, but then closed it. Ellyn was right. The first batch of ghouls they came upon would kill him off with ease. The damned troll had wounded him severely. So, instead, he nodded.

The next problem was there was something wrong in the air… Something he could sense. It was like being on the edge of a dangerous storm, and the clouds were starting to rotate faster and faster. You knew you should run, but realistically you knew you were already *Kurvad.*

"There is another problem, Aeric," Lydia said, stepping back from him. Worry was plastered on her scale-covered face.

"What is it?"

Ellyn was the one who answered. "The witch—I assume it was the witch—was watching us last night. I could feel eyes upon me right before I fell asleep."

"I was standing watch and I felt it, too," Lydia confirmed.

"She must have put a little too much power in her scrying spell, and the ward I placed around this tower picked it up," Ellyn said.

Aeric nodded. "She will be coming for us."

*****

Ellyn had healed Aeric and they had spent the rest of the day inside their tower, hiding behind Ellyn's wards that she had placed through Vala's magic. Night had come, and still they rested. The boredom they all felt now was laced with anxiety, and that anxiety was increasing with each minute closer to sunrise.

They had all agreed to face whatever there was to face outside their small tower as the first sunbeams peeked over the horizon.

Aeric watched from the window of the tower as the sun rose over the wetlands. He readied his bow, Lydia her short sword that she hadn't even used on this adventure, and Ellyn had Vala's magic. The only thing that worried him was that the fog that clung to the tower was thicker than ever. He had been about to suggest they wait until it dissipated, but Ellyn spoke up.

"I think the fog is her doing; it won't disappear."

Lydia and Aeric agreed with her, and they headed down the tower.

Somewhere down there in that fog, Aeric knew that the bitch who had taken his wife from him waited. Carefully planning her games. He only wished he knew what the hag was planning.

*****

Corina smiled; her body itself wasn't in raven form at the moment. But her eyes were still that of a raven, and those magic-induced raven eyes watched the trio slowly exit the tower, armed to the teeth. Her black eyes brimmed with a definite sheen of greed and hatred.

Licking her lips, over her few remaining front teeth, she started casting another spell and a powerful one at that. Her scabby connection to her liege began throbbing with the power she was calling on. Corina could feel her life force being sucked away, the scab feeding off her.

Taking a deep, giddy breath, the witch stepped forward and started chanting.

*****

They were about twenty yards down the street when Corina stepped from the fog, and her trap was sprung. Ellyn had been the first to shout out, as she could sense power being drawn from a dark entity. A perk of her goddess, Aeric knew she would claim. But he was aware that the woman's senses had most likely caught the slight stumble the witch had made coming out of her hiding spot. Or maybe even the deep breath the hag had taken before starting her wicked spell.

"Saiv, I pray Thee, break the Hunter's legs—"

Aeric's legs snapped at the shins with a sudden and jolting quickness. He didn't even have time to scream before he fell to the ground, his bones grinding together as they fractured. His mind didn't have a chance to wrap itself around what was happening.

"—Smite the scaly one's throat, so she chokes—"

Aeric watched through tear-filled eyes as Lydia started clutching at her throat, eyes bulging as she struggled for breath with frantic desperation. There was nothing he could do, the shock of his legs snapping still washing over him in waves.

"—And let Vala's chosen croak—"

Ellyn, Aeric's last hope, flinched, and a hint of intense pain bloomed on her face.

Maybe, just maybe, her goddess was real. Maybe Vala would save them. Aeric prayed, prayed that all the gods were real. He could have laughed, his thoughts were that muddled. They came to him through a dark, fog-packed tunnel of consciousness.

The pain was so bright and vivid, curses spewed from his mouth that he would never recall saying. Thoughts flew through his head, never giving a chance for them to sink in.

There was only one thing. Only one god that he knew of at this moment.

Pain.

Aeric groggily realized Ellyn's medallion glowed with a bright, vivid goodness. Like the sunset after a long moonless night.

The witch, however, wasn't done.

"—Curse I cast, so long ago
Dispel now, and let the chaos grow!"

With that, the witch's spell ended.

Ellyn stepped toward Lydia as if against a strong, unyielding wind. Ellyn needed help; she couldn't face the witch alone. Aeric stretched for his bow but it had skittered down the street, swallowed by the swirling tendrils of fog.

Aeric looked to Lydia and knew he was in trouble now, for he was beginning to hallucinate. He struggled to breathe; maybe it was something in the fog that was causing him to see these oddities.

Ellyn leaned over Lydia, but she was no longer Ellyn. She was Vala, though many features remained similar. Aeric had never seen, nor believed in this goddess, but he had seen more than one temple of Vala. Her statue was always out in the front, inviting all to enter.

Lydia's face was covered in Ellyn's blue light, but she was no longer Lydia. It was his wife, Nina. Her face was no longer scaly, and she was struggling to breathe as she clawed at her neck. Aeric blinked through the pain.

His long-dead wife.

Anger suddenly burned deep with Aeric. How dare this bitch cause him to see his dead wife and a goddess he didn't believe in. How dare the witch throw Nina's death in his face and mock his disbelief of the so-called deities, in a weak attempt to cause doubt in himself.

Realization was the next thing that hit him, boiling up through the anger in a swirl of understanding. The witch wanted him confused, angry, and hurt. He turned away from the three, sliding towards where his bow had slipped into the mist.

The words of the witch's spell tumbled through his head like a never-ending wheel.

Saiv, I pray
Thee break the hunter's legs.
Smite the scaly-one's throat, so she chokes.
And let Vala's chosen croak.
Curse I cast, so long ago,
Dispel now, and let the chaos grow!

His head was too clouded with the gritting pain of his shattered legs as he dragged them over the broken cobblestones. Aeric's mind couldn't piece together the spell to come up with a conclusion.

Aeric glanced over his shoulder and could see the witch open her mouth and let out a scream that was magically enhanced. It caused Aeric's ears to ring. Lydia dropped her short sword to clamp her hands over her ears, blood dribbling between her fingers. Her sword clattered to the ground, disappearing like his bow into the swirling mist.

Ellyn's aura of Vala protected her from the hideous scream.

The witch cackled and lifted her hand, pointing at Nina—Lydia. A reddish ball of energy shot from the palm of the witch's hand and slammed into Nina's stomach, where it instantly soaked into her.

Ellyn hefted the mace that she had summoned, its blue light holding the essence of Vala, and advanced on the witch.

Lydia screeched and convulsed, falling to the ground and flailing like a madwoman.

Lydia looked so much like Nina it caused Aeric to sob. He kept repeating in his head that it was just an illusion, but this was too much. Her scream broke off at its pitch as she vomited.

His hands finally curled around the cold wood of his yew bow. A bow he had made with his very own hands. Rolling onto his back and simultaneously nocking an arrow, he screamed in pain. In his excitement, he had forgotten his broken legs.

He fought to hold onto consciousness.

It felt like forever before that sharp, flaring pain began to subside and turn into a dull ache.

*****

Ellyn sent a silent prayer up to Vala for Lydia, who was attempting to suck in desperate lungfuls of air, still convulsing like she was having a stroke. She would have to hold on to life if she could, for Ellyn knew she needed all her strength granted to her through her devotion to Vala to beat the witch. There would be no healing now, most likely not after either. Weakness would replace the adrenaline that coursed through her body at the moment.

Ellyn waved her mace. The witch darted back out of range of the swing. The crone wriggled her fingers, and Ellyn dived at her with a wild swing of her mace. She was too late, though. A long, black-bladed dagger appeared in the witch's hands, black flecks floating in the air around the deadly looking blade.

The witch stabbed toward Ellyn's heart.

Ellyn twisted her body at an extreme angle to avoid the dagger, and felt a sharp pain in her back as she pulled a muscle. But she knew if she got even a scratch from that blade she would die, screaming in agony.

Ellyn swung her mace in a backhand strike, hoping to hit the witch and create some room. The blow wasn't a strong one, but blue energy crackled and the crone's shoulder smoldered.

Falling backward, the witch clutched her shoulder in horror, and an unholy shriek of pain was released.

Ellyn's hopes rose; perhaps the witch would flee. She threw a glance at Aeric, who moaned, inching across the ground. The poor fool had probably gone mad when the witch released the curse over Nina and it revealed his wife to him.

That thought left in a flash as the witch leapt back up and came at her with uncanny speed. Ellyn back-pedaled, and her ankle caught on the uneven ground. She flailed for a moment before falling to the ground next to a foam-mouthed Lydia. Ellyn's mace flew from her hand on impact, and as soon as the weapon touched the ground it disappeared into nothingness.

Ellyn looked into the eyes of the witch, who stood over her in terror.

What happened next happened unbelievably quickly.

A reddish stream of energy flew from the witch's outstretched hand, black flecks floating in and out of the magical current like tadpoles swimming about in a small muddy pool.

Ellyn felt an odd link to an otherworldly darkness. An entity that dwelled in the abysmal levels of the Nether. She felt her energy being sucked through the link. After that was gone, it would drain her youthfulness and then finish with a delicacy: Her soul.

Nina's mouth hung open in shock, pain, and horror next to Ellyn. They had come so far to remove this curse and bring Nina and her husband back together. It couldn't end like this.

Or maybe it would. At least Aeric and Nina would be together in death.

The witch shrieked as well, at first in exhaltation as the power flowed through her, then in pain as an arrow thunked into her stomach. She turned towards the broken hunter. Ellyn would swear on her goddess that the witch's canines elongated almost like that of a vampire.

The demon lord was projecting itself onto her features, though it couldn't enter this world. Even with that knowledge, Ellyn felt a bottomless pit of fear form in her gut.

*****

Aeric fumbled with an arrow as the witch turned on him and advanced. Nocking and drawing with a swift, but awkward, motion. He focused on the left eye of the witch, using the technique that his father had taught him so long ago.

Aeric's mind backtracked despite the pain and fear, to the beginning of this journey, to hunting the stag. Then to the many hunts before that. His heart warmed at the memory of his father the first time he taught him this technique. That was a memory he would hold in his mind right to the end.

The arrow's fletching zipped over his cheek, and through the air it flew. His aim was true. It sank deep into the witch's eye as she charged him, black dagger in hand. Falling head over heels, the witch landed on Aeric's broken legs.

The world slammed into Aeric, and he slipped into a hazy void. A greyness from which he was sure there was no return. Despite that knowledge, the void held a warm coziness that was seducing. He felt comfortable, even at home.

Clutched in this new home, Aeric drifted.

*****

Ellyn rolled Nina over with a sob. Nina's muscles were tight and her mouth foamed. For what felt like the millionth time on this adventure, she prayed to Vala.

The goddess' warmth did not come this time, though.

Ellyn sobbed a deep, hitching breath. So, this is how it would end. Nina wasn't dead yet, but Ellyn would get to watch the light exit those brown eyes. Red pockets were already forming under her eyes, and the whites of her eyes were dark red pools. The scales were gone from her body now, though, disappearing when the witch released her spell.

Ellyn stood up quickly and moved towards Aeric. The quick movement caused an explosion of stars to fill her vision, but she ignored them. She could not watch Nina die; her love for her friend was too great. Bile rose in her throat, her mind swam. By not being by Nina's side, she felt as if she was betraying her friend. But she just couldn't... Couldn't make herself watch that.

Ellyn's eyes fell on the hag that lay crumpled up on Aeric's legs, and she yelped.

Black-fletched arrow jutting out of her left eye, the witch was struggling to get up. Amazingly, the shaft had sunk deep, but somehow had not killed the crone. It must have missed the brain somehow. Ellyn felt panic following those thoughts, with rapid speed.

Ellyn approached, stumbling, too weak to do much. The witch was on hands and knees now. Ellyn did the first thing she could think of: She dove onto the witch, tackling her.

The arrow's fletching caught on the ground, and Ellyn leaned. The witch still struggled, though weakly. The shaft worked its way deeper into the crone's skull as Ellyn's weight shifted. Then the arrowhead burst from the back of the witch's head. Adrenaline controlled the cleric now, and she grabbed the witch's greasy hair and slammed the face of the dying witch into the ground several times with all the strength she had. Whether or not it was necessary, Ellyn wasn't taking any chances.

Blood pooled on the crone's broken face. The arm that ended in a stump, where Aeric had lopped it off so long ago, had an "S" shape that was smoldering. It left the smell of burning flesh in the air. Ellyn didn't know what it was; perhaps that was where the witch had been struck by the mace her goddess had lent her.

Ellyn couldn't hold it down any longer; flinging herself off the dead witch, she lost her stomach, disgusted with what she had just done. Still sobbing heavily, she paused. Not wanting to believe what she was hearing. Gasping and heavy breathing.

The witch! Why wouldn't she just die! Vala why? Please, no, no, no, no...

She whirled around, fear increasing her movements. Her heart was in her throat, and she knew, this time, fear would petrify her, and the witch would kill with glee.

The witch's corpse hadn't moved an inch, to Ellyn's surprise.

She let out a grateful sigh and almost started crying again. Until she realized who was gasping.

"Nina!" Ellyn flung herself towards her friend.

Her hands found the sides of Lydia's face, disbelief striking her dumb. All Ellyn could do was stare into Lydia's unconscious but alive face.

Alive.

She tried to rearrange her thoughts in her head. The knowing her friend was going to die, quickly turning into living, was still trying to find solid ground in her head.

Nina's face was pale, but no longer blueish. The red splotches under her eyes were still there, and Ellyn doubted they would disappear for a while. Her breathing was even now, and Ellyn knew she'd live.

Shakily, Ellyn stood and moved to Aeric. With a quivering hand, Ellyn bent down over him and felt for a pulse. Indeed, a pulse greeted her fingertips, and Ellyn felt a tear roll down her cheek. They had made it through.

It took a while, but Ellyn dragged the two back into the tower and started a fire. They both needed healing, but Ellyn was too weak and needed rest now. She made sure Aeric's legs were set, then checked Lydia one more time.

Turning, she stumbled to the doorway, calling on Vala one last time before her tired eyes claimed her. Divine wards in place, she fell asleep by the door.

*****

Aeric awoke to the most magnificent sight he had ever seen.

Nina lay next to him, sleeping peacefully as if she had never left him. His first thought was that it had all been a dream. But then he recognized the moss-covered room of the small tower.

He stared at her for a long time, trying to wrap his head around everything. Lydia had in fact been Nina all along. Questions raged in his mind, but he could not bear to wake her. Aeric felt that if he woke her up, the whole thing would disappear. He had checked her pulse when Corina defeated them, and Nina had been dead. So how had she ended up not only alive but covered in those hideous scales?

Nina's eyes fluttered open, as if feeling his heart calling to her.

He met those brown eyes with all of his love; it felt as if his heart would drown in it. By the gods, this wasn't a dream. His mind went back to the beginning of the trio's adventure and recalled all the times he felt he could fall for Lydia, but in truth, he had been falling for his wife all over again.

No questions, not now.

Not caring about the pain in his legs, Aeric leaned forward and kissed his wife on the lips with a deep passion that burned in his chest.

She had come back to him.

*****

Later, the trio sat around the fire, warming themselves and piecing everything together.

Nina explained how after the first battle with the witch, she had awakened after Aeric had left with their daughter, thinking she was dead. She told how just her face had been covered in scales when she had awakened. How, quickly, they had spread over her body like some form of leprosy.

Nina had wandered for a long time, going from place to place in a deep depression. She had not returned to Aeric, thinking he would not believe it was really her, or perhaps he wouldn't love her anymore in this scale-covered body. Just the thought of him no longer loving her tore her apart.

Finally, she had approached a temple of Vala in the hopes that she could find help. That was where she met Ellyn, and she had told her everything.

"I wanted to tell you so many times, but it just didn't feel right," Nina said to Aeric.

Aeric nodded; he didn't understand it, but he didn't care either. They were together again, and that was all that mattered.

Aeric turned to Ellyn and met her eyes. "I owe you and your goddess an apology. I've never been quite sure about the deities, but you have shown me time and time again. I was wrong to question your faith."

"You are forgiven, and it is forgotten. Vala, the moon goddess, loves all her children. Even those who don't love her." Ellyn's smile was sincere.

"And seeing how I was unable to believe in Vala when you had shown me so many times, perhaps I wouldn't have believed you were my wife when you were under the curse. Even when the witch revealed you, I thought it was an illusion."

Nina snuggled close, and all his worries lifted from his soul.

Everything would be better going forward. For Aeric had rediscovered his love.

His life.

His Everything.

The Dark Village

By Katie Lawrence

599AM
Age of Gloom

There was no wind blowing through the trees that evening. There were no sounds in the forest, save that of Taryl's barely-audible footsteps. The mountains loomed over the southern forests of Talanthus, allowing only scant sunrays to escape the foreboding shadows as the light sank down into the dark horizon. There was a darkness in these woods, a ravenous evil just waiting to awaken. It was exactly what Taryl was hoping for.

She had heard some rumors recently. Rumors that a couple of barghest had been prowling these woods. Often, rumors were just that—especially in the business of Valons. For not many would see such creatures and live to tell the tale. However, having just come down the mountain's edge, she could immediately feel a change in the atmosphere when arriving in this area of Talanthus, and it wasn't hard to believe that a pair of barghest may have chosen this area as their hunting grounds. With the many small villages in the area, and the plethora of caves to choose from to make their arrivals and exits from the underworld, it was a perfect feeding ground.

She continued her trek into the woods as the sun finally departed for the day. The forest was almost instantly blackened. It wouldn't be long now. The barghest would soon begin their search for prey, and the hunt would begin.

Just as Taryl was about to begin tracking she heard a scraping sound in the woods nearby, like something was being dragged across the forest floor. Soon after, she heard a muffled whimper. She made her way closer to the sound. As she did, she saw a pair of very large barghest dragging a villager through the woods, probably heading for their cave. She followed in the shadows, waiting for the right opportunity to attack.

One of the barghest had gouged its ferocious-looking claw into the man's leg, and was using the wound to drag the man. Tears were streaming down the man's clawed-up face, and onto his mud-covered, bloody tunic. It was a surprise that the man hadn't passed out from the agony of it all...or the blood loss.

The blueish-grey fur around the barghest's claws was covered in bright red blood, the mixture of colors giving the fur an almost purple tinge. The wind blew through Taryl's long brown hair; suddenly the monster stopped and sniffed the air, then lifted its lips, revealing its sharp, deadly teeth. It turned its head slowly until it was staring directly at her with its glowing, beady eyes, and it let out a deep, guttural growl.

It had smelled her.

Knowing she had no time to lose Taryl leapt out of hiding, heading straight for the barghest that was dragging the man. Before the beast had time to react to her charge, she pulled out her longsword and slashed down on the barghest's arm that was holding the man. The arm was severed at the elbow, leaving a bleeding stump to the beast, and half an arm protruding out of the man's bleeding calf where it had been gripping him. The barghest let out a blood-curdling sound that seemed to be a mixture of growl, yelp, and howl.

While the first barghest was still reeling from the shock of its severed arm, the second barghest charged Taryl. She dodged it easily, then turned around and placed a hard kick in its gut, toppling it over for a brief moment, allowing her the time to turn and plunge her sword through the chest of the first barghest. She swiftly pulled the sword back out as the monster crumpled to the ground, the light in its eyes fading.

She turned her attention back to the other barghest, which had just recovered itself. It began to circle her, waiting for her to let her guard down and give it an opening. When she didn't the creature lunged forward, slashing its large claws at her. As it did so, she dodged to the right and slashed at the beast's side. She just barely grazed it but it was enough to startle it for a brief second, allowing her to slam her hard boot into the side of its head. It fell to the ground, unconscious. Taryl stood over the barghest, and readied her sword above its chest.

Just as she was about to plunge her blade into the creature's heart she heard a man scream, "No!" behind her. There was an impact to her head and a sudden throbbing pain, and the world around her went dark.

*****

"*Mama! Mama! Watch how fast I can run!*" little Ariena yelled to Taryl as she tottered clumsily down the forest path. Taryl could see the little girl's breath huffing and puffing out of her mouth as she ran.

"Good job, Ari!" Taryl yelled back. "You're so fast, I don't think I could ever catch you; but Daddy on the other hand..." she looked over at her husband, Jorgan, as she trailed off. He winked at her.

"Uh-oh!" he exclaimed. His hands shot out of his pockets as he made them into claws. "I can feel it coming...I don't think I can hold it back...the tickle monster is taking over and it's coming to get you!" He started to run after her, and she squealed in delight as she took off running down the forest path, giggling all the way. Jorgan ran after her.

As they disappeared around a bend, Taryl yelled after them, "Not too far! It's not safe—" She was cut off by the sound of a man's scream. She ran as fast as she could toward the sound, feeling panicked. As she rounded the bend, she saw Jorgan and Ariena backed up against a large tree by a tall, furry, horned creature. A kralle.

She rounded the bend just in time to see her husband standing between the creature and their young daughter, and the monster slashed its long, deadly claw into Jorgan's stomach, thrusting him backwards into Ariena, slamming them both into the tree. Little Ariena slumped to the ground. Wide-eyed, Jorgan looked around in shock, and noticed Taryl standing paralyzed down the path.

She started to run towards them. Jorgan, his mouth agape and trickling blood, stopped her, shaking his head ever so slightly as he slumped and his eyes glazed over. She watched through tears and silent sobs as the creature dragged him into the woods, seeming to have no interest in the smaller prize that was Ariena.

Taryl darted to her little girl's side. "Ariena!" she screamed as she came to her little girl. There was blood *oozing down the back of her head. Her big blue eyes were open and unblinking.*

"*Ariena! No! My baby, don't leave me!*" *she cried as she cradled her daughter's still form in her arms.* "*Don't leave me alone! Jorgan! Ariena! Please! No, no, no, no, no...*"

*****

Taryl woke up with teary eyes. When she wiped away the blur, she saw that it was already late evening. She had been unconscious for almost a full day. She was in the center of a small town. Her legs were tied together and her arms were bound together in front of her, tied to a nearby pole by another longer rope. All her weapons were gone. There was a group of people nearby, seeming to be in a heated argument. The man she had saved was among them. They glanced over at her, seemingly surprised to see that she was awake. Surprise soon gave way to looks of fear and anger.

"Such hospitality," she said sarcastically. "Great way to thank the person who saved your life."

The man walked up to her and spit on her. "Do you even know what you've done?" he practically roared.

"I saved you from an agonizing death, you ungrateful fool," she said. "Those barghest would have devoured you."

"You've doomed our village," said a larger, middle-aged man, who Taryl guessed was the village leader. He was an unkempt-looking man, with scraggly brown hair and a thin beard. "Two months ago, the goddess Xanzith sent those creatures to our village of Felsron to collect sacrifices. You've interrupted a sacrifice, offending the goddess, and have surely brought doom upon our people. Xanzith will unleash her fury on the village, and we'll all be made a sacrifice to her! Don't you see? We sacrifice the few to save the many! Now we must sacrifice you to quell Xanzith's anger."

Taryl laughed. "You're insane. The barghest aren't creatures of a goddess, though they're malevolent beasts just as she is. Though they and she may be like-minded, barghest are no harbingers of Xanzith. They're slightly smarter than most animals but follow no orders, not even those of a goddess. They only continue to return to your village because it's close to their mountain caverns and you keep feeding them. Like all monsters, they're vile creatures which prey on the defenseless. They kill women, children, and entire families. They must be destroyed. All of them. People must be kept safe."

"Don't lie to us to save yourself! You've doomed our village, and we must make it right with your blood! It was you who desecrated her sacrifice, and so it is you who must be offered in return!" the village leader yelled. At that, the whole village cheered and roared. Their eyes were alight with lunacy and fear. It was as though they had been poisoned by a deep fear and superstition, which had sucked out all rationality. They were more a herd of spooked animals than a group of human beings.

"You'll be sacrificed this night for the good of the people of Falsron. Xanzith must know that you don't act for us," the man said. He pulled out a small knife. "As the village leader, I mark you for this holy sacrifice." He sliced deep into Taryl's right thigh, leaving a long, bleeding gash. "The monsters will smell your blood and come for you swiftly. By the time the sun goes down, you will have lost enough blood to not be able to fight back."

They left Taryl there the rest of the day, bleeding out under the hot sun with no food or water. Within an hour Taryl was feeling herself weaken, and none in the village would help her. They passed by as though she was nothing but a specter, meant to watch life continue around her as she slowly disappeared from existence. The afternoon continued this way until a little boy passed by. He looked no more than five years old, but his haggard eyes looked so much older than his age. Living in this village, she couldn't imagine all this little boy had seen.

He looked down at her leg then up at her face. Her lips were chapped and cracking; her face was no doubt bright red with sunburn. Then he looked down the road and ran into a little house close by. Within a few minutes, he came back out with a wet rag and some water. He looked around to be sure nobody was watching, then put the cup to her lips. She drank deeply.

"Thank you," she whispered.

The little boy smiled meekly then started dabbing the cloth on Taryl's wound. He packed the rag tight into her wound to try to stanch the bleeding. The rag was dirty, and the little boy was obviously too young to understand the risk of infection, but at least Taryl would be less likely to die of blood loss. When he was done he looked around, and ran off down the village road. She smiled after him. It was heart-wrenching to see such pure innocence corrupted by a place like this.

The sun began to set. As it did, all of the villagers quickly made their way into their houses. They didn't light any candles or cook any food, most likely in an attempt to draw as little attention as possible to anybody who wasn't part of the sacrifice. When the sun had vanished for the night, the village was nothing but darkness and silence. All Taryl could hear was the sound of her own breathing.

Then she heard a rustling in the woods, and the large, shadowy figure of the barghest appeared at the edge of the forest. It drew closer, sniffing at the air, taking in the scent of her blood. When it came upon her, it lifted its large claw and dug it into the calf of her already-injured leg. She screamed in pain. The creature then used the wound to begin pulling her into the forest. It pulled harder with the resistance of the rope binding her to the nearby pole, ripping her skin further until the rope snapped. Her leg was mangled.

Sticks and debris scraped and gouged Taryl's skin as she was dragged across the dirt. She struggled and bucked, but there wasn't much she could do while still bound up. She searched frantically for something to cut the ropes on, and found her salvation in a sharp piece of glass lying on the ground outside an abandoned village house. No doubt the owner was sacrificed, and the house was broken into and looted by the other villagers.

She cut the rope at her wrists then took the piece of glass and sliced the barghest's arm. It yelped, and released her for just long enough for her to cut the rope at her ankles. It then swiped down at her with its sharp claws, and she rolled to the side to dodge its attack. She then sprang to her feet, still holding the shard of glass, and almost immediately dropped down again at the pain that seared through her right leg. She managed to regain her balance, favoring her right leg.

The barghest snapped at her with its razor-sharp teeth. She dodged again, but couldn't keep her balance with her injured leg, and started to topple over. As she was falling, the barghest snarled and rammed into her, sending her flying into a nearby house and slumping to the ground. The beast came running for her, its jaws open. Obviously, this time it planned to kill her before dragging her off.

She tried to dodge again, but wasn't able to fully escape the lunge. The barghest's teeth sank into her right shoulder. It lifted her up with its powerful jaws as it stood. Screaming in pain, she jabbed the piece of glass into the monster's left eye. It yelped and flung her to the side, one large tooth staying lodged in her shoulder. As she connected with another nearby house a pitchfork fell, thumping onto her head.

Taryl pushed the pain aside, and looked at the pitchfork excitedly. Finally, she had a good weapon. She stood back up, feeling no pain, most likely due to shock, and braced herself. The barghest was still yelping and howling at the pain of her earlier blow but, seeming to sense her recovering, it turned to look toward her.

The shard of glass was still lodged in its eye socket, and blood was running in a stream down its face. It pulled the shard of glass out of its eye socket, and its eyeball came with it, skewered on the sharp glass edge. The barghest growled and howled, and in its rage it charged for Taryl.

She was ready this time. She stood, feet spread at a wide angle, bracing for impact. Just as the creature came within range, Taryl pulled out the pitchfork and thrust it out in front of herself at an angle. Between the force of her thrust and the creature's momentum from its charge, the tines of the pitchfork went straight through the barghest's chest and out of its fur-covered back. Taryl went flying backwards from the impact, covered in a mixture of blood from herself and the barghest.

The barghest began to topple over forward, but as it did it fell on the handle of the pitchfork, and its weight caused the pitchfork to sink even deeper into its flesh. She left it like that, dripping blood and propped up by the pitchfork like a mangled, gruesome scarecrow, and she made her way back to the center of the village.

Once at the center of the village, the village leader furiously came running out to her. His face was pale and his eyes alight with anger. He was carrying her sword at his side.

"What have you done! Now there will be no appeasing Xanzith! You've killed us all!" he blathered on.

"What have I done? I've saved you all. Your village is safe. There will be no more sacrifices, and if you wait and see there will be no retribution from Xanzith. Rebuild your village. Build a better life for your children," Taryl said, exhausted. "Now can somebody please treat my wounds?"

"Treat your wounds!? You've done nothing but endanger us since you got to this village. You lie to defend your evil actions and your bloodlust. You just killed the harbingers of Xanzith, and her retribution will be swift and merciless!" the man said.

Then the man and the villagers all dropped to their knees and prostrated themselves, praying for Xanzith's forgiveness, pleading for mercy and promising more sacrifices, even if they must kill their fellow villagers with their own hands. Then the village leader stood back up.

"We must offer another sacrifice right now if we're to have any chance of survival. It must be a precious sacrifice. Something to truly prove our loyalty... Bring the orphan boy."

Several villagers walked out of the crowd, and in tow was the young boy who had given Taryl water and tried to help mend her wounds while she was tied up. His big blue eyes were watering, tears falling down his pink cheeks. The poor thing was terrified.

"Look, boy. Just as your mother and father were offered to Xanzith as a means to save our village, so too will you. It's an honor. You'll be the hero who saved our people," the man said.

As he droned on, Taryl couldn't take his cowardice and ignorance. She walked up to him and spat in his face.

"You're despicable. You talk of saving your village from Xanzith and that which you believe to be her vile harbingers, but you're really full of nothing but lies and ignorance. You destroy your village in order to save it? What happens when you run out of villagers to sacrifice? Then, by your own hand you'll have brought about the very fate you claim you're trying so hard to deter. In your cowardice you've become no better than the monsters you feed," Taryl said.

Then she swiftly took her sword from the scabbard at her side, and stabbed him through the gut. "It seems that now the best way to protect your village is to save it from you," she said coldly. Then she abruptly pulled the sword from his stomach, and walked over to the little boy as the man sputtered out blood and fell to his knees, clutching his stomach.

"Don't worry. You won't have to follow your parents today. What's your name, little boy?" she asked.

The boy looked around nervously then said shyly, "Seth."

"Well, Seth, how would you like to come with me? I promise that I'll take care of you, and not a day will go by where you don't get to laugh and play. What do you say?"

Seth looked at her for a moment, studying her, then a smile lit his face "You promise?" he asked.

"I promise," Taryl replied, smiling warmly.
Seth bobbed his head, and took her hand, leaving behind the dark village and the monsters that lurked within.

Garrett's Tale

By Anna Warkinton

660AM
Age of the Dracon-esti

Garrett loved being up this early in the morning. The sun was just halfway above the horizon, waking birds and illuminating feathers of every kind as they flitted from tree to tree in a cacophony of song. Dew hung on the grass like jewels on a necklace, disturbed only by his boots as he trekked through the village of Sonarus, towards the woods where he would be spending his day. Smoke tendrils began to rise from chimneys, chatter and laughter heard from a few of the houses. For now, with everyone tucked away in their warm homes as they prepared for the day, the world was his.

One building he passed was cold and silent. His steps faltered as he took in the fading red paint of the small, one-room schoolhouse. Last month it had been full of life, children racing each other around in the yard, the bespectacled teacher looking on with a downturned mustache until class. Then, one foggy day, he had disappeared. Rumors swirled, whispers of murder, or elopement with a village girl who had disappeared at the same time. Garrett's brother, Tamasese, was among the ones old enough to start work in the fields at the sudden conclusion of their schooling. No one was happy about the change, but with a short investigation, they found no tutor willing to occupy the little red schoolhouse. At least, not for what the parents of the children deemed an affordable sum.

Rounding a corner on his way out of Sonarus, Garrett nearly strode headfirst into a small girl with jet-black hair.

"Terra!" he exclaimed, backing up and stumbling as he tripped over his own feet. "What are you doing up so early?"

"Oh, hi Garrett," she said, eyes fixed on the ground she sat on. The stick she held trailed back and forth in random patterns and swirls. The young man crouched beside her and lay a gentle hand over hers.

"Are you all right, Ter?" he asked gently. The girl was like family to him; seeing her so distant and distracted all the time worried him to no end.

"I miss 'Lala," she replied, staring at her shoes. Garrett sighed, and wrapped an arm around her narrow shoulders, pulling her into a hug.

"I know little one; I do, too."

'Lala was Terra's nickname for her older sister, Alaya, who had disappeared after rescuing her sister and several other women of the village from slavers. Many people felt her absence keenly, Terra and Garrett chief among them.

"She wouldn't want us to sit around moping, though, would she?" he said, trying to be upbeat. The girl beside him saw right through it, but pretended to play along. Garrett got the feeling she wanted to be alone.

"No, you're right. I'm waiting for Papa to call me, anyway. I've been helping fetch wood and water for the forge since I'm not in class all day anymore."

"That's good! I'm glad you're keeping busy."

"I'm glad I'm not in class anymore. The teacher was bad."

"I heard he was a good teacher."

She shook her head.

"Good teachers can still be bad men."

Placing his hands on his knees, Garrett pushed himself to stand and ruffled her hair. "In that case, I'm glad you're not in class anymore either. I'll see you later, all right?"

"Mm-hmm," she hummed, returning to doodling in the dirt. Hesitating a moment, he looked down at her, eyebrows pulled together in concern, and made a mental note to check on her more often. For now, though, he had more pressing matters.

The sun had fully risen by the time the last of the village faded from view behind him. Not too far away lay a freshwater called Aeth Lake and clearing, a favorite watering hole of local game. With a nod, he took his bearings from the sparkling morning sun and set off towards the lake, following a narrow deer trail while keeping an eye out for signs of fresh activity that could lead to an easier kill. As he struck deeper into the forest, something about it began bothering him, but he couldn't quite figure out what.

It took ten minutes of walking in silence, hair prickling on the back of his neck and skin crawling, before he put his finger on what itched at him.

Silence.

Not the quiet of the woods he loved, but silence. Not a single bird call or skittering squirrel, no woodpeckers or buzzing insects. Even the wind seemed unnaturally still. And yet, speckled yellow light danced across the ground like any other day. Despite the uneasy feeling wrapping its cold fingers around his spine Garrett pushed on, determined to bring *something* home and prove to his family that he could hunt alone.

Instinct and muscle memory made up for his distraction, and he spotted fresh tracks weaving their way across his path. He dropped to a crouch before they had even registered. The more the hunter studied the tracks, the deeper his frown grew. They were uneven and staggered, a splayed hoof here and stumbling cluster there. Garrett rose, stepping to avoid obscuring the tracks as he followed them down the path towards Aeth Lake. Eyes scanning for more signs on what was wrong with his quarry he picked up his pace, already several hours behind.

The sun had climbed nearly all the way to its zenith when the hunter broke through the underbrush and into the clearing around the lake. With the easy light, he identified a little more information on his deer. Streaks of dark colored blood across a few waving blades of grass told him that it had an injury, likely on its flank. The fact that there were no signs of it bedding down in or around the clearing confused him for a moment, until he realized he may not be the only predator hunting it. Something—or someone—had injured it earlier that morning. The only reason he could think that it would still be running, especially away from an easy source of water and nutrition, would be that it felt it was being pursued.

Tracking another hunter's prey wasn't Garrett's first choice, but a thorough check of the usually bustling lake area revealed not so much as a squirrel. So, he took off again, hoping to catch up with the animal before too long.

"Whatever scared this thing, scared it *good*," Garrett muttered to himself, if only to break the silence that hung over the forest like a heavy blanket. His feet ached in a way that told him he'd regret the long walk home with a hundred pounds of meat. However, a few drops of deep red blood on some shrubbery less than a mile away kept him putting one foot in front of the other. He was close. It wouldn't be an exciting kill, it hadn't been an adrenaline-filled chase, but it would feed his little brother and his mother and father. And that was something he could be proud of.

A turned-over rock with a few strands of coarse brown hair told him that his deer was fading. It wouldn't be long now. The animal stumbled downhill with the last of its energy, and so followed Garrett, careful and quiet. The absolute last thing he wanted to do now was disturb it as it began to bed down for the last time and have to track it for another few hours. Thanks to the silence he had now become accustomed to, he heard it before he saw it. The soft snapping of plant stalks and crunching of last fall's leaves alerted him to its nearness.

Freeing his bow from its place on his back, Garrett wrapped his hand around the wood, enjoying the familiar feel of the weapon. He pinpointed the copse of birch trees the noises were coming from, and circled around to find the high ground on it. As he drew an arrow and nocked it, he laid eyes on the animal for the first time. As soon as he did he wished he hadn't taken so long to find it, and put an arrow through its lungs without worrying about stealth.

Garrett bounded down the small hill, eyes watering as he came close to the now-dead deer. The smell of death perfumed the entire copse, along with a sickly-sweet scent, as if someone pumped liquid sugar into the deer's bloodstream. Pus and yellow froth was speckled around its nose and mouth, its bloodshot eyes rolled back and wide in death. Pulling his sleeve over his nose and mouth the hunter moved closer, swallowing hard as he inspected the wound that allowed him to spend the entire day on its trail.

The gash sliced, as he had guessed, across its flank. Blood stained the entire hindquarter, the wound itself black with some sort of gel-like substance. Not wanting to touch the deer Garrett drew another arrow, prodding at the unnaturally infected wound. Instantly the black substance shriveled, turning into a powder and exploding all over the area, causing the young man to backpedal and double over in a coughing fit.

"What in the Nether..." he muttered, glowering.

Shoulders slumped, he watched the black dust float into the air and dissipate. The sun seemed void of warmth as it shone down on his back, beginning to sink close to the horizon.

"A whole day wasted, with nothing to show but a worthless deer," Garrett spat, frustration bubbling inside his chest. His forest empty, the animals gone. Something was messing with his home, and the fact he knew next to nothing about what was going on ate at him.

*****

It took Garrett several hours to walk home, and by the time he caught sight of the first of the torchlight marking safety his nerves were thoroughly frayed. The eerie silence had been eating at him all day, and the entire way home he kept spinning around, sure that something followed him, just out of sight. When he stepped onto the familiar, hard-beaten road home, he had never been so relieved.

Far too few hours later, Garrett blearily opened his eyes to his mother's weary face over his.

"Time to wake if you wish to beat the dawn, my son," Caroline whispered, giving him a small smile through her tiredness.

Garrett nodded, still half-asleep as he swung his legs out from beneath the warmth of his thick blanket. The cold air hit his feet and raised goosebumps on his skin, causing him to shiver once while he adjusted. Shaking his head to free it of the cobwebs of sleep, he grabbed his boots and padded out of the room, easing the door shut to ensure his little brother didn't wake.

"How did you sleep?" Caroline asked in a whisper as she stirred the pot of oatmeal she had over the fire.

"Not enough, but nothing to be done about it," Garrett replied with a wry smirk.

His mother nodded sympathetically. "Here. To warm you for the road."

She handed him a bowl full of hot oatmeal, sprinkled with dried berries and drizzled with honey. He felt better the moment the first bite hit his stomach, warming him from the inside out.

"I may not be back tonight. The forest around here is sick and empty, so I'll likely have to range further afield to find anything," he told her, setting down the empty bowl. Caroline's mouth twisted in displeasure, but she nodded regardless.

"Be *safe*, Garrett. No hunt is worth your life."

"I will, Mother."

As Garrett made his way out of the village, he considered his options. The miles of forest he had seen yesterday were barren and dead; to find anything worthwhile he'd have to roam farther afield. So, he stuck to the worn dirt road, alert for anything that would speak to a successful outcome of the day.

Something tickled the back of Garrett's mind as he walked, a change in the environment that itched for his attention. Shaking his head clear of stray thoughts he paused for a moment, listening.

There!

In the distance, drawing closer, the sound of... music? Curious, Garrett continued down the road, as it seemed to be approaching from the opposite direction. As he rounded a bend in the path a bright procession came into view, a shock of color in the muted brown and green landscape surrounding them.

Wooden caravans, painted in many swirling colors and pulled by stocky horses, trundled towards him. Children clung to the sides or darted in and out of the line, a few wolfish dogs loping joyfully after them. Perched on the driving benches of a few of the carts were musicians. On one, an older man with a floppy brown hat strummed a lute. Walking beside him, a young woman with flowing golden hair restrained with only a crown of fresh-picked flowers kept beat with a tambourine. Another cart sported a boy with a pair of pan pipes. And at the head of the cavalcade rode a broad-shouldered man, somewhere in his early twenties, a scruff of beard around his face and wide smile on his lips as he raised his voice in song, harmony weaving in and out of the melody provided by the instruments. Catching sight of Garrett standing on the side of the road, his smile grew. He finished the verse of the song, then held up one gloved hand, and the group ground to a halt while he swung off his horse.

"Hello there!" he greeted Garrett, holding out a friendly hand, dark eyes sparkling.

"H-hello," Garrett replied, somewhat taken aback as he shook the young leader's hand.

"You are a hunter, yes?" the man asked in a conversational tone, as if an entire clan of traders, tinkerers, and nomads was not waiting quietly behind him.

"Well, yes. My name's Garrett. And you are…"

"Christus—a pleasure to meet you," Christus said, bowing. "Garrett, I hoped to ask you if you've had much luck hunting in these parts of late."

Garrett's face fell, and he shook his head.

"Some evil has befallen the forest, and it seems all the game has disappeared."

A shadow crossed Christus' face, and he pursed his lips. "I had feared as such. You live around here, yes?"

Garrett nodded, pointing the way towards the village.

"Keep heading down this road. It's not much, but it's home, and there are wells and fields for your horses to rest."

Christus brightened at this, clapping Garrett on the shoulder with a grin.

"Thank you, Garrett. I won't forget your help."

"Ah... sure, no problem," he replied, mildly bewildered by the charismatic young man.

Christus then turned back to his jet-black horse, who snorted as he mounted from the ground.

"Good hunting to you, Garrett!" he declared, and he urged his mount forward to music started back up as quickly as it had stopped. As the caravan made its way down the road, the hunter could hear Christus' voice floating back on the afternoon air.

Gather round me, friends, and listen to my tale
We shall dance through the rain and sing through the hail
No manner of weather, no storm and no fight
Will dampen our spirits or dim our strong light

The tune wormed its way into Garrett's head as he split off from the road into an unfamiliar patch of wood, and as Christus' song faded from hearing he began humming the bits and pieces he could remember, bow drawn and ready.

The more he walked, the more he felt watched. As he crossed a stream, the feeling grew so strong he would have sworn there was someone directly behind him.

Garrett returned his bow to his back in one fluid motion while he dropped to a crouch, eyes scanning every leaf for movement that may betray his predator. Hesitating only a moment, he leapt across the creek and drove further into the forest. Despite his speed, Garrett used every ounce of adrenaline flowing through him to his advantage, dancing between trees, vaulting fallen logs, and moving as quickly and quietly as possible. As he did, he pushed his panic to the back of his mind; instead, focusing on figuring out where he could run to, somewhere he could either rest in semi-safety or make a stand.

Although a fit young man even Garrett couldn't run forever, and as shadows began to lengthen he skidded to a stop beside a towering oak and doubled over, gasping. Raising his eyes to the near horizon, he prayed for some form of shelter. At that moment, as if the gods themselves were listening, a gust of wind fluttered through the leaves, revealing a small cave carved into the side of a hill not half a mile away.

Offering up thanks Garrett set off again, the feeling of eyes at his back never leaving or lessening for even a second. While he moved through the woods, he gathered twigs and sticks for a fire, picking up one here and two there whenever he felt like his lungs would give out if he didn't give them a short break. By the time he reached the cave he had a decent armload, which he dumped at the entrance with relief. After a cursory glance confirmed that the cave was empty, he turned and surveyed the countryside before him. Silent and still, as it had been for the past two days. Nothing so much as drew breath, and yet he felt as if he were under a magnifying glass.

Night began to fall, and Garrett built and rebuilt his unlit fire inside the entrance to the cave. Finally, when it grew too dark to see, he lit the fire, coaxing the flames to their height. The moon rose and still he sat, staring into the forest. But eventually his eyelids grew heavy, and he admitted defeat. Uneasy and cautious though he was, Garrett laid out a blanket and shaped his knapsack into a pillow, laying his head on the lumpy object and drifting into a restless slumber.

Tsk. Tsk. Tsssssk. Grrrr.

The sound of claws on stone and a low growl sent Garrett shooting straight up out of a shallow sleep, so quickly his head spun. Pressing the heel of his hand to his forehead, he peered towards the entrance of the cave. His eyes widened and he let out a yell of surprise as a giant lynx came leaping over the low flames of the fire. Brown eyes met lifeless, red ones for a moment, then the hunter threw himself out of the way just in time, fumbling to draw a long hunting knife from his boot as he did so.

The lynx landed heavily, claws gouging the stone floor as it regained its balance and turned to face Garrett, lips curled in a snarl that displayed a frightening number of razor-sharp teeth. Shakily unsheathing his knife and adjusting to an underhand grip, Garrett panted, brain struggling to catch up with the action while his body exploded with adrenaline. The lynx snapped towards Garrett, strands of saliva swinging from its maw. With no further warning it leapt once more, but this time the hunter was ready.

Stumbling to the side and just managing to dodge the outstretched paw intended to gore him, Garrett thrust his knife into the tawny monster, cutting deep along its shoulder and side. He could feel the muscle part like paper between his knife's honed blade and the momentum carrying the cat forward, warm blood spurting over his hand and arm. Wrenching the blade free before it got stuck in bone, Garrett pressed his advantage. The lynx unknowingly now stood a foot in front of the fire. Swinging his sleep-weighted arm in a wide crescent, Garrett forced the cat to take a large step back, and its massive paw landed right beside the fire. At that moment, a log cracked and collapsed, sending a flurry of sparks into the air. The lynx's ears flicked back, a tiny distraction.

Garrett leapt at it.

Wrapping his left arm around the lynx's neck he used its second of weakness to force its head up, following up with a deep slash to the throat to end it.

Or so he thought.

The giant lynx was wounded, badly. And yet it shook off the hunter, landing him on his back and winding him as he hit the stone floor. Garrett rolled as soon as he realized what had happened, and not a moment too soon, as the cat's jaws clamped shut where his own neck had been mere milliseconds ago.

Planting a hand on the oddly warm ground, Garrett went to push himself up and back into a combat position, but his anchor slipped. He looked down, confused, to see he was sitting in a large pool of blood. And yet the creature still circled, blood streaming from its wounds as it prepared its next attack. Its red eyes caught Garrett's attention once again, a suspicion growing in the back of the hunter's mind. If what he thought truly was the case, taking down this creature would be that much more difficult. But if, as he thought, the only way to stop would be to attack its eyes, then that's what he'd do.

The lynx pounced, and Garrett rolled, scrabbling at his gear as he did so, knowing he only had precious few seconds. The lynx turned back at him, seeming to smile as it growled deep in its damaged throat.

Calling on his years of knife-throwing practice intended only to impress his friends, Garrett flung the dagger. It flew true and, a second later, buried itself in the left eye of the animal. It roared in pain and Garrett made good use of the opening, jumping forward to twist the dagger in the giant lynx's eye.

The lynx's scream suddenly stopped, and it stood still for a moment, wavering, before crashing to the ground. Attempting to get out of the way, Garrett tripped and landed on the stone, tailbone going numb.

He just sat there for a moment. Clothes soaking in blood, muscles aching from being awoken and forced into action so quickly, and lungs still struggling to fill with air, he sat. After a long moment he rose to his feet, muscles aching and complaining.

The lynx lay as still as the rock around it, even the slight nighttime breeze barely ruffling its tawny fur.

Rolling his shoulders with a wince, Garrett set to work building the fire up in case of another animal attack. Once the flames were crackling high and shadows danced on the cave walls like drunken partygoers, he felt his heart begin to calm.

"Let's see here…" he muttered to himself, going to the large beast's corpse and rolling it over with a grunt.

"Pelt's not half bad. Plus, the teeth are massive, big enough to make jewelry out of. Perhaps Christus and his traders will be interested."

With only a few hours left until daylight, Garrett set about skinning the lynx and searing some of its meat for the way home.

Rejuvenated by the fresh morning air and a small meal, Garrett set the rising sun to his shoulder and began heading home.

Stepping foot back into familiar territory took a weight off the young man's shoulders, and even though it didn't ease the muscles' real load, it quickened his step and lightened his mood as Sonarus' smoke drifted lazily into view.

The first person he saw on his way back to the house was Terra and Alaya's father, working in his smithy on the outskirts of Sonarus. As he caught sight of Garrett his hammer froze mid-swing, and a wide grin spread across his face while he watched the hunter pass.

"A'ways knew ye could do it, lad!" he called out after him, then returned to his smithing with renewed vigor, a smile still on his lips.

His shout drew the attention of a few other people, who gathered around, offering congratulations or murmuring in awe oat the size of the pelt rolled up and balanced on Garrett's shoulders. Garrett turned to corner to the village square and stopped, surprised.

A cacophony of color had exploded over the center of the village while he was away, Christus' wagons scattered throughout. Between the bright wooden carts were tents of all colors and patterns, some patchwork and faded, others as vibrant as the day they were dyed. As the young man took it all in the leader himself emerged from a grey and purple striped tent, approaching him with an easy stride.

"Ah, you had good hunting then I see! There's a pelt and a half, by Jarak."

"Aye," Garrett replied with a lopsided grin. "The ganker jumped me last night while I was sleeping. Last mistake it ever made, I can tell ya that much."

Laughter rippled through the small group formed around him.

A few of the traders spoke up with offers to buy it from him, and Garrett ended up selling the pelt and teeth to a pleasant middle-aged man decked out in a well-feathered hat.

Stepping out of the trader's tent, Garrett weighed the silver in his hand. It would be enough for a start, at least. If he could figure out what was scaring all the animals away, he could continue hunting and earning enough to keep a teacher employed for Terra, Tamasese, and the rest of the village's children.

A proud smile on his face Garrett strode through his front door, just as his parents and brother were sitting down for an early evening meal.

"You're home!" Tamasese leapt to his feet in excitement.

"Aye, that I am," Garrett replied, setting the pouch of coins on the table.

"Well done, Garrett," his mother exclaimed, crossing to him and pulling him into a hug as well. With a boisterous laugh Garrett's father also stood, completing the group hug, and for a shining moment Garrett felt perfectly happy.

The sun set in a blaze of golden glory, but the colors in the sky went largely unnoticed by those in the village square. A bonfire had been lit, food procured, and it seemed half the village was sitting out with the nomads, eager for scraps of news from the rest of the world. Garrett made his way through the clusters of people, exchanging smiles and waves. He paused for a moment, watching as a well-muscled, dark skinned woman carefully allowed Terra and a few other children to take turns holding a shield as tall as they were. However, he didn't stop, as he was searching for a specific person. It wasn't his eyes that eventually led him to his target, but his ears.

Christus' distinct voice floated above the dozens of conversations, complemented by the trill of a flute and deep beat of a drum. Garrett found him sitting on the outskirts of the firelight, in a small circle with two of the musicians, surrounded by many of the younger children from the village.

Christus sat on the ground with them, teaching them one of the songs he often sang on the road, a blessing for travelers. As Garrett approached, he looked up with a smile. Garrett returned the gesture, beckoning the nomad towards him.

Christus nodded, indicating for the children to continue singing, and stood, making his way to the hunter.

"A beautiful home you have here, to be sure," he said, walking with Garrett as he made his way away from the music, so they could talk more easily.

"It is, and I love it dearly. But we've been having some troubles lately, and I was hoping you could help."

"Anything. You have all been very hospitable to my little band and I, and I do desire to return the favor."

Garrett then explained the situation in proper depth. Of the tutor quitting, the children having nothing else to do but go to work, the animals disappearing, and the strange black substance and red-eyed creatures he had discovered.

"You've traveled far and wide, Christus. Do you have any idea what is plaguing our forests?"

The young man had a grave expression as he nodded slowly.

"I have some notion. I've seen this before, when I was only a child. Do you know much of magic?"

A chill crawled up Garrett's spine and he swallowed, mouth suddenly dry.

"No... we here in the village stay away from such things. Leave it to the Circle of Magi, I say."

"As do many. But some who are so blessed run from the circle. They evade the red robes sent to capture them and hide away, growing their magic. Some lose sight of their humanity in their thirst for power. They become twisted creatures, capable of only greed and lust for control. The signs that you told me of, I believe that may be what's going on."

Garrett's stomach dropped, as if he had just fallen off a high place.

"But how...how do we fix it? Can they be killed?"

Christus gave him a small, sad smile. "Aye, powerful though they be, they can be killed. It is dangerous, though."

"Well, I have no choice, then," Garrett replied, resigning himself to the fact. "I must kill it. I won't risk the lives of those here." He blinked back tears of panic, forcing himself to take slow, deep breaths.

"You are only one man; you truly intend to face a renegade mage?"

"What else is to be done?" Garrett turned to Christus, pleading. "If there is something, anything else please, tell me. Because I can't sit by and let these woods stay empty. We may have food from the harvest now, but it won't last without meat from the forest."

"Nothing but destroy the source of the corruption," Christus said, laying a strong hand on Garrett's shoulder when he watched the hunter's face fall. "But by no means will you go alone, my friend. There are adventurers among those I have with me. Men and women who will help, of that I am sure."

"I can't ask you to come with me," Garrett said. "You all have lives outside of this village, places to go. I have to do this alone."

"Nonsense!" Christus declared brightly. "You'd die. We're coming. Now, let's go meet the rest of our merry little band."

Heading back towards the camp in the center of Sonarus Christus led him to a smaller, low-burning campfire outside the ring of tents around the main bonfire. Around it sat a mixed bag of characters, chatting and laughing, a bottle of dark liquor passing from hand to hand. A short cheer went up as Christus stepped into the light, dying just as quickly as Garrett joined him. Curious silence fell as they all looked to their leader, waiting for an explanation.

"Ladies and gentlemen, may I introduce Garrett..." he paused, turning to his companion. "What is your last name?"

"Tyrus," Garrett whispered back.

"Tyrus!" Christus continued. "He has discovered a rogue mage who is preying on the woods around this village. What say you we assist him in taking out this annoyance?"

His question was greeted with a rousing "aye!" from the group.

"Then, without further ado," Christus turned to Garrett, "may I introduce your companions for tomorrow's expedition."

"Tomorrow?" Garrett looked around, noting the mostly-empty bottle of alcohol and red faces around the campfire. "Will you all be... all right to fight?"

A stocky man rose from where he was hunched behind the fire. He towered over the others, even Christus.

"Of course, we will be! What do you take us for, children?" He let out a boisterous laugh. "I am Aslock, wielder of the sword Maturin, slayer of—"

Christus raised a hand, chuckling. "Thank you, Aslock. I'm sure tomorrow evening you'll start introducing yourself as mage-slayer."

Aslock chuckled in return and say back down. "Aye, you're likely right, Master Christus."

The figure beside him beckoned to Garrett, offering him a seat on the log they had dragged into place beside the fire. He picked his way over to them, only getting a good look at them once he had accepted the bottle and taken a sizable swig. He recognized her as the woman with the shield he had seen with Terra earlier.

"Nadia, shield-bearer and voice of reason to these maniacs," she introduced herself. Although largely shrouded in shadows, Garrett could appreciate that the woman was more muscular than most of the men he knew, including himself.

"Nadia keeps us safe and sane," a light voice came from behind Garrett's left shoulder. He snapped around, disliking an unknown person sneaking up behind him. The slight girl behind him doubled over with a peal of laughter. Although she giggled like a child, a quick glance placed her only a little younger than Garrett, maybe nineteen years old.

"Your face! Oh, gods, your eyes got so wide. Relaaax." Bouncing over the log, she sat on the ground beside the fire.

"I'm Milly—it's my job to sneak up on people, so don't feel too bad."

Garrett rolled his shoulders and tried to keep all the names straight. These people could possibly die helping him tomorrow; he would never forgive himself if he couldn't even remember their names.

A shorter man on the opposite side of the fire waved casually from his position on the ground, a jacket bunched up beneath his head as a pillow.

"James; archer. If you need something hit and you're too far away to smack it with a sword, I'm your man," he said, a small smile on his face as he stared up at the stars.

"James found some mushrooms while we were on the road yesterday," Milly informed Garrett in a loud whisper. "None of us knew what they were, but somehow I think he did and didn't tell us, so he didn't have to share."

Garrett nodded, overwhelmed as he took another swig of the bitter drink they had given him.

"And I complete our little group," Christus said, taking a seat. "Nothing fancy for me; I wield a normal sword and hope everyone else has my back for things I can't see or reach."

"It's worked out so far," Aslock said, and Christus smiled. "Aye, that it has."

The five of them sat around the campfire for several more hours, laughing and swapping stories of previous adventures. By the time Garrett took his leave and Christus walked him home to get a little more time to talk, he was far more confident in the abilities of his new companions. Falling into bed, he smiled at the ceiling. Perhaps tomorrow was beginning to look up.

Although it was only a few hours later, the adventurers were up with the sun. Each had their own ritual to follow before heading into combat, and they went about their various tasks by the cold light of dawn.

Christus was the first one up. In the twilight right before the sun broke over the horizon, he picked his way to the field that his group had been lent to pasture their horses. A single long whistle caused his own black steed to raise its head and prick its ears forward, trotting towards the fence. Lavishing the animal with quiet praise, Christus took a stiff brush from his pocket and gave its glossy coat a quick brush, sweeping away any dirt or sweat that had accumulated from the day before. Once he was sure his steed would be ready to ride that day, he gave its hindquarters a pat and slipped out of the paddock, on his way to rouse the rest of his group.

Milly was the first one Christus went to shake awake, only because he knew by the time he woke the rest of the party he'd have to circle back around and make sure she'd actually gotten up. To his surprise, she greeted him with a silent nod on his way back to camp. She stood, barefoot, in a dewy patch of grass. In each hand she held a long, curved, wicked-sharp dagger. Rolling her shoulders and head to loosen up she slashed once, twice, then began spinning the daggers in her hands. Once she got them up to a whirling speed so quick they were only a deadly blur of metal, she launched one into the air, swapping the other one to her free hand and catching the falling dagger perfectly. Despite having seen the young woman in combat, the feat was enough to make Christus step back. Stopping their spinning, Milly tossed each knife to the other hand simultaneously, meeting her leader's eye with a smile.

"Morning!" she greeted brightly, hands and knives never still as she tossed one into the air, catching it a moment later.

"Glad to see you're up," Christus replied with a smile. Milly shrugged. "Wanted to get a head-start on the day. Nadia has her brew warming up inside."

Christus nodded and ducked into the large tent Milly, Nadia, Aslock, and James all shared. Around the perimeter of the canvas room they each had a cot, and in the center there lay a bed of hot coals. Nadia crouched beside it, short hair tousled by sleep. A gust of chilly morning air entered with Christus, and she looked up.

"Ah, good, you're here. Maybe you can get them up."

She pointed a thumb at the two snoring men behind her.

"I see you have your poison already made this morning," he said, crossing behind her and shaking Aslock's shoulder.

"Aye," she replied. "I prepared it last night when I saw James brew those mushrooms into a tea. Then someone pulled out the liquor and I knew I was right in getting it ready."

"Always looking out for us," Christus said with a soft smile, retrieving a cup of water Nadia had left lying next to her and backing up a few steps.

"Watch yourself," he warned, and Nadia shifted to his side of the fire, away from the sleeping men. Christus then tossed the water out of the cup. It arched in the air for a moment, almost hanging there as if building suspense, then splashed onto Aslock's face.

"Eh, who's there?!" The giant man leapt to his feet, a short-sword somehow in his hand, although it looked almost like a long dagger rather than a sword beside him.

"Aslock, do you sleep with a short-sword under your pillow now?" Christus asked, holding back laughter. The man hemmed and hawed as he set down the weapon, passing a large hand over his face.

"No..."

"Liar," Christus teased, crossing to James' cot and shaking him. Eyes still closed, James raised a hand and, after a few times patting the air, found Christus' face. He muttered something in his half-awake state, frowned, then opened his eyes to his leader's amused expression.

"You're not a beautiful elf maiden," James said, utter resignation in his voice.

"Sadly not," Christus replied. "Up you get, now."

James sighed, then swung his legs out of bed.

"Ah, gods, my head aches. How much did I drink last night?" he asked of no one in particular.

"Here," Nadia offered, shoving a steaming cup of muddy-looking substance in his face. James' lip lifted, and nose wrinkled as he reluctantly accepted the cup.

"Always the charmer, Nadia."

"Mm-hmm," she replied, already serving up five more cups. "Drink up."

She handed Christus two cups, which he looked down at in confusion. "I didn't even drink that much last night; have I displeased you somehow to be blessed with double your concoction?"

She rolled her eyes. "Take one to Garrett. He drank, and although it wasn't that much you know this helps."

"Ah! Of course."

Before long he had Garrett by his side. They met up with the others, each leading their own horse, and a fine chestnut gelding for their new companion. The night before, in between amusing stories and tales of bravado, the group had agreed upon a plan for the next day. First, Garrett would lead them back to the cave where he was attacked. From there, the group would combine their formidable tracking experience to trace back the lynx's steps, find where it was 'infected' with the evil magic, and then, if necessary, track whoever infected it back to their base.

Garrett discovered that riding was much quicker and more pleasant than walking all the time. Between random outbreaks of songs and chatter, and re-learning how to ride a horse, he found they were soon back at the cave. However, all was not as he'd left it. The fire was kicked apart, staggered footsteps appearing in the charcoal. And the roof of the cave that had kept Garrett safe, warm, and dry the other day was blown apart. The rock had crumbled like last autumn's leaves, collapsed in what seemed to be a massive explosion. Scorch marks scarred the stone around the collapse, painting a picture of destruction and rage.

"Lovely," Nadia commented, dismounting. The rest of the party followed suit.

"Spread out, search for tracks, but tread lightly," Christus warned. "We don't want to destroy anything that could lead us the right direction."

It wasn't difficult to discover where the lynx had come from, and the owner of the footsteps. It was as if they walked a direct line from, well, whatever depths of the Nether they had emerged from. To the untrained eye there was nothing amiss, but the group of trackers, hunters, and warriors could see it as clear as if a line was drawn in front of them. Crushed plants from the weight of the massive creature, broken twigs, tufts of tawny fur caught in the bark of the trees it brushed by—it was all too clear. And so, riding single-file with James in the lead to make use of his sharp eyes, they made good time backtracking the steps of the giant lynx and its handler. As they rode deeper into the forest the trees grew older, larger, closer. Their thick leaves formed a nearly unbroken canopy above the party's heads, and the bright sun above them was all but gone; the only sign it was even there the strange grey-green light that filtered in all around them. The very plant life seemed to become hostile, the trees bending over and around each other in a battle for sunlight, starving the plants of the ground until none but the hardiest remained. The group rode in silence, as if straining to hear the scuffle of a squirrel or twitter of a bird. But the only sounds breaking through the forest's unnatural peace were the sounds of their horses, occasionally whickering uneasily to each other.

Just as Garrett thought they'd have to dismount and lead the horses to continue their path, the tree line broke as suddenly as a cliffside. Surprised by the unexpected amount of space, the horses stumbled slightly, spreading out as their riders looked ahead in disbelief.

The ruins of a great manor house stood before them. Perhaps once it was grand, ruling over all the land they had traversed, housing many people and striking awe in all who looked upon it. But now it was in great disrepair, the grey stone cracked and collapsing, the outer wings crumbled into the earth. The forest even seemed to reject it, forming a perfect circle around the property as if refusing to grow any closer. However, despite no trees growing within the circle, their ancient branches spread out and intertwined across the entire clearing, keeping it in eternal twilight.

"I think we found our evil lair," Milly choked out, voice unnaturally high. A deep frown etched lines into Christus' forehead.

"We certainly have. There is dark, forbidden magic here."

Garrett was glad he wasn't the only one who felt as if all the air had been sucked out of his lungs and replaced with ice.

"Leave the horses inside the tree ring," Christus continued, dismounting. Garrett did the same, although far less gracefully. As his boots hit the ground they sank slightly, the blackish moss that covered the ground cushioning his footfalls. Aslock had noticed as well, lifting a large boot and gingerly stepping back down onto it.

"Bad ground for fighting," he murmured, drawing nods of agreement from the others.

James and Milly collected the horses and led them back into the forest a bit, picketing them and making them as comfortable as possible before returning to the group. Garrett drew his bow, checking over the string and nocking an arrow, testing its draw to ensure all was as it should be. He then ensured that his long knives were still strapped inside his boots. Although he much preferred the bow, if worst came to worst (and, given what he was about to go up against, it likely would), he was handy enough with them to keep himself alive.

"James, eyes," Nadia said, nodding to a nearby tree. The man nodded, slinging his cloak over his shoulders to free up his arms and rapidly scaling it. Garrett quickly lost sight of him in the leaves, the only sign he was up there the occasional rustling of leaves and waving of branches.

"Damn squirrel, that man," Aslock commented from beside the hunter. "Climbs anything in sight. I once caught him running rooftops in Xerkas for the hell of it. Had the guards in a right tizzy, thinking he was trying to steal from the houses he climbed over, but he didn't take a single thing. He enjoyed the challenge of escaping the guards via rooftop."

Garrett nodded, lips quirked in a wry smile.

"I only hope his shooting is as good as his climbing," he replied.

"Better," Nadia assured him. "It's the one thing he takes seriously."

James reappeared on the lower branches of the tree. Winking at Nadia, he dismounted with an extravagant flip. It would have likely been more impressive if he had stuck the landing.

Instead, he landed, squished into the moss, and was sent tumbling to the ground face-first. An instant later he jumped back to his feet, as if electrocuted, sputtering and pawing at his face with an expression of horror.

"James," Milly darted to his side, trying to keep his hands from covering his face. "What's wrong? Are you okay?"

Slowly James removed his hands from covering his face. Aside from the little bits of moss, it was covered in a thin, orange-red liquid that was smeared everywhere from his attempts to remove it. The next thing he said confirmed what they had been dreading.

"Blood…"

Feeling his stomach turn, Garrett looked back down at the moss he stood on. His feet, having sunk a good two inches into the plants, created a dip, and liquid was slowly pooling around his boots.

"Let's finish this," Garrett declared in a low voice, disgusted as he realized just how much blood must be saturating the clearing. Even mixed with water, as he assumed it was, it was an enormous amount.

"Aye. Time to bring this to an end," Christus agreed.

"Did you see anything, James?"

James shook his head. "As dead as the forest."

Drawing their weapons, they moved towards the ruined manor as though they had been fighting together for years.

Garrett, bow drawn, felt like his heart was going to either stop or explode. Adrenaline replaced the blood in his veins, making his fingertips tingle as his ears rang with the strain of trying to hear anything that would give him an advantage over the enemy. As they stepped onto the overgrown path leading up to the surprisingly intact double doors, he caught something out of the corner of his eye.

"There!" he hissed, the others stopping immediately. "Top-right window. Something moved, I'm sure of it."

He hesitated then, unsure if they would disregard him, citing nerves or imagining things. But instead, Christus nodded solemnly.

"Nadia, watch front."

The armored woman nodded, hefting her shield a little higher.

"Aslock, left. I'll watch right. James, keep an eye on our rear, look for vantage points for you to shoot from. Garrett, with me."

Garrett nodded, feeling superfluous to their well-oiled unit, but determined to do his best regardless.

They made their way up the steps onto the porch around the door. The roof that used to cover the porch was long gone, the pillars that once held it up collapsed and broken.

"How do you want to enter?" Nadia asked, pausing at the door.

"They already know we're here," Garrett offered, and Christus nodded in agreement.

"No need for stealth, then."

Nadia nodded, and with a crash she booted the doors open, sending them swinging back with such force that one snapped off its upper hinge.

"Oh...oh, gods," Milly muttered, one hand clapped over her mouth. The doors revealed a small entry room and a long hallway. Paint peeled from the corners, the wainscoting badly damaged, weather-stained, or completely gone. Dust and cobwebs pervaded the interior, but what made every single adventurer's heart stop for a moment was what was on the walls. And floors. And ceilings.

Sigils, dark signs, notations in a language unknown to any of them, were painted everywhere. And, as they had come to expect, it was all in blood.

"Well, we're definitely in the right place," Nadia quipped dryly. "One rogue blood sorcerer, at your service."

"But where is the bastard?" Christus wondered aloud. "Let's move in."

Nadia raised her shield and they entered the house, leaving the doors still swinging slightly behind them.

They made their way down the hallway, Garrett shivering as a pair of eyes painted onto the wall seemed to follow him. The hallway opened into a medium-sized room, a grand staircase in front of them, banisters still mostly intact, although the stairs were badly warped. Half a chandelier hung two stories above them, the crystals long dulled and broken, wax marking much of it. Doors lay both to their left and their right, although the right-hand one was cracked open ever so slightly.

Christus silently gestured to it, Nadia nodding as she moved towards it. Each step they took caused the house to creak and groan like an old man's bones. The lead adventurer nudged the door open, all of them bracing for what may be behind it. But nothing moved, and so they advanced.

Garrett felt his face drain of blood as he entered the room behind Nadia. Scattered around the tatters of finery were bodies. Predators of the forest, creatures he had never seen or heard of before, monsters with their faces twisted in rage, eyes dead and bodies lifeless lay in every corner, draped over rotten chairs and even curled beside the empty marble fireplace. A quick inspection confirmed what Garrett and the others all suspected. Each body, from the smallest rat to the largest ithazar, was drained of every drop of blood. James was the last to enter, an expression of disgust crossing his face as he observed the contents of the room.

"What in the Nether..." he cut himself off, nose wrinkling. "Do you lot smell that?"

"Smell what?" Garrett asked, sniffing a few times.

"Exactly. We're in a room full of dead bodies, but all I can smell is dust, wood, and some spice or herb."

"No rotting bodies," Christus confirmed.

James took another step into the room, and as he did the door slammed shut behind him, shaking the entire house.

"Did... you do that?" Garrett asked. James turned from staring wide-eyed at the door, and shook his head.

Their attention was jerked to the other side of the room as a fire roared to life in the fireplace. The sconces around the room lit as well, until the large room burned with light, despite there being no fuel they could see.

"I think this is our welcome," Nadia said, circling slowly as her eyes darted around the room, searching for threats. She gripped her mace until her knuckles turned white.

"*Pfft*, some welcome," James mocked, crossing his arms. "A few dumb magic tricks—"

A low growl behind him cut him off.

Garrett raised his eyes to see the ithazar, a massive creature with the torso of a human attached in a centaur-like manner to the body of a spider, jerk to life, its eyes a solid crimson.

"You just *had* to say something, didn't you," Nadia muttered at James, leaping beside him and raising her shield just in time to block one of the ithazar's mandibles from slamming into James' neck.

"I'm sorry!" he squeaked, eyes wide as he fumbled for a moment with his bow. "It's not my fault we're in the house of a crazy sorcerer!"

Before he could spin and attack the ithazar, an arrow sprouted from its eye.

"I didn't do that," James said, confused.

"You're right," Garrett replied, already nocking another arrow. "It's not your fault we're here. It's mine, and now I'm going to make sure we get out, too."

"Good man," Christus praised, and the six drew into a circle as the rest of the room, quite literally, came to life.

The ithazar, although disoriented, still gathered itself to attack.

"The eyes!" Garrett called to the rest of them, remembering his fight against the lynx. "Go for the eyes!"

Although there was no verbal response an air of agreement washed over the group, and Garrett landed his second shot, felling the ithazar.

Another creature rose up in its place, this one towering over the hunter, mangy white fur covering its obscenely skinny body. It slouched over him, baring a row of deadly-sharp teeth.

"What in the Nether?" Garrett exclaimed, dodging as it struck out at him with long claws.

"Kralle!" Milly shouted, dispatching the large wolf she was battling and darting around in time to incapacitate the arm with which the monster was about to strike.

"Their claws are lethal—you can't let them touch you. Quick!"

Maneuvering her knives into position she twisted them into the shoulder muscles of the creature, breaking its concentration for a moment. Rapidly drawing his bow Garrett launched two arrows in quick succession, and the kralle dropped to his feet.

"Nice job," the younger girl commented, before dancing away to take on a giant ape pack that was giving Aslock some trouble. As his massive sword wasn't very good with precision piercing, he was electing to simply lop the heads off his enemies.

Garrett turned, and was relieved to see an enemy he was familiar with facing him. Although, most days, he would never wish to fight an angry sabretooth tiger, it was a relief to battle something he at least knew the name of. Grinning fiercely as he began to ease into the routine of combat, Garrett slid his bow into the quiver on his back and drew his knives. As he did so, the *woosh* of an arrow sped past his ear, the fletching tickling the skin as it drove home into one of the sabretooth's eyes.

"Figured I'd give a hand, or eye, as it were," James declared, before turning to parry a bite attack from a horrific, floating mass of reddish flesh. He darted around it, and the stalks that held the creature's eyes rotated to follow. However, it seemed to have trouble following his movements; by the time it turned to face him in one position, he was in another.

"Heh, Urlocks. Can't handle anything quicker than an old woman," the archer laughed, then called to his friend. "Christus!"

James dashed a short distance away, out of range of the monster's pincer-like arms. "Have a gift for you!"

Christus dispatched a possessed bear and turned, nodding his ready. With a wide smile, James launched himself at the confused urlock, shoving it into the waiting sword of his leader, who cleanly separated all its eyes from their stalks. The urlock immediately collapsed to the ground with a disgusting *squelch*.

Garrett turned back to his own foe, which had finally managed to snap the arrow shaft off after much pawing at its face. Tumbling to the left to avoid a swipe of its massive paw, he took a fistful of the sabretooth's ear and pulled sharply. With that, Garrett sank his knife into its other eye, letting it fall to the floor and pulling out the blade.

"How're we doing?" he wondered aloud, shaking the blood off his knife. While the lynx had bled a lot, these creatures seemed to have no blood except in their eyes. Garrett assumed it was a difference in the magic used to control the creatures. Whatever it was, at least the floor was not yet too slippery from the fighting here.

In answer to his question, he watched Milly and James team up on what appeared to be the last reanimated creature standing. The monster stood six-and-a-half-feet tall, covered in a greyish-white fur. It swung at them with powerful fists, but the agile fighters easily avoided its attacks. Near simultaneously, James landed an arrow in one of its eyes while Milly, who was clinging to its back like a spider monkey, stabbed its other eye. As it fell she jumped, landing clear of the creature, and the two high-fived.

"No problem," James said, a confident smirk on his face.

"Easy," Milly agreed.

"Hardly a challenge!" Aslock bellowed happily from across the room, where a pile of bodies and heads surrounded him.

"Hold up on the celebration," Christus said, exchanging a look with Garrett.

"He's right," Garrett continued. "We haven't killed the mage yet."

As if on cue, a scream grew in volume, climaxing as a blast of red fire appeared about five feet above the fireplace. The fire died out instantly, leaving behind a deformed, twisted figure of what may have at one point been a man. Once-blond hair hung in matted strings around its face, its pale skin stained to a rusty brown where visible. All over its arms, legs, and torso were open wounds, its skin sliced and cut so it seemed made more of cuts than skin. Blood flowed from each of the wounds, but not in such a way as one would expect from any sort of injury. Instead, the tendrils of crimson twisted and writhed around the body like a hundred crimson strings, levitating in the air.

As it looked down at the group they could see its red eyes burning with anger, as if it had taken the rage and life from every creature it had killed and absorbed it. Garrett felt his stomach turn as he looked in to the creature's eyes, studying it. The features, mangled though they were, were familiar to him.

Before them was the husk of the tutor who had abandoned their village.

It was then the blood sorcerer spoke, its voice a genderless screech of dark languages long-forgotten by people this side of Zhembium. Its mouth was deformed with thin, bloodless lips that stretched nearly the entirety of its face, and did nothing to cover its hundreds of tiny pointed teeth.

"Well, here's our chance," Garrett said, transfixed, barely able to breathe around the knot of fear in his throat. Dropping his knives to his feet, he drew his bow. The group took a collective breath, ignoring whatever scratches or bruises they had accumulated from their previous fights and, as one, launched themselves at the evil mage.

Aslock, having been closest to the fireplace, was first to reach the mage. With a deafening roar he swung his sword at it, the great reach enough to slice the figure from stem to stern. However, moments before the blade would have made contact, the blood tendrils floating around the mage circled around him, forming a chrysalis-like shell that sent Maturin bouncing off and slamming into the wooden floor, cutting into the floorboards a good six inches.

"What in Jarak's name…" James and Garrett exchanged a look, each running to separate sides of the room and drawing their bows.

"Now!" Garrett called, and they launched a few arrows each at the mage. However, the mage snatched each arrow out of the air with the blood surrounding him.

Screeching in anger, it sent the arrows whizzing back at their original owners. James and Garrett barely had time to dodge the razor-sharp missiles.

"All together!" Christus called. "On my count!"

Milly spun her knives, baring her teeth like an angered beast, every muscle in her lithe frame primed and ready to fight. Raising her shield, Nadia flipped her mace once, the most showmanship Garrett had seen from her the entire fight.

"One!"

Aslock finally freed Maturin from the floorboards, hefting the great-sword back into a fighting stance.

"Two!"

Garrett nocked two arrows, hoping at least one would hit his mark.

"You have the range covered?" James asked.

Confused, Garrett nodded. James then sheathed his bow and set it aside, drawing a strange, curved blade that the hunter hadn't seen before.

"Picked this beauty up in a gambling match with some traders," James said, rolling his neck. "I've been wanting to try it out."

"Three!" Christus yelled, and the six of them leapt forward as one entity. The mage screamed in anger, and its bloody tendrils sharpened to a hundred blades. Christus sliced through three which were trying to attack him from the right, but they simply reformed. Several tendrils came together to form a thick sword that jabbed and sliced at Aslock, who was forced to dance around and attempt to parry the much quicker blade. Unable to reach most of the mage due to its floating position Nadia moved with Milly, shielding the younger girl as she darted in and out of cover, slicing apart tendrils that were about to flank her teammates or attempting to cut the mage itself, although she never got close enough. Shouting something about elf maidens James launched himself straight at the mage's chest, but his powerful thrust was met with an immovable shield. Garrett loosed arrow after arrow, and although they hit the mage until his entire left side was as bristled as a porcupine, it didn't seem to make any difference.

Breathing heavily he looked over to Milly and Nadia, who were crouched behind the latter's shield, conferring. Nodding in agreement Milly backed up, while Nadia swung her mace at a few encroaching tendrils.

"Now, Nadia!" Milly yelled. Nadia instantly dropped to a knee, shield above her head as she braced herself. Quick as a striking snake, Milly darted from her position against the room's wall to Nadia. Planting one foot on the shield, she launched into the air with a war cry. Brandishing both knives in an aggressive underhand grip, she flew at the mage. The others had caught on only moments before and redoubled their efforts to attack on the opposite side, attempting to split the mage's attention. However, it caught sight of Milly and pulled all the tendrils in towards itself. Instead of shielding, though, the blood began spinning in a sickening crimson whirlpool. Just as Milly was about to connect it exploded outwards, slamming the girl against the wall, where she promptly crumpled to the floor.

"Milly!" Nadia screamed, racing over to her and covering her with her shield. Aslock and James fell silent, rage lighting their expressions as they continued fighting towards the mage. Christus, however, broke away from the fighting for a moment, making his way to Garrett's side.

"We can't defeat it," Garrett said in hopeless wonder, watching as James took a nasty cut to his ribs.

"Not like this," Christus panted. "Listen, Garrett. Sorcerers have an ancient practice, or had, of creating an altar or shrine somewhere in their home from which to draw their power. It's... well, it's possible there's one here, although I wouldn't count on it. You need to search the house, if this monster has one, then destroy the shrine. It's the only way we have a chance."

Garrett nodded, setting his bow and quiver in the corner in case James needed more arrows. Racing for the door, he only stopped long enough to swipe his knives up from where he had dropped them. Behind him he caught sight of Milly standing shakily, waving away Christus' offered hand, anger sweeping her visage as she glared at the mage. As he wrenched the door open, the mage turned and stared at him with the fury of a thousand suns. Not willing to stop, Garrett threw himself through the doorway. Not a moment too soon, too, as it slammed behind him so quickly it caught a corner of his tunic. The sounds of battle instantly faded, leaving the hunter's ears ringing.

Easily slicing through the fabric caught in the door, Garrett sped into the room across the landing. It was the remains of a kitchen, although any food had long since rotted away. No sign of any altar or shrine presented itself, and he was about to leave when he noticed a concealed door in the corner. When the manor was in its prime it would have been perfectly hidden, blended in with the use of paint and wallpaper, but with the way the house was now it was obvious enough. Garrett crossed the room and wrenched open the door, coughing as soon as he did so. The smell of spice that had been present in the living room wafted up a narrow stairway to him.

"Seems like the right track," Garrett muttered, turning sideways and rapidly descending the steep stairs.

He was right. As he laid foot on the packed dirt floor of what was once a root cellar, he saw it.

A massive stone block, every inch painted over with tiny sigils, sat in the center of the room. A shallow bowl was carved into the middle of the block, with individual human vertebra encircling it. Two skulls flanked the bowl, each holding a lit red wax candle, bundles of herbs in their mouths. But it was the figure slouched over the shrine that caused Garrett to pause. He hadn't known her well, but he was still sideswiped by a wave of emotion when he recognized the girl who had disappeared with the tutor.

However, his friends were fighting for their lives upstairs, and so without further ado he shoved the body off the shrine. Next to go were the skulls, smashed to bits and candles stomped out. Then the vertebra were swept off the shrine. Lastly, Garrett spat onto a bit of fabric sliced from his already-ruined tunic and smeared the sigils.

Deciding there was nothing to be done about the massive block of stone, he turned and sprinted upstairs. Expecting great resistance, he slammed into the door. Instead of having to force it open, he found it swung open easily at his touch, and so he ended up racing straight through the doorway and slipping on the floor, slamming into the other wall fairly hard.

He blinked once, twice, and took in the room.

Blood covered everything like someone had set off a bomb of it. Panic stopping his heart, he swept his head left and right, counting the drenched figures.

"One, two, three, four... Who's missing?"

He didn't even have to ask. The others traded glances, as if begging the other to speak. Then, silently, Nadia tensed and pulled her shield aside with effort. Beneath it lay a tiny, crumpled form soaked in blood. She seemed so much smaller now she wasn't moving, bouncing around and spitting witty quips.

"I wasn't... quick enough..." Nadia choked, looking down at Milly's body.

Christus moved next to her, a hand on her shoulder turning into a gentle hug as she leant into his chest, sobbing. "It wasn't your fault," he murmured, stroking her hair softly. "She was already injured, and we've never fought anything like this before."

Garrett blinked, surprised by two fat teardrops rolling down his cheeks and dripping off his jawline. Raising his hand as if in a dream, he touched the wet skin and watched the teardrops melt into the half-dried blood already on his fingertips. Cotton filled his ears; the only sound he could make out was the blood rushing through his veins. Somewhere to his right Aslock slammed his fist into the wall, shattering bone and wood alike.

"It's gone?" he turned to Christus, who seemed to know the most about these things. The man attempted to wipe blood off his face, but only succeeded in moving it around, as he also had blood coating his hand.

"It should be, aye. You destroyed its source of power. This sorcerer was so far gone he had bound his soul to his sigils. We should torch the house, though, just to be sure."

"I, for one, vote we first get the hell out of here and find the nearest water source to pollute so we can clean up," James suggested, shoulders slouched.

"Not with her in it," Aslock growled. Kneeling slowly, he scooped up Milly's small, broken body, turning her into a tiny doll in his massive arms.

"A funeral pyre is how we traditionally bury our dead," Christus prompted, but the large man just cradled her closer to his chest, tears streaking down his cheeks as he sobbed silently. "Not here, not in this evil place. She deserves sunlight and flowers; she deserves to be laid to rest beneath a beautiful sky, watched over by trees that birds build their nests in. Not a pyre made of corrupted wood, soaked in her own blood, surrounded by evil magic."

The others nodded, and together they exited the house.

It didn't take long for the somber group to find a water source, as James and Milly had picketed the horses near Aeth Lake. Shedding weapons and armor as they walked, the five began to run as soon as they saw the lake, diving in as if scrubbing away the blood staining their skin would scrub away the reality of what happened. Even once they had finished cleaning themselves they waited in silence as Nadia washed Milly clean, running her fingers through her hair as it floated in the lake, saying goodbye. As she finished, she bent and placed a soft kiss on the girl's forehead.

They returned to the house, each carrying a large armload of kindling. Aslock, ever prepared, produced a massive jug of clear alcohol that gave Garrett a headache just smelling it from a foot away.

"I made this a while back," the large man explained, soaking the kindling, "but no one would drink it, so we may as well use it for this."

After the kindling was laid upon every side of the house, Christus came forward with a torch he had lit off Nadia's campfire near the edge of the clearing.

"Would you like to do the honors?" he asked, holding it out to Garrett. The hunter felt a proud smile cross his face, nodding. Taking hold of the torch he walked forward, the rest watching in silence as he lowered it to the soaked kindling. It took the fire easily, spreading in a flash.

Garrett tossed the torch into the inferno, stepping back as he watched the flames crawl up the walls. He then turned and walked back to the group at the edge of the woods. Together, they sat and watched the house burn in weighted silence. The rotted wood didn't take long to crumble into the flames, and the moss made a good, wet fire barrier to the rest of the forest. Soon, they all knew it was time to return home. On the way back to the horses James passed Garrett his bow and quiver, which were only mildly bloodstained.

"I take it yours was totally destroyed?" Garrett asked. James shrugged. "I needed a bigger one anyway. Gotta have a bow to match these," he declared, flexing his arms. Nadia snorted in the background, covering it up with a cough, and although she had a shadow of a smile on her lips her eyes were still wet with tears.

The party mounted up and began making their way back to Sonarus. They hadn't ridden for more than a few minutes when Garrett noticed something.

"Stop," he called to the others. They pulled up their horses, looking at him in confusion.

Garrett tapped a finger to his ear. "Listen."

They did, and as each realized what he was talking about small smiles grew on their faces.

Birds twittered to each other from the branches, flitting back to whatever home they had before magic had infected their forest. A squirrel chittered at the mounted group, as if telling them to move along and get out of his woods.

They continued riding then, occasionally pointing out some form of life. Soon they were passing Aeth Lake where Garrett had originally tried to hunt at only a few days ago, although it seemed an eternity to him now. A deer raised its head, its eyes a clear black, unaffected by any evil.

As the sun kissed the western horizon, they broke past the tree line and onto the road, the village's smokestacks visible in the near distance.

"Well, friends," Christus said as they passed the first outlying farm, "it was an honor."

"Aye, that it was," Aslock agreed.

"I honestly don't know how I can ever repay any of you," Garrett said. "You risked your lives for me today. And it's my fault—"

"Nonsense," Christus cut him off, pulling his horse to a stop and turning to look at the hunter. "We are adventurers, Garrett. These sort of undertakings, these battles and hunts, these are what we live for. And we all know the risks."

The rest of his group murmured in agreement.

"You needed help," Christus continued. "Not only that, but you weren't even doing it for yourself. You were willing to put your life on the line for your family, your village. There is no better reason to fight."

With that, he motioned for Garrett to take the lead of their little band, and they rode into the village square.

A few quiet days later Christus and his band were bustling around early, collapsing tents and packing wagons. Garrett had risen with the sun, and stood near the edge of the hustle and bustle, watching.

"You're leaving," he stated as Christus approached.

"Aye. It's time we move on," Christus replied.

"Will you be back?"

"Perhaps..."

The two looked out across the people. On the other edge of the clearing Nadia was kneeling in a group of children, smiling and talking to them.

"It's the first time I've seen her smile since Milly," Christus said. Garrett nodded, watching Terra giggle over something Nadia said. Then, throwing her arms around her neck, Terra hugged her.

"She's good with the children."

"Always has been. Never had any of her own, always adventuring with and taking care of Milly."

They stood in silence for another minute.

"You know, Nadia's been across the country a few times. I'm sure she'd be able to teach the children a thing or two. And you wouldn't need to pay her as much as you would an out of town tutor."

"You're not wrong..." Garrett considered. "She'd be welcome, that's for sure."

"Aye. On the road there's too much time to think, but here she can stay busy. She can have a life. And who knows... you seem to have a knack for finding adventure. Maybe you two can save another village or two."

Christus pulled Garrett into a hug for a moment.

"I'll see you around," Garrett murmured.

"Aye, stay safe," Christus replied, a small, sad quirk to his lips. Garrett nodded, and they parted ways.

An unfamiliar dark-skinned man cleared his throat from the wall on which he leaned, a few feet away. Garrett glanced him over, assuming he was a part of Christus' group. The man was dressed in colorful silks, and a wicked sabre hung from his hip. The hilt of the sabre had a sigil of two crossed swords on it.

"Can I help you?"

The man pushed himself off the wall, strolling over with his hands in his pockets.

"Yeah, Garrett Tyrus. I believe you can," the man answered in a deep voice that was hard to understand.

He grinned, and Garrett felt a chill in the air. The man did not seem threatening, but something about him felt like a herald of change.

"My name is Ismail. A mutual friend sent me to speak with you. You're a man of many talents, and I'm part of a group that could help you make good use of those talents. I wasn't sure, but now I've heard of what you did at the manor...the Valons could use you."

Garrett's stomach twisted.

"I didn't do anything at the manor but get an innocent woman killed."

"You saved an entire village from being overtaken by a blood mage," the man insisted. "Think about it, yes?"

"Aye... I'll think about it," Garrett said, unsure.

Ismail started to walk away, then paused and turned back around, drawing a hand out of his pocket. "There's good money in it."

He tossed a jingling pouch at Garrett, who caught it automatically, the weight settling into his palm.

"A thank-you. For hearing me out."

He turned around again, but Garrett called after him.

"Wait! Who's the mutual friend?" He could think of no one who would associate with the Valons.

Ismail smirked.

"Her name's Alaya."

Fairy Trail

By Richard A. Knaak

733AM
Age of the Dracon-esti

The three mercenaries were an odd lot, with but one thing truly in common. They had all been part of a failed campaign. Only the chaos following the debacle that had been the losing army's grand charge had enabled them to depart the field fairly intact, once the overconfident Duke Idros had been decapitated by his rival's ax.

The human, dwarf, and minotaur rode side by side into the small village. The gray-haired dwarf, who prided himself on having not only collected maps of nearly all the known lands but also having memorized most of them, shook his head.

"We've already left Rast three days behind, and the mountains are just another two away! There's nothing listed here! I would know it!"

"Hardly a surprise, Gidrin," remarked the human, a lean, clean-shaven figure with two jagged scars on his right cheek. "Not much to look at." He sniffed. "Just so long as they have something that passes for a tavern or inn, eh,

Streit?"

The tan minotaur grunted. Well over nine-feet tall, he rode one of the massive steeds bred in his native Bolan. The horse itself was twice as large as the capable mounts of either the dwarf or the human. "So long as it isn't any of that swill the duke passed out before the battle."

"Oh, it wasn't the worst thing we've drunk."

The huge head turned, the yard-long horns with their so very sharp points directly facing the man. "Don't remind me about that, Herid. Don't ever remind me."

"Was it my fault that you—"

"Yes. It was." Streit snorted as he sniffed the air. "Although, from the smell of this place, we may find a new contender."

"Don't know what you're talking about," the dwarf muttered. "Not so bad here."

The minotaur and the human eyed one another, but said nothing more. The trio entered the dank village.

"Mud seems a common decorative feature here," Herid commented. "We should fit right in by this time."

"Hush, lad." The dwarf peered around. "No damned sign anywhere. Nothing to announce where we are."

"Would you announce this place?"

Streit grunted his agreement with Herid. Gidrin, not having a good counterargument, simply shrugged.

Not at all to their surprise, several villagers paused to stare at them. Herid grinned and nodded at several, including a passable young female. Under heavy brow, the minotaur's eyes darted back and forth, analyzing every potential threat.

"Still don't know why I can't place this village," muttered Gidrin. Finally exasperated, he gestured with one mailed hand at a pasty-faced youth. "You, there! What's this blot called?"

"Easy, Gidrin," murmured Herid.

"I just want to know! Well, lad?"

"P-Prebel, sir!"

"Prebel. Prebel. Prebel. Nope! It can't be. There's nothing on any of my maps called Prebel."

"Maybe it was built after your map, dwarf," Herid remarked sarcastically. "Of course, it can be. Just leave it."

"Need a new map..." the squat figure grumbled. "Must be one around here. Aye, that'll make up for it."

"Is there an inn here?" Herid asked the boy.

"Yes, yes! That way. Straight as you're going, sir!"

Herid nodded his thanks, then made a shooing motion with his hand. The youth scurried off.

They continued in silence until they came across the first wooden structure that stood more than a single story. A faded sign read Naylon's Folly Inn.

"Strange name for an inn," Streit muttered.

Herid nodded. "Maybe Naylon built the place."

"Or stayed there."

"Not like we've a choice, lads," the dwarf interjected. "After five months in the field, looks good enough for our needs this night while we figure out our next move."

"The next move is to stay in the south for a little while, until things clear up back north," the human remarked. "They didn't see any difference between loyalists and mercenaries. You saw them round up Orak and his bunch."

"Aye." That brought renewed silence to the trio. The other band of mercenaries had been forced to their knees and executed along with the duke's regular men, instead of being offered the chance to sell their services to the victors.

They pulled up in front of the inn. Herid and the minotaur dismounted while Gidrin took the reins of his companions' steeds. The human and Streit then proceeded inside.

Inside, a balding man who looked to Herid to be the proprietor behind a worn wooden counter gaped at the pair, and especially at Streit as the gargantuan fighter maneuvered his horned head through the doorway. Herid nodded as the two mercenaries approached the man.

"Good evening! It looks like you should have a room or two, I believe."

"A room?"

"Yes, a place to sleep. Probably upstairs where all those windows are."

The bald man recovered. "Ah! Yes. Yes, there are some rooms."

Herid retrieved some coins from a pouch hanging on his belt. He eyed the money. "How much for the night?"

Still staring at Streit, the proprietor blurted a price. Herid counted out the right coins, then set them on the counter. "We'll need a meal, too."

"Got some mutton and potatoes today," the other human answered as he scooped up the coins.

"No beef?" rumbled Streit. "I'm so hungry I could eat a whole side."

"Beef?" The proprietor gaped again. "But you're a—I mean you look like—"

The minotaur's brow furrowed. "Like what?"

"N-Nothing. Only mutton today. My apologies!"

"That'll do just fine," interjected Herid. "Won't it, Streit?"

"Sure."

"Let me see to that room." The bald man scurried away.

"I hate mutton," Streit muttered. "And why would he think I wouldn't want a good haunch of beef?"

The other mercenary kept his expression neutral. "I

have no idea."

The minotaur eyed him suspiciously, then looked up as the proprietor returned.

"You're in luck! There's one room that will serve all of you."

"That's fine. Streit, go help Gidrin. I'll check out the room with—are you Naylon?"

"Me? Naylon?" The other man laughed nervously, then touched his forehead twice with his index finger before doing the same over his heart. "No, I'm Riam, just like my father and grandfather! Praise be, Naylon's been dead for nearly two hundred years! Roundly defeated and slain by an alliance of men and dwarves determined to keep his ambitions from expanding! You've not heard of him?"

"No. A warlord, was he?"

"Worse! A wizard gone dark. Created a sanctum in the mountains yonder. Took much tribute from all around until he overstepped. He and those who served him were slaughtered in one great battle."

"Tribute?" Herid repeated, suddenly far more interested. "Treasure? Is that what you mean?"

Streit, nearly at the door, paused to look back. His ears were perked with interest.

"Oh, yes." Riam warmed to the subject. "Quite a lot, the legends say! Gathered from miles around! Most of it never found by those who took him down...and, of course, the fairy is said to be protecting it."

"A fairy'?" Streit asked. "A fairy guardian? Someone chose a fairy to guard their treasure?"

"Yes! Oh, yes!"

Streit and Herid looked at one another in disbelief. "A fairy," the minotaur said again. He fixed his gaze on Riam once more. "Gossamer wings. Flutters about like a huge butterfly. That sort of fairy?"

"Well, they're magical, too," Riam countered.

The horned fighter snorted. "Seen fairy magic. Seen a lot stronger."

The proprietor shrugged. "'Tis what my father told me, and his father told him. We're not folks comfortable around magic."

"So, no one's been there recently?" Herid asked.

"Nay! Besides, there's wolves and we're not warriors here, either." Riam frowned. "I must return to my work very soon. Will you see the room?"

Herid secretly winked at the minotaur, who silently turned and left. The human mercenary joined Riam. "Lead on! Oh, and while I think of it, we've depleted our supplies and still have a long journey ahead…"

*****

"So, finally found a map!" Gidrin declared triumphantly.

"Be sure to shout a little louder," Streit growled. "I don't think they heard you back in Bolan."

"Hmmph!" The dwarf spread it over the small table in the room, leaving only space for the candle that struggled to light the immediate surroundings. Besides the table, the room had two old chairs and three cots. The cots had proven too small for Streit, so now three blankets stretched across one side. None of the mercenaries had slept much, though, anticipation of a new course now driving them.

Herid touched a point on the map. "That where we are now?"

"Aye. There's Rast up there, and some old mines here."

"Is that a trail there?"

"From the mining days. Dwarven mines. Very old."

Streit leaned over them. "We do not even know where this dead wizard's abode is supposed to be."

The human nodded. "But the mines are older than his presence. Maybe his followers made use of them. Would make sense."

"What about this fairy? Does not seem like much of a problem. Why have none of these humans here gone after the treasure, magic or not? They cannot be that cowardly, can they?"

Gidrin tugged on his beard. "I already asked that of the old man I got this map from. The wizard's time has made them all shy from any magic since. Was a terrible period, apparently. Like a dog burned, you know?"

The minotaur snorted.

Herid grimaced. "Another good reason why there'll always eventually be work for mercenaries." He looked at his companions. "So, we're doing this? It's worth it? Streit?"

"You have to ask?"

Herid looked from the minotaur to the dwarf. "Gidrin."

"I side with Streit. We've now got the supplies and the map. We're all more comfortable outside than in here, right? Not worse than any of the mad causes we were paid to fight for, especially the last one."

"It's settled, then." Herid straightened. "Roll up the map."

Long used to keeping their gear ready for quick travel, it took only a few moments for the trio to depart the inn. The downstairs was dark and quiet, Riam having retired hours before.

Retrieving their mounts, they rode through the village in the direction of the mountains. Despite the absolute stillness surrounding them, the mercenaries kept an eye out for anyone who might notice their departure. Three riders heading into the desolation where the treasure of a dead wizard was rumored to be might attract a few unwanted followers hoping to benefit. However, once the three entered the mountains, it would be easy for them to lose those who could be on their trail.

"Too quiet here," Streit muttered. "And all the windows are shuttered tight."

"The stables weren't so shuttered," the dwarf replied. "Our horses were right there waiting for us."

"Just waiting for us," Herid repeated. "So, we're being set up for something. Are we agreed?"

Both Gidrin and the minotaur grunted in the affirmative. Although their postures were casual, all three already had their hands near enough to their weapons should trouble start. The mercenaries rode as if unconcerned, all the way to the edge of the village and then beyond, but even then they did not actually relax.

"Not one sound. Not one light. They've definitely got everything sealed too tight," Herid whispered.

What now?" asked Streit. "We do not go on like we planned, do we?"

"Not bloody likely." Gidrin peered into the darkness. "Looks like the whole wizard tale is probably just that. A tale. All to get us out. Work on our greed."

The human nodded. "And we did just like they wanted. We'd better head back the way we came to get here before—"

He stopped as a peculiar sound made all three mercenaries stiffen.

Streit peered around. "Was that a bird? It came from above, but it did not sound like a bird's wings flapping."

"Pretty large bird, if it was," the dwarf countered. "Pretty large for anything flying."

The sound repeated, this time from directly above.

With a swift motion, the minotaur unslung his ax and thrust the pointed tip skyward.

The sound shifted location, growing fainter in the process.

"What is that?" Streit growled in growing frustration. "Herid, you see it that time?"

The other mercenary already had his sword out. "No. Gidrin? What about you?"

"No, lad." The dwarf tugged a huge mace with a crowned head from the side of the saddle. "Don't rightly care. Just make sure one of us gets a good whack at it."

Fluttering filled the darkness above, the sound coming from several directions.

As the three mercenaries searched for the cause, they also had to struggle with their mounts. The horses, even more uneasy about the situation than their riders, fought the reins. That, in turn, forced the mercenaries to take their attention off the sky for several moments at a time.

Something dove at Herid. Something much larger than any bird any of the trio had ever come across before.

"Gah!" A face that had surely once been beautiful but now was scarred by rotting flesh, black eyes, and sharp, bared teeth made the human momentarily recoil. In doing so, he left his shoulders unprotected.

"Look out!" warned Gidrin, thrusting at the air near his human comrade.

"Hmm?" Herid started to turn—and four clawed hands grabbed him by the shoulders, easily lifting him from the saddle. The human thrust at one of the two winged figures carrying him, but while the sword penetrated deep into one, it did nothing at all to wound or even slow the foul creature.

Managing to gain some control over his horse, Streit used his great height to try to grab for his comrade. He snagged Herid's boot, and for a moment halted his upward rise.

Talons abruptly sought the minotaur's eyes. Streit instinctively batted at them, in the process losing his grip on the boot.

Hollering, Herid faded into the night sky.

Gidrin swung at the creature hovering in front of Streit. The dwarf chopped through a leg, but what should have been a grievous wound only made the winged form fly out of reach, then follow the others carrying off Herid.

The minotaur and the dwarf did not hesitate, the pair urging their mounts to a full gallop despite the animals' earlier skittishness. Herid's steed instinctively followed the others.

"You still hear him?" Gidrin called.

"Yes! This way!" Streit answered, gesturing to his left. "He is shouting at the top of his lungs!"

"He'd better! It's the only hope he's got!"

The pair continued their pursuit of their kidnapped comrade, at the same time doing their best to guide their horses through the dark despite the mad pace. Both strained to hear Herid, who did his best to keep shouting.

The path began to work against the duo, though, slowing them at critical moments. Finally, just in the mountains, the minotaur and dwarf had to slow.

"You hear anything, dwarf? Anything?"

"Your ears are far better than mine, Streit; you know that, you ornery bull. If you can't hear Herid, then we've lost the lad."

The minotaur snorted. "Damned things had to have wings!"

"Well, they *are* fairies... or *were*."

"They stank like the grave! What sort of fairies are they?"

Gidrin pulled out a long pipe. As he filled it, he answered, "'Course they stink like the grave. Have you never heard of blight fairies?"

"I care little enough about fairies. What are blight ones? Do they dwell in refuse or something?"

"No, you fool. They're undead. Tortured, murdered fairies turned into obedient abominations by some forsaken necromancer—"

"Necromancer?" Streit snorted again. "So, you mean that this wizard the innkeeper spoke about—"

The dwarf lit his pipe. The glow was strong enough to illuminate the upper half of his face. "Yes, this 'wizard' was a necromancer, evidently, something the good Riam failed to mention, damn his soul."

"But the wizard—the necromancer—is dead."

"So are the fairies." Gidrin took another strong puff, which caused the contents to glow even brighter. The dwarf reached over to the other side and removed one of several scrolls set in a long but narrow open pouch. "Let's see."

He unrolled the map he had gotten in the village. Using the pipe to illuminate portions of it, Gidrin eyed the contents.

Streit shifted uneasily. "Gidrin?"

"I'm not doing this for my entertainment—here! I'd say we should go this way! It's the only logical choice."

Leaning toward the map, the minotaur rumbled, "That one mine there?"

"Aye. It makes the most sense! It's the direction they flew, and undead aren't exactly known for deviating much from the path ahead of them. Blight fairies aren't really independent, like some undead."

"I do not care about that. All that matters is that we catch up to them." Streit bared his teeth. "They are just fairies. They will not stand a chance. We will crush them."

"Aye, keep telling yourself that." Gidrin rolled up the map, then doused his pipe. "Let's get riding. Herid's going to be impatient to see us, I think."

They urged their mounts onward, heading deeper into the dark mountains.

*****

Herid opened his eyes, to find his world upside down.

No, not his world. *He* hung upside down, his ankles locked in bracelets hanging from the ceiling. His arms were bound behind him, preventing the mercenary from doing anything to immediately free himself. Undaunted, Herid instantly began trying to loosen his arms.

As he worked, he eyed his surroundings. A dim, crimson illumination just barely allowed him to see the rock chamber that someone had hewn out of a mountain. The room was of a fair size, with several long tables or benches lining the walls. Various objects lay on some of them, most unidentifiable from his position.

Herid stiffened. Standing next to one of the tables was a familiar figure. The undead fairy stared with hollow black eyes at the empty air ahead.

The human swallowed, then noticed that the creature paid no attention to him. Even when the mercenary's efforts jostled him and made the chains above shake, the undead fairy did nothing.

No longer concerned about the fairy, Herid cautiously continued his survey of the rest of the chamber. One table beyond the still undead had some odd but vaguely familiar shapes set atop it. For some reason, Herid could not take his eyes off them. He knew those rounded shapes, and knew that they were out of place where they were.

The mercenary squinted. Slowly, his eyes grew more

accustomed to the strange illumination.
    And then he saw the heads.
    There were five of them, all in various stages of decay. Herid could tell little more other than that one head on the right looked fairly fresh.
    He grimaced, the potential significance not lost on him.
    Then, ponderous footsteps echoed through the chamber. Herid glanced at the undead fairy, but the creature had not moved.
    The footsteps grew louder, nearer. Herid tried to wriggle loose from his bonds, but failed yet again.
    Then, a new glow materialized from the other end of the chamber, where the entrance was. The glow swelled, as whatever caused it clearly drew closer.
    Eyes narrowed to slits, the mercenary watched as what at first appeared a floating yellow crystal entered. A moment later, it became evident that the crystal lay on a tray or platform carried by a hulking figure.
    Herid gasped, a sound that he felt thundered in the otherwise quiet room. The figure paused just inside, seeming to stare at the captive.
    Seeming because Herid could now just make out the lack of any actual eyes…or other features as well. The face was essentially flat, and of stone. Indeed, the figure was made entirely of *stone*.
    Still bearing its unearthly burden, the golem started toward the mercenary.

*****

Streit and Gidrin rode as swiftly as the path permitted them, which for the most part meant not nearly as swiftly as they would have liked. There were no new shouts by their comrade, nor any hint of the blight fairies. The mood of both fighters had only gotten grimmer in that time.

The dwarf raised his hand. Both riders halted. Gidrin took his pipe out again, lit it, then retrieved the map. In the glow of the pipe, he surveyed the path left to them.

"Should be pretty near here. Hell, it *has* to be near here. There's nowhere else!"

Streit nodded. "Notice something? No sounds. Should there not be wolves howling or night birds? The innkeeper Riam mentioned wolves, at least."

"I'm not likely to put much stock in *anything* Riam said. Still, this silence makes perfect sense, eh? No good beast would stay near this area." Gidrin put away the map, then doused the pipe. "Give me a good clean war rather than facing some damned magic."

"My people traffic little in magic," the minotaur replied. "A sign of our superiority."

"Hmm," his companion returned noncommittally.

"I know there is a reason we have not started moving again. What is it?"

"Oh, just being a dwarf. Noticing those rocks there don't read right. They conflict with the map."

"What rocks?" Streit leaned toward the indicated direction. "You mean those black mounds there?"

In response, the bearded fighter dismounted and led his horse toward the rocks. After a reluctant pause, Streit did the same.

Gidrin handed the reins to his comrade, then began feeling the nearest stone. He tapped it twice before moving on to the second. There, he repeated the tapping.

The minotaur's ears twitched. "That does not sound right."

"No. I'd think not. Give me the reins to both beasts and see what you can do with this rock here."

"This one?"

"That'd be it. Lean on the left and shove as hard as you can. Don't hold back, eh?"

"Of course." With a grunt, Streit threw his shoulder against the spot. At first, he seemed to be fighting a losing battle, but then, with a low scraping sound, the stone began to move.

Gidrin watched the minotaur's efforts, then said, "That'd be enough."

Streit rejoined the dwarf. Both stared at the tunnel entrance now revealed.

"Think that will take us to him?" asked the horned warrior.

"Would seem an odd thing to cover up such an entrance unless it had something to do with our dead spellcaster. It's fairly close and, well, let's face it, our best and only chance."

Streit snorted. "What about the horses?"

"We can't take them with us. Not much out here, as we pointed out. We'll just find them a reasonable spot and come for them later."

"'Later...'" the minotaur repeated, with far less enthusiasm.

They dealt with the animals as planned then, with the dwarf and his sharper night vision in the lead, headed into the tunnel. The path was utterly dark, finally forcing even Gidrin to seek illumination.

As he completed lighting his pipe, a macabre sight caught the attention of both fighters. Two skeletons lay sprawled to one side, but that was not what surprised the pair so much.

It was the lack of a skull atop either set of remains.

"Well, that bodes even less well for Herid," Gidrin murmured. "Not good. Not good at all."

"All the more reason to get moving." The minotaur shoved on ahead, only to have Gidrin pull him back.

"I'll get us to him faster. You know that. You've got the sharp ears, but I've got the bright eyes."

Streit grunted then, with a reluctant nod, retreated behind the other again.

With one last glance at the skeletons, the dwarf led the way. However, they had barely gone a few yards when both noticed a change in their surroundings.

"Where is the light coming from?" asked the minotaur.

Despite having no torches, the pair could now see for several yards ahead at a time thanks to a low, silver illumination that seemed to stay just ahead of them. There was no discernible source for that light, though.

Gidrin went to one wall and leaned close. After a short study, he stepped back and muttered, "Phos rock. Of course! A strong, natural vein over here."

"And the other side?"

The dwarf went to the opposite wall and repeated his inspection. "More of the same. A very large and very rare vein. Looks like the necromancer made good use of it, maybe found a way to enhance it. Not very bright, but bright enough for our needs, eh?"

"I'll take it. Let's move."

They had barely resumed their trek when they came across yet another skeleton, this one also missing its skull. The skeleton had a few bits of clothing on that reminded Gidrin of the manner in which the villagers dressed. He mentioned it to Streit.

"We need to move faster," was the minotaur's only response.

Yet, as if they were caught in some macabre game, they were soon again facing three more sets of remains—all headless. Now, neither could deny what all this meant.

"Poor Herid. Let's pray we're not too late."

"These are definitely not villagers," Streit pointed out. "Most look like outsiders like us. Even some mercenaries."

"There's more to it than that, even. Look. This one's missing both arms. The one next to it has the ribcage ripped open. Then, there's all these missing heads."

The minotaur clutched his ax tightly. "I hate fairies, dead or alive."

A crackling sound behind the pair made them look over their shoulders.

"And I really hate undead in general," Streit added grimly, readjusting his grip on his ax.

Three skeletons moved slowly and relentlessly toward them. The very same skeletons they had passed only minutes before. One wielded a sword while the others simply stretched forth bony hands ending in long nails. That they had no skulls did not appear to be a hindrance; the undead moved with unerring focus toward the pair.

"Leave this to me." The minotaur made one last adjustment to his grip in order to compensate for the tunnel, then stepped forward to face the undead. With a bellow, Streit swung at the foremost.

The ax chopped into the ribcage, shattering bones and scattering them everywhere. The lower half staggered forward, only to be crushed to fragments by the next blow of the horned warrior's weapons.

Streit did not pause. The ax made short work of the second skeleton, chopping free the rib-cage and spine, then cutting the legs in half. The minotaur stepped atop the pile of fragments and used his weapon to shove the last skeleton against a wall. He then twisted the ax, contorting the skeleton until at last the stresses on the bones made nearly everything break. Streit then kicked the remaining parts to the floor.

The minotaur snorted his disdain, then turned to his companion.

"Mind your back!" Gidrin shouted, pointing with his mace.

Brow wrinkling, Streit turned—just in time to evade a pair of bony hands reaching for his throat. The minotaur brought the ax-head between his throat and the fingers and backed away.

What faced him now was not a new skeleton, but rather a hodgepodge of pieces from all three. Worse, a second skeleton reformed in the same manner.

"I *really* hate undead!" he growled.

"Get to me, Streit!" the dwarf ordered.

Risking a glance, the minotaur saw the reason for the second warning. Gidrin now faced the skeletons they had just discovered.

"Whatever spell is on them must have activated when we got this far," Streit called.

"Aye!" Gidrin crushed a ribcage with his mace. "And it's also making them rebuild faster and faster!"

Sure enough, everything the two fighters had damaged had already begun rearranging into new bony shapes. Scowling, Streit grabbed one of those attacking his comrade from behind and threw it into the trio closing in on him again. The force of the collision scattered several pieces again, giving the minotaur the opportunity to slip past Gidrin's other foes and reach the dwarf's side.

"What do we do?" Streit asked.

"Hobble this pair, will you?"

'Hobble' was a mild word for what the minotaur did in response. One sweep of the wickedly sharp ax decimated the legs of the skeletons in front of Gidrin. The bony undead collapsed onto their ribcages, where the hulking minotaur then took one heavy boot and crushed the fleshless remains to rubble.

"Move!" he growled.

Gidrin was already ahead of him, several paces down the passage. He had not abandoned his friend, however. Instead, mace before him, he prepared to clear the way of any new attacker.

The dwarf did not have long to wait. Ahead, another bony corpse rose from the wall to the right. Gidrin wasted no time in battering it to fragments. By that time, Streit had already caught up to him.

"Is there an end to this?" Streit asked.

"Only one if we don't be careful!"

They continued their charge down the passage, decimating two more headless skeletons. One lacked a leg, another a hand, but all lacked the skull.

"I don't like the looks of this," Gidrin muttered as the duo moved on. "A part missing here, a part missing there... and always the head gone."

"What could all those heads be good for?"

"The real question is, what use could all those heads and other parts be for a necromancer who's supposed to be dead himself?"

Having no good answer, and fearing to hear one, Streit clamped his mouth shut. The two mercenaries continued their flight.

*****

The golem set the tray with the yellow crystal on one of the nearest tables, then turned its attention back to Herid. In the glow of the crystal, the mercenary made out even more heads and body parts behind it. Most were in terrible decay, but one looked all too fresh. Herid noticed that it had a resemblance to some of the villagers. The undead fairies were evidently frequent visitors.

Herid could understand the villagers' desire to save themselves by selling out travelers, but not enough to forgive them for doing so. Still, he felt a strange bit of comfort in having figured out even that much.

The golem reached a thick hand toward him. Expecting the worst, Herid gritted his teeth, but the golem only pushed him slightly in an apparent testing of the mercenary's bonds.

Turning away, the stone figure loomed over the table holding the most heads. After a moment, it seized the most recent one and set it right behind the crystal.

The eyes opened.

Herid struggled, again to no avail.

"*Mercenary...*" The voice was raspy, perhaps in part because, under the ragged throat, there were no lungs to supply air. "*Strength...*"

Herid turned his gaze away, or tried to. A compulsion came over him, a compulsion to *look* at the head. He could not deny it, despite his best efforts to do so.

"*A strong hea—*" Suddenly, the face twisted horribly. The sallow skin cracked. Out of the mouth poured a putrid, dark green liquid.

The eyes rolled into the head. Silence filled the chamber.

The illumination surrounding the crystal flashed—almost *angrily*, Herid thought. Simultaneously, the golem reached behind the crystal and swept the now-ruined head from the table with what was *clearly* anger.

The stone figure again turned to the mercenary. Herid swallowed, certain of what was going to happen next. Indeed, the golem seemed ready to confirm that by reaching for a long, rusty saw.

But the stone monster set aside the saw a second later,

to instead reach for what looked like a small box. It held the box before the crystal, which briefly pulsated.

The golem started to put the box to the side, only to have it hum, then faintly glow itself. Herid now saw it was not a box, but rather a cube of some iridescent blue substance.

Shifting with an ease its bulky form belied, the golem held the cube toward a puzzled Herid.

The cube flared brighter, its iridescence now dazzling.

Several seconds of utter stillness followed. Then, the golem hastily set down the box next to the crystal, which the mercenary noticed glowed much, much brighter.

A change seemed to come over the golem. It quickly grabbed the tray upon which the crystal sat. Whirling, the stone figure trod out of the chamber with more speed than Herid had previously witnessed from it. The mercenary was left dangling in the low crimson light, wondering what had just happened and suspecting that whatever it was could not be good for him.

Which was why he felt extremely relieved to finally loosen one hand.

*****

At long last, the passage ended. Streit and the dwarf peered around a large cavernous chamber, at the other end of which was a series of stairs carved into the wall leading to a gap far above. The chamber itself revealed nothing out of the ordinary save for some thick stalactites that the pair made certain not to cross under. With more than a little relief, they reached the other end without incident.

Peering behind them, Gidrin remarked, "Not a creak out of our emaciated friends. It appears that they will not or cannot cross into this chamber."

"Tell me that's good, dwarf."

"So far, it seems so."

They started up the stairs toward the center exit. Both minotaur and dwarf warily checked over their backs as they ascended. Not until they had exited the large chamber did they feel any relief.

The new chamber was not much smaller than the previous, but it did lack skeletons, which pleased both. The pair quickly went to the three passages ahead and peered down each.

"Any notions?" Gidrin asked at last.

"Yes. If we don't move faster, Herid's dead. Which way?"

The dwarf eyed the tunnels. Rubbing his chin, he finally answered, "This one on the left looks better-hewn. Seems more important."

"Lead on."

The passage led on for a distance, the path rising with each step. Finally, a crimson glow shone at the far end. Both fighters tensed.

The passage opened into a chamber that clearly held more importance, for not only were the walls smoothed, but ahead stood a great marble table. At the end was what might as well have been a throne, so large and elaborate was the high-backed chair.

Streit squinted. "Is that a body there?"

"Not just any body, I think. We've found our necromancer."

"Hmmph. And with no head again."

The dwarf made his way over to the corpse. "Still, a bit different than the rest. Note the fine quality ropes tying him to this magnificent seat with the gargoyle armrests. Note also that it appears someone really hacked away at the throat."

"And note the splatter of blood all over the front of the black robes, not to mention the gouges in those armrests from the fingernails," interjected his companion. "This was all done while he was still alive."

"Yes, well, necromancers don't bring out the best in people." Gidrin came around the great chair. "No sign of the head."

"No." The minotaur prodded the torso with the pointed tip of his ax. The chest crumpled in under the pressure of Streit's strength, even as restrained as he tried to be. "Gidrin, Herid might—"

"Don't go losing your own head!"

"Dwarf, we have a necromancer's sanctum, undead fairies. far too many heads missing—"

A familiar fluttering sound echoed from the passages beyond.

"Speaking of those foul butterflies," Gidrin muttered as he hefted the mace. "Go for the wings and the head, lad. We should be able to handle three—"

From the passages burst far more than *three* blight fairies.

"Damn it! Just swing as hard as you can, Streit!"

The minotaur let out a snort that made it clear he planned to do just that. In seconds, the pair was surrounded by what Gidrin counted as at least a dozen and likely more.

Roaring a challenge, Streit went charging at the nearest of the undead. He buried the sharp edge in the slim chest of the foremost fairy, then twisted the ax just enough to send his target colliding into a second. As that happened, the minotaur shook free his weapon and swung the flat of the head into a third.

Next to him, Gidrin was having a slightly harder time. The mace was a good offensive weapon, very useful for crushing things, but with threats from above the dwarf could usually only reach a leg or maybe a chest. It was hardly enough to stop something that did not feel pain.

Frustrated, the dwarf finally reached up with his free hand and, utilizing his own not inconsiderable strength, pulled down one of the undead by the leg. For a moment, Gidrin stared into the black pits that were all that were left of the fairy's once-beautiful eyes.

The dwarf quickly crushed the skull. The fairy dropped like a rock, enabling Gidrin to step over it and deal with the next.

Yet, the air remained filled with undead fairies who clawed at the duo and sought to grab their arms. Both fighters wore breastplates and leather guards; however, despite that it did not take long for them to suffer several bloody scratches each.

As Streit fended off another creature, he finally made sense of their grasping hands. "They are trying to grab us by our arms or shoulders! They are seeking to drag us into the air!"

"Aye! At the very least to drop us to our doom—" The dwarf's voice trailed off for a moment before he added, "—or maybe somewhere we actually need to be!"

Lowering his mace, Gidrin extended his arms.

"Are you mad, dwarf?"

Before Gidrin could answer, four of the undead grabbed him by the arms and carried him aloft. They did not concern themselves with the mace, instead seeming to only care that they brought him *somewhere*.

"Gidrin!"

"Follow us, Streit!"

The minotaur let out a growl of frustration. Taking a deep breath, he spun in a fast, hard circle, chopping through whatever happened to be in the path of his huge, sharp war ax. Legs, arms, torsos, and wings proved no impediment to

Streit's mighty swing.

The moment the path was clear enough, Streit bounded after his vanishing companion. As the dwarf and his captors disappeared into one of the passages, the horned warrior bared his teeth.

"I will kill you, Gidrin! So, I swear!" Streit muttered as he followed them into the passage. "Just you and Herid stay alive until I can!"

*****

Herid fought to stifle another grunt of pain as he swung his upper torso toward his legs. He had freed both hands, but it was proving very difficult to bend enough to reach the bonds holding his ankles.

Dropping hard, Herid took a deep breath. Still upside down, he quickly glanced at the entrance. How long before the golem returned, the mercenary could not say. Herid had to assume he had little time left to escape.

Bracing himself, he swung his upper torso forward as hard as he could. This time, his right hand came close to his leg. The human snagged his pants. For a moment he paused for air, then began trying to pull himself up enough to reach the bracelet holding that leg.

Herid was not ashamed of his path in life. Before he had become a mercenary, he had been a street child who had learned to pick pockets and locks. When, as a youth, Herid had been given the choice of prison or becoming a conscript in the local military. He had quickly chosen the latter. While there had been times when he had sorely wished for a nice safe dungeon, Herid had discovered a natural aptitude for war, especially the art of swordplay. Once freed of his initial obligation, he had gone on to find employ in that bloody field. Along the way, Herid had come to fight alongside Streit, a low caste minotaur seeking a personal glory he could not achieve back home. They, in turn, had joined up with Gidrin, who had fought in so many struggles for so many employers that he had lost count.

Despite being mercenaries, Herid had faith that the others were hunting for him. However, he did not have faith that they would find him in time. That sort of thing only happened in stories, he knew. It was up to him and him alone.

From his boot, he slipped out a tiny pin of his own design. It was a lock pick, one he had crafted after years of practice. Straining, Herid tried to keep from dropping the pick as he worked the bracelet.

Despite his best effort, he finally lost his grip on his leg and dropped upside down again. For a moment he hung there, catching his breath and trying to stretch his muscles. Then, ever aware that time was against him, Herid twisted upward again.

He managed to catch his leg once more. Immediately, the mercenary began working at the lock. Rust was a factor that slowed his efforts. He was just about to drop down again when at last he heard a clicking sound inside the lock.

With great care, Herid left the piece unlocked but still closed. Stretching to the side, he caught hold of his other leg with the hand holding the lock pick. Then, releasing his other hand, he plucked the lock pick from the one now holding the leg.

Gasping, Herid worked at the second lock. To his frustration, it felt more rusted than the last. Despite his growing agony, he struggled with the lock.

It clicked.

It opened.

Herid was unable to stifle a yelp as first the one leg swung free, then the second, tugging on the unlocked bracelet, opening it.

He struck the floor shoulder-first. The collision shook every bone in his body and made his head pound. Herid's vision went blurry for several valuable seconds and his shoulder screamed.

When at last he could suffer the pain, the human forced himself to his feet. Wobbling, Herid looked around for a weapon. To his relief, he saw his own sword and sheath resting on a table opposite from where he had hung.

On unsteady legs, Herid headed toward the sword.

Something moved at the edge of his vision.

"Damn!" He tried to run the rest of the way, but his legs still would not obey properly.

The winged horror fell upon him. In his haste, Herid had no longer paid attention to the still fairy to the side. Now the undead had him by the torso and, although he outweighed it, the creature had a proverbial death grip on him.

They fell to the ground. Herid did his best to drag himself forward a couple more feet, but was still short of his sword. The fairy's long nails raked his flesh. Grunting from the cuts, the mercenary managed to push himself atop the undead. He then pounded the head several times.

The creature's hold loosened a little. Herid used that to push himself forward. He nearly slipped free, but the undead fairy grabbed him at the waist. Fighting both the fairy and the ungodly stench it emitted, Herid managed to reach the table. Kicking at the ghoulish figure as best he could, the mercenary managed to stand. He grabbed the sheath—and then fell as the undead fairy pulled at him.

As the horrific mouth tried to bite him, Herid succeeded in drawing the sword. With all his strength, he thrust the blade into the fairy's gaping maw.

The point burst out of the back of the neck. Herid

shoved the squirmy undead back. Standing, he gave the sword one more shove, sending the fairy stumbling back.

The mercenary quickly withdrew his blade from the mouth, then swung it around.

The blade's keen edge cut through the dry, brittle flesh, then the bones.

Herid watched with morbid satisfaction as the head went flying. It landed on the floor with a wet thud, then rolled under a table. The body twitched and stumbled around.

Scowling, Herid tripped the body. Then, with some satisfaction, he chopped the legs and arms off.

Exhausted but hopeful, he wended his way toward the entrance.

The golem blocked his path.

Scurrying back, Herid brought his sword into play. He slashed and lunged, only to have his blade bounce off each time. Nevertheless, Herid had no other choice but to try to keep the golem at bay while he searched for some other way to either destroy it or escape... assuming either was even possible.

He desperately looked around for something better than the sword, but found nothing. The golem moved relentlessly toward him.

Herid backed into one of the tables. Legs still unsteady, he set his free hand on it to maintain what balance he had.

His palm pressed on something. Without thinking, Herid gripped it.

The stone figure reached for him. The mercenary made one more futile slash with the blade, at the same time growling, "Keep back, damn you!"

Lowering its arms, the golem took a step from him.

Herid remained still, waiting for whatever trick the golem intended. Yet, after nearly a minute, the stone figure had still not moved at all.

Finally, he tentatively tapped the point of his sword on the chest. The golem remained still.

Growing bolder, the mercenary reached toward his adversary. Only then did he pay attention to what he had been involuntarily clutching.

The cube. Nestled in his palm, it glowed just enough to let him see how it pulsated at the same rate as his heart. Herid eyed it cautiously. Finally, he gripped it tightly and said, "Raise your right arm."

After a few seconds, the golem did just as he commanded. Herid watched in utter fascination as the golem awaited its next instructions.

A scraping sound alerted him to the undead fairy trying to pull itself together. The mercenary eyed the golem one last time then, still gripping the cube, headed out of the chamber.

Unfortunately, once in the passage, Herid had no idea which way to go. Flipping a mental coin, he turned to his right.

A few seconds passed, the only sound the scraping as the undead fairy slowly pieced together.

Then, a slight grinding noise arose from the chamber Herid had abandoned.

A moment later, the golem stepped out, paused for a moment, then followed the mercenary.

*****

The blight fairies carried Gidrin deep into the wide passage. They made no move to take his mace. The dwarf doubted they were even aware of it. What will they had was very likely that of the necromancer who had created them.

The necromancer who had had Herid for far too long.

Suddenly, Gidrin and his captors entered another large chamber. There, the mercenary beheld what looked a library, the shelves carved into side of the cavern wall. However, the dwarf quickly lost interest in that upon noticing the display on another set of shelves farther down. To the necromancer, they had likely been magical artifacts collected for his dark studies, but Gidrin, as both a mercenary and a dwarf, could very much appreciate the gold, silver, and many glistening jewels that made up a good portion of those items.

Without warning, the blight fairies dropped him unceremoniously onto the cavern floor. The dwarf landed hard, but due to his compact yet sturdy build, did not suffer from the drop as much as a human or an elf would have. Thus, it was that Gidrin was ready for them as they descended upon him.

The dwarf brought the mace up at the nearest undead, crushing in the skull with one powerful blow. The damage only slowed the creature, but that was all Gidrin had expected. It still gave him the opportunity to deal with the next nearest. Gidrin rammed the mace into the narrow fairy frame, crushing in the decaying chest. As the blight fairy bent over from the force, the mercenary smashed the skull.

One of the remaining undead seized him by his weapon arm. The blight fairies had surprising strength, but still not quite enough to match the dwarf. Gidrin twisted, sending the blight fairy into the fourth one.

Just as the dwarf felt things were going his way, two more pairs of hands seized his arms from behind. Another pair of blight fairies alighted before him, the monstrous parodies of their once beautiful faces making even the hardened mercenary uneasy.

The two holding his arms pulled. Gidrin roared with pain as his arms nearly separated from the shoulders. One of the undead reached for his throat.

A roar resounded throughout the chamber. Gidrin thought at first it was his, so great had the pain suddenly gotten, but then something swept aside the undead in front. That was followed by a massive ax chopping through the arms of one of the blight fairies holding his limbs.

"These foul things fly fast, you know!" rumbled Streit as he knocked aside the armless undead. "Next time, no foolish stunts like this!"

Gidrin did not answer, instead using his free fist to punch the last of the four undead hard in the face. Dwarven strength was enough to make the ghoulish fairy loosen its grip, which was all Gidrin needed. Pulling his other arm back, the mercenary then delivered a powerful blow that snapped the neck and left the head tilted to the side.

Streit saved him the time of another blow by seizing the broken blight fairy by the ruined throat and tossing the creature into one of the others that Gidrin had damaged.

The two made short work of what was left of the band of undead. Streit took particular pleasure in crushing the wings.

"That won't last, you know," Gidrin told him. "They'll mend."

"It will take them longer."

"True."

Both mercenaries immediately turned their attention to the rich display. Streit grunted his approval before muttering, "After we find Herid."

"Of course."

"Don't bother," remarked Herid.

The minotaur and the dwarf spun to face their comrade, who stood leaning against the entrance to another passage.

"Lad! And with your head intact!"

"Yeah, thanks for trying, anyway." Herid's gaze shifted to the artifacts. "Can't say I entirely blame you, though. So, there *is* treasure."

"A nice lot of it, too. All we have to do is pick what we want." Gidrin gestured at the blight fairies. "This bunch won't be much trouble for a while."

Herid peered behind himself. "Yeah, well, Naylon may not like that."

Immediately, the other mercenaries tensed. Streit snorted. "You have seen him?"

"Well, in a manner. There's this golem wandering about."

"Golem?" Gidrin started to pull out his pipe, then decided against it. "You're sure about that, lad? A golem?"

"A walking statue. Not much to look at, but strong."

"Good thing you managed to steer clear of it, then."

The human grimaced. "Didn't really. Just happened to come across this when I needed it."

As he approached his comrades, Herid produced the small cube. Both the dwarf and the minotaur eyed it. They could see its monetary value, but they could also see the obvious.

"It is magic, is it not?" asked Streit.

"Yeah. Found that out at the last moment. It made the thing stop dead in its tracks. It'll probably even still be where I left it."

The horned fighter took the cube from Herid's open palm. "This is all you needed?"

"Worked instantly." Herid frowned. "Only, it looked brighter, more alive a moment ago."

Gidrin rubbed his chin. "Let me see that, Streit."

The minotaur handed it over. Gidrin turned the cube over, then over again.

"Well?" asked Streit impatiently. "It is a pretty bauble, but is it more?"

"For you or me, Streit, lad, it's a month of food, drink, and carousing." He blinked. "Well, for you, food and drink, anyway. For our friend Herid, though, it could maybe be a lot more." To the human, he added, "You never told us you had the gift, lad."

"The only gift I have is with my sword. I'm no wizard or sorcerer, and certainly no necromancer!"

"You've got something like it. Haven't you ever had a piece of luck at the untimeliest moment?"

"Sure. All bad. Like this is turning out." Herid glanced over his shoulder at the passage from which he had emerged. "We need to get out of here."

"Fine by me," Streit responded. "I have changed my mind. I want nothing of this so-called treasure."

"I'm of the same mind." The dwarf eyed the cube. "Best give this back to you, Herid. Just in case." He tossed it back.

The cube stopped just two inches from Herid's palm. Gasping, the mercenary tried to grab it, but the cube evaded his grasp.

"There!" growled the minotaur, gesturing at one of the other passages.

The golem stood there. One arm stretched out to the flying cube, the other held the tray upon which the crystal that Herid had seen earlier lay. The crystal glowed very brightly.

Herid made another lunge at the cube, but it moved too quickly. Streit barged past his comrade, his focus already on the golem. The minotaur crossed the distance with astounding swiftness, his huge battle ax already raised for a powerful swing.

The golem moved its free arm into the ax's intended arc. The sharp head struck the stone limb.

A small chunk of stone broke free from the arm.

A loud crack presaged the ax head breaking off and flying to the side.

Streit gaped at his ruined weapon, which had lasted through five wars and three decades of hard, almost daily, practice. The minotaur recovered quickly, tossing aside the ruined handle, and lunging.

The golem's flat palm caught Streit in the chest. The minotaur shook violently, then tumbled back.

"Streit!" Gidrin rushed forward. At the same time, Herid also turned to face the golem.

The dwarf only got a couple of paces before he tripped—or, rather, was snagged at the ankle. Swearing, the mercenary twisted to swing at the fairy hand clutching him.

Hearing the noise behind him, Herid looked over his shoulder. The reaction was a brief one, but Herid realized it was still too costly. He tried to turn back to the golem—

Something stung his neck. Herid let out a gasp and fell.

His last glimpse was of Gidrin struggling as more fairy hands grabbed his other limbs, and Streit…Streit lying limp and looking very dead.

*****

Gidrin let out a guttural sound as he saw Herid drop. Tearing off one fairy hand, the dwarf tried to claw his way to his human comrade. Unfortunately, there seemed more hands than there should have been. They grabbed his arms, his legs, and even sought his throat. Thanks especially to Streit, some of them were not even attached to more than a forearm, yet still they came for him.

Two covered his mouth while another grabbed his throat. Even as he fought in vain with the reanimated appendages, Gidrin still feared for Herid. The dwarf and the minotaur likely faced only death, but Herid, because of his newly-discovered unique nature, had a worse fate intended for him.

Older than both of his comrades by far, Gidrin knew a bit more about necromancers. Everything now made sense, even more so than the duplicitous villagers knew. They had been well aware of the blight fairies kidnapping those either ignorant or foolish enough to be out at night, but not the true reason. The necromancer Naylon had escaped death... barely. The crystal surely held his mind or his essence—Gidrin couldn't have cared less about the distinction—and the golem was as close as Naylon had been able to come to possessing a new body.

Until Herid had stumbled into the situation.

In this remote region, the chances of another spellcaster showing up had obviously been very slight. The necromancer had obviously been trying to create what he could from the victims his undead fairies had brought him, but they had always fallen short. However, with Herid's innate magical essence, clearly the spellcaster believed that he had at last found what he needed.

Gidrin managed to pull one grasping hand from his mouth. That enabled him to get a short breath before the hand around his throat cut off any further air.

He fought to his feet. A swipe of his mace enabled him to free one leg.

As if out of nowhere, the golem's fist struck the dwarf on the skull.

Gidrin collapsed into the clawing hands.

*****

Herid stirred, or at least he woke. *Stirring* suggested that he made some sort of movement, which he quickly discovered was not at all possible. The only part of him that could move was his eyes. That meant that he could only see above him and slightly to each side.

One thing he did know was that only a few minutes at most had passed. They had not even left the chamber. Herid knew that by the slightest of views of the shelves holding the necromancer's collection. Of his companions, the human could neither see nor hear anything. No help would be coming.

A slight grating sound warned him of the golem's return. It still carried the tray with the crystal. Herid wanted to look away when the crystal came into view, but found he could not. The mercenary felt forced to stare at it. And as he did, he started to hear a voice.

Mine... finally... finally...

Herid wanted to argue the point, but could not. He tried to at least glare, but even that futile act of defiance had been taken from him.

The golem shifted. With surprising caution, it took the crystal with its free hand and set it down on Herid's chest. Setting aside the tray, the golem then took a step back.

Despite the awkward angle, the mercenary could still not tear his eyes from the crystal. The voice continued speaking, but Herid could no longer make out exactly what it was saying. Nothing good, he knew.

Images flashed through mind, images he knew were not from *his* memories. They began innocently enough: displaying a town, some people, books. However, they quickly shifted to things more ominous, more disturbing.

They were the necromancer's memories.

The horrific realization made him want to shiver, but even that was not allowed. He could only lay there, listening to and seeing the life of the necromancer. What point that last served, Herid could not say for certain, but he had growing suspicions. Terrifying suspicions.

Then, a sense of drifting overtook the mercenary. Everything seemed to slowly disappear into the distance. Herid felt as if he drifted through an endless and thickening fog. Everything faded from view, save the crystal. In fact, the crystal began to grow, to fill his gaze. Soon, there was nothing but it. It surrounded him, became his world.

Herid knew then that he was lost... and his body was no longer his.

*****

Barely conscious, Gidrin stared up as Herid abruptly loomed above him. For a moment the dwarf took heart, but then he noticed two strange things. The first was that Herid's eyes had always been green, but now were a deep, deep blue.

The second was the sight—astounding even though half-hidden by the human's shirt—of the crystal *imbedded* in Herid's chest.

Herid said something in a tongue the dwarf did not understand, but instinctively knew was something no mortal should have been speaking.

Gidrin felt his limbs go rigid.

Glancing to the side, Herid snapped his fingers. With a slight grinding sound, the golem stepped into the old mercenary's view. If there was any need to verify Gidrin's worst fears, this did it. The golem leaned down and lifted the sturdy dwarf, as if Gidrin weighed no more than a cat. Gidrin felt the blight fairies release their hold on him, but could take no comfort in that. The dwarf could not budge; worse, he knew that death would be no escape from the necromancer. What the sinister spellcaster had done to the fairies, he could easily do to a dwarf.

Gidrin expected to be carried to one of the other chambers, but the golem only went so far as a flat surface in front of the collection of artifacts. There, the dwarf was tossed down like a sack of flour. The drop left Gidrin in pain for a short time but he paid little attention to it, more concerned with what Herid appeared to be doing. The possessed mercenary walked into and out of the dwarf's view, at last reappearing wielding a dagger with an onyx blade.

Gidrin struggled to move something. *Anything.* Yet only his eyes could move.

Once more, Herid appeared. He again spoke in the same mysterious language. As he did, the dwarf felt a constriction around his throat.

The possessed mercenary leaned over him. Now, not only were Herid's eyes the wrong color, but they were even the wrong shape. Herid's had been almond; these were rounder, wilder.

Herid raised the dagger. Gidrin glared, not wanting the necromancer possessing his comrade to see the dwarf's uncertainty and fear.

Then, what looked at first like another undead rose up behind Herid. Gidrin could not stifle his surprise, though he wished he could have.

Eyes red and chest heaving, Streit grabbed the wrist of the hand wielding the dagger and squeezed. Herid cried out and the dagger dropped free.

Streit suddenly looked to his side. Gidrin could not see what so caught the minotaur's attention, but heard the telltale grinding sound that presaged the golem.

Worse, from above the minotaur descended two blight

fairies. They seized Streit's arms, tearing his grip from Herid.

Herid reached down, rising a moment later with the dagger. Now, however, his intended target was Streit, whose earlier escape from what the dwarf had believed death looked soon to be short-lived.

The possessed mercenary turned on the minotaur.

*****

Streit *felt* like death. He still was not certain what had happened to him, only that for a time he had felt as if he had fallen down an endless hole. Then, he had managed to wake up enough to notice the threat to Gidrin.

It had taken the greatest of efforts just to rise, but the more immediate the danger became for the dwarf the more Streit's blood surged. He had managed to reach the possessed Herid just as the latter had been about to sacrifice Gidrin.

Streit had put what strength he could into squeezing the wrist. Had his might been at its peak, he would have crushed the bones. Instead, he had at least managed to force the dagger free.

And then everything had gone awry.

First, he had been distracted by the oncoming golem. That had enabled the necromancer to catch him by surprise with the blight fairies. With their own surprising strength, they had easily pulled the half-dead Streit back from Herid.

The possessed mercenary had reclaimed the dagger. He now turned to use it on Streit instead.

Snorting, the minotaur grabbed one of the blight fairies and ripped it free from him. That left blood and torn flesh, but the new wounds only served to push the exhausted fighter onward. He threw the one fairy into Herid, then grabbed the second by its wrist and swung it at the golem.

The stone figure brushed aside the undead fairy with ease, then continued toward Streit. However, the minotaur paid the golem no mind, only interested in Herid. He reached for the possessed mercenary, dragging the human to him.

Herid tried to stab him, but Streit was prepared this time. He twisted Herid's arm, once again forcing the dagger from his hand.

Herid glared defiantly at him. Streit peered down at the slighter figure.

"You will not—" he began, only to find his limbs stiffening, his breathing faltering. Streit tried to look away, but the blue eyes that were not Herid's held sway over him.

Strange and unnerving words spilled from Herid's mouth. Streit could barely breathe.

Something jostled the human. Herid's gaze abruptly slipped.

It was all Streit needed. Turning his gaze slightly to the side, he evaded a second attempt to ensnare him. The stiffness swiftly left his body.

A glance down revealed the cause of the minotaur's reprieve. Gasping, Gidrin kept his fingers wrapped around Herid's ankle as best he could, although it was clear that the dwarf had even less ability to move than Streit had had moments before. Only Gidrin's indomitable will had enabled him to manage even this much.

But it *was* enough for Streit.

"Sorry about this, Herid," the minotaur muttered.

The horned fighter grabbed the crystal and, when it would not come easily, ripped it from Herid's chest.

Herid cried out, then shook. A large, black outline had been burned into his chest by the crystal. The human grasped futilely at the injured area.

"Hope I am right." With that, Streit threw the crystal to the floor. It bounced twice, then settled.

With a frustrated grunt, Streit tossed Herid out of the way. He stared at the golem, which was nearly upon him.

Eyes narrowing, the minotaur gave the crystal a sideways kick. It slid just as he'd calculated, ending right underneath the golem's descending foot.

The heavy foot crushed the crystal into countless shards.

A mournful wail rose around the minotaur. It echoed through the chamber, seeming to come from all directions. For a moment, it grew so loud that Streit wanted to cover his ears.

Then it ceased.

The golem teetered. The grating that often accompanied its movements grew more pronounced. It managed to start one more step, then halted as the necromancer's power faded from it.

The imbalance proved too much. The golem tipped over. It hit the floor with a hard crash. One arm and one leg broke off and a fissure cut across the head, splitting it open.

To Streit's left, a blight fairy dropped like a wet sack. The undead lay there, looking... dead. It was followed by two more. Looking around, the minotaur saw that the pile of undead the mercenaries had earlier battled had also ceased moving.

Streit's legs finally gave out on him. He dropped to his knees even as Gidrin managed to roll to a sitting position.

"Thought you were dead," the dwarf commented as he fumbled for his pipe. 'Mind you, you still look it. Just too stubborn, I guess."

"You talk too much sometimes," Streit replied without rancor.

A new moan caught the attention of both. The two

grabbed for their weapons.

Herid pushed himself up on his elbows. "I-I'm back. I'm here."

"Yes, glad to have you back, lad. The other one, he didn't take too kindly to us."

"My head pounds," the minotaur interjected. "I could use a drink."

"You and me both. What say you, lad?"

Herid nodded. "Once I get my legs back."

"There is that." The dwarf lit his pipe, then pointed it at one of the shelves. "Don't suppose that bottle there might contain some drink. Or maybe that nice gold one up the next level."

Despite their condition, the other two straightened.

"There is another bottle on the left," the minotaur offered. "That one with the intriguing jewels around the base. We should really try that one."

"And, of course, we'll need something for the road, too. Pity we don't know what's with the rest of those items. Seems a shame to leave them for those villagers. I especially like that emerald thing on the top shelf."

"No! We don't want that!" Herid blurted. "Don't even think about it!"

Streit and Gidrin stared at him, at each other, then at him again.

"How do you know that?" the dwarf asked between puffs.

Herid blinked. "I don't—I just remembered—his memories came first."

The minotaur straightened. "You know it because you have the necromancer's memories?"

"Some. They pop up without warning." Herid grimaced. "Not *all* of them, fortunately."

"You have the necromancer's memories," Gidrin mused. "What's in that ruby thing on the upper right? Anything nasty?"

"No. A little lingering magic, but nothing for us to fear. It's old and pretty valuable—" Herid's grimace became a grin. "Yeah. Very valuable. Like that one and that one and that one..."

The dwarf chuckled. "You just keep them straight for a few minutes, all right? Streit, we're going to need your legs. Are you up to snuff?"

"I am better now. It seems what was done to me has faded now that the necromancer is no more." The minotaur pushed himself up. "Where do I start, Herid?"

"Go to the third shelf, second item. We definitely do not want to leave that."

"We won't."

As Streit went to work, both Gidrin and Herid also succeeded in standing. The dwarf continued to eye his human companion, who now began looking for something near the golem.

"What're you searching so intently for, lad? What?"

"I was just curious where that cube ended up. Should be around here somewhere."

"And what would you be needing it for?"

Herid looked up at him, his expression all innocence. "Thought it might be of some value."

"To whom? You?"

"Well, I guess maybe me, too. If I've got some magic in me, maybe I should see what I can do."

Gidrin took a long puff on his pipe. "You do recall what we just went through, don't you, lad? Or a couple of times in the past?"

"Yeah, but just think if we had some magic on our side!"

"I am." The older mercenary doused his pipe. "Streit! Leave all that! We're getting out of here right now!"

The minotaur eyed him suspiciously. "Why is that?"

"Because our friend here is thinking of taking up magic."

Streit snorted. "No. Not that."

"Exactly my thought. Come on, lad. Leave that cube wherever it is. The sooner we're out of this place, the better."

Exhaling, Herid finally nodded. "Whatever you say, Gidrin."

Packing away his pipe, the veteran fighter nodded. "Wise."

"But what about all these valuables?"

"Leave them for the villagers," the minotaur rumbled as he joined the other two. "They deserve them."

Gidrin chuckled and Herid grinned. Weapons ready, just in case, the trio looked at the many passages.

"That one," Herid said with the utmost certainty. "That's the best way out."

"Good to know." The dwarf glanced at the human. "Herid?"

"Yeah?"

"Once we're out, try *real* damned hard to forget again. All right?"

"Already starting to blur."

"Good. Let's be off then."

The three mercenaries exited, with Streit and his ax leading, Gidrin next, and Herid taking up the rear.

"Soon as we get to the horses, I'll check my maps," the dwarf commented. "There must be a better place in this region than that village. Somewhere with some food and drink, at a reasonable price considering our circumstances."

"Food, drink, and rest," Streit corrected.

"Aye, that. What do you say, Herid?"

"It all sounds great. Let's just get there. Maybe our luck will change for the better then."

"Maybe so, but never count on it. I've learned that along the way." Gidrin laughed briefly at some old memory. "Oh, I have."

Herid echoed his laugh. "Still, you never know." He took a surreptitious look at his left hand. The cube, which he had located just as Gidrin had told him to forget it, pulsated quietly. Herid admired it a moment more, imagining how impressed the other two would be once he proved to them he could safely wield magic. Then, not wanting to be careless, he slipped it into the pouch on his belt. "You never know."

Requiem For A Fisherman

By Chanté Van Biljon

734AM
Age of the Dracon-esti

Softly the sun shone down on the crowns of their heads, and against the bright blue sky they gleamed like royalty. They bathed in the crisp ocean breath, and in their timber carriage they sailed the whale-road. That morning, Shilantar commanded light and song over the Storm Coast and all was good.

Blackness.

Yuri opened his eyes with agonized slowness; the thick blanket of night rested heavy on his lids. He heard no more song, felt no more warmth, and saw no more light—only a numb silence, a hard wooden bed, and a sleeping dog in the corner of his room. He could feel the bed creaking as he turned over on his other side to face the small, round window; there he lay, just staring through it as he awaited the dawn. In that little room he wasted away, doing what the deaf did best, he supposed. Died

With much self-contention, Yuri lifted himself out of bed. His clothes hung loosely on his body; the strength he'd built the last two years, melding with his confidence, had drearily dripped away during his catatonic days. Kalko, his canine companion, licked his toes as he tried to get his boots on. It was ticklish and slobbery but Yuri smiled, and he stroked Kalko's thick black fur, thinking about the moments in which his furry friend had been by his side. It had been many years since he found Kalko as a pup, and he hoped—no, yearned—that he would be by his side for many more. He was the only reason Yuri had not wasted away entirely by that point. Yuri had hope that they would share many more moments in the future, somehow. Kalko quickly lifted his snout in the air and ran to the door, scratching to be let out. Breakfast was sniffed.

Yuri's room exited to a long and dim passageway, which led to a narrow, wooden staircase. As Yuri and Kalko headed to the stairs, Yuri felt a light pat on the side of his leg. He turned around and there it was—the brownie. An ugly little thing about the size of a child, with blemished dark brown skin and brown strands of hair like straw. Quite a contrast to Yuri, who was a tall human man with pale skin and light brown hair. Yuri was about the age of his father at the time of his father's death; thirty summers since the day he was born. Kalko barked at it and showed it his fearsome teeth, but the brownie gave him no mind. It just bowed its head, stretched out its arms, and in its palms lay an envelope with his name on it. Yuri carefully lifted the letter out of its hands then gave the brownie a slight kick, urging it to get back in its cupboard, or at least just out of sight.

Who would be sending me a letter? Yuri thought as they headed down the wooden stairs of The Skinny Hill Giant Tavern.

The tavern was small, its floors were sticky more often than not, and it had a damp smell from all the rain over the last few months. Yuri wasn't sure who christened it; he had faced hill giants in the past and they were, for all their flaws, positively not skinny. The tavern's sign, with the image of said skinny hill giant, swayed on rusted hinges outside the main entrance. It was a splintery piece of art and the paint had long begun to peel away, but even though the sign that marked the tavern was faded no one ever struggled to locate it. The Skinny Hill Giant Tavern was situated near the city walls to the south, and it was one of the most renowned and oldest drinking holes in Darvalon. It was there Yuri had been renting a small room for the past three months. He was a trained Valon, hunting monsters for the past two years. A vocation that imbued him one day as he sat on a rock in complete despair, staring out at the fearsome Oritheon Ocean.

Yuri sat at a small table in a dark corner, furthest from the tavern door. The serving wench placed a plate of bread and butter in front of him, along with a tankard of ale. She was a heavy-set young woman with long red hair, and there wasn't a breakfast that passed without Yuri discovering a fiery strand of her hair baked into his bread. He stared at his food and believed today would be no different. Today, like all other days before, had a sticky floor, a loaf of bread, and the essence of a melancholic existence for Yuri—a day like any other except for the letter. He brought the envelope up to his nose to ease his olfactory curiosity. Lilac. Didn't smell like anyone he knew or would know. The envelope contained a letter which read:

Yuri,
We didn't part on good ground when last I saw you. I was your partner, and I feel that I failed you. I am partly to

blame for the condition that now inflicts you and the hopelessness you feel. Your drive for vengeance is not lost on me, and were I in your boots I might have given up my sword as well.
I write to you to ask for your help. A bounty has been offered for the heads of a group of hobgoblins and the safe return of the children they have stolen from Bela, a small village in southern Duskvar. Please join me as soon as you can. I could really use a good tracker.
–Esten

    Yuri picked up the hefty pewter tankard to take a sip, but only felt the coldness of the mug on his lips as he tilted it. He looked inside, and it was a quarter full. Confused, he stared over to the serving wench standing at the bar, and she just shrugged her shoulders. The ale had run dry again. He felt it was quite festive last night; the music and merriness had reverberated through his wooden floors until the early hours of the morning. Yuri's sigh fell hard upon her ears at the hands of another defeat. There would be no bitter victory for him that morning; no bitter ale to wash away his bitter existence. He tore off a piece of bread and put it in his mouth, then threw the rest on the sticky floor. Yuri gently lay his head on the cold wooden table as he watched Kalko devour his breakfast. He got up from the table as the wench approached, with a broomstick in hand and foul look for Yuri. He felt her angry glare sting the back of his head as he passed.

    Yuri struggled to imagine picking up his sword again as he headed up the stairs, back to his room. With each step he recounted each beast he had slain since he joined the guild—from the most grotesque ogre to the tiniest of goblins. He wouldn't be able to take up the title of Valon again, not with his deafness, not by being broken. Broken like the artifacts on his bedroom floor. He stepped over his long, steel sword—Oathkeeper—and past his wife's silver locket with the broken clasp. He sat on his bed and beheld all the facets of the life he'd led, threw Esten's letter onto his graveyard floor, and then went back to sleep.

Just as quickly as his new world went black, his old one lit up.

Yuri saw how softly the sun shone on the crowns of their heads, and against the bright blue sky they gleamed like royalty. They bathed in the crisp ocean breath, and in their timber carriage they sailed the whale-road. That morning, Shilantar commanded light and song over the Storm Coast and all was good. Kalko chased his tail and then some seagulls that dared to fly over their boat. Yuri basked in his good fortune as he watched his beautiful wife, her gorgeous dark locks dancing in the breeze, her beautiful smile mirroring his. Elaina held their beautiful blond boy in her arms as she sang him a lullaby. Her melody curved with the contours of the waves, and was carried by the currents in the air. Her song traveled along every ray of sun and flowed to every point the sun touched—far beyond the horizon.

But beyond the horizon there was another sound, and it wasn't long until Yuri could hear it pulling. A hypnotic screech that played puppet master with his hands, leading their ship along to a rocky coastline. The crisp ocean air quickly became a fog, and the ocean waves that gently rocked their boat now crashed against its hull. In the distance, the mist cleared a bit, and Yuri could see the siren that serenaded him. All he could hear was her as he navigated through the rocky ocean to reach her. With every rocky hit, their boat took on water. He could feel Elaina tug at him in a panic; he could hear the faint cry of his little boy and see Kalko barking in distress. Suddenly, the boat's keel howled as it dragged along underwater rocks. Rocks that scraped and shredded it until their timber carriage slumped over in defeat. Yuri and his family fell into the water, and the siren's song stopped. Elaina reached out to her son, but was violently swept away by the angry ocean. Yuri used all this strength to fight the sea to get to his boy. His boy, who was only three years old, couldn't swim. He cried and gulped as he bobbed in and out of the ocean's salty jaws. His little hands tried to grip onto Kalko's slippery fur, occasionally pulling Kalko under the water.

Yuri, his son, and Kalko washed up on the shore. His body was numb from the cold water; he could only feel the rough grains of sand graze his cheek as he lay dazed. It was not long, however, until he remembered what had happened, and saw his son lying on the beach not too far away, small waves washing over him. Yuri crawled across the sand until his knees were raw, to get to him. His son's body was colder than the water. Yuri wept as he ran fingers through his boy's hair, as he put his ear to this boy's chest to hear his heart. Yuri held his boy's cold body in his arms as he yowled into the air.

Blackness.

Yuri woke up in a cold sweat, his eyes wet with tears and his body was shivering. When he looked through his window he found that the sun was low in the sky; he had slept away the day just like many other days before then. He felt a knot in his stomach when he thought back to his dream. He had set out from Ishar two years ago to join the Valons, to learn how to avenge the death of his family, but nothing had come of it. He was now less useful than the fisherman he was before he came here, and that siren remained alive. Perhaps going to assist Esten was the only good he could do, the only way he could salvage some meaning in his broken life. He peered over at the letter that lay on the floor, and decided to leave at first light.

*****

The air seemed almost hollow as he looked back at the dry blue sky over the city he called home. A grey city, built with old grey stones on old grey ground, cowering beneath The Valonholm—House of Valons. Its size and beauty could not be contested. Some parts of it rose up to ten floors in the sky, and unlike the city stones its stones held majesty and splendor. It reigned over the crippling grey, and its tall towers leered at Yuri as he crossed the moat to leave Darvalon. Once again the city walls were at his back, and with Kalko by his side Yuri embarked on his next commission. From the map that Esten had left him on the back of the letter, Yuri estimated that his travel to Bela would last about five days. Heading south, Yuri moved away from the Duskvar's northern tundra. The path to the village wouldn't be strenuous that time of year, nearing the birth of summer. Yuri moved with haste, as he felt the sense of urgency to recover children held by hobgoblins. He had encountered those creatures before, and knew they thrived on terror and were prone to take slaves in times of war. They were well versed in the use of whips and chains, shackles and cages. Whatever the reason they were taking children, avoiding the worst outcome for them was Yuri's top priority—which meant finding them as quickly as possible.

By the late afternoon of his fourth day of travel, Yuri reached the tiny village of Bela. The sky had begun to yellow and felt warm, and the buildings were built with old sandstone which stood on the ancient ground. The dry-stack stone houses looked so serene below the setting sun; in the distance he saw the head of a hobgoblin propped up on the prongs of a hayfork, and knew all was never as it seemed. There was no one in sight, and he wasn't sure how he would find Esten. He roamed around for a bit, but there wasn't much ground to cover. As the sky became increasingly dim, however, he began to see village men with torches and farming 'weapons' begin to surveil the area. Yuri deducted that a curfew had been implemented, and that those men were out protecting the village from any more hobgoblin intrusions. One man saw Yuri and his dog roaming about, but instead of confronting him he alerted Esten of their presence. Esten came out with torch and ax in hand, but other than that he wouldn't have been hard to miss anyway. He was a large, middle-aged man with a big black beard, and he always wore an intimidating bear pelt across his shoulders. It was a trophy of his first kill. A bugbear's large black bear pet terrorized the village he grew up in. At the time, only dreaming of becoming a Valon, he didn't know a bugbear from a bear because he had never seen one before. He had only heard stories of them as a child. He wondered why there was such an unusually large bounty for the head of a simple bear, so he had ventured into the bear's cave, wholly unprepared for the maze and the traps that awaited him. Nonetheless, he made it through, and even though the bugbear escaped him that day he slew that mighty black bear.

 Yuri had a trophy of his first kill as well, although the story wasn't nearly as heroic as Esten's. Yuri and Esten stumbled into the territory of a hill giant while they were tracking a pack of ogres in the northern tundra of Duskvar. The massive giant had terrified Yuri with its dark grey skin and pitch-black hair, and Yuri froze on the spot as it charged towards him. Just as the giant was about to reach him, it tripped over a rock and fell hard on the frozen ground. As the giant started to rise to its feet, Yuri's courage kicked in and he sliced into the giant's neck, releasing a spray of blood that drenched him. He had kept the giant's left big toe, but it went missing a few months later. Yuri suspected Kalko of eating it.

Esten had a broad grin on this face as he approached Yuri and Kalko. He gestured for Yuri to follow him, and so they did, into the home of what Yuri guessed was one of the village elders. The elder was a jolly old man, and his wife was a silver-haired, petite lady with a welcoming smile. As they entered the home Yuri felt the warmth of the fire, and could smell the glorious aroma of roasted chicken and potatoes. There were smiles all around. The elder and his wife were delighted to see him. They greeted him with handshakes and pats on the back while they poured him some ale and dished him some food. Kalko sat ready at Yuri's feet, waiting for a piece of chicken. The chicken wasn't dry like that served to him at the tavern. It was delightfully delicious, and its skin was wonderfully crisp—the best meal he had had in months. The elder's wife poured everyone another round of ale as Esten told, what seemed to Yuri, a fantastic tale about himself. In fact, Esten explained to the elder that, although Yuri was deaf, Yuri was the best tracker of all the Valons currently living, and that the village children would not be missing for much longer. Yuri could see their relief and could feel the worry that occupied the room fade away.

After an exuberant evening, the two hunters were led to their beds that the elder's wife had made up. Soft beds, not like the one Yuri had to endure at the tavern. He lay his head down and sank into the feather pillow. The exhaustion of the journey engulfed him in a flash, but before he could pull the soft wool blanket over himself the elder's wife knelt beside him. She had a cup of what appeared to be warm tea in her hands. She urged him to drink it, and he wouldn't usually refuse if he were not so full. She kept offering it, however, so he begrudgingly took it. He held it in his hands, but she did not leave. He cautiously investigated the tea; it was a bright yellow liquid with three different types of tea leaves floating in it. Yuri didn't recognize the leaves, and the tea smelled of nothing, but he slowly put it to his lips. She placed her hand below the cup and forced it to his mouth until he had gulped down every drop. Yuri pulled his face in disgust—somehow the tea tasted bitter and sweet at the same time. She just smiled, and then she said something as she rose to her feet. Yuri couldn't read lips, but he hoped it was something along the lines of "Hope you sleep well," and not "Enjoy the poison."

That night, Yuri's dreams were those of a great abyss—a vast, black void in which he drifted. In the distance, beyond what he could see, he heard a faint melody. It was a familiar lullaby that sounded like a mere whisper. It brought warmth to the cold vacuum, and tugged at his leg. It pulled harder and repeatedly, and then it started to shake his leg. Yuri slowly opened his eyes, and as he did so a loud scream filled his head. He gripped his ears in pain. Esten let go of Yuri's leg and went over to assess Yuri's obvious pain, but the scream stopped just as swiftly as it started. Esten touched Yuri's hands and tried to look in his ears, but Yuri quickly shook him off. Esten gestured to Yuri that it was time to leave.

As they stepped outside, the elder's wife called them back to the door. She had a wrapped loaf of bread in her hands that she handed over to Esten. It was freshly baked and still warm, and it smelled delicious. They didn't stay for breakfast, and decided to eat as they tracked the hobgoblins; they wanted to get tracking as soon as possible. As they walked through the village, all the peasants stood outside and wished them well. The villagers threw lilacs in their path as they headed towards the woods, southeast.

Yuri and Kalko followed Esten's lead. Esten had scouted these woods before, and had a relatively good idea in which direction the hobgoblins took the children. The only problem was that the creatures had covered their tracks well, and the rain that fell three days ago obscured their trail even further. Tracking was one reason Esten urged Yuri to join the search. The other reason was his concern for Yuri's well-being. It was not uncommon for a member of the guild to retreat into isolation for a lengthy period of time, but Esten knew Yuri. He knew that Yuri's isolation was more than a simple withdrawal from the world—it was a withdrawal from reality.

Just over three months ago, Esten and Yuri answered a call to slay a group of sirens on the coast of Fragmar. These sirens caused the sinking of a number of ships carrying gold and jewels from Ogena in Fragmar to nobles in Isatarist. Other than the significantly large bounty, Yuri jumped at the opportunity to face a group of sirens. All his studying and training would finally be put to use in slaying the creatures which had caused him to join the guild in the first place.

Their nest was in a shallow cave atop a low cliff, on a rocky part of Fragmar's coast. The cave was damp, and smelled of rotting fish and seaweed, and although the cave wasn't deep it was exceptionally dark. The sun never shone upon its mouth, and made an attack during the daytime particularly risky if the sirens were awake. Esten and Yuri had agreed that a stealthy nighttime assault would be safer, while the creatures were asleep. They expected to kill of twenty-four sirens from the count of their initial scout. The moon had been full that night, and the skies were clear. All they could hear were the waves crashing against the cliff. They trod silently into the beastly nest as the creatures slept, blissfully unaware of their fate. Esten and Yuri targeted the sirens closest to the mouth of the cave, and with one swift pierce of the chest the first two creatures were dead. Their swords, which earlier glistened in the moonlight, were now bloodied as they moved on to the next pair. Two by two the sirens were slaughtered, but Esten and Yuri's treads weren't as silent as they thought; the sound of tearing skin every time Yuri pierced a creature titillated the ears of the sleeping sirens ever so slightly. When they reached the back of the cave there were no more sirens left, but their count was only twenty-two dead.

From the darkest shadows at the edges of the cave wall they heard soft screeches, and out of the shadows charged two sirens. They swiped at Esten and Yuri with their lizard claws. For all the beauty of a nude woman they possessed, they were equally hideous. Scaly green wings protruded from their shoulders. They walked on the legs of a lizard, and had long tails which pierced like a whip. Esten dodged their claws, and with one fell swoop Yuri dismembered one. The siren screamed with pain as she pursued Yuri with her tail, and with a fearsome crack she pierced his leg and dropped him to the ground. The other continued to swipe her claws at Esten, gashing his sword arm, but it would take more than a mere scratch to slow him down. He quickly grabbed his sword with his other hand, and as he leaned in with a forceful swing he slashed her belly open. She fell to the ground in crippling and fatal pain. The golden-haired siren that whipped Yuri to the ground leaned in for a final swipe, but just as she exposed herself Yuri thrust this sword into her neck. With her last breath, she released a trembling scream that shook the cave and nearly caused Esten to lose his footing. Her cry was so incredibly loud that it permanently deafened Yuri.

The days following the encounter Yuri visited many healers, but none could restore his hearing. His hearing was gone for good; a numbing death. He couldn't hunt anymore, he felt. He wouldn't be able to hear an oncoming creature, track monsters using the sounds of nature, or even effectively communicate with others. He spiraled down a hole of deep depression and misery. That was, until five days ago.

Yuri tracked the hobgoblins until sunset, then they decided to make camp and rest for the night. They slept in their tents, on the hard ground, and even though there weren't feather pillows and woolen blankets they were comfortable enough. The temperature of the air was just right—not too warm and not too chilly. Again, that night, Yuri dreamt of a tremendous abyss—a vast, black void in which he drifted. In the distance, beyond what he could see, he heard a faint melody. It was a familiar lullaby that sounded like a mere whisper. It brought warmth to the cold vacuum. Like a feather, he swayed in this warmth, but it didn't last for long. From the darkness came a loud scream; a scream so loud that he woke up gripping his ears, and then it was gone. Through the opening of his tent, Yuri saw Esten dishing up some breakfast and Kalko sitting right by their little campfire, waiting for his portion of bread and eggs. Esten held out a wooden plate as Yuri slowly emerged. Yuri, as always, threw some food on the ground for Kalko. Silently they ate, and quietly packed up their campsite and went on their way.

Just before midday, they reached the hobgoblin encampment at the mouth of a cave. There were five of the foul-looking hobgoblins sitting around a campfire, preparing a filthy-smelling lunch. They had flabby grey-green skin and piggish, sunken yellow eyes. Their teeth were as sharp as daggers; all the better for biting. The children were nowhere to be seen, but Esten suspected that they were being held in the cave. The cave was quite deep and dark, but as they snuck closer they could see the children locked in a sturdy wooden cage. Esten thought it wise to sneak into the cave to release the children first, before they made their attack on the hobgoblins. Yuri and Kalko remained where they were, in view of the hobgoblins and cave. The creatures sank their teeth into the meat that they roasted over the fire, and seemed relatively distracted by their lunch, except for one. Just as Esten entered the cave, the single hobgoblin alerted the others. Jumping and screaming, it pointed in the direction of the cave. They all got up, picked up their rusty short swords, and headed in Esten's direction. Yuri burst out of the bushes, and Kalko barked to divert their attention. Three of the hobgoblins charged at Yuri as he drew his sword. The first he sliced into quite quickly, but the other two put up more of a fight.

In the cave, Esten used his ax to crack the skulls of those attacking him. Soon they were bloodied and dead, and with no hesitation Esten brought his ax down on the cage's lock to free the children. In the meantime, Yuri was fending off the blows of the hobgoblins. They felt stronger than the hobgoblins he had encountered before; then again, he had gotten significantly weaker the last few months. However, he still had the skill to defeat them. As he pierced one in the chest the other rammed against him, and they both toppled to the ground. Yuri opened his eyes, head throbbing in pain and a ringing in his ears. He saw Esten remove his ax from the skull of the hobgoblin that had pushed him to the ground. The four children ran over to Yuri; they were skinny and dirty, and showed great concern for his well-being. Esten helped Yuri to his feet and gave him a congratulatory pat on the back.

In single file, Esten led the children back to the village. The youngest was six and none were older than ten. Yuri and Kalko trailed behind, on the lookout for any hobgoblins that might still be out there, but the woods were quiet, and by sunset they reached their old campsite. At the ashes of their past campfire, little birds were pecking the bread on the ground. The children hadn't lost all their sense of play; they ran to chase the birds, which scattered in all directions. The children helped set up camp, and it was not long until their dreary faces had smiles.

Yuri and Kalko took first watch for half of the night as everyone else slept. He leaned against a large rock as he looked to the sky through the canopies of the trees, and felt the ancient light of the distant stars caress his cheeks. His ears hadn't stopped ringing since his fall at the hobgoblin encampment, and it started to become painful. Kalko could see his master's pain, and began to lick Yuri's ears. Yuri just laughed through the pain and gave his big, furry friend a kiss on the snout. He gave a sigh of relief when his watch was over. Hopefully, some sleep would relieve his pain.

Once again that night, Yuri dreamt of a great abyss—a vast, black void in which he drifted. In the distance, beyond what he could see, he heard a faint melody. It was a familiar lullaby that sounded like a mere whisper. It brought warmth to the cold vacuum. Like a feather, he swayed in this warmth, but it didn't last for long. From the darkness came a loud scream, an all-encompassing shriek that shattered his hearing, but when he opened his eyes it was gone, and so was the pain. The numbness in his ears had disappeared.

For the first time in months, he could hear the birds chirping high in the trees. He could hear a crackling fire, Esten's wooden spoon hitting his metal pot as he stirred breakfast, and the soft laughter of children. As he stepped out into the light, he could almost hear the sunlight glistening through the treetops. Yuri could listen to himself chuckle as the tears flowed down his cheeks. Then he heard another sound; a sound that didn't come from anywhere he could see. It was the sound of Elaina's lullaby. It was just as beautiful as the last time he heard it. It was an enchanting melody that curved with the contours of the trees and was carried by the birds. It traveled along every ray of sun and flowed to every point the sun touched, and all seemed right.

Esten rushed over to a weeping Yuri. He took him by the shoulders and scanned his body for any injuries. "I," Yuri stuttered. "I," he tried again. Esten looked up in surprise, uncertain what he heard.

"Yuri?" he asked. His voice was deep, and had an almost calming effect on those who heard it.

"I can hear," Yuri said. Esten backed away, stunned. "I can hear!" Yuri exclaimed.

"Yuri!" Esten grabbed him and lifted him up in a big bear hug as he laughed and rejoiced. "How can this be?" he asked.

"I don't know," Yuri said as he swept away his tears.

"A good knock to the head, perhaps?" Esten smiled, thinking back to Yuri's fall the day before.

"Perhaps. Perhaps a strange tea I drank," Yuri wondered out loud.

"Let's pack up, my friend. We need to get these children back to their parents." Esten mirrored Yuri's smile. "It's good to see you smile again, Yuri," Esten said as he patted Yuri on the back.

"It's good to hear again, Esten."

They reached Bela the following evening. The villagers didn't expect them back so soon, but rejoiced at their return. Immediately, a feast was planned for the next evening in their honor. Esten led Yuri to the elder and his wife, and was finally able to properly introduce them.

"Yuri, I would like you to meet our hosts, elder Ered Greywater and his wife, Menha."

"We've already met Yuri," Menha laughed.

"But now I can hear," Yuri said. Ered's jaw dropped.

"It is a miracle! How did this happen? What happened in those woods, my man?" Ered leaned in and bombarded Yuri with questions.

"Whoa, whoa, wait right there, Ered," Esten interjected. "It's been a long journey, and we could all use some rest right now."

"You're right, you're right." Ered held up his hands and backed away.

"Come inside, you all," Menha said as she headed into her home.

"Any more of that tea, Menha?" Yuri asked. Menha stared at him and smiled.

"You have had all you need, young hunter."

The following morning Yuri and Kalko sat outside, enjoying the morning sounds. The rooster crowed, the birds chirped. Soon the villagers started to awaken, starting their work for the new day. Yuri felt a tap on his shoulder.

"You're up early." Esten sat down next to Yuri.

"I couldn't sleep. Too many sounds. I forgot how loudly you snore," Yuri explained.

"You'll get used to it again." Esten smiled. "Soon everything will be back to the way it was." He yawned, and stretched his long arms. "Speaking of which—we've gotten rid of those hobgoblins, but we still don't know why they took the children."

"Yes, they're usually not this organized."

"We should stay—go back to their camp and see what we can find."

Yuri stared off into the distance, to the far trees. His wife's song was still in his head, and he couldn't figure out why or where it was coming from. "I have a job to finish."

"A job?" Esten asked.

"I need to return to Ishar. I need to face," Yuri paused, "you know."

"I know. If you can find it."

"It's there." Yuri threw a stick for Kalko, who sped off after it. "I can hear it."

*****

Bela was at his back, and with Kalko by his side Yuri embarked on his next commission. A self-commissioned job, rather. There wasn't a bounty, and he wouldn't receive any compensation. The only reward would be justice—an age-old incentive better known as revenge. The journey to the fishing village he once called home wouldn't be a strenuous one. The land was mostly green and flat on the southern side of the Frostridges, but the trip would be a long one. Yuri estimated he would travel for eight weeks, but he was determined to get there in no more than four.

Yuri and Kalko only ate what Yuri took from the village and what he could forage. Kalko was fortunate enough to catch a rabbit or pheasant every so often as they journeyed. Yuri didn't sleep much, and traveled at night while the moon lit his way. Before he knew it, they had skirted down the entire Storm Coast and could see the great city of Isatarist in the distance to the south. Isatarist was the most significant city on the continent of Draston, and it was indeed marvelous. It was home to all races, and boasted massive religious temples and various institutions of learning. It had extensive trade centers, where Yuri often brought fish to be sold. That was where he had met Elaina, an ironmonger's daughter. Yuri didn't linger long; he didn't want to become lost in memories as he stood atop a green hill, watching the city. The coast was not far.

The road turned back to the north from Isatarist, but this was the quickest way, and on the morning of the twenty-ninth day Yuri collapsed on the outskirts of Ishar. His body was frail and so was his mind; delusional from thirst, hunger, and exhaustion. Fortunately, it wasn't long until an elderly couple found his body baking in the summer sun.

"Come on, boy; here, Kalko," Yuri called as they carried him to their home.

"The heat has taken him; fetch me some water, my love," said the elderly woman as they placed him on their bed. Shortly after that, her husband rushed in with a cup of water.

"Who do you think this is, Jane?" her husband asked as he slowly fed Yuri the water.

"I don't know, Arthur." She slid her fingers across Yuri's sword sheath. "He's not from these parts."

Yuri was in and out of consciousness for the next two days. The couple had moved him to a bed of hay in their shed and meticulously cared for him. On the third day, Yuri asked where he was.

"You're in Ishar, son," Jane answered as she was clipping Yuri's beard.

"What are you doing to me?"

"I thought I'd clean you up a bit." She clipped another piece of his beard. Yuri saw Kalko sitting at the foot of his hay bed, and immediately felt safe. "You're in bad shape, son."

"I've traveled a long way to get here."

"Is that so? Where from?" Jane lifted his head to meet the cup of water in her hand. Yuri swallowed.

"Darvalon."

"Never heard of it." She lay his head back down. "What brought you here?"

Yuri paused for a second. "The ocean."

*****

For a week, Jane and Arthur brought him food and water. Yuri would eat and drink half, and left his bowl and cup on the floor for Kalko.

"You need to eat all your food," Arthur said one evening as he brought Yuri his dinner. "You need it to regain your strength; you were hanging by a thread when we found you."

"I'll be all right. I think tomorrow I should get out, get some fresh air."

"That's a good idea. Just don't go too far; wouldn't want you getting lost."

"I won't. I grew up here," Yuri explained.

"You did?" Arthur was taken aback. "I thought I knew everyone in Ishar. What's your name?" he asked.

"Yuri."

"Yuri." Arthur pondered on the name. "Yes! Yuri!" Yuri nodded.

"You're meant to be dead, son." Arthur leaned in. "You and your family were taken by sirens. How did you survive?"

"Survive is a strong word. My wife was swallowed by the sea, and I had to bury my son. In many ways I didn't," Yuri looked down, "survive."

"But you're here. Why are you here?"

"I've come to kill a siren."

"There are no sirens here, son," Arthur chuckled. "Not for a couple of years. In fact," he paused, "not since you and your family were seen last!"

"There have to be!" Yuri's eyes filled with panic. "I know they are still here. I know!"

"Calm down, son. Even if they are, no one has ever found their nest."

"We will."

"We?" Arthur laughed. "Oh no, son. I'm not getting involved." Arthur left the shed shaking his head.

The next morning Yuri gathered his strength and equipment, and headed out. Yuri and Kalko's search would start on the beach that they washed up on. He dreaded going there, and he didn't know how he would react once he got there—it was there that he'd buried his son.

After a two-hour hike, the beach's steep ridge was in sight. As they approached, the large white stone that marked Yuri's son's grave became clear.

"Tane," Yuri said as he stood in front of the white stone. Tane was his son's name, and that day was the first time he'd uttered that name in two years. Yuri dropped to his knees and wept for his son; he ached to see Tane one last time. Slowly, he began scraping in the dirt with his fingers. He dug and dug until he unearthed Tane's little hand, and there he left it. Yuri couldn't bear to uncover any more. He reached down to touch Tane's hand, and he felt something soft tickling his hand. He grabbed the tickling thing buried next to his son's tiny hand and pulled it out, and what he pulled out was a clump of black fur. Yuri's eyes widened, and his heart began to race. He threw the fur to the side and started digging again. He dug and dug until he unearthed that corpse of a dog—a large dog with patches of black fur. Yuri looked up at Kalko, who sat across from him. His dead dog. The dog that lay dead beside his son all those years ago.

"I buried you," Yuri whispered. An unsettling reality set in, and a blanket of anxiety began to suffocate him.

Yuri got up and ran. Kalko chased after him, then past Yuri. And as Kalko ran by, the lullaby in his head became louder. Yuri continued to run, following the sound of his wife's song and the specter of the dog.

Before he knew it, Yuri followed Kalko right up to a cave entrance just above the crashing tide, tucked into the bottom of a tall cliff. The dog walked up to the opening, sat down, and eyed him with a calm gaze. Yuri wasn't sure how far he had run, but he walked by the ghost of the dog and into a shallow cave.

It was damp and stank of death. Yuri counted only six creatures. Most were just lying on the ground—they seemed almost as if they were in a trance, rocking back and forth on their backs. Yuri counted three babies; they were eating the flesh of another dead siren. On the far side of the nest, he saw an iron cage with a woman inside. She had dark locks like his wife had, and sang the lullaby that echoed in his head. Her melody curved with the outlines of the cave walls and was carried by the gulls. It traveled along every ray of sun and flowed to every point the sun touched, but nothing seemed good.

Yuri drew his sword and carefully made his way to the cage. He moved slowly between the entranced sirens and past the feasting hatchlings.

"Elaina?" Yuri reached the cage, and he couldn't believe his eyes. His wife was alive. She was incredibly skinny, and her once-luscious black locks were dull. "Elaina?" he asked again, but she just continued singing. Yuri pried the cage open with his sword and reached in for her.

"No, no, no," she whispered as she stepped back against the cage bars.

"Elaina, it's your Yuri. Don't you recognize me?"

Elaina saw the sirens come out of their trances, and began singing again.

"Elaina, we must go." Yuri grabbed her by the arm and pulled her out, but as he did so she uttered a yelp. The entranced sirens came to, and in seconds they surrounded Yuri and Elaina.

Yuri lashed out at the one in front of him, slicing it open. He turned to another and pierced her chest. They began to swipe with their claws and whip with their tails, but Yuri managed to bring down another one. When he looked over, Elaina had run back into her cage. He moved towards her, but as he did the siren closest to the cage released a mighty scream. Her scream vibrated violently through the air; echoes bounced off the walls and rocks and shook the ground of the cave. Yuri fell to the ground in agony when his eardrums burst. Elaina fell, too. She opened her mouth and tried to sing, but she couldn't hear herself. The sound that she made repulsed the sirens. Yuri saw the panic in her eyes, but as he tried to reach for her he faded out of consciousness.

The sun was setting, and gleamed off the calm ocean when Yuri eventually opened his eyes. There were no sirens in sight; even the babies were gone, and only the dead remained. It seemed that the few that were left went in search of another nest. Why, he would never know.
"Elaina!" Yuri shouted. He shouted, but he couldn't hear himself; he couldn't hear anything. He crawled over to the cage where Elaina lay dead. Razor-sharp claws had slashed her open. Yuri began to weep as he crawled into the cage with her. Her blood covered his hands and knees as he moved towards her. He lay behind Elaina and held her tightly like he always used to—he knew it made her feel safe. As Yuri started to sing her the lullaby, Kalko loped into the cave and entered the cage, where he lay down at Yuri's feet, and all was good.

Bloodied
By Stuart Thaman

734AM
Age of the Dracon-esti

"If the Order finds out what you've done, they'll kill you."

"I know, I know, just... hand me that beaker."

The taller of the two sorcerers bit back a cough as a wisp of vile gas escaped from a nearby jar. "And you do all this for what? Money? There can't be anything in it for you."

Ezznar snatched the vial from the sorcerer's hand. "You know they don't trade in gold coins," he half-sneered, though he didn't really mean all the venom in his voice.

"I don't know," the tall one said with a disapproving sigh. "You reek of blood. I don't even know why I'm helping you."

"You'll have my eternal gratitude," Ezznar said. "Besides, you have to admit that you've always been intrigued by these sorts of things, right?"

"As an academic!" the sorcerer countered. "Not like this. Not down in the bowels of the Order, brewing potions and hoping we don't get blown to the nether in the process."

Ezznar drew a thin knife from his waistcoat. The tool was delicate and elaborate, designed for a singular purpose. Placing the point against the flesh of his palm, he applied just enough pressure to break the skin. "One, two, three, four," he counted carefully as the crimson droplets fell. He stopped quickly at six and pulled back his hand, making sure he had exactly enough of his blood in the tincture, and not a drop more.

"This whole business feels like a dangerous path to be walking, Ezznar—one that does not well suit a sorcerer of Dunarth's Order," the taller man concluded. He shook his head and turned, but a quiet pop caught his attention.

Ezznar's smile was impossible to conceal. "There," he said, happily pointing to the now-smoking vial. The wooden table was covered with a thin layer of purple liquid that had splattered all over it. "Dunarth can have his books and his secrets. The goddess Falthi rewards those who practice her lost arts, and she rewards them well."

"I don't need to tell you how the Order would deal with a blasphemer such as yourself, do I?"

"You are my only friend," Ezznar said, his voice somewhat sullen despite his minor success. "I know how much danger this puts us both in, that *I* have put us both in, but please... you will understand when I have succeeded. For now, your trust and your silence are sufficient."

Again, the tall sorcerer let out a heavy sigh laden with regret and a hint of fear. "If you die down here doing one of your experiments, I will not try to salvage your reputation," he said after a moment. The smell in the small, nearly-lightless chamber was starting to wear thin his nerves.

"I accept your terms, good sir," Ezznar replied. "Now, be ready tomorrow at dawn, or perhaps an hour before. It will take some time to reach the trolls, and I have need of another subject."

*****

At dawn, Ezznar and his tall friend met their driver in front of the Order's tower. They both wore cloaks designed for the road and sturdy boots, an altogether unusual ensemble for sorcerers to be seen wearing. Once alighted in the carriage they took it only a few blocks, as they had not actually told the driver where they were ultimately headed.

"Here will suffice," Ezznar said when they were several streets away from the Order. The driver looked curious in response to their short trip, but his expression faded when the sorcerer dropped a few coins into his pocket.

Ezznar waited for several minutes on the side of the quiet, dreary street before motioning to a second carriage that had been parked fifty feet away, in front of a brothel. The driver pulled his horses close, and Ezznar nodded to him, producing a tightly rolled scroll and handing it up as he climbed inside the closed compartment.

"Just how far is it?" the tall sorcerer asked.

The carriage lurched forward, and Ezznar pulled a short curtain over the only window to further conceal them. "We will likely arrive sometime close to dusk," he said with a frown. Travelling to the troll-populated areas was a lengthy endeavor, and he didn't like being cramped inside the small carriage for so long.

"You've brought food, I trust?"

Ezznar smiled, and lifted a small panel next to his seat. Inside was a rather abundant selection of pastries and dried meats that he had arranged for the driver to provide. "I've planned it all," he said with confidence. "You needn't worry."

The village of slender trolls was small and rustic, nestled in a broad bend of a river and surrounded by woodlands. Civilization only extended so far into the wilderness, and there was no road that led all the way to the trolls, so Ezznar and his companion stopped a few miles from the nearest hut and told their driver to wait. The man was a bit of an unsavory type, someone Ezznar frequently called upon to procure more illicit ingredients.

The forest path leading from the nearest bit of road to the troll village was one Ezznar knew well. He had traversed it several times in the past month, always for the same reason. His magic, his *blood* magic, required fuel. As they hiked, Ezznar thought of all the decisions that had led him down such a dark and twisted path. He didn't consider himself evil though, if his actions were ever brought to light, there would certainly be those who did attach the moniker to him, and he resented it. To Ezznar, an academic through and through, blood magic was simply another pursuit to be mastered.

The pair reached the outskirts of the village of slender trolls when the sun was high overhead. Ezznar's head glistened with sweat, and the back of his robe was wet all down the center. Near a large white birch tree atop a small crest in the land, the two sorcerers crouched to observe the trolls.

"How much do you think you need?" the taller one asked.

Ezznar fished in a deep pocket of his robe for a bit of parchment and then read a few numbers to himself. "Just one should do, but it will need to be a tall one," he said, once he had run through the calculation twice to make sure he had it right.

Down below, the trolls seemed to be celebrating some sort of event. Their language, if the noises they made to one another could even be called such, was far too unrefined for Ezznar to have the slightest clue what they were saying. In the center of the shoddy huts and tents, there was a large pile of dead fish, and none of them had been cured or prepared for storage in any way. Ezznar wondered if the trolls had figured out how to smoke meat, for they at least had become proficient with fire, though little else.

One of the troll leaders, adorned with a colorful headdress and several necklaces made from shells and other bits of wilderness windfall, was orchestrating the strange event with a short staff in his hand. He arranged the other trolls into rows around the dead fish, and then each member of the tribe was permitted to select a single carcass for themselves. The smell from the fish pile was overwhelming, and Ezznar's gut churned when he saw one of the trolls happily devouring his prize.

"Some sort of food ritual?" Ezznar guessed. He had observed the trolls for some time, and often he returned to civilization shaking his head at things he had seen.

"Your guess is as good as mine."

They waited at the edge of the village for some time, watching the strange spectacle before them, until finally one of the trolls wandered away from the tribe, in their direction.

"Look alive," Ezznar said, sliding a long-bladed knife from his robe.

The tall sorcerer gave him a concerned look.

"All for science, brother," Ezznar said with confidence. "I do it all for my research."

A moment later Ezznar exploded from the underbrush, a spell lingering on his fingertips. He conjured forth a bit of sorcery, and the troll became encased in bone-chilling frost. Ezznar felt a bit of his inner strength, his *will*, fade from his mind as the magical ice spiraled out of his fingertips, and he knew the cost of such a spell was steep.

The troll's movement halted at once, and only the faintest echo of a scream managed to escape the large creature's lips. Luckily, the troll did not fall to the ground, and for that Ezznar was thankful. On previous attempts, he had seen more than one creature shatter on the forest floor, its precious blood wasted.

After casting a quick strength spell over the both of them, the taller sorcerer moved to the troll's legs and lifted, bringing the frozen humanoid several inches from the ground. Ezznar caught the head, and together they began to carry the terrified, immobilized creature back toward the road. The journey took considerable effort, but the two sorcerers returned before nightfall to meet their driver.

Once returned to the Order, Ezznar dragged his fresh catch unseen to the bowels of the building, using a little-known entrance he had recently discovered behind the noisy tavern next door. The troll was heavier than most of the others the sorcerer had stolen from the tribe, and a smile crept across Ezznar's face when the thought of all the blood there was to harvest. Down in his makeshift basement lair, he set to work at once.

Falthi, the forgotten goddess of tyranny and control, demanded exacting precision from her disciples. Ezznar kept a small, painted portrait of her hidden in a shallow drawer at his workstation, and he fetched the item gingerly from its place, careful not to let his flesh brush against the oiled canvas. He placed the painting horizontally on his desk, and then set to work on the troll.

Long blade in hand, Ezznar inched closer to his unconscious prey like a leopard stalking some lesser beast. The troll was very much alive, though it would remain magically asleep for quite some time. Ezznar worked his blade quickly, and two slender fingers came free of the troll's hand. Ezznar held them upright until they stopped bleeding, then set the digits on top of Falthi's image. Returning to the troll, he moved a metal bucket beneath the two stumps he had created to begin collecting his precious fuel.

After an hour, a fine layer of sweat had built up on Ezznar's forehead and back, and the troll was nearly unrecognizable. The same spell that had frozen it had also stopped the slender troll's regeneration abilities. Its hands and feet were completely gone, and its large, dark eyes were resting on the top of Falthi's portrait. Against one corner, three buckets of troll blood waited to be used, still warm.

Finally, Ezznar set down his bloody knife. He had a short bookcase against one wall with several alchemical implements on top of it, and he took a blue-bound book from the shelf, quickly flipping to the page he needed. He had read the recipe at least a hundred times, though he still could not calm his mind and take away the sinking feeling that he had forgotten something critical.

"Two fingers..." he muttered, his voice trailing off as he read aloud to himself. "Got it. Three gallons of blood..." Ezznar went back to his buckets and dipped a graduated wooden stick into the center of the nearest one. When he pulled it out, the stain on the wood told him his calculation had been correct. "Exactly three gallons."

His fingers traced over the final ingredients, and the last one gave him pause. "Protection from Chaos," he repeated. He knew the spell, but Ezznar also knew that the spell's sorcerous words would be erased from his mind the moment he spoke them. He only had one chance.

When he had all the necessary objects neatly arranged on his desk, all three buckets of fresh blood arranged in a triangle around Falthi's portrait, he spoke the words to Protection from Chaos. There came a shimmer, a faint purple glow, and the blood began to vibrate.

The vibrations grew stronger and stronger until Ezznar feared they would shake the rafters down atop his head and bring the entire Order crumbling onto the street. He felt confident, yet utterly terrified at the same time.

Then the blood spoke to him. "Ezznarrrrrrr," it hissed, bubbling and splattering the walls behind the buckets.

"Falthi," the sorcerer gasped, falling to his knees before the quaking blood. "My goddess, I have sought your favor."

The blood boiled and burst outward again, and some of it landed on the portrait with the severed troll fingers.

Then the light of the world extinguished, bathing all of Duskvar in silent, oppressive darkness.

*****

Ezznar awoke in utter darkness. His throat was dry, and his feet felt heavy like he hadn't used them for days or even weeks. He opened his eyes, but the darkness did not extinguish. The wind hammering his face told him he was no longer beneath the Order. Perhaps he was no longer even in the city. Maybe he was dead.

Then he heard it. He heard *her* voice, drifting through the wind like a plague come to corrupt his mind and destroy his body.

Falthi.

The goddess had come to him, or maybe he had been taken to her—it did not matter which. Ezznar knew he was in the goddess' presence, and it shook him to his core. All the confidence he had felt, all the surety he had known before casting his spell, was gone.

A drop of liquid fell onto his forehead. Ezznar brushed it away, and he could smell its metallic tint. *Blood.*

"Am I... am I dead?" he asked the darkness. His voice was soft, and scratchy in his throat.

"Ezznarrrrrrr," the goddess whispered, her voice so close her lips brushed against the sorcerer's ear.

"Y—Yes?" he stuttered. "Where am I?"

"You are not one of my disciples," the goddess stated.

Ezznar heard her footsteps, and he crunched himself into as tight a ball as he could manage. Desperate for a way out, he tried to remember the spells he had dedicated his life to learning, but their words would not come to his mind. He was trapped.

"You do not bow before me," Falthi continued, prompting Ezznar to roll to his knees in supplication.

"What have I done?" the sorcerer whispered. He brushed a tear from his cheek, his forehead pressed firmly to the ground.

"I know your thoughts, Ezznar," the goddess went on, "and they are not pleasing. You wanted to summon me and use me. You wanted to steal my knowledge."

"No!" Ezznar was quick to correct. "I would never! I merely wanted to learn *from* you, to know if the blood magic was real, Your... Highness?"

Falthi laughed, and her sickening voice echoed around the walls of Ezznar's mind—until he was delirious, his thoughts completely scrambled by the sheer intensity of his experience.

"You are too weak to learn from me," the goddess stated, her voice returning mercifully to a less painful level. "And now you are in my debt. I own you, Ezznar. I *control* you."

For a moment, the sorcerer thought of disobedience. And then the thought was gone, erased by his unending will to live. "Yes, Your Highness. It shall be as you say."

"Of course it will," Falthi spat back at him with a sneer. "The only path before you is mine. All others lead to destruction. And with your destruction will come an eternity of servitude. Do not forget that."

Ezznar could not lower his head any closer toward the ground.

"You're mine."

*****

Ezznar awoke with his brow covered in sweat, safely tucked into his sheets in a small chamber near the top of the Order's headquarters. The room was his own, and it took him several seconds to realize that he was not trapped in some dungeon or imprisoned within the dark reaches of Falthi's mind.

Slowly, Ezznar extricated himself from his sheets and inspected his body. He was all there, unscathed as far as he could tell, with nothing whatsoever amiss. When he was dressed and more or less composed, he made his way carefully down the stone stairs outside his door to the main level of the building, listening for Falthi's voice after every step.

Upon reaching the Order's main hall Ezznar saw several other sorcerers eating, and idly chatting as though nothing was wrong. Still, Ezznar could not keep his eyes from darting around each corner, probing every ounce of darkness for the hideous blood golem he had crafted.

Falthi was nowhere to be seen.

"Ezznar, come! Join us!" one of the sorcerers sitting at a nearby table called, motioning to an empty seat.

Ezznar shook his head and turned, finding his only trusted friend among the others. He grabbed the tall sorcerer by his arm and pulled him aside, trying in vain to keep the fear from his face.

"What do you want?"

Ezznar waited to respond until he knew his voice would not carry far enough to be heard by the wrong ears. "The spell..." He drifted off, unsure how to describe what he had seen. "It worked!"

The taller sorcerer's face showed his confusion. "What spell?" he asked.

"The *blood* magic," Ezznar whispered. "It worked!"

"Blood magic?" the sorcerer exclaimed a little too loudly, surprise in his eyes.

Ezznar clamped a hand over the man's mouth to silence him. "Keep it down!" he urged. "What I've been studying, all my research... You helped me! It worked!"

The taller sorcerer backed away, his hands in front of him. "I—I don't know what you're saying," he stammered.

"You *helped* me... The troll?" Ezznar asked. "You don't remember any of it? Falthi? The blood?"

Then he could smell her. He could smell the blood-tinged scent of the goddess, and it was pungent in the air. *Close.*

The corners of the tall sorcerer's lips curled up into a knowing smile as he backed away.

"No..." Ezznar gasped. He couldn't believe what he was seeing. "What have you become? What have I created?"

Turning quickly for the staircase, Ezznar bolted down several levels until he was once more on the street. He ran to the rear of the building and stopped.

Several sorcerers stood around a small wooden door, the same entry the knowledge of which Ezznar had thought had been his alone.

One of them turned as Ezznar approached, and the unfamiliar sorcerer raised a hand to point in his direction. "There!" the man shouted. "That man is the one I saw!"

Ezznar whirled and took off the opposite way, his heart pounding in his chest. He thought to the spells he knew, to the decades of research and study he had conducted—and all of it was gone.

In its place, occupying a huge swath of his memory, was the knowledge of blood magic.

He knew there was more to blood magic than just what had been placed into his mind, but it did not matter. He had enough, and he knew what to do.

All Ezznar needed was blood.

Without the time to harvest another unsuspecting slender troll, Ezznar shouldered through the nearest open door he could see, staggering into a building he didn't recognize. Inside, the structure was populated mostly by women, and the two nearest the door shrieked at Ezznar's violent entry.

"Blood," he growled, and his own voice sounded somehow foreign to him. *Is this it? Have I lost my mind?* he silently thought, unable to comprehend how his entire life's work had so quickly gotten so far away from his intentions.

Before Ezznar could fully understand what he was doing, he had a hand around a young girl's throat, pulling her to his body. The others screamed, and one of them tried in vain to push him back with a broom, and then the girl in Ezznar's clutches was dead, her throat shredded to ribbons.

In his hand, the sorcerer held a sticky, warm chunk of human meat, and he could feel the power of the torn flesh waiting to be released. Waiting to be consumed and utilized. Waiting for his *command.*

Ezznar turned and propelled the blood in his hand behind him, toward the door he had barged through just a moment before. When the red mass splattered against the wood it came alive, writhing with magical energy and pulling itself together into a roughly humanoid shape the size of a tiny dog.

Two of Ezznar's pursuers were nearly upon the door frame when the bloody homunculus leapt into action. The little beast vaulted through the air, trailing a steady stream of blood behind it, and latched onto the lead sorcerer's chest, digging through the man's flesh. As it worked its murder, its body began to grow and shift, adding layer after layer of mass that it was stealing from its victim.

Ezznar could barely fathom what he was witnessing. He wasn't sure what made his hands shake more: watching the putrid golem at work, or knowing that he had been the one to give it life.

Thinking almost entirely of his own survival, Ezznar pushed through the terrified women in the building to reach the rear exit, eager to turn his back on the killing he had wrought. Once more on the city streets, he didn't know where to turn. So much of his life had been spent in the Order that he barely had any acquaintances outside his fellow sorcerers, much less friends he could rely upon to hide him.

Turning to his left, he ran for the only place he knew well—the Order.

It didn't take more than half a minute for Ezznar to reach the complex once more, and he was relieved to see no guards or sorcerers outside patrolling for him. Counting himself lucky for the first time all day, Ezznar barged through the front door and made straight for his chamber, the beginnings of a weak and disheveled plan starting to come together in his mind.

He flew up the stone staircase to his room, then stopped in his tracks. The tall sorcerer, one of the few people Ezznar regarded as a true friend, was leaning casually on the door frame as if he had been expecting Ezznar the entire time.

"You're back," the sorcerer said. Ezznar could hear Falthi's voice underneath the man's, and a shiver ran up his spine.

"What have you done?" he pleaded.

"Me?" the goddess laughed. "I haven't done anything. But you, *you* have done things the bards will sing about for years."

Ezznar staggered backward, putting one hand against the wall for support. "Jus—Just leave me alone! Let me live my life!" he stammered.

Falthi took a step toward him in her stolen body. "You belong to me, remember? Or have you so quickly forgotten our little arrangement?"

"I—"

Falthi's hand shot out and wrapped around Ezznar's throat. "Either serve me, or you die right here on these stairs. Those are your only options," she sneered.

Slowly, Ezznar nodded. He knew he wasn't cut out to be a hero. He would never be able to muster the strength to resist a goddess.

"Good," Falthi cooed, turning her stolen face into a smile. She gave Ezznar's neck one final squeeze before she let him go and the sorcerer fell to the floor, gasping for air.

"Now," she went on, "the task I have for you is one of paramount importance. Do you understand, mortal?"

Ezznar nodded, but he did not meet her gaze.

"You have summoned me, and I have given you the tools necessary to aid me," she said, walking in tight circles in the narrow hallway, her hands on her hips. "I need you to find someone for me. Her name is Elaná, and I have been searching for her for some time. She stole something from me, something I hold very dear, and you, Ezznar, are going to return it to me."

"And... and why must it be me?" he asked weakly.

Slowly, the tall sorcerer's skin began to melt, revealing Falthi's horrid body. It sloughed to the floor as the goddess spoke, revealing the bloody amalgamation beneath. "Because you can use the channels to find her, and I cannot. In this form, the pathetic attempt you offered in your dingy workshop, I am not capable of creating blood magic. But you are. You will be my vessel, and through you I will fully enter into this plane."

Ezznar couldn't imagine the weight of the task being thrust upon him. When the final bit of his friend's flesh dropped to the floor, he finally looked up. "And what then?" he dared to ask.

The blood golem smiled wickedly, and the goddess' voice was overwhelming. "Then the world shall kneel!" she bellowed.

Ezznar fell backward, rolling painfully down the stairs behind him, and crashed onto the landing with a thud. He glanced back once to see if Falthi was following him, and when he saw she was not he leapt down the next staircase as quickly as his feet would take him.

Deep in his mind, Ezznar knew he would be able to find Elaná. The knowledge of the spell he needed had been planted in his mind; he only had to find a suitable place, compile the components, and he will have fulfilled his debt. Though he knew, deep down in the recesses of his whirling mind, he knew he would never *truly* please the goddess. His servitude would never be enough. His obedience would never satisfy her lust for dominance, and Ezznar knew he was doomed.

Once more on the street, the terrified sorcerer continued to run. He darted past a few businesses, stealing glances in their windows as he ran. When he reached the end of the street, he was panting and soaked in sweat. His body was not very accustomed to physical exertion, and it let him know with each heaving breath.

And then he heard shouts from behind, and set his feet in motion once again, turning down the nearest alley to try and confuse his pursuers. His ploy worked, and the men running after him went past the alley, continuing down the street in the wrong direction.

Ezznar sighed in relief. He let himself fall to the ground, his back against the stone behind him, and closed his eyes. Resting just beneath the veil of consciousness, Ezznar sensed the blood magic spell he needed to cast. The spell he was required to cast. It wasn't very complex, but he would need a mirror. With them being so expensive, he wasn't exactly sure where he would find one.

Slowly, the muscles in his legs and sides aching, Ezznar got back to his feet and looked around. He was between a tavern and a half-timbered building that looked residential, so he decided to investigate the home for the component he needed.

The rear side of the house was tall, fitting neatly between the other businesses in the cramped city center, and a single door was the only point of entry. With his ear to the wood, Ezznar listened for any sounds of movement inside. He heard nothing.

There was a knocker set into the center of the door, and he pushed on it gently, smiling when the wood moved beneath his touch to allow him entry. The interior of the house was sparsely decorated, a handful of tapestries and some small paintings hanging in wooden frames down the main hallway to the front door. Behind him, Ezznar found the locking bar for the back door and dropped it into place.

He moved as quietly as he could through the lower level of the house, though he was still breathing heavily from his run. To his right, he found a small kitchen area, and the fireplace was cold. To his left, Ezznar entered a small sitting area with an elegant rug covering the floorboards. The rug gave him a bit of hope that the owner of the residence was wealthy enough to own a mirror, though he shuddered when he thought about the amount of blood he would need to provide for his spell.

Making his way upstairs, Ezznar paused every few feet to listen for activity. Still hearing nothing, he reached the landing and winced when the top stair squeaked under his weight. Something moved inside one of the two rooms at the top of the stairs. Ezznar inched backward, and the stair creaked again, perhaps even louder than the first time.

Finally, when the door did not open, Ezznar let himself breathe again. He crept up to the door, carefully stepping over the final stair, and stood as still as possible to wait and listen.

A dog barked from the other side of the door, and Ezznar felt his body physically relax more than he ever thought possible. He pushed open the door, and a small, yappy dog scampered out and jumped up to the sorcerer's knees, happily slobbering all over his robe.

Inside the room, a tall mirror stood on wooden supports behind a posh, embroidered dog bed. A four-poster bed dominated the rest of the chamber, along with a set of drawers against a wall beneath a frosted window. "That should certainly work," Ezznar said cheerfully as he gently pushed the dog away.

"But I need blood. Lots of blood," he said. The list of components for the spell flashed through his head. He let his eyes drift back to the dog happily barking at his feet, but he pushed the grim thought far from his mind. *Besides, the dog doesn't have enough blood to cover the entire mirror,* he told himself.

So, he waited. Ezznar wasn't exactly sure what he would do when the owner of the house came back, but he needed blood, and he dreaded the thought of leaving the building. If the sorcerers were still hunting him down, it wouldn't take long for him to be found. Their magic would certainly locate his position, especially since he was still so close to the Order.

You can hide, a deep, sinister voice echoed in his head. Ezznar was crouched next to the front door of the residence, a kitchen knife held in his hands, and the words made him nearly stab himself with fright.

You have it within you, slave, Falthi's voice said.

Resigned, Ezznar searched his newfound knowledge of blood magic until he thought of the correct spell, a magical means of concealing his existence to the world.

With a grimace, Ezznar ran his stolen kitchen knife along the side of his forearm, cutting the flesh enough to bring forth some blood, but not enough to cause any permanent damage or impairment. The blood beaded on the surface of his arm, and he could sense the power it held. A quick series of runes flashed in front of his mind's eye, and Ezznar knew they were committed to memory. Using his blood as paint and his trembling fingers as the brush, he drew the three runes he had seen on various parts of his body. He made the first on his forehead, using the reflective glint of his knife to follow his work, and the second and third runes he affixed to his arms, one on each.

You cannot be scryed, Falthi told him, almost congratulating him on his amateur blood magic.

For the briefest of moments, Ezznar let a smile play out on his bloody face. Blood magic was useful, he knew, and he *almost* gave himself over to its strength. Then

Falthi's voice laughed in his head, reminding him of his eternal servitude, and his spirit fell once more.

Several hours crawled past as Ezznar waited with his knife. The dog he had left upstairs occasionally barked, and the house was otherwise totally silent. Then he heard someone coming toward the front door, and his muscles tensed in anticipation.

A key rattled in the lock.

The door swung open, and Ezznar jumped out as quickly as he could—and there he skewered a little girl's chest. The knife sank into her body, up to the hilt, and she dropped to the floor a book she had been carrying, her eyes wide with horror.

"N—No!" Ezznar shouted, but it was too late. The girl was dead, or else she would die very quickly. It did not matter. The deed had been accomplished, and Ezznar was a murderer twice over. His mind raced, and Falthi imparted more images of the slaughter that would befall him should he be captured. Thinking once more of nothing but his own survival, he dragged the girl by her feet, into the house, leaving a smear of blood on the front steps.

He took her corpse up the stairs, pulling her unceremoniously to the bedroom where her parents likely slept. Taking the mirror from its supports and laying it flat on the bed, Ezznar struggled to hoist the dead girl on top of it. She wasn't heavy by any means, but the sorcerer was tired. When he finally had her arranged as best he could, he pulled his knife free from the girl's chest and set to work. He needed the mirror covered, and the mirror was unfortunately quite large.

After almost half an hour of cutting and slicing, the girl was in pieces on the bed and the mirror held roughly an inch of standing blood. The spell was almost complete.

"Elaná," he spoke, drawing her name in the center of all the blood. There was too much liquid on the mirror's surface to get the letters to stay, but it did not matter. He knew he was completing the spell correctly.

After a moment, the mirror began to shake. The blood vibrated, and then it scattered to the edges of the frame, some of it spilling out over the sides to further stain the sheets.

In the center of the mirror, a face appeared. She was pretty, with auburn hair, and large, round eyes that danced in the sunlight. Ezznar watched as the girl worked, dipping strings into candle wax and hanging them on a rack to dry. He pushed some more of the blood away to reveal the rest of the room the woman was sitting in, and he recognized the street from one of the windows. It wasn't far away in the city, perhaps a dozen or so blocks, and the woman appeared focused on her task. She'd likely be there for quite some time.

A pang of sadness welled up in Ezznar's chest. It was different from the terror he had felt before, when he'd killed the girl in the doorway. That terror had been quick and painful, but had subsided in a blur when he had realized he couldn't go back. Standing above the mirror and Elaná's beautiful face, he knew he had a choice. Going to her candle shop would be an active decision, and it would take him long enough to get there that he would have time to consider his actions.

"I'm already a murderer," he needlessly reminded himself. He thought back to the first innocent human he had killed, the woman whose throat he had ripped from her neck. But then he thought of all the trolls he had captured, the trolls he had *harvested*, and shuddered again. His stomach turned in nauseating circles.

An image of Falthi in the form of a hideous blood golem danced behind his eyes, and Ezznar vomited onto the floor. "What have I become?" he gasped, wiping his mouth. "This isn't how it was supposed to go!"

He heard the front door open on the floor beneath him, a pair of agitated voices accompanying it. *The parents.*

Ezznar didn't know what to do. He was aware that he was still hidden from magical means of detection, but anyone looking at him would still see him just as easily as they would anyone else. And he was covered in blood. The blood of the household's daughter.

Taking up his knife, Ezznar ran for the staircase. More shouts came from below and were aimed in his direction, but he ignored them all. At the bottom of the stairs, a middle-aged man blocked his path. The father was bewildered, his eyes full of surprise and fury, though his physical stature was far larger than Ezznar's short frame.

"I—I'm sorry!" Ezznar stammered, holding his knife in front of him. "I didn't mean to do it!" Then he lunged forward, trying to push his way past the man, and his blade found flesh. Ezznar tore a ragged, bloody line into the shoulder of the father, and the girl's mother shrieked wildly from her curled-up position on the floor nearby. Thankfully, the bigger man fell back against the staircase banister, and Ezznar was able to rush past him to the back door.

"I'm sorry!" he yelled one last time over his shoulder as he unlatched the door and exited. Back in the street, he knew which direction to run to reach Elaná and her candle shop.

They saw my face. They saw my robes, Ezznar thought as he pumped his legs along the alleyways. *They'll know I was from the Order, and the Order knows I've turned to blood magic.*

Ezznar was in too deep. With only a single murder on his hands, he might have been able to negotiate for a quick death with the city magistrate. With two murders, a dead troll, and a blood ritual in his wake, he knew they would torture him. They would make it public, and his torture would last for weeks, if not years or decades. His name would be chiseled in stone as one of the vilest creatures to ever walk the streets.

He used the hatred and fear swirling around his mind as fuel, and it worked. He ran harder than he had ever run in his life, and he reached the candle shop before long. He stopped behind the building to catch his breath, and he tasted some of the blood from his forehead mingling with his salty sweat and running into the corners of his mouth.

There was no going back.

Carefully, Ezznar peered through the rear window of the business and saw the woman he knew to be Elaná. The woman Falthi wanted him to kill.

A smile grew on Ezznar's face, but not from the prospect of what the goddess wanted him to do. He smiled because it was nearly over. The vile things he had done would soon be in the past, and with a heavy amount of alcohol, Ezznar even entertained the notion of one day forgetting the things he had wrought.

Once he had rubbed the majority of the blood from his skin, Ezznar entered the candle shop as nonchalantly as he knew how. Luckily, the pretty girl making candles behind the counter didn't pay him much attention, and he was able to lock the door behind him without her notice. "Elaná?" he asked as he approached the counter.

She looked up and smiled, her hair falling just slightly in front of her face as she moved. "Yes?" she replied. Her voice was melodic, like she was singing a song just under her breath.

Or maybe Ezznar was simply entranced, and the woman was some sort of demonic sorcerer who knew exactly what the sorcerer was there to do. But then her eyes went wide, and Ezznar knew that she was just an average commoner, perhaps more attractive than most, but she was terrified of the blood staining his robes. She wasn't some witch or agent of the goddess, she was just a frightened woman.

Ezznar raised a hand to hopefully quiet Elaná, but it did not work. "You have something I need," he said quickly, over her terror-filled screams. "Calm down, Elaná. I won't hurt you!"

Finally, the woman stopped yelling, though her eyes darted all around the shop.

"An associate of mine needs something you have," he went on. "Do not be afraid."

"What do you want?" Elaná demanded, a bit of resolve entering her voice.

Kill her, Falthi said in the sorcerer's head. *Send her my regards.*

"Falthi..." Ezznar trailed off. "She... she wants you..."

Elaná pushed herself back from her work, her back hitting the wall behind her. "Falthi?" she repeated. "You're in league with evil?"

Slowly, Ezznar nodded. "I'm so sorry..." he whispered, moving closer and cutting off the woman's only route of escape.

"Get aw—" she screamed, but her voice was cut short as Ezznar's knife ripped into her neck.

The blood golem walked into Ezznar's view from around a corner that led to the store's reserve inventory. Falthi clapped her hands, throwing blood all over the floor and walls.

"Congratulations!" the goddess said in a mocking tone.

Ezznar fell to his knees. "You have what you want," he muttered.

"Indeed," the goddess concurred. "I wanted you."

"What?"

"Elaná was nothing," the blood golem continued. She placed a hand on Ezznar's back to guide him to his feet. "She was just a girl. I've never seen her before in my life. But I needed you, Ezznar."

The sorcerer's mind spun. He looked with horror at his hands, his bloody hands, and wished for death to take him from his nightmare.

"You've been a good servant, Ezznar. You have proven yourself most capable, and you do not shy from the most demanding of tasks. Look," she said, turning the sorcerer's face to behold the dead woman on the floor. "Look at what you did. And you did it only for me. Only because I asked."

Ezznar shook his head. "No... You made me do it," he stated.

Falthi laughed. "You're mine, sorcerer. Your mind is shattered, and every single piece, every broken fragment, belongs to me."

She Called From Below

By Aaron Wulf

708AM
Age of the Dracon-esti

Ransden was a bastard. His mother was a harlot who went by the name of Violet Grimtrue, and worked at a dismal and decaying brothel on the north end of Orcan's Grove. In her controversial line of work, she shared herself with many clients. She eventually became pregnant, to which she responded with mixed emotions.

The birthing process was overly onerous, and Violet almost lost the baby. He was born breathing, however, but with complications. His breathing was never that strong; even months later, his breath was often short and weak. Baby Ransden's eyes were filtered with cloudy cataracts, and he had eleven toes.

By the age of five months the cataracts worsened, and Ransden was officially deemed blind.

He was raised in the brothel, yet Violet kept him away from the business aspect of it. It was a shame she had to live like this, she thought. She wanted to escape and make a better life for them both, but hated the near impossibility of trekking through the desolate mountains, or across the treacherous sea.

Despite her living conditions in the corrupt and decaying town of Orcan's Grove, Violet still did her best to raise Ransden as well as she could.

The brothel was known to most civilians as The Inn of the Dancing Specter. A creaky, dark oak sign hung loosely over the front steps, inviting in only the most wretched and lustful. Most of the women who worked at the inn were humans or outcast Eltharian elves, but were not wretched and lustful. At least not by nature. They considered themselves lucky to even have an occupation. This may not have been the case if they knew how well most other women had it beyond the mountains and sea, and in the many cities and capitals of Draston.

Within the past several decades, Orcan's Grove had seen a rise in local governing and religious powers, and a recession from their former governing kingdom of Kal.

The great book of The Orcanami was reintroduced after being found hidden away in the ancient annals of the local library. It had been translated and rewritten countless times by priests, philosophers, and scholars, and Orcan knows who else. Little known to the current generations, the meaning of the words in the book mirrored the original intentions not even in the slightest.

The most recent publication was only held in the Church of the Great Orcan—formerly a church of the old gods—and only read by those educated enough to read. Unfortunately, the city of Orcan's Grove had an illiteracy percentage near seventy-nine percent.

The Book of the Orcanami, year 708AM edition, spoke of the roles of women and men, which could be found in sub-book VII, chapter XI, page I, line I.

Simply put, The Orcanami stated that men were the superior gender, and women were meant to marry by the age of 16, conceive children, and raise them to be what The Orcan expected of them.

Violet Grimtrue did not marry by the time when she was 16. Nor did she ever marry, even by the age of 26, which would be the age of her death.

At 20 years of age, Ransden was born. This was not planned, of course, for her line of work made it fantastically difficult to know who the father had been. Still, this fact placed a heavy hulking burden on Ransden's shoulders. Little did he know that that very topic would illuminate the truth of fate, as well as revelation.

It could be said by most that Violet was a bad woman, but in those days, in that particular Netherish city, a single woman had to buy her own passage out, and in the concealment of night. She would have to either cross the treacherous mountains, sail the open seas, or attempt passage through the elven regions to the North.

She, regrettably to herself, did what she had to do to survive without being under the control of another. But when her child was born, any plans of escape were now just a fantasy.

She raised Ransden as well as she could. In the daytime, she would teach him the histories of Draston, basic math, and what little alchemy she knew. Aside from proper morals, she believed these were the three subjects that would be the most important for survival.

Late at night she would cry for hours, hoping and praying for a better life for her and her son.

It was hard on Violet, and harder on Ransden.

The other women supported Violet, to her face at least. But behind her back she could hear them whispering secrets of damnation, calling her demon spawn, and woman of evil.

Ransden was the blind boy who shouldn't have been born.

Ransden would hear this phrase every so often up until his sixth birthday. A few weeks after that is when *They* came.

The self-appointed high officials of Orcan's Grove caught wind of rumors that The Inn of the Dancing Specter was, in reality, a brothel. Sir Anton Duffry of the council could have vouched for that based on his personal experiences there, but decided to let that detail slip unknown.

Violet grabbed Ransden's wrist with urgent demand and led him down to the cellar, which was mostly empty and smelled like dead fish, barley, and piss, but had many dark alcoves to hide a boy of only four-feet tall.

Upstairs, bursting through the front door, they invaded. Soldiers and civilians, all screaming profanities in the name of The Orcan, declared ownership of the establishment and ordered all harlots to be put to death.

The next day, as the sun rose and the cock crowed, not a body lay breathing in the ransacked hole. None but one.

Beneath the tattered remnants of curtains, busted and broken chairs, the mangled and lifeless corpses, in the overlooked basement, breathed a little boy.

His breath was slow and heavy, counting his breaths as time passed since the last voice was heard. His nostrils flared, searching for the smell of his mother's perfume. Sweeping his hands across the dusty floor, he searched for the staircase somewhere along the perimeter of the room.

His temples throbbed, and his chest tightened with heartbreak. His dirty fingernails scraped to find ascending wood planks. His wobbly knees inched forward ever so carefully.

When he finally stumbled upon the decayed wooden steps he fell to his back, too grief-stricken to climb. His arms and legs swept up and down like bats kicking up dust on the floor.

If anyone would have seen this, they would have sworn the image he created on the dust-covered ground resembled an angel, like children would make in the snow.

Without a mother, he would never feel like a child again. No more building sandcastles, no more happiness.

Ransden was alone. He felt beaten. He felt dead.

TWO
738AM Age of Oddities
Thirty years later

The streets of Orcan's Grove twisted and turned beneath ghostly, bending buildings. The rooftops seemed to arch toward one another, creating a manmade canopy.

Little footsteps splashed in puddles with the deliberateness of city guards on patrol duty. The tiny feet doing all the marching belonged to a little girl, not much older than 12. Her wheat-colored ponytail bobbed up and down, tapping the nape of her neck. Her downturned eyebrows and crooked smirk suggested that she was concentrating extremely hard on something.

Her right arm crossed her blue coat to grip the strap of her horsehide satchel, and her left hand balled up into a fist at waist level as it swayed like a pendulum on beat with her feet and her ponytail. She was on a mission; a very important one, too. She was to deliver a letter to a Mr. Matchersnatch on Brookshollow Way, toward the southern end of town. The first of many letters on her daily routine. But, as children often do, she became excruciatingly bored.

Whenever this occurred, she would always stumble upon a detour which would normally set her back by about an hour or two, and perhaps pick up an item or two that caught her interest.

She was working for her uncle, and every day she would come back late he would be furious. "Margaret!" he would say, "how many times do I have to tell you to fulfill your daily duties, report back to me, and then you can go out and play."

Her Uncle Strombough's cheeks would blush red, but soon his pupils widened and his face was no longer rosy. He would breathe out a surrendering sigh, and continue in a more moderate tone of sympathy.

"Mar, listen. You're only here for a few months. I know it's not the most exciting city and, yes, it has its faults, but you should feel privileged." Privilege was not something she felt. She felt... well, bored.

She opened her letter bag and moved around many bundles of letters, a carved stone face she had found a half an hour earlier of some important man from another time, a copper-plated compass, a hairpin, a hairbrush, a butter knife, blank parchment, a short knife, a ten-foot bundle of thin rope, a handful of raisins, and then placed her hand around something squirming and alive. She smiled, nudged the living thing aside, and pulled out a bright yellow apple. She took a bite.

Mar was proud of her duty as letter carrier, she supposed, for most women and especially little girls would never be trusted with such a task in this city. When she did pass by another girl, or a woman, she was met with scowls. They envied her freedom.

This young rebel wasn't raised in this city, and had only resided in Orcan's Grove for two months. Once her parents were done with the mission they had set out to accomplish, they would return to her and be back on the road to the gods only know where.

Nope, even after sixty excruciating days she didn't give in to the "norm" of a womanly way of life because, frankly, she didn't care. She wanted to be happy and free, so that's what she did.

She would march around Orcan's Grove on a mission, saying "Good day!" and "Top of the mornin' to ya!" as she passed friendly-looking citizens.

As she lifted her chin while greeting a cabbage vendor, she was struck head-on by a crazy man who knocked her down into the wet and muddy street.

"I smell them!" he screamed, paying no mind to the girl. "She is close! I must answer her call! When two are one, a new life's begun!"

He hobbled away rapidly, running into people, boxes, and carts along the way. He even ran into a wall.

This was more excitement than the girl had experienced all week.

The little marcher sprang to her feet, brushed off what mud and filth she could, adjusted her satchel, and ran in the direction the crazed man had taken. The letters she had to deliver had already been forgotten.

It wasn't hard to find where the man went. His cackling squeals echoed off the stone walls. A parade of toppled jars and broken glass drew her closer to his location. Margaret followed his manic yells, leaped over angry cats, down to the port, where ships had once set out to fish. But it had been nearly ten years since any ship had set out to sail too far off the coast.

She passed by the last building in town, an abandoned trading post, and followed a mossy boardwalk through a slim gathering of oak trees, and onto to the docks. What she saw when she cleared the trees were about 50 people gathered around in a circle. They were all observing something... odd. And smelly.

As she got closer, the pearl-white sails seemed to tower over the crowd, making the entire scene much more intimidating than the little girl expected.

Then she noticed the sky. She hadn't paid attention to it earlier, but now that she wasn't surrounded by buildings she could feel an actual breeze. Instead of blue, it was the color of muddy pomegranate, unusual for this part of Draston, or anywhere in Harthx for that matter.

The sails fluttered like violent doves. She counted the boats, beginning from the right end of the docks: one, two, three, four, five, six, seven. Four of these once were trading and cargo ships, three were smaller fishing ships. All the ships were large and extravagant, a reminder of how profitable Orcan's Grove used to be, before it even received the new name. They all looked rather run-down, and not well cared for.

At the furthest docking station to her left sat a dark ship floating silently in the water like an abstract shadow. Its grey ropes and knotted ratlines sagged down from darkened sails like weathered spider webs.

Pirates! she thought to herself, and walked across the smooth stone landing and into the crowd. She began pushing and shoving her way through smelly men, and brushing up against their rough clothes. Soon enough, the crowd allowed her through.

Mar stepped up on her toes, still trying half-mindedly to appear noble and stern, and scanned the crowd for the dirty seafaring type.

It was not hard to spot the captain. Nobody in Orcan's Grove had set sail on the ocean for longer than a day, and any time spent on the water at all was even slim. Since the town's main source of trade had disappeared, that being fish, no outside traders would travel to the town anymore, not even by land.

The filthy pirate stood on the far north side of the crowd, not speaking a word to anyone, just smoking a pipe and tapping his peg leg on the cobbles. He was shorter than the rest of the men, and Mar realized that he was not a man, but a hill dwarf, standing just a foot taller than herself.

The dwarf captain was staring not at the spectacle in the center of the circle, but at one man in particular. His baggy eyes pierced the back of the head of a man who did not grow his hair long, like most others, but wore it short and above his collar. Mar could see, on closer inspection, the short-haired man had a rag tied around his head, like a bandanna. The same head that was attached to the body she saw running through the streets after it had just knocked her into the mud.

It was the crazy man, and he was stepping into the center of the ring.

Mar pushed past three more people, and could finally see what everybody was looking at.

Not more than five feet in front of her, standing with a shrunken posture and a chain around its neck, was the slugman.

The slugman is what she decided to call it, for she couldn't think of anything better than that. Its skin was grey and slimy, and looked like a slug. Only this creature's skin didn't look tough; Mar could see right through it. She saw hundreds of blue and red veins, purple muscles, pink organs, everything, pulsing with life.

Its legs looked like two human legs sewn together, and its feet reminded her of a mermaid's tail. It had no arms, and the head was nearly featureless: no ears, no nose, no mouth. The eyes terrified her more than anything she had ever experienced before. Eyes so big and black she feared she would fall in if she got to close. They stared unblinking toward the ground, defeated.

The crazy man stepped in front of the chained slugman, blocking her view of the onyx eyes, and as a sudden chill up her back, the fear was washed away. The man muttered something unintelligible.

"What was that?" said the strong man who held onto the chain.

The crazy man spoke louder. "I said, I will buy him off of you."

"Oi, you can't sell that thing to a lunatic, you'd be out of your mind," said another man, this one with a bushy black beard and a heavy accent.

The strong man studied the crazy man. "How much?" he asked.

He pulled a sack out of his shirt that was bigger than Mar's two fists. "This enough?"

The man opened the bag and inspected it. His eyes widened. "Yes." Then he handed the chain over to the crazy man.

He pulled the creature away. It was somehow slithering like a snake, but remained upright like a man.

When the man turned to face Mar, she let her jaw hang slack in astonishment, for the crazy man had no eyes.

THREE

Well, he must have eyes, Mar thought. They were probably just hidden away nice and snug underneath the burgundy cloth he had wrapped around his skull.

The crowd quieted down, until only whispers were heard in the back. The ships creaked, and leaves rustled. Then, like a clap of thunder waking the night, he spoke.

"I've waited long for this. Please, I implore you all, give me this opportunity. This is the sign I have told you about, and it's here. The tpka was washed ashore from the east, you say?" After strenuously stretching out his words, the crazy man paused in wait for a reply.

Everyone shifted on their feet, until the black-bearded man replied.

"Aye. Warshed up right over there he did, all kickin' and flappin'. I'm willing to bet The Taker sent him 'ere. Bad voodoo on that thing, I'm afraid." The black-bearded looked around nervously, then back at the blind man. "If the Orcan were to send us salvation, it would not be in the form of this abomination."

The slugman made a noise that sounded like the purr of a kitten, yet the growl of a bear.

The crazy man rubbed his brow, smearing dirt and grime over the wrinkles. He bit his lower lip, and Mar could have sworn his chin quivered. "I need this," he said.

No one replied, they just looked at one another aimlessly.

"Yeah, all right," said the strong man. "Have it your way. We ain't got no use for that thing. You got it."

Men began to walk away, no longer interested in the fate of the slugman, and annoyed by the blind man.

"I need a ship," the crazy man said. I need someone to take us to The Taker." But no one answered him. People flooded back into town, leaving the tall transparent creature to the blind man.

Mar stood still, wishing she could help the man.

The dwarf captain had remained, however. He walked up to the blind man, tapped him on the shoulder, and whispered something in his ear.

The two men walked over to a grouping of benches, all the while ignoring Margaret. Then they sat and held palaver, the slugman standing behind them like a servant awaiting orders.

What is this? Mar wondered. Her mind was such a tsunami of questions and ideas that she couldn't contain herself. She stormed over to the men, and surprised both them and herself.

Words spat from between her teeth like angry bees, pleading them to let her go with them, to get her out of this dreadfully boring city. After ten minutes of the two men telling the girl to get lost, they finally gave in and let her sit and listen to them talk, only if she would speak when spoken to.

"What's yer name?" the pirate dwarf finally asked.

"Margaret," she said, holding back excitement. "But most people just call me Mar. And you are?"

"My name's Captain Admiral!" He stood up so fast and with such enthusiasm that Mar thought he was about to perform a song, like in the plays her mother used to be involved in.

"And that's your pirate ship over there?"

Captain Admiral's face went slack with horror. "Good heavens, no! We are not pirates. We don't pillage villages. We don't kidnap maidens and rape them. Dear me, no. We ain't no pirates at all, lassie."

"Well, what are you?"

"We be adventurers!" His bulky arms spread out before him, petting the air, or painting an invisible canvas. "Wanderers of yonder blue sea, we be. We have sailed from Draston to Pargon and back again. We have coasted through the rivers of the underworld, found the lost city of Ta'hi, and drank rich bourbon with the high lord Kumba himself. And now, we set off to seek the end of the world! Where at last my shipmates and I will be greeted by our god Jarak, the god of adventure, and live forever in the land of Yenun, surrounded by many maidens and merry courtship."

During his heartfelt speech, Mar noticed that Captain had almost abandoned his pirate accent completely. Once he was done, he looked back and forth at Mar and the blind man, expecting applause or cries of astonishment.

When they said nothing, he reluctantly sat back down in silence.

Pargon? Ta'hi? What a loon, Mar thought. She had never heard these words at all in her short life. But, with everything that she had seen and heard, she couldn't just dismiss them as possible truths.

Now she turned her attention to the blind man. "And what's your story? Are you really blind, or do you wear that rag as punishment for some moral sin you've committed?"

It was not uncommon for cultures to temporarily rid persons of one of their senses. Some had wax poured in their ears for spying, others had their tongues wrapped in bandages for committing gluttony, and some were blindfolded for viewing things they should have avoided.

"It is not polite to ask a man if he is blind," he said calmly.

"And it's not polite to go ranting through the streets and alleys of Orcan's Grove, knocking over little girls either," Mar retorted.

He was silent, and for a moment Mar thought he was about to apologize. But instead, he huffed, "I'm Ransden."

"Ah."

A longer moment of silence continued for what seemed like ten minutes. Eventually, Ransden spoke in his smooth and yet gravelly voice. "So, you're really not leaving."

"Nope."

Geeze, did this guy ever smile? The corners of his mouth had lines from frowning so much.

Silence.

"Is she gone?" Ransden turned to ask the hill dwarf.

"No. I think the lassie is deep in thought about something or another. She's just staring off into your face. No, she's lowered her eyes to the ground now."

"Perhaps she'll fall asleep," Ransden sneered.

What she was really staring at was the slugman, who was now lying down behind the bench.

"What-what is that thing?" the girl asked.

"A tpka," Ransden said.

Tpka. The word didn't sound like any common language Mar had ever heard before. It sounded off, like it was missing one too many vowels. And the way Ransden had said it, the way his breath created it, made it sound evil.

"What is it?"

"It's what I've been waiting for," said Ransden. "I've known them in my dreams. It is to lead me to Beastmother. She will cleanse me of all my sins and grant me eternal peace from my damnation." He said this passively, like he'd told the story every day of his life.

A shudder ran down Mar's spine.

Beastmother.

This guy may be crazy, Mar thought, but he needed assistance. Besides, it was only Tasarsday, and she didn't have anything to do. Did she? She couldn't remember. What she did know is that she was bored in this rotten city. She wanted to be brave and courageous like her parents, who were Valons. She wanted to help people, and this was her opportunity to do so.

"What's The Taker?" Mar asked the Captain.

"Ye never heard of—"

"I'm new around here. And won't stay for long," Mar remarked. "But if I may travel with you, I want to know the facts."

"Ah. Well, The Taker is a gargantuan storm over the Sea of Sangu. It popped up, oh, I'd say thirty years ago. Been eating up ships ever since."

Mar wasn't scared of a sea storm. She was brave, like her father. She felt her bag still hanging by her side, and remembered the letters she was to deliver. She figured they could wait.

"Can I go with you two?"

"WHAT?!" Captain barked, and nearly choked on his tongue. "I be not even taking this fellow here, not for free."

"What? I figured you two were making plans to set sail."

Ransden said nothing.

Captain Admiral said, "Aye. I told him I would take him if he could give me something of value. And he has no more money."

"What if I paid for his fare?" She could see a grim look of despair sneak onto Ransden's face. He was losing hope.

"Sure, if you have the funds."

Ransden got up and began to pace back and forth behind Captain Admiral.

Margaret felt bad. She knew she had to help him, as nobody else would. Plus, just thinking about the adventure she could have made her blood run hot with excitement. She had to do something other than deliver mail for the next month. Her uncle was an all right man, but he had no children for her to play with, and the women in this town had very little freedom, which made her sad. She would rather be off with her parents, hunting monsters, or on a pirate ship that was not a pirate ship, sailing toward The Taker, with a captain, a blind man, and a dead slugman (tpka) in tow.

"I don't have much coin," Mar said, "but I do have this." She pulled her pet creature out from a bag at her side, and Captain was captivated by its ugly beauty.

"My," he said, with a twinkle in his eye.

"Here, he's yours."

The pirate took the creature and placed it on his shoulder. Its many little legs clicked around the back of the man's neck and snuggled up close to him, nuzzling its face inside his beard.

Ransden sniffed the air, and then spoke.

"Is that..." he paused. "A Giant Western Cenepede?"

"Yup." Mar grinned ear to ear. "I named him Wallace, but you can change it if you want, Captain."

"Dear gods," Ransden said. "Those are near extinction. And they are one of the only creatures I know of that create magic when they die, but only for one."

"I believe that's a myth, lad," said the dwarf. "But they are worth a lot of money to the mages; only if they die from natural causes, of course."

"So, does that payment suffice?" Mar asked. "Will you take us both?"

The pirate stopped stroking Wallace's clicking head, and rose from the bench.

"We set sail in two hours. Oh, and uh, get yourselves enough food. We be short on supplies for both of ya."

The pirate-not-pirate hobbled away toward his ship, taking the tpka by the chain, leaving only Mar and Ransden.

He was again silent for a while.

"I need to purchase new clothes," Mar said with absent-minded confidence. "I'm not returning to my uncle's today."

Ransden stood with a grunt and said, "Follow me. We will return within an hour and a half."

"Follow you? But you're blind."

"Am I? One doesn't always see with his eyes. You'll do best to remember that if you're coming with me."

And off he ran into the town. Mar stood in astonishment for a moment, and decided she was wasting time. She bounded along after him.

Behind her, she could hear the scraping and squishing of the slugman being dragged aboard the pirate ship. To her, it would always be a pirate ship. Otherwise, that would be no fun.

No fun at all.

FOUR

"How long have you lived here?" Mar asked coolly as she rummaged through sticky drawers and opened squeaky cupboards. "The town, not this home."

Ransden's home was a lower-level hole-in-the-wall apartment between two abandoned buildings. The street was more a back alley than a main road, and if Mar had not been following Ransden she would have missed the steps leading to his darkened front door.

What she did notice about his home were the rows of lavender, jasmine, and roses strung across his door frame and down the sides. The scent was pungent and welcoming. After they stepped inside, the warm and comfortable feelings were gone, but a glow of calm fell on Ransden's face, seemingly changing his character completely.

"As long as I've been alive," Ransden said gleefully. His voice rose in pitch when he said this, and his eagerness to talk calmed Mar's nerves, for the time being.

"What does the name mean? Orcan's Grove."

"It used to be called Puffin's Point, years ago. But we separated ourselves from Kal, a new religion took over, and we renamed it after The Orcan, our god," he said as he found a matchbook under his bed and tossed it to her with surprising accuracy.

"Thank you." She lit the lantern in her hands, illuminating the far corners of the room. "So, my uncle explained some of it to me already, but what happened with all the ships being grounded?"

"The waters on the banks of Orcan's Grove were the richest in sea life in all of southeast Draston. Or so I've heard. That's back when it was still Puffin's Point. Then, one day at peak fishing season, boats began to disappear."

"Like, they never came back?"

"Yeah. Pass me that matchbook, will ya?"

She did. Ransden wedged a fat dark cigar between the scruff on his upper lip and chin, and drew in smoke.

"After a few days, fewer and fewer ships dwelt in the harbor, and the ocean life on our coast grew less and less in a matter of months, until they were all gone. Then out of godsdamned nowhere, pardon my words, POOF." Ransden spit out his cigar with an explosion of smoke, reminding Mar of the dragons of legend, as he clapped his hand together. "The town turned to squalor."

He rose from his bed and picked up his cigar, not even feeling around for it. Margaret watched the blind man with awe as he navigated to his cookware, deliberately grasped an iron pot off a hook on his first try, and set it above a fire.

"How can you move around so easily without being able to see?" Margaret mused.

"The Orcan blessed me with a superior sense of smell, which is the only compensation for my damnation."

He drew out the word "only" and began stirring ingredients into the pot. Ransden lifted the lid off the boiling brew, wafted it to his vigilant nose, and nodded to himself in satisfaction.

"Is that what we came here for?" Mar asked.

"Yes."

"What is it?"

He paused, and the glow on his face faded into shadow.

Come to me.

She heard a voice that seemed to come from everywhere, yet nowhere at all. It was not Ransden's, not her own, yet—

When two are one, my child, a new life's begun.

Suddenly, Margaret didn't feel so great anymore. It was cold; all the light in the room seemed to fade.

"Nothing yet," he said in a barely audible hackle, "but in the end, it will be desperately useful to me."

As the tar-like liquid cooled, he poured it from the pot, through a funnel, and into a tiny ceramic jar about the size of a pear. He sloshed the thick substance around and smiled as if to acknowledge the sound was right.

"Let's get back to the docks; I've had too much of this place." Mar said.

"Very well," he said. "My deed is done. Now it's time to go forth into the open everythingness."

They both stood. Margaret stepped up and out of the door. Ransden stopped and turned back to the flame still burning under the empty pot.

"Or nothingness," he whispered as he said this, and kicked over the bundles of fags onto a pile of woolen blankets, and stepped out the door as well. Behind him, smoke trailed out from underneath the rotten wood door and disappeared onto the fading daylight of the evening sky.

FIVE

After purchasing new clothes, two weeks' rations of food for Mar, and only Mar, the sun had set on the ghostly docks of Orcan's Grove, causing the pomegranate hue to transform into an almost bloodstained obsidian.

Captain Admiral stepped down onto the gangplank, with Wallace still around his shoulders, and said, "There ye both be. Hurry up, now; the time to set sail is upon us." They walked aboard.

The crew members, this being the first time Mar had seen them, moved across the deck like shadows. Ropes were pulling with strain. Rotten wood boards groaned with the weight of the heavy sails.

The crew's faces were shadowed, leaving no face that Mar could see at least. With the lack of moonlight behind the sails, she wasn't surprised.

Captain gave his orders, and the crew followed. There seemed to be a hundred men on deck, maybe more. After a time the vessel pushed away from land, and drifted out into the unknown beyond, to where Mar knew hundreds of ships had been lost forever.

As the sea breeze kissed her face, Margaret wondered if she hadn't made a grave mistake. What if she was gone for longer than a month? What if she never returned from this voyage? She didn't think of the possibility of dying—that topic was usually moot for a twelve-year-old girl. But she did feel a bit guilty for leaving her uncle behind, without even a goodbye note. And what of her parents? If they were to return before she did they would be furious, and heartbroken.

Ransden followed the sound of the dwarf captain's boots, or more likely he followed his nose-prickling body odor, to the stern where Mar assumed the captain's quarters was.

She stood like a statue among a hurricane of activity. Men swarmed around her this way and that, like gnats swarming around a rotten apple. Her caramel eyes disappeared behind her heavy lids, and she sat and meditated, right there among the chaos.

Her father had taught her this trick.

When you feel overwhelmed and helpless, he would say, *close your eyes and rediscover your center. Your body is your axle of consciousness in this world of disorder. And once this is known, order can be found in chaos.*

The little girl breathed in, then breathed out, and she remembered her purpose.

SIX

Margaret was bored. Nothing exciting had happened in the last six hours since she had been on 'The Bender', which was the ship's name. She wasn't even sure if it had been six hours.

In normal circumstances, she could tell time by the sun and moon. However, most of the time the sky was blotted out by heavy purple clouds, reminding her of bruises on a dying fruit.

Now, the only way she could measure the passing of time was to watch Ransden. When the moon was still in sight at their journey's beginning, about every hour for five hours, he would make his way to the front of the ship and "smell" for whatever he was looking for.

Every hour he would do this, and if they were off course Captain Admiral would hear about it with a curse and a scream.

After she slept for a whopping eleven hours, she ate handfuls of dried beef and a crunchy carrot.

She rummaged through her sack, staying out of the way of the shadowy-faced crew. She found a space underneath some steps that served her liking. Then she remembered the letters she had never delivered. She flipped through the names and addresses, until she came to the largest envelope of them all and pulled it out.

Her old friend's name was on the top left.

Milo of Evesburg.

A family friend.

She didn't know he was in town before her uncle gave her the heavy letter. And it was only this letter she regretted not delivering.

What if it was important? Milo would never forgive her. Well, he would, knowing his character, but she knew she would feel guilty for at least a month. If it was important, and the man was expecting it, what would happen if he never received it? He most likely knew that she was in town, Mar thought, and he knew her parents very well. Would he come looking for her? The unopened envelope was shoved back into her brown bag.

The moon had shone on 'The Bender'. None of the crew talked to the girl, probably because she was only a child. Men both tall and short, lengthy and stocky, ran this way and that across the deck. She didn't know what they were doing. She didn't know a thing about being at sea. She was lonely, and was forgetting her soul purpose on this vessel: to help Ransden achieve his goal.

So, she still didn't know much. Did not know who or what this Beastmother was. Didn't know what that potion or whatever the liquid was that Ransden had made was. If she was going to help, she wasn't going to be treated like a child; she was going to understand this mission for what it was, and was not going to be underestimated.

It must have been three hours past noon, or six past, she didn't know for sure. But the hour was upon them, for who stepped up to the bow but Ransden.

His silhouette was all Mar could see in the growing fog. With that defeated crouch, the sad swagger as he shuffled his feet, it was him all right, and she was going to get him to talk again.

SEVEN

"When two are one, a new life's begun. When two are one, a new life's begun. We come to thee, oh, Beastmother, Queen of the sea, and bearer of life. The Orcan cursed me, the city broke me, but you will restore purpose to my soul. When two are one, a new life's begun."

Ransden repeated this in a rapid cadence, but spoke so softly that no human ears could pick out every word.

"What's he blubbering about?" The dwarf captain's voice cut through the thick air like a knife through velvet, causing Mar to start.

"Who, him?" She pointed up to the forecastle deck. "I don't know. He's been coming up here every hour."

Captain grunted, then bent down to scratch his wooden leg, stood upright again, and removed Wallace from around his neck, squirming and moving his hundred legs in an insectile dance. The centipede's name was still Wallace, Margaret noticed, which made her slightly cheerful inside.

"They say this creature has magical properties when it dies," said the dwarf, in more of an inquiry than a statement.

"Yes," said Mar.

"Do ya know how it works?"

"I've only heard stories. Some say that they were companions of the gods, long ago. When the bug dies its spirit lifts to the sky, and you can ask it to take a message to the gods for you."

"Hmphh," the dwarf scoffed. "Well, let's hope that tale of yours is true. We may need it later." Captain paused, and looked at the rambling man on the upper deck.

"Yer friend," he said to Mar. "Is he stable?"

"I don't know." She didn't consider Ransden a friend, but didn't argue this point.

"Then answer me this, dearie. Why did ya follow him out here?" The bulky seafaring dwarf allowed his new pet to weave in and out of his fingers, from hand to hand, but his pondering eyes never left the little girl.

"I... I don't know. I wanted to help him. Find something. Ransden seems to need my help."

"We both know he needn't need your help. All the man be asking for was a ship. You know that all the same as I."

Margaret studied the dwarf captain's weathered face, trying to determine what he was getting at. Under his bushy eyebrows she saw honest and sentimental eyes, like those of her father.

"Yer bored, that's all. But adventure can get a girl yer age killed. You be only a little lass. You needn't be out on dangerous waters on a brigantine full of rough-necked men and barely any food and water to last yourself a few weeks. How old are you?"

"I'm twelve. But I've traveled—"

"You still be a child," he interrupted, repeating himself. "Don't convince me why ya need to be here. If you be needing to serve a purpose, go talk to the man up there."

"Ransden," she said.

"Be warned," the captain spoke as Margaret was about to walk up the stairs. "He may very well lead us into danger. I'm a man of my word, and I'll help him, but if the rumors of The Taker are true, which I believe they are, he's leading us right into death."

"What?" Mar stammered, but regained her confidence right after. "How has he even been leading the way?"

"What, because he's blind? That man can see more than you and me at times, lass."

"Captain!" A grimy crew member popped up from below deck. "Best get your arse below deck. We be having a situation you need to see."

The urgency in his voice scared even Mar. Captain Admiral fled away from her in a way that made her fear the boat had sprung a leak and was sinking. Or, maybe a mutiny broke out below deck, and the devilish crew were killing the remaining loyal ones in their sleep.

Everything was quiet when the captain left, everything was still. The floor shifted evenly below her feet from one side to another. If the brig was filling with water then the rhythm of the ebb and flow would have changed, for there hadn't been any major change in waves within the past few hours.

The few crew members above deck, Mar counted only eight now, continued about their daily duties as if nothing major was happening.

So, what was it?

Mar figured she could head down and see for herself, but she wanted a chance to speak with Ransden first, before they got wherever they needed to go.

She ascended the stairs to the foremost deck, step after rotten step. When she got to the forecastle deck, her face was greeted with a fresh dose of sea breeze. The air currents pelted her nose, and tossed her hair past her cheeks and above her ears. Her eyelids closed, and she rejoiced in a private symphony. She loved the sea. The sound of the water splashing against the bulkheads. The smell of pure salt and potent ocean life. The sound of—

"When two are one..."

"Excuse me."

"We come to thee."

She tapped his right shoulder.

"Beastmother."

Thunder cracked, and light illuminated the fog all around them. At that very second, the blind man snapped his whole torso around like a murderous Jack-in-the-box. Mar started back a step, but not because of the sudden twist, as unnatural had it been, nor was it because of the simultaneous crash of thunder.

It was his eyes.

Ransden's blindfold had been removed, and to her horror so were his eyelids. What stared back at the girl were two globes, void of anything but haunting foliage of mist and vapor. They were like portals to another realm.

Before Mar could decide whether to defend herself or run, Ransden's face muscles relaxed. He fell to his knees, and began to weep into his dirt-streaked palms.

The little girl stared back shocked, not knowing what had just occurred. She just knew that she was here for a reason—so she decided to speak with him in hopes that, through a better understanding, she could make a change.

EIGHT

Ransden told her of how his mother bore him, an illegitimate child. He spoke of The Orcan, the god of his people, and how he cursed those who disobeyed his high command.

"My mother wanted to provide for herself," Ransden said. "She never wanted to marry a man; no man who was raised in Orcan's Grove at least. The Orcan left his male children in charge, and to provide. He commanded the females to serve their purpose and..." he paused. "Multiply."

"That's stupid," Mar said.

"Yeah," he said. "My mother thought so, too. Which is why she went against The Orcan's command and began working illegally. Come to think of it, it was rather ironic. She disobeyed both the word of The Orcan and the law of our people. The officials discovered her blasphemy, and that she had a child out of wedlock, and had her murdered."

Margaret sighed. "So, you were deemed an abomination."

"Yes," he said. "And it was after her death I realized it to be true. I was never accepted anywhere, and never allowed to leave the city."

The thunder continued to crack while the blind man spoke. The low clouds still hung heavy on the ship, but Mar didn't focus any attention on either; her soul concentration was on Ransden as she tried to understand this undeniably complicated mess of a man.

"They couldn't have me put to death," Ransden said, "because even The Orcan says that a dumb and deaf male can work next to a mule in the fields. I wasn't dumb or deaf, but I was blind. That was my curse for being born into this world through the act of evil, and I am to carry on with this curse for the sake of my mother. But there is a passage in the Orcanami which states that the damned can be forgiven if they find a purpose to serve until death. Only then will my soul be cleansed."

"Wow." She breathed deeply, and exhaled. "So, you're following your path to forgiveness?"

Thunder rolled again, this time nearer.

"Yes," said Ransden. "But it's much more than forgiveness. It is my redemption."

"Before, while we were at your home, you mentioned dreams. Can you explain that?" Now she felt like an interrogator, but Ransden didn't seem to care.

"Yes. In my late teenage years, and I'll get to the dreams in a moment, I had a friend. My one and only friend. His name was Khatvif. He was an outcast, as he was half-elf, but he was also an alchemist. Many called him a sorcerer, but he was not. He taught me all I know. He even knew my mother, and spoke of her often. They were childhood friends. Anyway, he took me in after the religious extremists took my..." he touched his lidless eyes, and did not finish speaking.

She waited, then asked Ransden to continue with his story.

"He taught me how to mix potions, and create recipes," the man continued. "I learned this all by smells and it came naturally to me. But the dreams all began a week after I began to live with Khatvif. I heard voices from the heavens. I smelled something so unnaturally euphoric that I knew it had never existed in this realm before. But something had indeed crossed over, and has been with me ever since, in spirit, and in my dreams."

"This Beastmother?" Mar asked.

"Yes. She is where I will find my refuge. My redemption. She is where my soul will be cleansed."

"Who or what is she?"

"Some say that she is a living goddess, right here in our very own plane of existence. The gods did create her, but only so that they may work through her, like a prophet. Though she lives long she is mortal, but through her we can become one with The Orcan."

"And by doing this, answering her call, this will bring meaning to your life again?"

"Again?" Ransden stammered in surprised shock. "Not again. When I join her, I will have purpose for the first time in my life. When I join her, we will become one. When two are one, a new life's begun. When two are one, a new life's begun."

He reverted to how Margaret had found him not more than twenty minutes ago. Shaken. Distant. And peering off into a not so far distance, where the fog had begun to lift, where the horizon seemed to twist into a nightmarish trick of the eye, and caused Mar to feel fear rise like a living boulder inside her tiny throat.

NINE

Imagine, if you will, a long and endless hallway.

See it splayed out before you as far as the eye can see, until what seems like the end is only a pinpoint in a cloth the color of coal. There are no doors in this hallway, only walls.

Now, rotate the hallway ninety degrees. It shifts before you like a slow grinding stone. As it locks into place the walls are above and below you, endless and expansive beyond space and expectations.

The wall below you melts into a roaring, churning body of water. Its dark waves tackle one another in an endless battle of supremacy. The wall above you begins to wave and ripple, not like water this time but like rolling storm clouds. Purple and black, breathing with faint, glowing light from the imperium and dark, roaring thunder from the Nether.

This is what Margaret saw from the forecastle deck. The sea storm was less like a natural phenomenon, and more like a leviathan. A beast whose mouth they were sailing straight into.

Her hair whipped around her face. Raindrops began to fall onto the wooden boards under her leather boots.

"Ah," said the captain. Mar didn't notice his arrival, but was glad he was here. "I believe we have found The Taker."

And so they had. Mar imagined all the ships that had traversed upon this gargantuan tumult. Their hulls and sails overtaken by the fate of the wind and currents of the sea.

It was too late for them to turn back. The world was swallowing them, and the dark below the sea was its stomach. This was now their fate.

Ransden's babbling faded to a blur behind Mar's conscious thoughts. Regret and horror washed over her like a tsunami, and she broke.

"Shut up!" she screamed. "Shut up, shut up, shut up!"

The girl clutched the collar of Ransden's rain-soaked shirt and shook him vigorously.

"What did you do?" she cried. "You call this your redemption? You're going to get us killed! Someone turn the ship around!"

Ransden's speech ceased. His face twisted, not with malice, but into a face of scary serenity.

"It is time. It's me that she wants. I shall have her spare you. I promise."

"Forget your promise!" she screamed over the roaring storm. "You can't change nature!"

"Aye, that we can't," said the dwarf captain, speaking louder over the erupting cacophony. "But maybe this bloody creature can."

He lobbed a sack of blubber onto the deck with a wet smack. It began to wiggle and squirm like larva. A large nub the size of a melon twisted around and revealed two eyes. Two very large, black, lidless eyes.

It was the slugman! Mar thought.

A groaning hiss escaped from the slimy captive, followed by a shrill banshee screech. The top of its head cracked in four lines like a rotten egg and split up the sides, meeting at the center. The top of the head opened for what at first reminded Mar of a tulip blooming in spring, but as the orifice widened it was more like a Venus fly trap with rabies.

It flopped like an eel out of water. Which was pretty much what it was, Mar would soon realize.

"This be the time, then?" Captain Admiral asked Ransden.

"Yes," he said flatly.

"Time for what?" Mar cried.

Captain picked up the writhing tpka, which in length was taller than he was.

"I'm sorry, lass," Captain Admiral said. "This has to be done. But I promise I'll do everything in my power to turn this ship around soon. If that fails, we may still be able to use a bit of magic. It's almost over."

Then Captain tossed the creature into the churning water below.

Everyone heard the splash, and they leaned over the railing to see what was to become of the slugman. Everyone except Ransden.

"Which way did it go, Captain?" Ransden asked, sounding a bit impatient.

Mar saw it glide on the surface of the water. In normal circumstances, with storm waters as dark as these were, no one would be able to see a thing. But the creature began to glow like a lightning bug.

Slowly it pulsed, going directly northeast. The further it got, it pulsed faster and faster. The water around its body seemed more and more clear as it increased its distance from the ship.

Rope rapidly unspooled overboard until it snapped tight, tied onto a cleat. The slugman swam far away at the end of the rope, but they weren't going to lose him. They were following it right into the mayhem of the storm.

Water sprayed up from the bulkheads, and everyone stepped back. One crew member up on the crow's nest shouted down.

"I see it!" he exclaimed, tipping a golden spyglass from his one good eye.

"Are we on the correct course, Jacoby?" Captain yelled.

"Aye!" he yelled down. "No more than two-tenths of a league. He has slowed his velocity and now it appears he has made rest no more than two fathoms below sea level, sir."

"Much gratitude," said Captain. Then to Ransden, he said, "He's stopped. This is as far as I be taking you."

"And my word is my bond," said Ransden. "I thank you."

This wasn't what Mar had planned. How was this helping the blind man? She hated him now for dragging her into danger such as this. Even her parents would never put her in this kind of situation, and they hunted monsters for a living. They at least would give her a fighting chance, or a failsafe. And if those failed, they would put themselves in harm's way.

No, she was alone here, it seemed, and her patience had reached its end.

She marched over to Ransden, with greater purpose and wider strides than she had marched only two days ago on the streets of Orcan's Grove. Or was it three days? She didn't care, she was mad. She still wore her satchel around her shoulder, but all former duties had been forgotten.

She pulled back her little fist. It reversed its direction and cut through the rain-filled air.

White knuckles crumpled into a rain-soaked coat. She punched him until her hands went numb, blaming him for everything, regretting her part in all this, wishing to go back home.

She choked on her tongue, and finally stopped hitting Rensden.

"I-I'm sorry," Mar stuttered.

Ransden sighed. He seemed to gather his thoughts for half a breath, then said, "When a girl punches like a warrior, she is no longer a girl. She is a woman. But when she attacks me out of ignorance, she's still a child."

Mar stammered, but said nothing audible.

"You're ignorant to my motives. You're playing checkers while I'm playing chess. I tried explaining myself to you, but you are too young and lack the capacity to understand, I'm afraid." Turning to the dwarf, Rensen said, "Thank you for your help, Captain, but don't share with me your own thoughts and opinions, for that is where my interest dies. Now, this is where my ride ends, and my purpose begins."

The ship bobbed over choppy waves. Below the waves was a rapidly pulsing light. The slugman.

Everyone leaned over the edge again, and saw that Ransden was right. Somehow, he knew they had reached their target.

Ransden pulled himself up on a ratline, and hoisted himself into the railing.

"Wait," Margaret said too quietly.

"When two are one," said Ransden.

"Wait!" This time the girl was louder, but her voice still could not cut through the pelting rain and screaming thunder.

Ransden's right hand reached into a hidden pocket inside his shirt and pulled out an object that Mar had forgotten about. It was a jar.

He bit into the cork, popped it out, and spat it into the hungry sea. He lifted the jar to his mouth, and drank.

He gulped the last of the liquid. The ceramic jar shattered on the deck behind him.

"A new life's begun," said the man.

His boots pushed off the rain-slick railing, and Margaret watched as first his legs disappeared, then his torso, then his head.

Margaret screamed in defiance, but defiance of what she did not know.

Children don't need to justify their actions. They don't think of the consequences until after the fact. Young ones act on impulse. If a reason could be concluded, perhaps they will either act out of boredom, or hunger. In this case, Mar was not on a ship to scrap rations for her next meal. She had been a bored child in need of excitement.

In hindsight, perhaps it wasn't the best idea for her to leave town without telling a soul. Maybe it had been a bad decision to go sailing with a bunch of filthy pirates, no matter how much they denied it, and with a self-centered crazy man.

Remember, she told herself, *you first met him when he knocked you down in the alley while talking to himself.* Yeah, great choice in companionship.

Still, children need to see purpose in everything, even if they don't realize it themselves. And it was because of this that Mar couldn't let all this happen in vain. That is why she chased after the man when he jumped overboard. That is why she was ready to risk her own life, just like a Valon would, just like her parents would.

If she could just save his life, maybe that would be her purpose. She had to try.

But huge arms wrapped around her midsection and held her firm.

"Let go of me!" she screamed. "He needs saving!"

"Let him go, lassie," Captain Admiral said solemnly. "We must each go our own path. He chose his."

"No," she said, her tone all but hopeless.

Every ticking second, she imagined him drowning. Swallowing pint after pint of salt water. Choking. Gasping. Dying.

"No," she repeated.

"We must let those go who don't want help. We can't be letting them drag us down with them," the captain said. "If that were to happen, then we can't help anyone else."

In a moment of trust, the captain released his hold on the girl. She shivered in the pouring rain. She was crying, but didn't think anyone would notice anyway. She was tired of trying to be strong. She was sick of trying to live up to her own expectations. So, in one last effort to fulfill her duty, she ran to the ledge and jumped overboard after a man who may very well have already been dead.

On her way over, her satchel caught on a pulley and was ripped from her shoulder. The bag and all its contents followed her into the water, every letter, including the one addressed to Milo of Evesburg, her friend.

She no longer heard the storm; all she could hear was the echoing silence of a universal expanse, an alien wasteland to those above.

She opened her burning eyes, and what she saw would haunt her dreams for decades to come. Her lips parted in horror and fear of her own insignificance. She felt her consciousness stretch further and further from her body, pulsing in and out like a dying heartbeat, as she could not comprehend what she was seeing.

It was bigger than a mountain.

Its shape eluded her ability to construct a description of any kind other than a mountain, an ugly bastard chunk ripped out of the earth.

It stared back at her through misty linings of polluted water. It stared with its eyes... and then it stared with its ALL.

This concept hurt Margaret's head. At this moment she wished she had never followed the blind man out to the sea. She wished she had never left her uncle back in Orcan's Grove. She wished she could see her parents one more time, the once-mighty Valons, and her most dedicated friends.

Bubbles forced their way from between her pressed lips. Her nostrils flared as more bubbles ejected themselves. But she was losing this fight.

As a shadow above her blotted out whatever light was left, Beastmother looked up from the dizzying depths and into her soul with hungry disparity.

TEN

Margaret's throat clenched, and she felt herself being pulled. Down to the bottomless eyes that gaped like volcanos.

What she thought was the darkened ocean floor was really a grainy secret formation of something alive. She was looking at nothing, it seemed, but it was also everything. The black mass below her invaded her every thought. The space in the dark water breathed with not life, not anymore, but death.

The desire to sink deeper into the cold sea overtook her; her skin felt like it had been pierced by a hundred fishhooks, forcing her to come home to the void below, the nothing that was everything.

Come back to me, the ocean said. *Come home.*

Margaret struggled to hold her breath; her lungs had begun to burn. She had been under water not more than twenty seconds. But to her, she could barely even remember what dirt and grass smelled like anymore; she could not remember the faces of her parents or the taste of crisp air caressing the plains of Draston with its sweet tinge of pine and daisies. She could not remember the face of the dwarf captain on the ship above. All her thoughts were diverted to the thing below her.

She no longer wanted to escape the hollow eyes. She didn't fight the pull downward—she didn't want her flesh to tear away from her bone.

The yearning for deliverance was everything to her now. If only she could dive into the cavernous eyes and enter her rebirth, she could finally live for the first time. She would be forgiven from running away from her uncle and her letter carrying duties. That letter she was supposed to deliver to... she forgot his name. But none of that mattered to her. She would join Ransden, and the slugman, and be freed. When two are one.

Bubbles exploded from her nostrils again. Acidic salt water burned her lungs when she breathed in.

Who are you? a voice asked. A voice she had heard before.

I am no one, the girl replied in her mind. *I am yours, Beastmother*. And just as she was about to inhale for the last time...

*****

"Margaret! Margaret!"

Ears popped with spastic ripples and lightning flashed directly overhead, echoing off the barnacle-encrusted hull of The Bender. Waves arched over her head as she was pulled from the water, and crashed back down onto her.

"Girl!" a man's voice crackled. "Pull 'er up, me lads! I don't see her breathing."

Dwarves hate water. No dwarf would be caught dead on a ship, but Captain Admiral was not like most dwarves. He was the first to jump in after Margaret, taking with him a long strand of rope. His crew hoisted them both back aboard the boat, and Captain never had the look of fear in his aged eyes. Her body was thrown on the deck with a wet smack that sounded like raw beef being prepared on a butcher's slab.

"Stand back, lads."

The crew stood in honorable silence, giving their captain space.

The dwarf placed both hands, palms down, on Mar's chest, the fingers of each hand pointing like a compass needle toward her armpits, and applied frantic force.

He did this repeatedly, all while keeping her right cheek close to the deck of the ship. By the sixth push, ugly water spewed from between her cracked lips, followed by violent fits of coughing and choking.

Captain sat her upright, pounding a fist into her upper back to counter her hacks and wheezes.

Moments passed as the girl recovered her bearings.

The storm still thrived. Waves were careening higher by the minutes, and vortexes could be seen a mile away to the east. Rain pelted down in fat helpings of grief and agony, and slowly, ever so slightly, the ancient vessel began to rotate clockwise in the water like a spinning top nearing its final revolution.

ELEVEN

"Here, let me help you up," Captain Admiral said. "We be needing to get moving."

He helped her up and brought her over to a stool, offering for her to sit. She declined, and Captain asked the helmsman to reverse their course back to the mainland.

"Reverse the ship one-hundred-and-eighty degrees," Captain shouted over the storm. "Take us out this demonic typhoon, then take us around south."

The peg-legged captain hobbled to the stern's castle deck, and continued giving his directions.

"Wait, we must drop the lass off first, back to Orcan's Grove. Then we head south, to the end of the world!"

The crew cheered at the news as lightning flared, filling the inky sky with the tears of the dead. But the helmsman looked to the compass at his left, and his face melted.

"Come on, lad, what's the hurry?"

Captain called attention to all hands on deck to prepare their rotation out of the storm. Mar didn't understand half the words he was using, but by the look on the helmsman's face she knew the crew's actions would all be in vain.

"Captain," he said.

"Yes, Tog?" The rain was forming into hail, and every minute the men had to raise their voices even higher than the last.

Tog, the helmsman, showed the golden-cast compass to Captain. The girl's curiosity moved her feet swiftly to the two men.

Mar's emotions, however, were not that of excitement and splendor. Her curiosity stemmed from the root of fear, from the tree of the knowledge of evil and death. Her eyes watched the jagged needle spin slowly behind the scratched glass. Around and around. Slowly increasing its speed counterclockwise.

She saw that the wheel Tog had been holding remained as steady as a sword stuck in stone.

They dropped the compass, shattering the glass into glimmering dust, and raced for the edge.

A whirlpool.

They all could see it. Manipulating the brig like a potter molds a clay jar. The sea shifted the ship's weight ever so slightly between its swaying, watery palms.

And that's when things became much, much worse.

"What's that?" Mar pointed to a dark form in the water no more than twenty feet from the ship.

"What's what?" Captain asked. "The sea be too choppy to see very far."

"That dark shape, it's... growing."

"Could that be Ransden?" one man asked.

"Nay," said Captain. "That boy cannot still be alive."

Then they did see it, all of them did, and it was growing, expanding like a bloodstain on parchment. Coming straight for the ship.

As they rotated to the northwest the shadow remained in the same location, putting it further away from their view.

"Hold on tight," Mar said, though she didn't know why. She had no clue what was about to come forth.

Everybody was silent, watching, waiting helplessly.

Then the ocean exploded.

Towering, wavy stalks shot up from the depths like pythons with the girth of sycamore trees. Hundreds of them sprouted like rapidly growing grass, lethal grass, evil grass, all surrounding The Bender.

As each stalk broke the water's surface, a lightning bolt skewered down from the sagging purple clouds to smite it. The stalks of otherworldly origins climbed upward to dizzying heights, above the storm clouds even, like unobtainable pinnacles of misty mountaintops.

Mar guessed she now knew what it felt like to be a petty little insect in an expansive field of weeds. These stalks were not green, or earth-like at all, however. They were purplygrey, the hue of internal organs. They squirmed like earthworms, and rippled like a jellyfish.

Still, they were solid, but malleable.

When the sky could no longer contain their gruesomeness, the tips curled down like dying roses. Faster and faster the pointed heads barreled for the sea. They splashed, making an echoing KAPLOOSH, and the sound itself rocked the ship.

They rose from the water, and plummeted again. KAPLOOSH. As if they were searching for a target.

The rotating current gyrated The Bender directly at a fat, beefy stalk, crashing the ship like a bartering ram and shifting it into the tallest of the masts, rupturing the wood, and raining down splinters on all those aboard.

"Run!" Captain yelled, grabbing his hat as he did so.

The wind gusts punched the black sails headfirst, making the broken mast lean, and pushed it toward the stalk, luckily away from the ship itself. The stalk dipped its tip down, this time aiming for the far side of the ship. It dove and submerged. The mast snapped, cracked, and split apart completely this time, sending eight-foot sections flying across the deck.

The stalk had finally wrapped itself around the ship. They were not getting out of this.

A bestial roar. A noise that only moving mountains could make, reminded Mar of an earthquake she once experienced in the Rhoben Mountains with her parents.

Could there be an earthquake in the ocean? Mar did not know, and the crew of The Bender did not care to set their minds to this possibility.

"What's going on?" Mar asked.

Captain looked down to his boots in defeat. "It be a Soul Snatcher," he said.

"A what?"

"They go by different names in different regions. The don't just eat bodies. They eat souls. Each one takes a different form, but they all do the same thing"

"You mean a Soul Eater?"

"Aye."

"Those are myths."

"All myths have truths, as all fruit has roots," Captain declared.

"Meaning... if you're right, and we die... then—"

"There be no Empyrean, nor Nether for us. No Yenun. No Lands of the gods. No rest. Nothing. We will be nothing."

We will be nothing.

It was like words on a stone, whispers carried by the passing wind.

He smiled. But it was a passive smirk. Wallace crawled out from his hiding spot under the dwarf's coat, and rubbed its face on his beard. "We have no choice," he said, petting his centipede. "We have to try something, or cease to exist."

Mar could have asked him any question, she could have remained silent. But this man intrigued her. Ransden had intrigued her with his mysteriousness, just as his disappearance into the deep blue struck her with horrible wonder.

But this man, the pirate who was not a pirate, who sometimes spoke like a sea man, and sometimes spoke as if he was from the northern plains, or didn't know what dialect to use, he was more mysterious to her, and yet, she felt like she had known him for a very long time. A good friend. A friend she must fight side by side with.

Wallace suddenly fell from the dwarf's neck as the ship rocked violently. The captain and the girl gained their balance, but the insect skidded down the inclined floor.

"No!" Mar shouted, and chased after the creature alongside the peg-legged dwarf.

They almost had him, but another jolt flung them backward, and Wallace the giant centipede fell through the hole and into the water below. The two of them raced back to the edge and peered over. Wallace was dead and gone. Now they would never discover whether the tales of magic were true or not.

What they saw in the water instead made them want to retreat.

Great triangular monoliths jutted out of the wet body below the floating wreckage. Fifty– maybe more—rose just as the stalks did, their bases getting wider with their ascent.

The stalks retreated to make way for these new anomalies, all but the one holding the ship captive. They kind of looked like teeth. Teeth to eat bodies with. Teeth to eat souls with.

"Margaret!" Captain called.

When had she reached the edge of the ship? Why was she stepping onto the ledge again? Why, to go home, of course.

Come home, said an oily hush, silencing the calamity of the wind, waves, and thunder into the ears of the little girl.

"MARGARET," yelled the dwarf captain.

Strong and sturdy hands guided her back on deck. "You be stronger than the voice of Beastmother, okay?" Captain said.

She knew he was right.

"I'm sorry." She blinked, coming back to reality.

"I just need you to do one thing," he said.

"What's that?" she asked. Her determination to stay alive returned to her soul. "Anything. I trust you, Captain."

He smiled a warm smile. "Don't let her get inside your head. You keep her out, and I'll get us out of this. We can't lose you."

Shadows of the crew danced from deck to deck, securing sections of the ship so far undamaged, preparing for the next move, the next attack, the captain's orders.

Stress fled from Mar's body as she sat in the center of all the chaos. She sat on the soaking-wet planks just as she did three days ago when she first boarded The Bender.

First you sit, back straight, her father would say on training day.

They practiced monster hunting in a meadow, with long flowing rivers of goldenrod.

Before you face your foe, he would say, *you must understand their place in this world. And before you understand the minds of evil men, you must also see your place in this world.*

She would sit in the grass, thin shimmering stalks ticking her ears.

Her father would say, *Close your eyes.*

She softly closed her eyes.

Good, he'd say. *Now, look inward. Watch your breath. Once you see it, feel it, then look no further. Once you feel it, grasp it, become it. The breath becomes solid, something tangible.*

But how do you control something you can't touch? she said, opening her eyes.

You will know soon enough, my goldenrod.

She would close her eyes again, and she became her breath.

Her breath was her, and that was everything. And with every inhale and exhale her being grew, and expanded into an all-powerful force of knowing.

Her father would speak and say these words: *Now evil is like smoke. You are like a stone. You stand steady and it sifts around you, not harming you. If you throw a stone at smoke, it scatters.*

This is your place, as well as the place of evil and chaos. Remember this, remember that like smoke, evil always fades away and disappears into nothing. But the stone remains.

But the girl was educated.

But what is the stone to water? She would ask.

The stone is the student, the river is the teacher.

The lesson would go on, followed by a battle with a little monster here and there, but this memory was all she needed.

She was a stone among smoke.

She sat on the ship amongst chaos, unfazed, unmoving.

Returning to reality, the voice from the sea fell silent. The only voice that spoke now was the waves, the real voice of the sea. She was ready for anything now. She would not be dragged under as easily as Ransden.

As she meditated, the shadows of the teeth swallowed the ship. They were beginning to close high above them and then the last remaining stalk slightly loosened its grip, ready to retreat.

She had trusted Captain to rescue them. But there wasn't much he could do against a monster of this magnitude. The gaping maw of Beastmother was rising from the depths, blocking any wind to thrust the sails.

The thunder echoed from what seemed like other lands away. The purple clouds were replaced with enormous, thick fangs, curling upward to the crest of the sky where the sun or moon should have been. The bone-yellow monoliths curved down to form a new horizon all its own. It looked like a bowl about to extinguish a flame. The flames of their lives. The flames of their souls.

And as the teeth from the north clashed with the teeth from the south, a resounding boom shook the steadying water.

Their stomachs flipped and the water began to go down, the ship with it. Down, most likely, into the throat of Beastmother, like a dying well.

All was black. All was indeed bleak. But in the girl's mind was a glimmer of hope. A pinpoint of light at the end of a tunnel, so to speak. She felt a certain presence the same way she could feel the emotions of Captain and his men, the same way she could feel the desperation of Ransden back in his home.

Call it intuition, call it mind reading, she didn't know. But in her deep meditation, she could in fact hear a true voice of hope that Captain and his crew could not hear.

A voice that was not Beastmother.

It said, *I'm sorry.*

The voice in her head said, *Forgive me.*

The voice crawled nearer to her consciousness, and was clearer.

Let me now serve my purpose. The voice spoke like sand.

Let me serve you, or let me be damned.

And then the voice dematerialized and broke apart, flying around her like a million lightning bugs under an overturned bowl. Or like the smoke of an extinguished candle under an overturned bowl.

Or... like smoke passing around a rock, minding its own business, paying the rock no mind. Mar opened her eyes.

TWELVE

He had to make things right again. He was never supposed to live in this world, let alone serve any purpose. He shouldn't have existed at all. And in the words written in The Orcanami, the most magnificent Orcan spoke through his disciple Jesibelle, and said: 'If you are born into life through sin and lust, let it be known you are damned.

'If mother and father are not bound by wedlock, may their bodies suffer the everlasting agony of a thousand years in bitter torment. For this blasphemy, may their souls experience tenfold that of their former bodies.

'As for offspring, may they live and suffer the truth spat upon them by their brothers and sisters in skin and blood, but not in soul. Living this way is torture twenty times that of their seed curators.

'Let it be known, there is a way to salvation for these innocent souls; though they were brought into life in sin, they do have a chance to serve The Orcan, but only after death.

'Let them follow the voice of his bidding. Let them hear his words, and never tarry to his call. In the world of dreams, purpose awaits. A life-long purpose after death to serve The Orcan and to make right what their seed curators made wrong.

'This is the only way; The Orcan is your true seed curator. Only through The Orcan can you be set free.'

Ransden set himself free.

He removed the elixir from a hidden pocket and drank heavily. He drank it all. It tasted like bile.

The girl who had followed him on this adventure to the end was screaming somewhere behind him. Screaming his name, begging him not to jump.

She did not understand the meaning behind it all. He hoped she would make it through alive, but the Orcan came first. His destiny always came first.

A fraction of Ransden felt regret for letting the girl follow him. She seemed to be innocent, living a life sheltered from evil such as every child should grow to be. But the other She called to him. Beastmother beckoned, destroying any other thought he had.

Forget the girl, he thought. *The time of the beast is now.*

After the warm, prickly liquid was drained from the powdery container, time had slowed for him fourfold. The rushing of the raindrops backtracked their progress in midair, somewhat apprehensively. The thunder shook, not with hysteria but in trepidation, fearful to strike the water lest it be the end of its existence. Screams wrapped themselves around Ransden's neck and crawled their way like spiders into his ear canals, but they sounded muffled and damp. He locked the screams away in an iron box, and sank into the thick stillness below.

He jumped.

Weightlessness.
Spinning, headfirst.
Cold.
Wet.
Sweet droplets of hydration flicking the skin, awakening the consciousness.
He breathed. And he could breathe very well. Water ran down Ransden's throat and filled his chest, but he still breathed and lived. He never doubted that the potion would work; it had to. He'd worked so hard to memorize the ingredients and incantations while studying under the shadow of Khatvif the half-elf. Since The Beastmother called to him in his dreams, he knew this was kismet. To dwell in the sea moments before he transcended to a higher life. A life living as one with The Orcan Almighty.

He collected his bearings, and six breaths later swam down toward the putrid smell of death, feces, and decay.

But to Ransden, this all smelled of sanctuary.

THIRTEEN

Hundreds of slugmen, tpka, surrounded Ransden, all pulsing with an eerie blue glow, like burning stars in a black sky. All followed the same course toward the fleshy body of the unearthly Beastmother.

When the slugmen twisted their way to the outer skin of the Mother, their heads opened and latched on like leeches. Clinging to her like parasites.

Ransden swam, still breathing in the thick burning water, continuing to live.

He swam until his hands hit the sea floor. But it wasn't the sea floor his hands had touched. It breathed with life. Even in water, he could smell her sweet calling. He was touching the flank of Beastmother herself.

He yearned to keep going to her, past the barricade of flesh and muscle. Reaching her wasn't enough. He needed inside of her. He needed to breathe with her as one, to pump the same blood, and feel what she felt.

Ransden bit down on rubbery skin and tore off a fleshy chunk, chewing and swallowing what remained in his mouth. Then another piece, and another. He began to claw a hole in the Beastmother's body with his dirt-packed fingernails. The thirst for life and power pulsated from within her; he felt it absorbing him into Her.

For two-hundred beats of his heart, he burrowed into her. He was a worm eating his way into an apple. He was a seedling, breaking through the earth to one day become an apple tree. He was a termite, eating the apple tree. He was the dirt, eating the decayed wood of a long-dead apple tree.

He was inside Her now.

Only his kicking feet and calves were still outside the body, and the rest of him was crammed in tight, nestled between slabs of rotting muscle. His dying body cradled into hers like a hungry baby against her mother's bosom.

Then the walls around him squeezed. He struggled to gain control, but the flesh of the Beastmother ordered him to be still.

It will all be over soon.

Ransden's hair melted like sugar in hot water. Liquified follicles trickled down his waxy face. His face was reshaping itself, fusing to the flesh of Her, stringy tendons now connected one life to the other.

Ransden's belly bulged, then exploded, but only after it met with the outer wall of his tomb, and then it all happened as quickly as a bag being slipped over a man to be hanged.

One heartbeat later, he was alive.

He felt his whole body drifting afloat in the sea; no agonizing pressure blanketed his body anymore. He was no longer Ransden.

He was Beastmother—devourer of souls, deceiver of men. It could feel the thousands of male counterparts buried into her flesh, tpka, pumping the same blood, filling their stomachs with the same nutrients. They were all totally dependent on Her for survival. They lived only to serve Her. They would provide her the seeds to conceive children, and in return the children would find their way back to Her, only to serve their purpose just as their fathers had done.

Ransden saw all this; no, he knew all this because She knew this.

With more tpka came more power to The One and Only Mother.

For centuries she has thrived deep in the sea, pulling down the power from the sky to create an everlasting rapturous storm, which would snare travelers in her trap. Then, she would feast.

Those fortunate enough to be considered prophets of The Orcan, or Beastmother herself, followed Her call, or followed Her scent. Even mysterious rumors of her existence, or the rumors of the storm known as The Taker, had led many souls to their death. Her body would be filled with the dead trees creating the structure of the seafaring vessels, and her life would prosper due to living souls, which in return would be given to the one and only Orcan, or Xanzith—goddess of hatred, destruction, and wrath.

Beastmother was thought to be a goddess among mortals, but the truth is that She was no goddess but an abomination. She was the only female of her kind, and she was only to bear male counterparts. They, in turn, would navigate the seas until they reached adulthood, and heed to her call. The sole purpose of the tpka, or so-called slugmen, was to attach themselves for the rest of their lives onto Beastmother, and bear Her more children.

Thus would be the fate of Ransden. Now that two had indeed become one, he shared with her all that was his: his nerve endings, his consciousness, his memories... his bloodstream.

FOURTEEN

Beastmother could feel the motion of the oncoming ship above Her, and She was hungry.

The stalks on Her back were used as hands, to grasp the victim floating high above Her. Then She would rise and swallow the vessel whole, people and all.

She had done the same routine all around the oceans of Harthx for the last seven hundred years or so by the time she attacked The Bender. This time, however, she did not feel as strong. She was never supposed to grow weak, she thought. She had done her duty to deliver the souls of men to Xanzith. She strained with all her might to push herself up, to open her gaping orifice as wide as was possible. But pain shot like poison daggers across her bones. Her island-sized lungs did not work like they were supposed to. Her heart slowed down its time.

In frantic fury she cried out to her mother, Xanzith.

The goddess responded with a vision. A memory. A boy, born out of wedlock to a mother who knew many men. This boy's mother had exchanged much more than conversation, and much less than true intimacy. Before the seed of Ransden was planted, another seed was planted inside of her. A seed of rot.

A virus, from an infected phallus, poisoned Violet Grimtrue's immune system, and she began to grow sick much slower than she could realize. Her immune system began to wear down, and she was unwell often.

Soon after, she bore a child. The child, Beastmother saw as her vision expanded like a growing fever, had unfortunately contracted the infection during birth, causing him to go immediately blind. The evil seed of rot was primarily a female-based disease, and did not favor men as much as it did women.

Some scholars in Orcan's Grove later found evidence to support a claim that a cleric had created this disease by order of The Orcan, to rid the city of evil woman who retaliated against his wishes.

Violet was one of those unfortunate women.

Now that Beastmother and Ransden shared the same bloodstream, all of it was controlled by the organs of the Beastmother. In no more than fifty beats of her heart, the virus was spread through her entire body.

Ransden's consciousness faded in and out. He hoped he had made The Orcan proud, as was his only wish until this point.

Visions of a girl, from what seemed like lifetimes ago, materialized in his mind. She was young, and determined. Her hair was that of goldenrod, which was the name her father would call her. Others knew her as Mar.

He remembered her diligence, and willingness to help. He remembered his mortal selfishness. And for the first time, he felt pride for another. But he feared her death so he reached out to her, calling her name through the arteries of life, searching for her mind. He called to her.

He said, "I'm sorry."

He told her, "Forgive me."

His voice crawled nearer to her consciousness, and he knew she heard him.

"Let me now serve my purpose," he asked of her.

"Let me serve you, or let me be damned."

Just outside the skin of Beastmother, as the mind of Ransden was calling out to Mar, a tiny creature floated by. The creature was dead, and had many legs. Many people in history claimed that the Great Centipede had magic properties after death, and perhaps it did. For when Ransden said, "Let me serve you," the body of the insect disintegrated like sand, leaving behind a blue orb. It pulsed once, then blinked out of existence, hoping a god would hear a dying man's final wish.

Ransden fought with all his will to overcome the morbid evil that was Beastmother, and with one last conscious effort he reached his mind out to the beast, like a fisherman drawing a line for trout. He caught hold of her mind, which was also the same as his at this point, he became her, and let himself go.

Ransden died.

*****

Beastmother had the sea vessel in her maw, she wanted to swallow, but her throat was so swollen from the virus now that she could barely breathe. Any water than did go down felt like tar, or acid.

She held on to hope, repeatedly asking for forgiveness, but after giving her the vision of the boy who contracted a sexual disease, her mother ignored her plea. She was dying, and it was upon her faster than she ever thought it would be. So, she did not resist the inevitable. Having lived in the world for a few breaths short of a thousand years, she realized that everything died. She just didn't know it would happen this quickly, so anticlimactically.

She remembered every ship she ate. Every sailor, merchant, explorer. She remembered their thoughts, those souls kindled in her mind like lucid dreams, of families on dry land, free to run and play. The happiness they shared with friends. Their feeling of happiness is what she thought she would miss most of all.

She willed the hulk of her body up one more time toward the sky above the sea's surface, calling to the gods above for one last chance, but no thunder rolled this time. So, surrendering to the inevitable, the heated darkness in her eyes went cold. Her heart beat its last thump and she simply went to sleep, forever.

Eighty-two breaths later, just as her mouth closed upon the ship called The Bender, Beastmother died.

FIFTEEN

Mar opened her eyes.

Everything was still. Everything was silent, except for the gentle lapping of water against The Bender's bulkheads. They were no longer spinning.

Margaret lifted her weary head. Above her sagged a jumbled mess of splintered wood, torn and shredded canvas, and what seemed like miles and miles of spidery rope. Beyond that, a crack split the sky.

She felt very small. There was no sky above, only teeth. Their curvature looked like the inside of an overturned bowl, and she imagined a giant placing a ceramic bowl over top of them like an insect he wanted to keep from escaping.

If someone were to come along and take a very large hammer to this very large overturned bowl, and cracked it, she guessed it would look something like what she saw above her. Obviously, it was no bowl; she hadn't yet forgotten the beast which almost swallowed her and the crew. What amazed her was what she saw through the crack in the teeth.

Light. Natural, gleaming sunlight poured through the crack like a golden waterfall.

Heavy footsteps shuffled behind Margaret. A callused hand welcomingly placed itself on her shoulder.

"What happened?" she asked.

Many silent breaths rose and fell before Captain said anything. His feathery hat has fallen off his head some time ago; he held it at his left hip as the two stood together, gazing up at the rescuing light beyond the confines of their cell.

"That I don't know, lass," he finally said, this time sounding more like a pirate than ever. "What I do know is this: she ain't gonna take our souls. Look."

Mar's gaze followed his finger to the teeth high in the sky, and was shocked with utter delight to see them parting away from each other, blue sky expanding as darkness diminished.

Blue sky. No longer was it purple and dark, no more did it ripple with thunder and flashes of lightning.

The crew members were on deck, cleaning debris, securing salvageable sails, pushing water overboard through the scuppers. A sliver of sunlight cut through the brig's midsection, welcoming Mar and Captain with its grace. As the mouth high above began to open, slowly and groggily, the shadows on either side of the ship were pushed outward to both the bow and the stern, and for the first time Mar could see the crew's sunlit faces.

They were no longer shadow-like, or formless, but were much like carved granite blossoming into busts of beautiful beings. She couldn't believe what she saw. Some of the crew were men, but many were dwarves just like Captain. There were elves among the crew, even dark ones. She hadn't noticed the small ones before, but now she noticed there were gnomes as well.

"They're ghosts," she said.

"Aye," Captain said. "Some of them, at least."

"Who were they?" Mar asked. "Before they joined your crew, that is."

"Well, many of them searched for an end in their past lives. They shared a common goal—to find the end of the world, a land with no more suffering, no pain, no more searching. A place of rest. They just...found me, I suppose. They follow me, not really knowing why, just feeling it's right, I suppose. I gotta tell ya, I don't know where the end of the world is. I don't even know if there is a Yenun. But it gives them hope, and that makes me happy. That makes this life worth living. Perhaps one day they will pass on. Perhaps one day I will have had enough adventure, but today is not the last."

The last of the jagged teeth sank back into the ocean. There was no more rain or storms, or strong winds, even. Just a steady breeze coming in from the northwest.

Captain inspected the wreckage of the ship, and labeled it a total loss.

"We still can't sail back?" Mar asked, not letting her fear seep through.

"In time," he said. "But I'm afraid this will take months to rebuild, depending on the supplies we have on board. I'm so deeply sorry."

"It's okay," Mar said. "Maybe there's a chance that a miracle could happen."

Hours passed, and the wrecked ship seemed to be floating nowhere. They had been at least two days out to sea, but Mar could have sworn she saw land on the horizon.

"Is that..."

"Draston." The dwarf scratched his head.

"How did we get back so soon?"

"I don't know; could it have been that centipede of yours?"

"I never made a wish when it died."

"Maybe you didn't have to. Maybe he just knew."

"Maybe," Mar said.

"Everything okay?" asked Captain.

"Yeah," said Mar, but she gazed out toward Draston with a blank expression. "It's just, I don't know if I'll ever be the same after what we just went through."

"Aye, that you won't be. But you can't stay a child forever; change is inevitable."

"You're right. I'm happy I went on this adventure."

"Me, too."

They stood on the forecastle deck, silently, and watched the shore grow closer until The Bender was a shipwreck on the shore.

Nobody ever believed Mar what had happened out at sea, but it shaped her life for years to come.

DRAGONBAND Books

Tales

Crossroads of Draston

The Hunters and the Hunted

Women of the Crystal Coast (Hits Kickstarter June, 5th!)

The Companions Cycle

Wayward Companions (Coming Winter of 2019)